UNTIL THEN

Also by Gail Kittleson

Women of the Heartland Series

In Times Like These
With Each New Dawn
A Purpose True
All for the Cause
&
Kiss Me Once Again
a Women of the Heartland story

and

In This Together
Catching Up With Daylight

Until Then

a novel

GAIL KITTLESON

WordCrafts

Until Then
Copyright © 2019
Gail Kittleson

Cover concept and design by David Warren.
Cover photo of Dorothy Worst (ne Woebbeking) courtesy the Worst Family.

Published by WordCrafts Press
Cody, Wyoming 82414
www.wordcrafts.net

Dedication

To Dorothy Worst (ne Woebbeking), who gave so much to the American soldiers fighting through North Africa, Sicily, Italy, France, and Germany. Also dedicated to the brave London constables who persevered through the daunting trials of World War II.

With grateful thanks to Dorothy's daughter Sandra and son Marc for so much information about their mother's service. What an incredible woman!

Thanks also to an anonymous descendant of a Bethnal Green tragedy victim I encountered at the tube station in spring 2018.

A hearty thank you to the faithful readers who perused this manuscript before publication—what an encouragement you are to me!

Chapter One

March 1943 French Morocco

"Sent Jerry packin', didn't we?" Still focused on the battle, a burly sergeant ignored his wounds.

"You showed 'em what we're made of today." Dorothy slipped the doctor's order of meperidine solution into the sergeant's mouth when he opened it again.

He sputtered, "Yeah. The Kasserine Pass taught us a couple things. Next time, we'll—"

"You'll soon be back in the thick of it, but this shrapnel has to come out first. Open your mouth, Sarge." She stuck a thermometer in and he closed his eyes.

The GI on the next litter mumbled, "No use fightin' her. She's the one those pilots took to..."

Dorothy checked the sergeant's pupils and dabbed grit from his face as the other soldier continued, despite his severe shoulder injury.

"I hear she even navigated a C-47."

The sergeant fought to maintain control as Dorothy checked his temperature. Here in the Eleventh Evacuation Hospital, tough guys rarely went down easily. "You... you're..." The medication took hold, and Dorothy moved to the next casualty.

"She's cute too, and man, is she ever stacked."

She had half a notion to scold the mouthy GI, but her training took over. Deep down, he was scared to death.

1

Not a second to lose, with a hundred emergencies in this surgical tent alone. Several doctors, corpsmen, and other nurses worked from litter to litter set up on sawhorses. When her last 18-hour shift ended, Lieutenant Eilola, the nurses' commander, had to remind her to leave.

Another GI clawed the air while Dorothy cut away his uniform. *Snip, snip... rrrrrip.* Unrecognizable Army khaki dropped into an overflowing hamper.

"Hang on—we'll get you into surgery as soon as we can." The poor fellow's eyes glazed over. That might be a good thing.

A tap on her shoulder revealed a nurse and a surgeon. He gestured for Dorothy to follow, and the nurse took her place.

The doc stopped near a patient whose chest barely rose and fell. Worse, what was left of his body took up only a third of his blood-soaked gurney.

Sometimes you will see a basket case with all limbs missing...

The surgeon lowered his voice. "The tourniquets failed. He's bled out." He drew a long breath. "Sodium pentathol to the jugular—lethal dose. Pronto."

En route to the supply tent, Dorothy passed a grimy chaplain. Good—at least she wouldn't be facing this all alone.

Against North Africa's flat horizon, stifling heat enveloped encroaching darkness. In a smaller tent lined with cabinets of jars and bottles, she rubbed her trembling hands.

Craaack... Someone smacked into something near the tent—hopefully not with a loaded gurney. Profanity echoed as she located the right bottle.

Breathe. Steady, steady... Pull back the stopper. Wait for the glass tube to fill.

Careful to protect the syringe, she pushed a mass of thick damp hair from her forehead, and through a morass of sweaty litter bearers, re-entered the surgery. Halfway to her GI, a tipped-over waste receptacle blocked the aisle.

A corpsman grabbed the handle. "Sorry, nurse."

2

Beside her patient, the haggard chaplain touched the patient's head and studied his dogtags. When the GI's eyelids fluttered, the chaplain whispered, "Psychological shock, but perhaps he's still cognizant."

He eased his hands under the patient's neck. "The Lord is my shepherd..."

Suddenly wide-eyed, the young man shot Dorothy a searching look as she grasped a small pouch of skin below his chin.

"Need a boyfriend?" His jaunty tone matched the light in his eyes, and the chaplain's slight nod called up her voice.

"Yeah. Yes, I do."

Pimply blue-gray epidermis accepted the needle. Above, on a wire between two tent poles, a single light bulb revealed the instant effect.

Ever so gently, Dorothy removed the needle. Labored breathing tapered into full silence, and she sought the hankie Mama gave her before she left home. But blood coated her fingers, so she ran the back of her hand over her eyes instead.

The soldier's head slipped sideways as the chaplain made the sign of the cross. "May you rest in peace..."

"Nurse—on the double!"

Setting the syringe in the TO BE STERILIZED bin, Dorothy answered the call—then another and another. Hours later, things slowed down a little, and one of the surgeons sent her to get some sleep.

Outside, she washed her hands and took a deep breath. Against a slim golden line in the east, a few litter carriers still bore patients from a deuce-and-a-half. Though she longed for sleep, a strong coffee aroma drew her to the mess a few tents away.

Truck lights flashed through the canvas walls as she sank at a table and lowered her head. A yell sounded from the entrance, where sand formed drifts much like Iowa snow.

Someone yelled, "We're running short of bandages—anybody have any fabric stowed away?"

Nothing in her duffel but her wool Great War-issue uniform—a lot of good that would do. Dorothy buried her head even deeper until a familiar voice rallied her.

"Hey, Moonbeam, are you in there?" Shrouded in cigarette smoke, her friend Millie commanded, "Drink this."

Pungent caffeine cleared Dorothy's head enough to digest the conversation at the next table. "Rommel won on Valentine's Day, but Patton's back in charge. From now on we'll show the Desert Fox what's what."

The speaker's facts and figures drew listeners, but something else caught Dorothy's eye—a neatly folded Wrigley's gum wrapper chain around his neck. Millie noticed it, too.

"That's the new mail officer—seems like a nice guy, and smart. I'll get us some breakfast."

A quick bowl of oatmeal later, Dorothy lurched up at a call for incoming, but Millie grasped her arm. "Remember, we've got two shifts now. Come on, kiddo—time for a nap."

Dorothy followed, but her heart dragged, and Millie paused. "You have to let that basket case go, Moonbeam. You did your best. The last thing he saw was your big brown eyes."

"True. And I'll never forget his."

"I know. Come on."

American bombers hummed overhead, like her younger brother Albert's in the Pacific, where their older brother Vernon also served as a tank buster. The youngest, Ewald, recently graduated from medic training.

Heat welled behind Dorothy's eyes. Mama must be beside herself with worry.

"Hey chickadees, looks just as messy as ever in here." That would be Henrietta—Dorothy knitted even faster. Millie stopped writing her daily letter to Delbert long enough to react.

"When did you last straighten up *your* tent?"

4

"It's hopeless. My new roommate's such a slob." Henrietta perched Indian style in the doorway, her bony legs sprawled across the tent floor. The unit's wire terrier mascot wriggled from her arms and scurried to Dorothy.

"Good to see you, Eric. Is Hank keeping you cool?"

Henrietta eyed an envelope on Dorothy's cot. "Writing to that Paul guy again?"

"No, to my sister."

"Don't neglect Paul. Not everybody gets to date a university professor, you know."

"How many times have I told you we're not dating?"

"Oh, about 60, but mark my words, nobody writes to a girl that much for nothin'." Henrietta fingered the packet of Camels in her breast pocket, but Millie shot her a severe look.

"Hey, not in here. You know Moonbeam hates smoke, even if the Red Cross supplies our cigarettes."

Henrietta growled. "Anybody up for a card game, then?"

Millie shook her head. "Sorry, I need to get another letter written. There's so much to tell Delbert. I just got started on our trip across Algeria, all those rivers we crossed on pontoon bridges—"

"Thanks to Jerry for blowing up the real ones. Fording the Atlas was the worst." Henrietta's scowl deepened. "Wasn't that when somebody started calling me Hank?"

"Who knows? But it fits you." Dorothy touched noses with Eric.

"My folks'll think I made this all up—40 nurses in Army truck beds for 1,200 miles from Morocco to Tunisia."

Hank's sneer could have boiled dragons. "Your folks've never met Colonel Scott. I'll bet the old curmudgeon's proud of that move."

"Shh!" Millie held her finger to her lips. "Remember, he *is* a Great War veteran."

"If anybody could find something positive about him, it'd be you. But don't worry, he'll never pass by our little ghetto. He wouldn't lower himself."

"Well, Lieutenant Eilola might—"

"She's on our side, remember? I doubted her when she told us to hunker down and wait after Scott's so-called welcoming speech, but she was right."

That memory produced groans, but Millie grinned. "Enough smoke puffed out of her ears during that speech to burn down Casablanca." She stuck out her chest and lowered her voice to mimic the Colonel.

"Well, you made it here, but you're not welcome. We don't need you. We've done fine without you, and you'll all be going home soon—most of you will probably be pregnant."

"You memorized it, Mil? To Scott, we're lower than Rommel. He's the Desert Fox, but we're desert rats."

"Yet we're still here, right?" Dorothy snuggled with Eric. "We kept a low profile like Lieutenant Eilola said, and kept doing our best. It didn't take long for the doctors and corpsmen to see how much they needed us. And only eight girls were sent home."

"True enough. Eight out of forty-eight, that's..."

"One sixth."

"But my tent mate was one of them." Hank could whine better than anybody. "After that first night when we froze to death, she figured out how to make a cocoon from three wool blankets. Saved my life."

Her voice took on a harsh note. "The Colonel sent her back just when she recovered from being so seasick."

"I know. But if he tried to get rid of us now, the docs would rise up and rebel. So would the corpsmen." Millie stretched her shoulders. "Lieutenant Eilola's orders to do only what we were asked and be pleasant worked, didn't it?"

"Yeah, and now they've piled all kinds of responsibilities on us. The other day, a corpsman asked me to show him the proper way to give an injection—they'd only trained him using oranges." Hank knocked some sand from her saddle shoes and Millie cuffed her shoulder.

"Will you cut that out? At least we try to keep our abode clean."

6

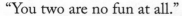

"You two are no fun at all."

"Anybody for a swim? We're takin' a load over to the beach in five minutes." The generic invitation was shouted from the walkway near the women's tents.

Hank scrunched up her nose, Millie looked thoughtful, but Dorothy leaped from her cot and dragged out her duffel.

"Good thing I sewed a swimsuit from those parachutes we collected on the way."

"And if there's one thing we have plenty of, it's suture thread."

"Yeah—I feel naked without my spools in my pocket. Out with you, Hank. Gotta get my suit on." Dorothy handed Eric over. "Are you coming, Millie? We don't get a chance like this very often."

Millie bit her lip.

"Hey, a girl's gotta have a little fun once in a while."

Millie made a quick decision to join her as Hank got to her feet. She tapped her cigarette package. "I'll stay around here with my Camels—never know what Scott might be up to. Somebody's gotta guard the fort."

After a bumpy five-mile ride through sand dunes casting mountainous shadows, the truck lurched to a halt. Dorothy jumped down onto hot sand. By the time Millie joined her, she'd slipped off her fatigues.

The sparkling Mediterranean beckoned, so she tore across the beach and plunged in. After swimming the safety zone and back, she dropped down beside Millie, who leaned her head back.

"What a perfect day!"

"Out here, you'd never know how close the war is." As Dorothy dried her hair, a tall redheaded pilot approached with a towel slung over his shoulders. He dipped his head and saluted.

"Houston Pinkstone, here—they call me Pinky. And you ladies are?"

"Millie and Dorothy." Millie answered for them both, and Dorothy took in this fellow's jovial smile.

"Nurses with the Eleventh Evac, I presume?"

"How did you guess? And you're RAF?"

"Ah, 'twas my hair that gave me away." His grin highlighted his dimples.

"Quite the sunburn you're developing." Millie's comment teased out another smile.

"One day soon, this will peel into the best tan in all of Scotland. Of course, it may be years before I get back there."

His freckled nose and forehead, also burned, brought out the sea shades of his eyes as he turned to Dorothy. "Where did you learn to swim like that?"

"In the Cedar River back home in Iowa. The mud held me up when my brothers tried to drown me."

"Jolly good. Here, the salt water attends to that, righto?" He pointed out to sea. "See the chap out there in that boat? Why not swim there? Maybe he'll invite you in."

"He's past the safety line."

"But you're a strong swimmer, and he's there to save you." The dare in his eyes proved irresistible. In spite of the warning written all over Millie's face, Dorothy took him on and jogged to the shoreline.

In minutes, she grabbed the rowboat's worn gunnel, and a dark-haired, mustached occupant greeted her in an unfamiliar accent. "Lovely day, Miss. You must be with the American hospital unit?"

She answered his questions about her background, but when she asked about him, he merely squinted into the sun. He looked at least 40, with a bit of white above his ears. Seeing he had no intention of inviting her in, Dorothy swam back to Millie and the pilot, who chatted about Delbert, also a pilot.

Dorothy waited for a pause and asked, "Did you think he would ask me in?"

Pinky's robust laugh declared good-natured trickery. "I had no idea, but thought finding out a worthy quest. You have encountered royalty, my friend."

"What?"

8

"You just passed the time of day with King Zog of Albania. When the Italians invaded in '39, he fled his country with his wife and son. He'd already become a pilot, and once he got his family settled in old Blighty, he joined the RAF."

Maybe he was still joking—his laughing eyes made it impossible to tell. Dorothy circled her hair with a towel and settled on the welcoming sand, but Millie stared at Pinky in wonderment.

"The King of Albania?" Her shocked expression could have sold for thousands of dollars. "Blighty?"

"Our most affectionate term for old England, dear." Pinky ignored her other inquiry as he surveyed the Mediterranean. "Strange how this war brings us all together, kings and paupers alike."

Then he asked about their homes and the States in general. By the end of their chat, Dorothy still wasn't sure if she'd met the King of Albania. But one thing she knew for sure—she wouldn't mind seeing this cheery fellow again.

Chapter Two

March 3, 1943 Bethnal Green, London's East End

Shortly after the hall clock struck a quarter past eight, a siren split the air. Marian Williams lifted her sleeping daughter and darted down the stairs. Her mother and father-in-law, off on air warden duty, had left the front door unlocked.

The shrill *wheeeee* ascended the scale, so she hugged her youngest child close. The blackout made the going difficult, but she reached the pavement along the street as twilight darkened into night.

Careful to avoid a bomb crater's rough edge, she raced toward the tube station as Melvin had instructed before he left for the war. "Whatever you do, get down inside the station fast as you can."

For a time, a searchlight's roving circle of light guided her. Abreast of the tube station entryway, she hurried the last few yards to the stairs. A growing crowd jostled her from behind, and her little girl cried out.

"There, there. Mummy's here, precious. We'll be safe soon."

Very few others preceded her, so she hoped for a spot near the canteen, with access to milk. Uneven light shone over the paved steps, so she counted the remaining stairs before the landing—three.

Then she tripped.

With nothing to latch onto, her knee hit the concrete. Then something heavy bashed her left side. Someone cried out. Pain lanced Marian's chest, and another blow scraped her arm on the landing floor.

A bevy of scents inundated her—sausage gravy, perspiration,

boot leather—but where was her baby? She attempted to get up, but an even heavier weight slammed her face down. Voices echoed the deep structure, and frantic screams.

Groping in the darkness, Marian choked out, "Mummy's here, where are you?"

But liquid filled her mouth, and a crushing burden descended. Something snapped in her chest, in her hip. Then all went black.

Police Officer Rupert E. Laudner closed his hand over the spine of a stained cardboard notebook filled with names, over 150. All citizens of Bethnal Green—his people.

The oppression in the stairwell made him stifle a retch. Surely he must have imagined the human mass here less than an hour ago. He squeezed his eyes shut, only to have the scene replay. Arms, legs, crushed torsos, heads—trousers and sweaters and dresses and shoes all mashed together.

Helpless, he stared at his dripping hands. What had happened here—and how? His first recollection was an odd-sounding siren as he made his way to the volunteer fire watch station midway through the evening. Who had set it off?

Staring at the emergency workers scuttling about the stairwell made him dizzy, but there was nowhere to brace himself. The walls were awash with—words failed him.

Adept at handling crises since the Blitz, the workers went about their work stone-faced. Hadn't he glimpsed Vicar Towsley a while ago? Rupert surveyed all around in vain. Probably out on the street or at the morgue consoling survivors.

Dizziness struck again. Just when the stairs seemed an interminable climb, familiar footsteps approached. Chief Constable Derby. Rupert stumbled forward.

"Laudner." Despite the shadows, the Chief's eyes glinted. He screwed up his face and cleared his throat. "How long have you been—"

"Sir, I—" A sob threatened. "On my way to my evening duty, I—"

"What have you got there? Is that the casualty list?"

Numb, Rupert handed over the stained record, and a great wave of relief washed him.

"Everyone has been accounted for, then?"

"No. We had trouble putting... ah... things together. That is, no one knows yet how many people made it down into the tube before the blast. They've transported many to the hospital—upwards of 50 I should say, and the rest to—"

"Indeed." The Chief worked his lips, and a fiercer light shone in his eyes. "You have done remarkably well, but you must go home. I shall proceed from here."

Home? Rupert's knees trembled at the thought. There, Madeleine and their youngest children enjoyed safety and warmth. He backed toward the wall, but with a look of revulsion, the Chief pulled him back again.

"Oh my—some were even crushed up against here?"

Mute, Rupert nodded.

As if he were a child, the Chief propelled him up the stairs by the elbow, past workmen balancing sloshing water pails, mops and scrub brushes.

"Come now, Laudner. The cleaning crew is upon us." Chief Derby rubbed his forehead. "Oh my. This takes me back to the trenches. Do come along quickly." He half-pushed Rupert up into cool night air and faced him.

"You have carried out your duty, Officer Laudner. Now listen to me. This is a direct order. Go home immediately."

His words issued from some distant place. The misty late winter air, so much cooler than down below, made Rupert blink.

"Do you hear me? You have done all you can here." Skilled in obedience, Rupert nodded. The Chief bodily turned him toward his house. "Off you go, then. We shall sort all this in the morning."

Rupert started off, but his knees belied his determination. Could he make it that far?

Following the afternoon meeting, the Chief Constable summoned Rupert into his office and gestured him to a chair. Taking a seat behind his desk, the Chief wrenched his hands.

"Such a grisly business. Until now, our citizenry has retained the right to chat about our losses. But not this time, lest the enemy hear and believe they have finally conquered the stubborn British morale." His logic, a repeat of the presentation to local officials, made perfect sense. Each official decision revolved around *Herr* Adolph's ever-present spies.

"It falls to us to enforce this rule, Laudner, though it shan't be easy. The Prime Minister himself has forbidden conversing about this event. This means we must educate the populace face-to-face; speak with workmen on lunch breaks and women out hanging their washing."

Once again, the Chief scrubbed his hands in the air.

"Quite the task, considering the shocking number of deaths. I have asked you to stay because, well, since you witnessed the scene and so many victims live on your beat, I am entrusting this charge to you."

What minutes ago had sounded so rational now lodged like a stone in Rupert's chest. "Sir..."

The Chief's sigh attested to his concern. He pushed back his chair and stood. "I realize the heaviness of this load. But I simply cannot divide such delicate duty amongst the force. Everyone must be informed, and you know how Fletcher would—"

At the name of his scrupulous fellow officer, Rupert cringed. *Fletcher* was all he needed to hear. "Of course. Exactly, sir."

Chief Derby rounded his desk and settled his hand on Rupert's shoulder. "I can rest assured you will see to this, and have assigned Officer Young your area, including the tube station, for the next two days."

Typical for this time of year, a sodden haze shrouded Bethnal Green. The rattle of the back door latch called Rupert from his second miserable night following the tube station debacle. *That must be Anna coming in after her second shift.* Hearing the back stairs creak confirmed his judgment.

"Was that Anna?"

Rupert patted Madeleine's hip. "Undoubtedly. Rest a bit longer, love."

A dull throb pounded behind his left ear. Most of the time he relished his work, but would rather do anything else today. In India, men walked barefoot on nails and broken glass—petty pain in comparison.

As a loyal servant of the Crown, he must, as always, represent the government, be its ears and eyes—and voice. But today, this duty required unthinkably punitive obedience from ordinary Bethnal Green citizens.

Coming home last night, he had passed Queen Mary University, dating back to the founding of London Hospital Medical College in 1785. Here, the Green chummed with Shoreditch Park off Cheshire Street, and he paused near the institution's gate to survey the institution's motto embedded in stone—*Conjunctis Viribus*—With United Powers.

Yet this task, he must undertake alone.

Such a harsh blow for this corner of the great old city, he could scarcely take it in. The Chief Constable appeared stunned also, under a calm exterior. He had instructed the force, "As with all else this bloody war thrusts upon us, we shall prevail."

Dawn air seeped through the crack Rupert left in the window last night before hunkering down for the impossibility of rest. But long after Madeleine drifted into sleep, he stared wide-eyed at the cracked ceiling.

As he stuck his feet out, she stirred again. "Are you sure?"

"Certainly, fully capable of..."

She rolled over. Good. She needed her sleep. Besides, time alone might help stir up his courage.

14

Since the war began, the constabulary had asked more and more of its officers, and he hadn't minded. Anything to hasten the demise of that German fiend. Surely this blistering war must end by Christmas. That's what some politician burbled over the wires, but last year they touted the same, and the number of fronts had only increased.

Navigating the short hallway stocking-footed, Rupert peered in at little Cecil and sweet Iris, nestled in sleep like bunnies in a burrow. The rise and fall of their chests piqued dark visions of those innocents perishing in the stairwell. With a shiver, he continued out into the beckoning garden, sequestered by vines along the back wall.

In spare moments, he'd begun widening the vegetable plot of an evening. The sweetness of fallowed-over soil, even this poor London clay, soothed him. He walked to the overturned sod, grasped a clump and inhaled.

Oh, the sheer simplicity of this dank, mulchy scent bespeaking springtime's arrival. His sigh carried an echo, cast back by an unseen guest.

The grit in his palm transported him to his growing-up summers at an uncle's farm, rising before dawn to embrace new-mown hay, chickens at their perennial scratching, and cows mooing with full udders.

From some quarter, perhaps the munitions factory, came distant clatter. He hated the idea of Anna working there such long hours, but Rupert Junior, *Junior* for short, kept an eye on her.

The Beckton Gas Works whistle blew. There, in the last century, the city had transformed marshland into housing for gas and sewage workers. 'Twas a good walk through Victoria Park, down to Poplar, and eastward at least as far.

Great War sentry duty taught him how sound travels at night, when all lies still. How true that proved in the blackout since the Blitz, though searchlights still scanned the heavens. On the Luftwaffe's rare night off, London reclaimed its midnight serenity, but pre-dawn quiet magnified each noise, including some shuffles next door, where Milford Beavens readied for his day at the grocery.

Somewhere down the lane a baby cried, but not Rupert's cheerful grandson Henry, ensconced up on the third floor with Junior and his wife Kathryn. Before stooping through the kitchen doorway once more, Rupert stretched, aware of the cold claiming his toes.

Madeleine would not appreciate garden dirt on his socks. Setting the kettle to boil, he dabbed the muddy toes with a dry rag. Not a bad job of it, but before pulling on his boots, he slipped down the hall again to listen to Cecil and Iris breathing in unconcerned abandon.

The slumber of the innocent. A few minutes later, Madeleine touched his arm as he donned his long wool coat.

"Finally, a night without those Nazi blighters, yet you could not sleep?"

No need to reply, for she knew. The finality of the edict he bore to their fellow citizens struck him once more as he buttoned his coat, replete with badges for faithful service.

Madeleine plied him with an extra cup of tea, quite the treasure these days, but his thoughts still went rogue. Hadn't everyone been grieving since Dunkirk in '39? Then the Blitz razed whole households, blotted out entire neighborhoods and landmarks, the skyline he'd cherished. A wonder St. Paul's had survived—so far.

Comrades died fighting the great dock fires that threatened to consume the Thames, a cruel naval yard accident felled workers in Portsmouth, a district nurse traveling between patients was blown up, a Yorkshire friend of Gran's taken while on air warden duty. The list continued, *ad infinitum.*

But this—helpless people suffocating as they sought shelter from a would-be bomb attack—mothers, babies, school children. And today, he must instruct them to swallow down their anguish.

The blessed hot tea fortified his nerves. He might have downed another, had they extra, but the rationed Earl Grey tin stood close to empty. Rising from the table, Rupert accepted Madeleine's embrace, but kept his emotions tight.

"I will keep you in my prayers today."

He dared not meet her eyes. Murmuring a thank-you, he plastered on his policeman's face, secured its tense line behind his ears, and entered the veil before daylight. March 5, 1943—still, no official word had surfaced. Surely, the report must come out soon. Rupert fell into his long stride and covered several blocks.

As he approached the tube station entrance, the sun made its lingering appearance far across the island. Perhaps that stranger would visit this beleaguered island today—any bit of cheer would help.

Chapter Three

Dear Dorothea,

Thank you for your letter. It took three weeks to get here. It is difficult to imagine you in the desert, but you still find ways to enjoy life... this is goot!"

Picturing Papa sitting with Mama at the dining room table brought a smile. The two of them compiled letters that Papa rewrote in English. And always, they called her Dorothea, even though they had Americanized all the family names and removed the umlaut from Woebbeking.

Somehow, the censors had overlooked *goot*, Papa's only slip. Dorothy held the letter to her lips and whispered her response in German for Mama's sake. "Even though I'm in the middle of sand dunes, I have trouble picturing myself here, too."

The newsman says Benito Mussolini has pulled Italy's surviving soldiers from the Eastern front, and our troops battle in the Bismarck Sea.

Perhaps you know that General George Patton now commands the Second Army Corps? We also heard that General Rommel will be replaced after his latest defeat.

Here, Congress has moved to extend the Lend-Lease Act. How proud we are to support the supply of war materials without expecting repayment. How else will this war ever come to an end?

We welcomed Ewald home on leave two weeks ago, and he tells us the Army will keep you and the other nurses away from danger.

We can only hope you are far from the fighting. Write us what you need so we can send it with the next box we send from the bakery.

With our daily prayers and love...

Repeating Papa's usual closing to the four tent walls, Dorothy slipped the letter back into its envelope. His carefully penned letters touched her like nothing else. After a hard day of work, he spent hours with Mama composing this.

Reading the *Waterloo Courier* and listening to the nightly newscast kept him up-to-date. Interesting that he'd mentioned the two commanders responsible for the daily toll of casualties arriving at the Eleventh Evacuation Hospital—the censors let that through, too.

Of course she'd heard Patton now commanded the Second Corps. His gutsy reputation preceded him. After the disheartening defeat at the Kasserine Pass, General Eisenhower himself had taken control of the command structure and created the Eighteenth Army Group under British General Alexander as the new Allied Headquarters in North Africa.

Now, as that wounded sergeant had said, Rommel had a taste of American determination and fortitude. Word had it that soon the Nazis would be ousted from this continent altogether.

Next, Dorothy turned to the other treasure from Mail Call, a letter from her older sister Elfreida. As she read, a steady wind blew sand into ever-increasing tufts beneath the floor, making the perimeter as puffy as Papa's hand-fluted pastries.

"What are you smiling about?" Millie stood in the doorway.

"My parents are sending us another care package. My older sister works at the bakery and she knows all my favorites."

"All right! The last one was made in heaven!"

"Did you get a letter from Del today?"

"No, but I know he's busy, and it's only been two days since his last one." Always positive, Millie wrote her fiancé every day. "I just heard something really great in the mess. Overheard it, I should say."

"If anything was top secret, it'd be blown in the mess."

"That's for sure. I think people figure we're out in the wilderness and no Germans can possibly hear what they say. Ever heard of Operation Mincemeat?"

"No, but the name tells me the British must've dreamed it up."

"Right. They dressed a corpse as a British officer with falsified war plans." Millie plopped on her cot. "They set things up so the Germans would find the body washed up off the coast of Spain."

"And what did the plans say?"

"That we're going to attack Greece and Sardinia instead of Sicily. According to the officer I eavesdropped on, Hitler has suspected the Allies will invade Sicily, but the command is hoping this will convince him to add more defenses in Greece and cut Sicily short. Wouldn't it be something to be involved in that sort of stuff?"

"Mmm... I'll say. You and me and Hank could come up with some doozies. Sounds like it's a good thing we're headed to Sicily, huh?"

This uncompleted section of London's Central Line Extension once stirred such pride—even the lowly Green would finally enjoy underground train access. But this morning, muffled voices rose from the tunnel—families who had spent the night here in safety.

Soon, parents and children, grandmothers and grandfathers would emerge onto the street like moles. Their appearance had long ago become a daily occurrence. Even yesterday, children bobbed up stairs behind their parents, sleepily unaware of the disaster the night before on these very stairs.

The tunnels held 5,000 and a good portion of London had gone underground. Many spent nights there as a matter of course since the Luftwaffe first struck. "What a blessing," Vicar Towsley said, "that the digging reached here before then, as if Providence had prepared us for the worst."

Each morning since then, Rupert visited the tunnel to manifest the arm of the law—to quietly proclaim all was not lost, and that in the end, all would be well. In this time of trouble, the Chief said, his presence had become even more important. Even yesterday, he acted his part, twiddling his keys as usual, ruffling the hair of a youngster here, giving a salute to a freckle-faced lad there.

Under his uniform, though, his heart had run wild. Could these citizens not smell the hydrogen peroxide as they navigated the steps to the outer world?

As soon as possible, he fled up beyond the sharp scent that still pervaded the landing. As he bolted, though, he spotted a small grey wad balled up in the corner.

He paused to retrieve a hankie, squashed and stained as it was. A woman's hankie, he presumed. At street level, morning light clarified the handmade piece. On one corner, dried blood obscured some embroidered letters. Could this have belonged to one of those obliterated by that impossible twisted mass of humanity?

With a shiver tracing his backbone, Rupert carefully pocketed the swatch to show the Chief Constable. Perhaps this evidence might aid in the complicated investigation. When he presented the hankie an hour later, the Chief Constable stroked his chin.

"In the corner, eh? On the landing, you say?" His forehead flooded with thought lines. "Perhaps it flew from someone's hand—someone near the bottom. We'll see what it has to tell us. Good work, Laudner. Always about our business, you are."

This morning Rupert hurried past the tube station entrance, set like a gaping hole in the block. Thank goodness Chief Derby had the foresight to assign his beat to Sergeant Young. New to the force as he was, the fellow appeared quite proficient.

As dawn outlined the streets of the Green, Rupert turned past a set of red brick flats—rare, indeed, to vary his morning route of shops, bakeries, markets, and eateries. He passed pubs and back alleys where sots wallowed in their filth, St. Peter's church and schoolyard, and several buildings newly claimed by the military. Not a figment of this area escaped his notice.

Any other time, the reassignment of his neighborhood would have troubled him, but this morning, the Chief's action brought only relief. The regulars down in the tunnel would wonder at the alteration, but so be it.

Past the brick flats, Rupert pressed on toward a stone edifice adrift from the regular small shops. With singular determination, he aimed for a wooden side door framed centuries ago by a mason. *Intriguing how the fellow puzzled together such rough hewn pieces.* Behind this door waited the only hope Rupert knew.

Rattling the latch proved futile, as all around people ventured out into St. Peter's Street. Used to his route, the milkman's pony trotted over uneven cobblestones, and a shaft of first light made a glory of the small creature's tangled mane.

Wriggling the sacristy key from his pocket always posed a challenge, for Rupert kept it separate from the rest of his ungainly assortment—a key for each business along his route. Perhaps the vicar had considered the growing criminal element and decided to bolt this side entrance.

Asked why he stored this particular key in the long rectangular slot inside his coat, Rupert might say, "To keep it close to my heart." And his reply would scrape the truth, for something about this structure drew him.

Perhaps it was the quietness—ethereal, shadowed—or Vicar Towsley's unflappable exterior. The white fluff grazing his ears gave undeniable testimony to his age. Still, he manfully tackled whatever fresh misery this war presented.

No telling how many mass funerals he had officiated since the Blitz, or the amount of bad news he'd carried to families. How could he hold up through it all?

No sign of him now, so climbing the narrow back stairway to the sanctuary, Rupert took opportunity to consider this friend. Yes, he counted Towsley a comrade, but their connection also held a certain mystery.

A small door opened into the preaching stanchion, and from that height, glossy pews claimed filmy light from high stained glass. Here, he and Madeleine had married. Here, the Vicar had baptized their children.

The half-door of the simply carved pulpit swung open with ease, and the oak floor, swept and scrubbed by devoted parishioners, beckoned. With several members of the constabulary deployed with the army, the stability of setting aside all else to attend Sunday service had vanished.

Truth be told, some days he might have joined Madeleine and the children, but chose nature's company instead. Accountable to no one, he wandered at will for an hour or two. This luxury he kept to himself.

At the back of the sanctuary, six high windows above the front door let in more light—such utter quietness here. But without warning, Rupert's phantoms recurred, even stronger in this place, unthinkable images that played with what he'd always called *faith*.

Through the long nave and out into the narthex, he opened the custodial closet. Ah, there it was, a one-word note propped against the FLIT disinfectant sprayer. Towsley knew he'd not give up until he found their word.

In large square script, black ink upon white scrap, *BEHOLD*. Rupert drank in the letters as he would a fragrant swallow of tea. He could scarcely recall how this daily practice of sharing words originated, but treasured the ritual.

"Thank you, old chum, wherever you've gotten off to."

Returning to the side door, he paused. Through the ages, how many faithful had climbed these stairs to pray in solitude?

Turning the key in a strong *click*, he set out on his route. At one house, someone's wash took advantage of the early breeze. Hung in careful rows, babies' nappies, boys' trousers and men's pants, shirts and girls' dresses in various sizes, and far to the back, a line of underclothes and hankies fluttered.

Small details, those hankies, nearly hidden by all the rest, but what a tide of tears they absorbed. That hankie he had found in the stairwell at the tube station—

Ah... no. No. He now had different to consider. *BEHOLD*. By this evening, what might he have beheld? Most likely, more destruction, plus stricken faces when he delivered this latest injunction.

Later in the afternoon, he met Vicar Towsley.

"My friend, you've just come from telling someone?"

Rupert nodded and Towsley waited. When no words came he continued. "I have informed those in our prayer group. That makes ten with whom you needn't trouble yourself."

"But—"

"No buts. They all understand."

Rupert raised his hand in protest, but the Vicar held him off.

"Deputize me if you must, but the telling falls to me as well."

As Towsley listed those he had notified, Rupert breathed deeper with each name. Among them was Marian Williams' mother-in-law, the worst assignment of all.

Behold—Towsley was even now acting out the meaning—*Look, see.* More than one method may produce the desired effect. His next thought reminded him that Marian's husband, off with the Navy, had yet to be told.

"Will Mrs. Williams inform their son?"

Towsley stated what Rupert already knew. "Melvin. Only that she perished, no information concerning how her death occurred." He ran his finger along his collar. "I know Melvin well enough. Watched him grow through the years, and married him and Marian. As I recall, the Navy sought his expertise with engines, even though he was above age for the service."

"How will he take the news?"

The Vicar eyed the heavens for a second or two. The lift of his shoulders accompanied a heartfelt sigh. "People react so differently, but at least he has some time to accept that she's gone before he comes home." The way his voice drifted off gave Rupert a nasty sensation.

"Has official notice come down yet, Laudner? Almost 36 hours have passed. The wartime reporting restrictions allow for this, but—"

"I looked for that yesterday, but nothing. Certainly today."

Towsley drew him aside. "It has come to my attention that some are blaming the authorities, my friend. Even the police force—"

"Rightly so. We ought to have prevented—"

"But what might you have done?"

24

Rupert threw up his hands. "Surely something."

"Those who think clearly have no complaint." Towsley cuffed him on the shoulder. "How is Madeleine taking the loss of her friend Violet? I must pay her a visit soon."

"Violet? Violet Burns?" Rupert shrank back. *Madeleine. Violet. Yes, they'd always been such good friends.*

"Oh my. Violet was one of...? I was not aware."

"Understandable. Indeed, the list was so long. I saw her daughter this morning and explained the need to keep mum."

"My word, Towsley." Rupert groaned. "How could I have missed her name?"

The Vicar commandeered his gaze. "*Behold*, my friend. Behold your humanness, as we all must in these trying times."

"But I must have gone doolally not to have noticed."

"Not at all. You might well be the sanest man I know."

The kindliness in Towsley's tone touched Rupert. Then he pointed out a sign in a recruiting office window to their left.

"Look there—a new sign, Rupert—read the note down there at the bottom: *Ministers of Religion and other fools need not apply.*" His chuckle called forth a smile in spite of Rupert's disgust with himself. "I should say, old chap, this puts me in my place."

"And me as well. If only these young recruiting blokes had seen us in our day. Back in the War to End All Wars, the forces wanted us!"

"Indeed they did. And we answered the call." The Vicar tapped Rupert's elbow. "Oh, we've come to my corner, so I'll be off."

As he continued on his way, Rupert's anger flared again, and for the rest of the day, he rehearsed what a dullard he'd been. Keeping her sorrow to herself, Madeleine had been supporting him since the tragedy.

Two more stops, and at his last one, the man of the house had just returned from work at the munitions factory. Still smelling of ammonia, he looked up from removing his boots.

"Good day, sir. How does it go at the factory?" Feeling foolish, Rupert added, "I have a son and daughter working there."

"More's the pity. Oh for the day when all of this will be shut down for good."

"I must agree." Rupert delivered his news, and hearing the edict, the man gave him the evil eye. He turned away with a, "We can no longer speak of our lost ones? What next?"

His wife touched his arm and attempted to blunt the sharp tension.

"'Twas his closest sister who passed, sir."

If nods of commiseration counted for anything, Rupert would be a rich man.

On the way home, the new library site caught his attention. Bless Mum, who often lamented the lowly Green being the only borough without a library, and bought or borrowed books wherever she could. After the Great War, she celebrated the opening of the first public library in the old asylum grounds, aptly named Barmy Park.

On September 7, 1940, the first day of the Blitz, how she would have wept at the direct hit through the roof. Precisely at 5:55 pm, the library fell in ruins.

Thereafter, the London Civil Defense Region allotted £50 for temporary tube station shelves, and the police helped librarians carry the surviving 4,000 books down there. Madeleine and Cecil made frequent visits from 5:30 until eight o'clock of an evening and would continue in the new library, now nearing completion in spite of the war.

Turning onto his street, Rupert's spirits altered. He'd learned on deployment that even the slightest change could upend a ship or right it again. Was that the way with things on land as well? Each seemingly insignificant action made a difference, and perhaps led to some other movement.

Lifting the back door latch, he willed away the killing sentiment in the factory worker's eyes and pondered how he might acknowledge Madeleine's grief.

Words forsook him far too often this day. Perhaps he would suggest a quiet after-dinner walk.

Chapter Four

A few feet behind the mess tent, Dorothy gave one of the surgeons a haircut.

"Just think how many nests the birds can line with all this hair—always wanted to donate my hair to Sicily."

His joking nature made it easy to get to know him, and earned him the nickname *Abner*. The first doc to befriend the nurses, he'd won everyone's heart. Well, except Hank's—she groused that he probably wanted something in exchange.

"Like what? He's got a wife and three children back home—he needs friends like everybody else. Human companionship, you know?" Millie, true to her nature, took Abner's part right away.

"Ha! *Female* companionship, you mean?"

"I mean somebody to talk to—can't think of anybody who doesn't like Abner. He gets along with everybody. It's going to be a long war, kiddo, so the more friends we make, the better."

"Somebody named after L'il Abner is no friend of mine! That lout's a dull-witted, lazy mountain man without an ounce of sense."

"Exactly—in the comic strip. But our *Abner* is brilliant. Can you name a surgeon who works harder? And he's so innovative—remember in North Africa how he made a frame for his wife's picture out of shrapnel fragments?"

"Guess I didn't hear about that. So how'd he get the nickname?"

"Who knows? They dubbed Dorothy *Moonbeam McSwine*, and the only resemblance is that she gets muddier than the rest of us."

"That, her dark hair and eyes, her figure, and her perfect complexion."

"True, but she's nothing like Moonbeam in the cartoon—not *inside*. Same with Abner. Maybe his height connected him to L'il Abner in somebody's mind. All it takes for a nickname is one little trait in common."

Hank seemed unconvinced, and Dorothy didn't even try to enter that conversation. Today, she relished cutting Abner's hair out in the sunshine and hearing about his family.

"My oldest son's 14 today. Missed his birthday last year, too. I sure hope we make faster progress from here on, or he'll be out of high school when I get to see him next."

"Must seem even worse to the troops."

"Definitely—I can hardly imagine. When we all get home, I'll look twice every time I see a guy walking with a limp, knowing I might've contributed to it."

"Better than not being able to walk at all. How many bones do you think you've set so far?"

Abner crossed his arms. "What a question! We could look it up in the records, but I'd rather not. Three hundred, maybe? That's a wild guess, and would only be counting legs, not arms and noses and—"

Somebody racing between tents noticed them and shouted, "Hey, I just heard Mussolini's been arrested. The Italians have relieved him of his offices. Best news since we bombed Rome."

As he ran on, Abner gave a wolf whistle. "That can only mean we ship out of here pretty soon. Never'll be so glad to leave an island—of course, this is my first."

"Mine, too."

On Dorothy's way to her next shift, excited discussion created a celebratory air around the surgery tent entrance. A nurse asked, "Did our Air Force really bomb Rome?"

"Don't you nurses keep up with things? That was almost a week ago. Must've shaken the Italians up, since they all thought we'd never bomb the holy city."

Somebody added, "But we only hit the rail yards, right?"

"I dunno. Who cares? What matters is the Italians got our message. A couple of days ago, we bombed Hamburg, too—Operation Gomorrah, they're calling that one."

Somebody else asked, "I wonder who picks these names?"

"General Eisenhower?"

"I doubt that, but somebody on his staff must have a gift for words. Who would ever have thought to call a Sicilian invasion *Operation Husky?*"

Hank's sarcastic humor surfaced. "Should've been *Operation Paradise.*"

Inside, the conversation continued and cheered Dorothy's first patient, who rested in a shady corner. She unwrapped his leg burns and started debriding. He said something, so she leaned closer in spite of the sickening odor.

"Paradise. That's a laugh. Up in the mountains, the litter carriers had to buy or borrow farmers' mules to bring our wounded down here. Jerry had demolished the mountain roads the whole way, and they were barely passable to begin with."

"Did you ride a mule?" Dorothy shuddered at the thought—no wonder this GI's legs were in such bad shape.

"Yeah. They sorted us into *severe* and *slightly*—wounded, that is. Guess I looked like a *slightly.*"

"Somebody must not have checked you very closely."

"Oh, I don't know. Some of the others—" A faraway look filled his eyes. "You can't imagine the chaos up there, taking prisoners at the same time they evacuated us. The medics had no chance to set up clearing stations, and night was comin' on. They knew they had to get the wounded down quick. The carriers even forced captured Germans to haul some gurneys."

Not too much of a stretch to think one of those enemy litter carriers might have been her schoolmate during her year in Bremen. The soldier winced when Dorothy pulled away a length of skin.

"Sorry."

"That's all right. Just hope I heal fast enough for the next fight. Then it'll be up the boot for us, and you can bet Hitler's gonna divert some troops from the Russian front to make up for all those Italians he's lost."

"Where are you from?"

"New Mexico. Most people would see it as wasteland, but there's almost always sunshine, and red cliffs everywhere you look."

"Sounds spectacular. Have you always lived there?"

"My folks moved down from Minnesota in '29. My Grandpa got a wild hair and bought a ranch. I was a little kid but I still remember riding down through the Midwest. What a sight we must've made parading through Iowa and all the other states. Grandpa sold out lock, stock, and barrel—sent some stuff by train, but loaded most of it in an old farm truck and a trailer he pulled behind." He gasped as she pulled off some dead skin.

"I know this hurts a lot."

"Yeah, but what's gotta be has gotta be, right?"

"If we keep at this, you'll be able to walk without a limp."

He grunted, and Dorothy urged his thoughts back to New Mexico. "Do you raise longhorns down there?"

"Horses. Grandpa used to sell 'em to the Cavalry, but now.... You know, I almost went to the Philippines with a lot of other New Mexico boys. If I had, I'd probably be in a Japanese prison camp right now. Got a buddy over there. Haven't heard from him since General Wainwright surrendered Corregidor."

When Dorothy smoothed olive oil on his wounds, he closed his eyes. Quietly, she dressed his legs. Burns sickened her as much as anything she'd seen on this tour. Almost.

Crystal blue eyes flashed before her as she hurried to the next patient. The chatter outside still centered on what had happened here in Sicily, and why. That always interested her, since the overwhelming patient load made it hard to keep up with recent Allied progress.

"Someone told me the commanders saw this operation as practice for invading France across the English Channel. Remember watching the ships converging in the Strait a few weeks ago?"

"Quite the armada."

"Yeah. One hundred eighty-thousand soldiers—Canadian, British, and ours. More than 2,500 vessels landing infantry on ten different beaches—it's tough to grasp all that went on that day."

"They say nothing like that ever happened before. But it will again, which is probably why Ike and Monty came to Malta to direct the thing."

Hank must've joined the group and took the opportunity to throw her dart. "You guys got to watch the beginning of this mess? Lucky you—we were *in* it."

"True, and you took fire waiting for us to bring the hospital on the 13th. The whole thing went kind of backwards."

"Kind of? As in—get the nurses killed off first, and then..."

As she checked temperatures and changed bandages throughout the tent, Dorothy pictured Hank's sneer.

"The Colonel made a big mistake, that's for sure. I'm glad he got canned for sending you nurses in with the infantry. Is it true you only had the water in your canteens?"

"If we had any left after the crossing. At least the engineers were already there. They had a fit and loaded us in trucks. After they dug us in, we calmed down. Later, we even found some gardens and gorged on local vegetables."

"Hating the idea of women here is one thing, but Colonel Scott went way too far. I've heard they sent him stateside—something to do with recruiting nurses."

Hank's sarcasm could have cut a thick steak. "Sounds like another brilliant Army idea."

"It's me." Hank's voice, though bedraggled, had lost none of its strength.

"Hank?"

"No. Santa Claus." Her irritated tone was nothing new.

Dorothy glanced at her alarm clock. Two am. Henrietta ought to be fast asleep—so should she and Millie, but Millie was already sitting up. She always wakened with such clarity.

"What's that smell? Hank, you didn't—"

"Just don't laugh, that's all I ask. I don't think you'd want me to come in, because…"

Dorothy leaped from her cot and threw open the tent flap. Peering out into the night, her nose explained what her eyes could not. The latrine—Hank must've fallen into one of the slit trenches the engineers had dug—one set for men, one set for women.

"Oh no. You actually slipped out there and…?"

Hank shrugged her bony shoulders. "It's raining, of course, and that makes everything like glass, how could I not?"

Millie wiggled in beside Dorothy and gasped.

"Come on girls, you see worse than this every day, all day long. So are you going to help me get cleaned up or not?"

"Sure. Mmm… I'll run down to the mess and see if there's any warm water left from the dishes.

"Good idea." Dorothy stepped out so she could get a better view in the moonlight. No use getting that slimy stuff on your pants all over. "We'll all go. There's bound to be…"

On the short trek, she refrained from asking how this could've happened, but Millie didn't. "Did you really just slip, or—"

"No." Of course, Hank had to wisecrack. "You know how sure-footed I am, right? So I decided to check out the depth of the latrine. You know, just out of curiosity. In the middle of the night, when I've got early duty this morning."

"But—"

"B-u-t-t, you mean. Mine's covered with the leftover meatloaf, or whatever that was, from last night's meal. Probably horse flesh. No wonder so many of us were racing to the trench during the evening."

Wally, the cook, was nowhere in sight, and one whiff of Hank was all it took to convince the guard this emergency required soap and clean water.

"Not exactly *warm* water," Hank pointed out as Millie shielded her with a sheet while she wiped her legs down. Meanwhile, Dorothy doused Hank's filthy pants and washed them in a scrub pail.

"Good thing it's summer and we're on a hot island, huh?"

"Yeah. Otherwise you'd be shivering by now, kiddo." Dorothy went for more water. "I suppose somebody on the mess crew will be cursing us when they come in to work. Oh well. At least these ought to be dry by noon tomorrow, but what do you have to put on now?"

"My seersucker uniform. It's on the stool at the foot of my bed." Every line in Hank's forehead proclaimed she detested depending on Dorothy and Millie.

"I'll be right back. Don't go anywhere."

"Right." Hank started in again and Millie tried to sooth her as Dorothy made for the nurses' tents.

Halfway there, a soldier met her. "Beautiful night, isn't it?"

"Yes." He paused and touched something around his neck. Ah, the officer with the gum chain. What was that about, anyhow?

"You're on a mission, I see. Wouldn't have anything to do with the latrine, would it?"

"How would you—"

He held up his hands. "You know how fast news travels around here, and day or night, there's never a quiet moment at the latrines."

"Umm... I'd better get going."

He made a sound in his throat. Was he clearing it or stifling a laugh? No time to figure it out. If they could hurry and get Hank situated, maybe they could still get a couple more hours of sleep.

Hank's fall was still the talk of the camp by the next afternoon. Snitches came to Dorothy and Millie during the noon mess, accompanied by guffaws.

"She's the tallest nurse—the one with the smart mouth."

"Such long arms and legs, a lot of area to cover—" Snickers and snide remarks floated all around them.

Dorothy turned to Millie. "There's no big war news, obviously. Guess Hank's adventure tops anything else people can think of to discuss today. I have to admit it's funny in a way, but I'm glad she's on duty. She wouldn't take all this lightly, and maybe it'll all quiet down by the time she gets off."

"Just so they remember how hard she works." Millie's eyebrows took a conspiratorial curve. "Say, we could try to do something about it. What if we start another story—something even more exciting?"

"Great idea. But what?"

"I don't know. We could say—umm—somebody's come down with bacillary dysentery and the docs have put them on sulfaguanidine."

"That'd be nothing new. We've treated plenty of cases like that already."

"Or we could start a rumor that there's a new breed of super-mosquito here, even bigger than the ones in Africa."

"That's probably true, too."

"Right. Somebody was talking yesterday about the lucky American docs and nurses set up in Palermo—we could make a big deal about them living in comfortable quarters and getting to use some great modern equipment. They even have prisoners cleaning up bomb damage for them."

"Where'd you hear this?"

"Right here, at lunch."

"I mean, who told you?"

"Nobody *told* me. The officers at the next table were talking about it. Just our luck to be an *evacuation* hospital, they said, a *mobile* medical unit. And then one of them told how one of those docs in Palermo took out somebody's lower left wisdom tooth during a storm aboard ship before they got to Casablanca. Had the guy lie down on a mess table and went to work."

34

"With nothing for pain?"

Millie shrugged. "The soldier was already hurting so much, he figured nothing could be worse." Some of the staff left their tables and she glanced at the clock. "Oops, almost time to go, and we didn't come up with anything. Guess Hank'll just have to take whatever comes."

"Don't worry. She can handle it. She's tough."

Chapter Five

T his war rather resembled a sea voyage with the ship making slow progress, yet always in danger of sinking. In the midst of it, Rupert determined to live out the middle name his mother chose for him. She named him after his father's father, but added *Ernest* for Sir Ernest Shackleton, explorer extraordinaire. His exploits captured her heart, and seeing her firstborn son, Mum declared her intent.

His father banished the idea, since the name originated in Kilkea County, Kildare, Ireland. But Mum won out—only just, considering the birthing nearly killed her—the luck of the Irish.

She went on to deliver three more strapping lads who served in the Great War. The two middle ones died in the Z attack from Dover, when the Navy engaged Rupert on the other side of the Channel. They'd been so desperate, they used sailors to dig trenches. And he almost died in one.

After the war, he'd planned to take Mum to Dover to pay last respects to "the boys" as she called them, since Pa had died by then, but the dreaded influenza swept her from this world too soon. One day he might still go, and perhaps his remaining brother Shelby would come over from the opposite coast, though that seemed unlikely.

Over to Dover.

The thought of Shelby, such a dramatic little boy, initiated something akin to a chuckle, the closest Rupert had come since the tragedy. The eruption startled him as he neared the station—how

36

could he indulge such extravagance, when all those victims at the tube station had lost their ability to laugh and cry, to see and hear?

The other night when he and Madeleine discussed Violet's death, Madeleine's strength shone through. "I must be calm for the children's sake, and one of the other ladies helped me gain perspective. She told me an aunt in the Cotswolds has taken the children—at least they'll be in the countryside now."

Perspective. How could he ever regain his own? Even thinking of the tragedy brought him low, and pursued him to the end of his own private tunnel.

Grateful for Madeleine's levelheadedness and understanding, he turned to today's word, exchanged verbally with Towsley hours earlier. *WONDER*—from the go, the utterance charmed him.

Interesting that Towsley suggested they consider a word each weekday when his vocation already centered on verbiage. He insisted they take turns choosing. Yesterday's had come to Rupert too randomly, in bleak morning chill, when he voiced it to Towsley without thinking.

WAR. What a foolish choice, far too close to the reality buckling hearts all around them. The three strung-together letters brought nothing but palsied attempts to make sense, paramount to *ICE* for Sir Ernest, for it was ice that crushed Shackleton's ship, the *Endurance*.

But the day passed and when Towsley delivered today's word, he added a story about a mystic of old who admonished her Maker after an accident on a muddy road, 'If this is how You treat Your friends, no wonder You have so few of them!'

"What does this have to do with *wonder*?" Rupert questioned as they walked together from the church on a misty spring morning. "The fierce rainstorm she experienced fits our circumstances, true. But this *Therese* lived four centuries ago."

"I thought you would see it instantly. The weather has dampened your mind."

"*No wonder*, as in *of course*? Just how...?"

37

The clock struck seven and the Vicar halted. "I've a meeting this morning at St. Paul's, a fitting locale to ponder London's future."

"Ah, yes, especially after—"

Towsley groaned. "I have visitations from that miserable night, too. Such a distress, but perhaps the worst is over, yes?"

He gestured to a shop window bearing one of the War Ministry's signs.

DON'T HELP
THE ENEMY!
CARELESS TALK
MAY GIVE AWAY
VITAL SECRETS

"All but two family members have been notified, a young woman up north with the Land Girls, and Marian Williams' husband." Rupert's sigh mingled with ever-moist air. "Letters might be intercepted."

"Ah, Melvin. Imagine coming home to such loss." Towsley shook his head, spraying dewy drops from his mustache. "I must be off."

Rupert saluted him.

A few steps down the way, the vicar half-turned. "Think on *wonder*. The meaning will come."

As Rupert continued on his way, recollections of reactions to the PM's edict troubled him. Some people nodded in compliance, as if this might have been expected, while others muttered against the powers that be.

A few pounded their fists and roared at him until he ducked his head. Several took to the far side of the street now when they saw him, but their loathing crossed the cobblestones like a putrefying odor. Grateful for a diversion, Rupert turned to the odd story Towsley had told. All the way to Cambridge Heath Road, he mulled the long-ago mystic unafraid to raise her voice to her Maker.

Mist turned to miserable drizzle, increasing his general disgruntlement. "*Wonder*—we've nearly lost the sense. But what does Towsley's tale have to do with it?"

Twice, umbrellas poked at him, but at least he avoided colliding with women and children. Finally, 214a Cambridge Heath Road, the B.G. Infirmary, now used as a military hospital, came into view.

Once inside, he almost neglected to remove his helmet, which made him appear a good three inches taller. In an instructional meeting, the Chief had warned, "Some are taken aback by an officer's mere appearance. For example, Officer Laudner, merely by his height, might seem imposing."

When he flipped up the strap, water spattered, and a young nurse trainee patted his arm with a cheery, "Good morning, Constable. Wet out there, eh?"

She hurried down the hall, and shaking rain from his coat, he approached a granite-faced nurse who failed to greet him from behind the counter.

"Ahem." She perused him through glasses much in need of cleaning. "Your business?"

"We have received a summons to transport a patient to Bethnal Green."

"They keep the police busy with this?"

Rupert maintained his composure. "The patient's name is Willoughby."

"Aha! Good riddance, I must say. He is your relative?"

"Not at all. I have never met him."

"A sorrier sort I never did see, no doubt he'll break the other leg on the way home. These men choose the gutter—what are we to do with them all?"

"Leg?"

"Broken. Three places. Sour temperament."

"I'd no instructions to bring an auto, and now we've a rain out there." A barrage of pecking on the window certified Rupert's admission.

"We cannot keep him even one more night. Glance into the ward and you'll see why." She walked away, so Rupert made his way down the busy passageway.

The occupants' very postures cried out their distress. A pair of brown eyes glistening in the closest corner stopped Rupert's heart. This young fellow with his head bandaged could easily pass for his baby brother—surely he might spare a minute.

But before he could advance, the head nurse appeared. "We can keep Willoughby until noon. Might you secure transport by then?"

"Yes, mum."

"Follow me." She led the way past some soldiers with a loaded gurney, and Rupert bit his lip at the copper taint. Even after all this time, such encounters held power to return him to the trenches.

Through another ward teeming with wounded, she pointed out Willoughby, stuck up against a moldering wall, with a massive plaster cast covering one leg.

An odor not unlike pongy cheese emanated. Rupert looked away, breathed in, turned back. "I shall fetch you later, sir. Where will you go?"

With shuttered eyes and breath steaming with fermentation, the fellow gave a shrug. "The Marquis of Cornwallis, if y' please."

Backing away, his own Mum's oft-intoned statement riddled Rupert. "Earnestness, this is your calling. To do your duty, unflinching." She'd uttered this like a benediction after the war, when he received news of his installation in the police force.

But this Willoughby had given a tavern's address. Perhaps he rented one of the rooms above. *Withhold judgment when possible.*

Outside, the dripping seemed less unpleasant, and Rupert devised a strategy, though assistants were sadly lacking at the station. "Perhaps the Vicar can help." The oppression of the Infirmary passed over him again. "No wonder that nurse snarls like a cougar."

Just then, Towsley's point emerged—an odd angle on *wonder,* indeed. *No... wonder.*

To live a life without wonder, with no awe—the discordant concept struck in like a barb. Would such a life be worth the pain?

Chapter Six

Santa Agatha, Sicily

In the battle for Messina, the latest casualties included a GI with a devastating chest wound. A few feet away from Dorothy, the docs deliberated—should they attempt a near-impossible surgery, when at least ten others needed immediate attention?

A few minutes later as Dorothy categorized more patients, one of the docs delivered her orders. "Stay with him."

No doubting what that meant. She set her mind.

This boy looked to be about 18. His closed eyes belied the chaos all around as severely wounded patients writhed on litters. Close enough to the white-masked surgeons who had secured one such litter on two sawhorses, Dorothy envisioned the internal injury they attempted to mend.

"Clamps!"

"Suction!"

"Pull this flap over. There, that's better—hard to see down in there."

A few feet away, hidden by the canvas walls, truck doors kept slamming, boots shuffled against uneven terrain, and curses flew. Litter bearers had it rough—a dangerous, thankless job, with much of their work in fading light or full darkness, when it became safer to retrieve the dead and wounded.

No one would envy their rugged front line treks, especially under the enemy gun sites on Mount Etna's steep slopes. A medic armband provided no guarantee, but load after load after load, these men returned to the front and bore their precious cargo to one evac hospital or another.

Sitting with her charge, Dorothy recited the Lord's Prayer and Luther's small catechism from her confirmation days. Then she rehearsed all the Psalms she'd memorized.

I will lift up mine eyes unto the hills, from whence cometh my help. My help cometh from the LORD, which made heaven and earth. He will not suffer thy foot to be moved: he that keepeth thee will not slumber. Behold, he that keepeth Israel shall neither slumber nor sleep. The LORD is thy keeper: the LORD is thy shade upon thy right hand...

No reaction from her patient, and no chaplain in sight. She dabbed the young man's forehead with a cool cloth, as his mother or sister might. The lapses in his breathing declared it wouldn't be long now.

Surrounded by so many litters, the most common ones ran through her mind. Her patient lay on the wooden number 7844000, almost identical to its Great War counterpart. That one, the collapsible aluminum 9935000, seven pounds lighter, from 22 pounds down to 15, was nowhere to be seen right now.

The newest wooden version, number 9936200, introduced this summer for cavalry and airborne use, collapsed too, and weighed only a half-pound more than the aluminum. It also folded in the center at a socket–type joint near the middle of each pole. So far, only a few of these had come in.

A few weeks back, Lieutenant Eilola briefed them on another model, number 993600, made of steel due to the aluminum shortage, with galvanized metal for the stirrups. This made it much heavier. She commented, "They ought to have known better. The last thing medics need is more weight to deal with."

As the timing between her patient's rasps lengthened even more, this seeming trivia kept Dorothy's mind busy. But litters could never be insignificant, since they helped save lives. Throughout this whole time, Dorothy prayed. Chaplains' prayers had reinforced the idea that short and succinct often meant more than long and flowery.

"Help him," and "Help them," for patients, docs, nurses, and litter bearers—this became her most frequent plea.

The other day, a couple of bearers had been restocking a truck with washed litters when she ventured out for fresh water, so she took a moment to thank them for their work. Their raised eyebrows told the story. Who ever thought to acknowledge their contribution? But without their faithful service, where would the wounded be?

Her patient's breathing stopped, so she checked his heartbeat. Nothing. She eased a sheet up and made the sign of the cross on his forehead.

"I commend your soul to God. May you rest in peace." She lifted his dog tag, but his name swam in blood.

Eventually his family would receive his simple metal ID, along with the contents of his pockets and what he carried in his knapsack. In some American kitchen, his mother would hold this cold tag to her heart and call out his name. Long before his effects reached her, somebody would have cleaned it up.

Turning toward the fresh influx of wounded, Dorothy focused on the first GI she came to. Not that she left the other one behind—not in her heart.

"Hey, our guys are about to overrun Messina! Somebody up there's on our side, doncha think?" One of the drivers stuck his head into the mess tent.

Somebody outdoors yelled, "Maybe the ghost of Mount Etna."

"I've seen that driver before, haven't you?" Hank kicked Dorothy under the table, forcing her to look up from her newspaper.

"Ouch!"

"Who are you talking about?" Millie set her section of the paper

43

aside as Hank pointed toward the entrance. "Oh, yeah. He drives for one of the commanders—I forget which one. I talked with him the other day and he's a farm kid, a little shy. Kinda cute, isn't he?"

"He'd come up to my naval—maybe." Hank changed the subject to Mount Etna. "Pretty spiffy we get to see an active volcano, huh?

Dorothy went back to reading while Hank cited facts about Mount Etna; tallest in the world, killed tens of thousands in the 1600s. How would they like to hike up there—

"Why so intent, Moonbeam?" Millie must've tired of volcano talk.

"Just catching up. It says here that on April 18th Allied planes shot down German troop-transport planes on their way to pick up the Germans we cornered in Tunisia. This article calls it The Palm Sunday Massacre."

Hank put her hands on her hips. "Don't you remember that?"

"Dorothy and I like to get the full picture. We never really know what's going on at the time it's happening—a little about this, a little about that, but I don't always understand what it all means."

"But that was four months ago, for Pete's sake—"

"Go on, Moonbeam. I'm all ears." Millie draped her elbows on the table and wrapped her hands behind her head.

"Well, we carried out two operations, Flax and Retribution."

"Flax? What's that about? Retribution I get, but—"

Millie's practiced scowl quieted Henrietta, at least for the moment.

"The terrible state of Algerian roads and railway lines created logistical challenges for the Allies and prolonged the Axis defense—"

"Oh yeah, we've been on those roads. Terrible isn't the word—"

Millie's put a forefinger to her lips. "Shhh."

"...taking into account the Allies' inexperience, as revealed at the Kasserine Pass and in its aftermath." Dorothy cleared her throat as the stunning eyes of that basket case reappeared before her. Even with all the patients she'd sat with until they died, his final gaze stayed with her.

"Inexperience, was it?"

"Nevertheless, the Allied forces finally squeezed the Nazis toward

Tunisia's northern tip, while from bases in Malta, the RAF and Royal Navy took a heavy toll on Axis shipping."

"Yeah, that was when they shifted us all the way from Rabat to the north. I counted every cotton-pickin' mile in that truck. My rear end has never been the same. See if I ever sit in the back of a truck again."

"Go on, Webbie." Millie held her hands up. "I keep hearing the corpsmen calling you that—it fits you as well as Moonbeam."

"My brothers used to call me Webbie, too. Okay, here we go. Because nighttime Luftwaffe transports could act with impunity, supplies still reached the Afrika Korps, so the RAF and US Army Air Forces began conducting operations both day and night to prevent their resupply or withdrawal. This led to unrecoverable enemy losses and the Axis surrender in North Africa. The Allies took upwards of 250,000 prisoners from the Afrika Korps and Italian army combined."

Someone at the next table gave a shout—should've known a private conversation was impossible around here. Now, some soldiers took up the topic.

"Wouldn't you think Jerry'd run outta soldiers?"

A doc chimed in, "They're extra prolific, the master race. Hitler's created a blonde, blue-eyed super people with better genes. Besides, the Nazis have had a long time to brainwash the citizens. They organized Hitler youth camps way back in the '20s. There's even some in the United States."

"What? You can't mean that."

"Oh, I do. They're out east, but I know of one in Wisconsin—"

"But Hitler has dark hair."

More people joined the discussion as Dorothy sat back to consider her family's time in Bremen. Had she ever seen a swastika or heard of a youth camp? No, her memories of Germany included only kind neighbors bearing *kuchen* and other baked goods when they arrived, and friendly children. Her teacher never mentioned anything about the Nazis. She had been strict, but no more than some back home.

As for everyone being blonde, that simply wasn't true—the little girls she played with down the street had both blond and brown. Although Elfrieda and her two oldest brothers Otto and Karl had been born in Germany before Mama and Papa emigrated, she and the rest—Vernon, Albert and Ewald, were born in America, and everyone had dark brown hair and eyes.

She smoothed the widow's peak inherited from Mama—was that characteristic under scrutiny, too? What was all this about the master race, anyway?

But another question bothered her far more. What had happened to the Germany they knew back in her childhood? People took Sunday afternoon walks, filled their window boxes with bright flowers, and aired feather beds over second story railings each morning in Bremen.

Being such a vital port, how could her neighborhood there have escaped the propaganda this doc mentioned? Maybe she simply hadn't been old enough at the time, but Vernon never mentioned anything like this, either.

Probably a good thing to keep quiet about speaking German. You never knew when somebody might take something wrong and sound off. Just the other day, a fistfight developed over something or other right here in the mess.

Meanwhile, two corpsmen carried on. "Enough about what went on in North Africa. I want to know what's slowing us down right now? Messina should've fallen to us long ago."

"It would have if those Brits would've put Patton in charge. He's a born warrior—you've gotta surge forward no matter what. Sitting still is the enemy."

One of the older docs spoke up. "In battle, yes. But his style does leave something to be desired. Have you heard how he slapped that poor soldier who was shaking so badly he could hardly stay on a cot? The guy had malarial fever, but Patton ordered him back to the front lines and called him a yellow coward."

"But don't you think some of them try to fake it to get sent

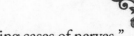

home? Commanders can't have everyone claiming cases of nerves."

"Maybe a small percentage, but we've chronicled battle fatigue since the last war. Men get to a point where they can't take any more. Some have actually run into the line of fire just to get it over with."

"Well, what they've seen here can't be any worse than Rommel getting reinforced and sending his tanks after us in Tunisia. Remember all those GIs in such bad shape we couldn't do a thing for them?"

"I sure do."

"Things were just as tough in that godforsaken desert as they are here. Where were all these shakers back then?"

"My point exactly. The pressure keeps mounting. The more battles a person experiences, the more likely he'll crack." The doc made a steeple out of his fingers. "I can't begin to imagine what it would be like out there, and wouldn't want to try it. Would you?"

The speaker fell silent. Millie and Hank had long ago disappeared to get ready for their shifts, and as the talk became more heated, recollections surfaced of several poor fellows who shook worse than anybody Dorothy had ever seen. No amount of blankets helped. Lieutenant Eilola said she would crawl onto their cots and hold them if it would make any difference. Those men couldn't have been putting on an act.

Word had it that Patton had treated another GI in an evac hospital the same way. The docs had routed the patient back to North Africa for more care, but General Patton ripped the poor guy from his cot, pulled his gun on him and threatened court-martial.

"Glad I didn't witness that," she muttered as she stood to leave. "I don't know if I could've kept my mouth shut, and Patton would've sent me packing. Sure hope the docs still sent that poor fellow back to Africa."

Darkness nearly engulfed the tube station entrance on this cloudy summer afternoon as Rupert made his rounds. Where the stairs turned, a 60-watt light bulb now guided citizens to their nighttime abode instead of the former 25-watt one. Workers also had installed two sturdy iron railings.

With all windows covered in black and the street lamps turned off, lest some dastardly German pilot note a likely target, this entrance proved only one of many dangers along the street. One might stumble into a jutting wall or lamp-post. Some people had, indeed, walked into canals or suffered grievous falls.

"I ought to know, as I'm the one called out with the district nurses, bless them." Rupert's murmur carried in the relative stillness, since many regulars had entered the tube earlier than usual in this dismal July weather.

A Wednesday it was, almost four months since the nightmarish scene that still raged before his eyes. Rupert sank against the cement wall as those sickening images arose before him once more. One hundred seventy three souls fleeing to this shelter at the sound of a bomb siren—or so everyone surmised.

The final mortality number, entered in the ledger after morticians finally finished reassembling body parts, stood higher than an earlier estimate. One hundred seventy-three—Rupert could scarcely repeat the figure.

Only a few feet away, the hungry shadow of death had snatched them all. The smells of that night made his stomach lurch even now. He'd always imagined death by drowning or fire to be the worst, but had relegated being crushed to death to the top of his list.

You would attempt to wriggle free, but one by one, your extremities would go numb. Then your bones would smash to bits inside you. All the while, you would be unaware of the cause until finally, you lost consciousness.

No wonder Marian Williams let loose her hankie. A few days after the tragedy, the Chief had delivered that remnant to the corner of Rupert's desk. He so rarely entered this small space, but on that occasion, he took a seat and began to explain.

"A few more details have been compiled. In the noise of those new artillery guns, three extra busloads of passengers got off at the Number Eight stop next to the station, boosting the numbers seeking safety. The 15 X 11 foot tube station opening could hardly contain them."

"As you know, the Metropolitan Borough and the Mayor have often campaigned for better access, but the Home Office repeatedly turns them down." The Chief's sigh went straight to Rupert's heart. "You recall the early evening shower that made the concrete steps even more treacherous."

He slid the hankie onto Rupert's desk. "This hankie belonged to Marian Irene Williams, whom workers found at the bottom of the pile-up. I wonder if you might return it to her family—when you see fit, of course. Heaven knows, not much else survived the crush."

Laundered and folded into quarters, the hankie stared up at them. It still occupied the far right-hand corner of Rupert's desk, for he had yet to deliver it to the Williams family.

Why put off that duty? Why not return this reminder of that horrible day to where it belonged? Perhaps it might offer the family a bit of comfort.

In quiet moments when few voices carried from the front of the station, the answer swelled within Rupert's consciousness. The thought of touching the hankie repulsed him.

Since March third, he'd learned that other occurrences had also led to great loss of life on the same day. For one, Australian and American air forces had devastated a Japanese navy convoy in the Bismarck Sea, killing more souls than had died here.

But this sort of logic did nothing to assuage his aversion to the hankie. Those who lost their lives in the stairwell weighed on his conscience beyond all rational thought—if only he had happened along earlier on his trek toward the volunteer fire station. Perhaps he might have met Marian and delayed her entrance to the station. Perhaps he might have—

Even now, he barely shut his eyes at night, lest the phantoms of the lost float before him. He had failed them utterly, along with their families. The memory clung like blood to concrete.

49

Walking through the tunnel as people began to gather for the long night, no one spoke of that pivotal event. Did they even think of it as they ate their evening meals at the Canteen? Ascending the stairs again, no odors remained. Rupert steeled himself—he must still the insistent urge to race to the top like a frightened child.

From the street came an Air Raid Police Warden's yell. "Put out that bloody light!" Someone had forgotten to pull their blackout drapes, though by now, most citizens followed this sunset routine as a matter of course. Rest assured, the culprit would soon read his name in the *Hackney Gazette* summonses to court.

But seeing one's name in the paper was preferable to having it inscribed on a cross near a mass grave. Rupert glanced at his watch. At home, Madeleine would be pulling their drapes, calling Cecil in from play and preparing supper. Perhaps some poor woman was late to leave for the tunnels today because her baby had fought being placed in its 'Mickey Mouse' capsule in case of a gas attack. In trying to console the child, she had momentarily forgotten the blackout and reaped the warden's cry.

Still transfixed by that horrible night, he wiped his eyes. Little school lads and lassies, sent ahead by their parents to claim a family sleeping spot, mothers with babes in arms, aprons smelling of yeast and mash, vinegar liquor, and tinned beef. Many still gasped for air by the time he arrived.

Against the far wall, a boy of 10 or 12 stood immobilized against the far wall, aghast at the scene around him. That lad had survived, but how could he ever forget?

What if he had been Cecil?

Grasping the need to search out those still breathing, two emergency workers had teamed with Rupert to disentangle still-warm bodies that hung heavy and limp in their arms. He had no idea how long they worked until at last, the Chief Constable found him.

A tap on the shoulder shook Rupert from his reverie. "Blockin' the route for late comers, are you?" The least friendly of the fire wardens spat sideways. "Need I report ya, too, off'cer?"

Rupert contained his irritation. "Thank you kindly, but no. I shall be off now."

Visions of the tragedy accompanied him home, into the cozy kitchen, and quelled his normal urge for a game of checkers with Cecil or a bedtime story with Iris. The images drained his normal sanguine cheer, even his longing for Madeleine's touch.

Towsley kept assuring him these reactions would pass, but he wondered. One thing he would never whisper, not even to the vicar: the tube station carnage carried him back to what he had witnessed 20 years ago and thought he had buried forever. Inside his being, the Great War resurrected.

At night, gassed soldiers appeared before him, pleading for aid, and it was all Rupert could do to shake them away. Even in the daytime, those mangled wretches sometimes turned his stomach into a mass of barbed wire not unlike No Man's Land.

This afternoon, unable to touch the hankie on his desk, he had simply sat and stared at the initials. That one small object now embodied the tube station tragedy, and seemed to hold even more power than his memories from the war.

Chapter Seven

"**H**aven't had a minute to do this tapin' m'self, off'cer. My youngest takes everything I've got, and soon there'll be another, what with Danny's furlough in February. The District Nurse said I must see the doctor once a week, so between getting back and forth to the Infirmary—"

"Yes, I understand. I don't mind helping at all." Rupert wet a length of brown gummed paper and stuck it to Mrs. Evans' kitchen window in a diamond pattern. The sticky stuff most locals called scrim was heralded to keep glass shards from flying into the room during a bomb blast.

"So you visit the infirmary once a week?"

"And what a jog that is."

An idea began to take shape, a way to employ the citizenry in detective work, as the Chief recommended in their last meeting. Sixty-five sticky pieces of scrim later, Rupert dipped his hands in a water basin and dried them on Mrs. Evans' proffered towel.

"I've an idea, just now. Would you mind assisting the force in our official duties, Mrs. Evans?"

"Why, of a certain. But what can I do?"

"Have you heard of a man named Avery Ritter?"

"Ah, that's the wide boy sellin' horse flesh for beef. Black market, off'cer. My Danny cursed 'im and said to stay clear."

"Precisely. The authorities doubt Avery has curtailed his actions, so we keep an eye on him. To be honest, though, our resources are running quite short with all of the deployments."

"Some of the force had sons off to the fight, eh?"

"Exactly. But recently we have been informed that Ritter carries on his business over toward the Infirmary."

"I shall take extra care, officer."

"Good. But suppose you kept an eye out for him on your trips to and fro?"

"Me?" Mrs. Evans slapped her cheeks with her hands. "Like a spy?"

"Somewhat along that line."

"What might I do?"

"As Danny instructed, stay clear of Ritter, but observe and report what you see." Rupert angled his head. "Women's powers of observation often far outweigh men's."

Mrs. Evans brushed back her hair and stood a little taller.

"Let me know whom Ritter speaks with, for example, or if you see him exchanging packages with anyone, things like that."

"But what if I don't know who he deals with?"

"Simply bring me a description—his clothes, shoes, height, unique markings, things like that."

"Like if he had a scar on his face?"

"Yes, exactly." Rupert readied to leave, and Mrs. Evans nodded, not once but three times.

"Every bit of black market goings-on here hurts our boys. The more of these skivs we apprehend, the more goods become available to our troops."

"True, but I never—"

Two young children raced in and attached themselves to her skirts. She wiped the youngest one's nose with her long apron, patted the other one's head, and sent them back outdoors.

"I will do what you ask, Constable. You can count on me."

She went inside and Rupert started off toward home. Soon, he spied Gran coming toward him down the pavement, with Iris in her arms and Cecil in tow. Cecil broke into a run, landing in Rupert's grasp. Then Iris wriggled, and Gran had all she could do to keep the child in one arm and her shopping bag in the other.

Rupert reached for his baby girl and Gran gave a sigh.

"Are they wearing you out, then?"

His mother-in-law wrinkled her nose. "These youngsters do have a great deal of energy."

"It's a blessing you live with us, such a help to Madeleine."

"Papa... papa..."

"A moment, Iris." Rupert turned to Gran. "I've gotten off a bit early today. Let me take them for awhile."

With Cecil clutching two of his fingers, Rupert juggled Iris to his hip. "What say Papa takes you to buy some candy?"

Four eyes popped—this was unheard of.

"Say goodbye to Gran, then, and we'll be off."

A certain shop owner owed him a favor, so Rupert started off toward St. Peter's Street. Passing St. Peter's Church and school, where Junior had attended, and Cecil too except during the evacuation, a sense of calm settled over Rupert.

Children First, announced the sign in the candy shop window.

A small amount of Cadbury's chocolate has been made. All the food value of the milk is in it, a glass and a half in every half-pound. Supplies are limited, but are being distributed fairly in the areas we supply. When your turn comes, please remember that growing children need this extra refreshment most.

Sniffing the rich, tempting chocolate satisfied him as much as if he'd enjoyed a piece himself, and the obvious delight on his children's faces as they partook of the fruit and cream filled his heart to overflowing. Maybe it was the lights in the shop, but Cecil's cheeks seemed ruddier, and Iris—did her eyes always shine this much?

Perhaps if he bought just a couple of sweets every payday, they would remain healthy until this bitter war came to an end. If he failed to provide a bit of a treat for them, who else would?

Returning home with tummies full, plus a piece each of Cadbury's Chocolate soundly bitten into and tucked into their pockets for later, the children slowed Rupert's footsteps. He stopped to greet passersby as he used to, addressed them more heartily than he had since springtime. The autumnal scent of gardens in their final burst of life touched him anew. Another growing season nearly at an end, awash in life's rhythm.

A fortunate man was he, trekking about with his son and daughter. During the evacuation, he and Madeleine had sent them to a farm near Whittlesea, north of London. Weeks without Cecil and Iris had turned into months as the bombing continued, and when they returned, they seemed almost strangers. But he'd been so occupied with his work that their absence affected him less than it did Madeleine.

On the day of their return, how she wept to see them again! He'd gone with her to meet them at Victoria station, and oh, the hubbub as parents reunited with their youngsters. That day's palpable joy must have been a foretaste of what Towsley referred to as the reunion with our loved ones in glory.

For the serenity that claimed Rupert on this short journey, the Prime Minister or the King might have announced the blackout lifted, the troops brought home, the war over.

Ah, the late day sunshine casting its rays over his children on the way home from that small shop. Oh, the telltale signs of waning summer in the foliage, and the twinkle in the eyes of Londoners they met, wholly beyond reason, for some of them had lost all.

Vicar Towsley's unflappable spirit seemed to have overtaken Rupert. Was this how he saw the world when he wakened each morning? At their street, Cecil ran on ahead, so Iris slid down, too. Madeleine met them at the door—what a capitol mum she was, she must've been watching.

"My, my—what a mess your faces are. What have you been eating?" The low ripple of her voice alerted Rupert's senses even more. A fortunate man indeed.

July 22, 1943 Agrigento Sicily

With the nurses bivouacked in a large tent until they could set up regular tents and settle more-or-less permanently, everyone discussed the news of the day, a visit to the Bishop of Agrigento. Dorothy's deuce-and-a-half had been bringing up the rear when a priest dashed out into the street and waved them down.

Somebody understood enough to establish the Bishop's desire for a photo with the Americans. So they'd trooped out and lined up against an imposing wooden door, with the Bishop in the middle.

Friendly and white haired, he seemed more than pleased, and communicated his gratitude for their arrival with a great many hand signs and smiles. His brief speech pointed out that he and many other islanders were anti-fascist. Someone also interpreted that he had cousins in the States.

"Sure you do—the Mafia." Thankfully, Hank's comment escaped the Sicilians.

The Bishop insisted on taking a photograph with the nurses and corpsmen on the steps of the Cathedral. At the last minute, a few shy, black-haired local boys got in on the excitement, too. A corpsman slipped them chocolate when they ran up to get into the picture, and Millie poked Dorothy.

"They're cute as can be, but awfully thin, don't you think?"

As twilight fell a few hours later, talk about the day's events persisted, but Hank had had more than enough of that. "Okay, so we met a Bishop. It was more exciting when you started petting that farmer's goat and he offered you some milk, Moonbeam."

"He was really generous—probably had very little to share."

"When you said *yes*, I figured, 'Why not? If we get sick, we've got doctors handy.' The stuff really didn't taste that bad."

"Nope—a little oilier than what we're used to." Dorothy gave a big yawn—tomorrow would be a long day of setting up the surgery and pharmacy, starting at the crack of dawn.

But Hank had a terrible time falling asleep. Oh yes, during their first days in North Africa she'd often wanted to talk into the night.

"Tell me about your brothers and sisters again."

"You must be desperate. You sound like a little kid who can't sleep."

"Fifty percent correct. Now start talking. There's seven of you, I remember that..." She could probably have listed them all herself after all the times they'd bivouacked together across North Africa.

"Let's see. What can I say you don't already know? Elfrieda was born in 1910, Otto in '11, Carl in '13, and Werner the next year. I came along in 1916, Albert was born in '22, and Ewald in '24. Got it?"

"No. Tell me again."

"Carl and Otto work in the bakery with my father. Werner—he changed his name to Vernon in English—he's a tank buster in the Pacific. The last I heard from him, his unit was aboard ship again and kept crossing the International Date Line. He'd changed the clock ahead and back three times in two days."

"What? I don't get it."

"Me neither, but that's what he wrote. He also said he was losing his hearing, after all the shooting he's already done."

"No wonder. A tank buster—that must be some massive gun."

"Right. Okay, back to Waterloo. Mmm—we lived at 418 Cherry Street."

"What kind of house?"

"Wooden. White. Big." It was tempting to say, "Now roll over and think about your own family," but Hank's childhood left a lot to be desired. Nothing anyone would want to think about to put them to asleep, and some of her experiences no doubt led to her insomnia.

"And Albert's a Marine pilot, right? What a gorgeous guy—those flight suits do something for a man. Vernon's handsome too, but Albert has that adventurous look, like he'd take on the entire Luftwaffe singlehandedly. You'd better show me a picture of Ewald one of these days."

"I wrote home for one—we'll see. He's really tall, and the last time I saw him, he still had his chubby baby face."

After a while, Dorothy nearly fell asleep mid-word, so Hank changed course.

"Millie—you awake?"

"Mmm..."

"It's your turn. Give me the low-down on your folks and grand-parents and ancestors, back to the fourth century."

"All right. My grandma spent weeks at the library going through our family tree, certain she'd find something exciting. You know how people claim they're direct descendants of a king or queen? Well, my relatives have a higher distinction. We're related to one of the witches in the Salem witch trials."

"You made that up."

"Not really."

"If that's the case, we're related. My family has plenty of witches, too."

Hoping Millie's voice would put Hank to sleep, Dorothy let herself drift. The Eleventh had been re-designated as a semi-mobile hospital and would follow the troops all over the island.

Scuttlebutt had it there was a big white hospital in Palermo that managed to survive the Allied bombing, though it took a couple of hits. But Palermo was clear across Sicily, and who knew what shape it would be in by the time the Eleventh got there?

Finally, silence reigned except for Hank's snore. There was no better nurse—if they could only retrain her mind to sleep. At least warm weather had arrived, which dried up the mud and made everything easier. The Evac's new semi-mobile designation brought a sense of satisfaction. That meant they'd be as close to the troops as possible, and could save more men.

A couple of other nurses grimaced when the word came down, but in the darkness, Dorothy whispered. "This is what I came for. We're right where we ought to be."

One other positive—the mail caught up with them today, including a package from home with several skeins of yarn, homemade grape jelly, and pickles.

Those pickles transported her right to Mama's kitchen, where she probably was busy preserving this year's cucumber harvest. Oh, the tantalizing scent of dill, garlic, and vinegar! Dorothy opened one jar in secret, though she shared most of the contents.

Something about biting into that first crisp taste brought exquisite comfort. Life burgeoned with ambivalence these days—knowing she was exactly where she needed to be cohabited with her longing for home. When she'd volunteered for duty back in '41, no one had any idea they'd be sent to Africa or Sicily, or how long this war would take.

Her first trips to Fort Leonard Wood for her induction and then later for R & R were close enough for regular visits, but the next orders took the unit to New Jersey, where there'd been no chance to take the train back home.

Tonight, she shared the jelly with Millie and Henrietta on some crackers Millie produced. While they ate, Dorothy scanned the packaging—copies of the Waterloo Courier. Millie asked her to read it aloud.

"You're sure you don't mind?"

"Are you kidding? My sis packs everything in popcorn."

"And we get to eat it—that's worth a lot." For once Hank found a positive slant, but not for long. "My little town has a newspaper the size of a toilet paper square. Bores me stiff with Mrs. Mosely's prize roses getting trampled by some wayward dog, a soldier coming home on a nine-day leave, or a change in rationing coupons. Your town's big enough to have important things going on, Webbie."

"Listen to this. 'PFC R.W. Handel, former East High basketball star, has arrived safely in England, according to word received by his parents, Mr. and Mrs. C.W. Handel, 416 Placid Avenue. Private Handel, who is with an army infantry unit, entered the service in June 1943, following his graduation from West High.'"

"Sounds pretty much like our paper." Millie spread a little more jelly on another cracker. "Editors have it easy right now. People want to hear that a PFC from their area made it to where he was going without his ship being torpedoed. Even if they don't know the family personally, they can relate."

"Here's a headline from June 18. 'Allies Pound Italian Boot Bases, Naples.'"

"Wow, Naples ought to be rubble by the time we get up there. Or over there." Hank rubbed the back of her neck. "And I was looking forward to a night out in that old city—thought we could dance and live it up."

"Right. It'll probably look just like this island—producing rubble seems to be Jerry's strength."

"We'll see. Italy's a long country." Millie stretched her arms wide.

"Yup, it's one high-topped boot we've gotta climb."

Millie and Hank—at least the three of them could make a home-away-from-home wherever they happened to land.

"Anybody here speak German?"

Working with a patient nearby, Hank nodded in Dorothy's direction. Drat! With hardly enough water to douse a puppy, she'd been attempting to bathe a wounded GI. He stirred and his eyes shuttered open. What did he see? Definitely not khaki canvas, a pole holding up the roof, and a whole lot of commotion—no, in his mind's eye, he traveled far, far from this tent.

Awaiting transport to a British hospital ship, he hovered between consciousness and coma. Like so many others, this patient sometimes burst out with unintelligible words and phrases. Once, he called out for his mother. Did a woman with his blue star in her front window sense his need right now and pray harder?

One of the teachers at the Lutheran school in Waterloo declared that such things happened. "The world around us has unseen spiritual connections and communications. We have no idea how many angels attend us here on earth, or the ways our prayers might affect others."

This soldier's skin, so clammy Dorothy bit the sides of her cheeks when she first touched him, had warmed a little. Even if he died soon, maybe wiping mud from his face, humming "Don't Sit Under the Apple Tree," and praying he would live created invisible results.

"Sure hope so." At her whisper, his eyelids twitched. At the inevitable tap on her shoulder, she smoothed the sheet under his chin and turned to see an officer's liaison.

"You read German, Miss?"

No point in arguing. Might as well just follow him. This translation might make a difference for some GI somewhere.

A few minutes later, an officer she'd seen in the mess invited her to pull a chair up to a table positioned behind a tent flap. "We're moving to Qualiano tomorrow, and an advance party has confiscated these papers from a captured enemy stash. We need to know if there's anything vital here, but our normal interpreter has influenza. We hope you can..."

Thankful for Mama clinging to her native tongue and for that year of school in Germany, Dorothy set to work. She made sense of the notes without much trouble, and transcribed them while the officer went about some other tasks. He questioned only one translation before letting her go.

Grateful he asked no questions, she paused outside the tent, letting her imagination run. Minus its present devastation, this island would be so beautiful. Clear blue-green water, phosphorescent in midday sun, beckoned her to swim. Sky so blue it hurt her eyes smiled down on scattered olive trees.

On the walkway back to the hospital tent, a tiny yellow wildflower peeped from between two rocks. Squatting, Dorothy supported the blossom with her finger. A glossy patina covered each miniature petal. Where had she seen this plant before?

Ah—behind the house in Bremen. She often went out to help with the weeding, and Nana had pointed out these flowers, insignificant in the landscape's grand scheme.

Diese Blume ist hier seit ich ein kleines Mädchen war, Dorothea. Während des Krieges, als deine Onkel in Frankreich kämpften, war ich so verängstigt, aber eines Tages, als ich hierher kam, jubelten mir diese gelben Sprites zu.

A scuffle broke out somewhere, but Dorothy stayed beside the walkway. That day, Nana had described her fear during the Great War. She'd been so afraid her brothers would never come home, but one day a tiny, bright flower had cheered her. Interesting that this memory would surface today.

Under sky as blue as any she'd seen, Dorothy breathed, "Oh, Nana, I wonder if your house on Admiralstrasse still stands. You were so good to us—what a beautiful place."

The answer had to be *no*. Close to the shipping yards along the Baltic Sea, where so many Allied bomber pilots trained their loads, how could that structure possibly survive?

A GI passed by and broke the spell. Tempted to pick the fragile bloom, Dorothy decided against it—maybe someone else would spy it and receive just the boost they needed. That proved true on the spot, since Millie happened along.

"Look at this little flower—isn't it a beauty?"

"You notice everything." Millie reached for a petal. "*Earth laughs in flowers*, you know."

"That's poetic."

"Emerson." Millie took a long breath. "When we were in fifth grade, Delbert brought me a handful of flowers like these. That was the first time I realized he cared about me."

"Fifth grade. And you two have been an item ever since?"

"Not exactly. Del's pretty shy, so years passed before he gave me another sign. But those first flowers still had a hold on me. At our ninth grade dance, I waited and waited for him to take me out on the floor, but his bashfulness won. Walking home, our paths crossed, and I asked him if he'd had fun.

"He said no, because we hadn't danced."

"And you said?"

"'Well, why didn't you ask me?' He scuffed around in some fallen leaves and finally whispered, 'I was too scared.'"

"That's shy, for sure."

"Yeah. Of course, my heart went out to him, and we took in our first movie the next Saturday night."

"And went together to the next dance?"

"From then on, I was hooked. He was like the brother I never had, the best listener ever, and he still makes my heart go *pitter-pat.*"

From the area of the nurses' tents came a welcome yell—*Mail Call.* "Oh, maybe there's a letter from him." Millie darted away.

Dorothy trailed her to where a private set down a leather mailbag slung over his shoulder. A bevy of nurses squeezed around him, hoping for news from home or a beau somewhere around the world. Eager hands reached out as he called names.

Nothing for her this time, but she'd received two letters at the last call. She'd been hoping the next delivery would bring Millie one from Delbert, and her wish came true. Millie ran off somewhere to savor the news while the girls who'd been overlooked slowly meandered away. Whew—no one commandeered Millie and forced her to read her letter out loud, as sometimes happened.

Beside their entrance, Hank slumped on a canvas stool, letting her long legs sprawl.

"So, did you hear from your great big happy family?"

"Nope. Not today."

"How about your secret lover?"

Dorothy ignored that. Paul's latest letter had hinted at romance, she had to admit. But he was far too old, and he also shared that he'd decided to join the Catholic Church. She could never hurt Mama by marrying him.

"You didn't even bother to go over?"

"Give me one good reason I should."

Better change the topic. "I'm hungry. Do we have any of those eggs left?"

"You bet. That was our best find in months, and the islander seemed happy with your scarf in exchange."

63

"If the nights get any colder, I might be sorry I sacrificed Mama's handiwork."

"In Italy, the temperature's bound to drop."

"Yeah. But I think Mama would understand my reaction when that lady showed us her eggs."

From under her cot, Dorothy pulled the treasure. "I'll light the stove. Do we have anything left from last night?"

"Are you kidding? The termites took off with the leftovers hours ago—the joy of island living. Oh, to be in Italy, with grapes hanging from the vines and apple boughs heavy with fruit." Hank's snide expression belied her words.

"Yep, and somebody to drop those grapes in our mouths. All our troubles will be over once we get to Italy—it'll be heaven on earth."

Chapter Eight

A letter lay on the table in the narrow front passage that during childhood had struck Rupert as so large. Now he must cramp his head and shoulders each time he entered. He picked up the letter Gran had retrieved from the postbox.

From the kitchen emanated cooking aromas, sizzles, and pops. Madeleine went about her perennial task of making everyone's plate seem full.

Held to his nose, the letter smelled of labor and purposefulness, but the handwriting and return address looked utterly foreign. Harwood. Should he recognize this name?

"Intuition—we use this resource every day, and you especially, seek out crime and working for justice." Vicar Towsley's philosophizing came to mind from earlier in the day.

The urge to toss the letter into the rubbish bin—could this be intuition? Or could Rupert's first instinct simply signify fear of the unknown? Realizing he had pressed his lips together, Rupert thrust in the opener and began to read.

Perhaps you recall my name from when your children came to us during the evacuation. Due to the recent loss of our youngest child to scarlet fever, my wife has been ailing, and often speaks of your Cecil and Iris.

Would you be looking for a place for them for the summer?

They might help my Eloise through this sadness, and enjoy mushroom hunting in our vales. Cecil might also join the local boys in fundraising.

With hopes that a visit might be possible,

Yours sincerely,
M. Harwood

Aha... the Harwoods, who cared for Cecil and Iris during the Blitz. A moment's reflection on their sorrowful circumstance and this man's kind intentions took Rupert back to those harsh days when Adolph had gone berserk trying to uproot England from her moorings.

Surely nothing could ever strike such terror again. Starting in September, for 56 days, hundreds of bombs had rained down each night, leaving devastation at every turn. They caused impossible rubble, terrible fires, and so many deaths. In the Green, streets lay gutted, gas mains ruptured, and plumbers heroically attempted to get to broken or blocked pipes.

In all, 'twas a hellish time.

When the Nazi effort to annihilate the Royal Air Force failed, fear still lingered, as tangible as London's perennial haze. Welcoming the children home came with added trepidation for their safety, but the Harwoods' generosity could not be overestimated. Along with hundreds of rural inhabitants, they had opened their home to London's children.

Cecil's animated expression when he'd returned flitted before Rupert's inner vision, and also the permanent shadows darkening the fragile skin under Madeleine's eyes. In those terror-filled weeks, her busy fingers flew through endless evening stitching, with no one to cuddle in the rocker, no small hands and feet to scrub, no need to toast two slices of bread over the fire to satisfy the children through the night.

When Cecil and Iris returned whole and happy, she simply could not get enough of them—their voices, their smiles, their scent. How often had he caught her breathing in their essence? He shared her loneliness, but faced extra duties at work, earlier mornings, later evenings, and constant emergency calls in the night.

The mass graves—oh, my. Who would have imagined how many would be necessary? To make one's living digging was one thing, and honorable, but to join in the vast excavation necessary to bury a whole block full of your friends and neighbors, quite another.

And that row of rabbis, priests, and vicars lining the edge of the long gravesite, the survivors on the other. How could anyone forget such scenes?

Remembering them unearthed the tube station horror—yet another mass grave, with Madeleine attending the service. Lately, her growing weariness had become evident, so he had taken over part of the children's bedtime ritual.

Stooping here in the hallway, he calculated his pay and her sewing earnings. Plenty enough to manage, but standing in weekly ration lines for their paltry seven eggs—one per person—took its toll. She was always stretching the household's scant weekly 18 ounces of tea or butter. What might he do to lighten her load?

Once, he'd come across her in the butcher's line, her meat bag tucked under her arm, knitting a stocking while she waited. All for a section of brisket, if good fortune shone, but more likely some offal from a recently slaughtered animal—sweetbreads, brains, pigs' trotters...

The tube station loss had carved a deeper hole in Madeleine's reliable, easygoing nature. After that evening, a frantic look sometimes entered her eyes. What if she had been carrying Iris there, stumbled and fallen like that poor woman?

In addition, her dear bandage-rolling comrade lost her life that night. Rupert had stopped in a time or two when they'd first begun the rolling, and their friendly banter always made him chuckle.

"Here you go, Duckie," one would say, and the other would respond in kind. Violet taught Madeleine to improve efficiency by rolling each bandage from her ankle to her hip. But Madeleine no longer frequented the bandage rolling. Instead, she threw her fury into knitting more socks and caps and sweaters for the troops.

Besides losing that chum, she'd known many of the children lost on those stairs. Of course she had—one grew accustomed to their voices at play in the gardens and out in the street.

Would allowing Cecil and Iris to stay in the country trouble her more than help her?

The gold watch that had belonged to Rupert's father showed enough time to consult Vicar Towsley before supper. Perhaps he could offer some insight.

A few minutes later, Rupert presented his dilemma.

"Ah—opportunity and loss cohabit like spiders and flies, do they not?" He changed the subject. "I shall attend a meeting very early tomorrow near Westminster, at St. Matthew's Church. What say we take this opportunity for an early word? Shall it be *opportunity*?"

Towsley leaned back in his wooden desk chair. "Or we might consider *nature*. That brings to mind Aristotle. 'In all things of nature, there is something of the marvelous.' Hard to disagree with that, eh?"

What could be better for Cecil and Iris than time out in nature, so meager here in the East End? Did not Mr. Harwood's letter thrust opportunity under their noses?

"So then... *nature* or *opportunity*?"

"You choose."

"Nature." Towsley made the decision and saw Rupert to the side door. Though he'd circled 'round a direct answer, the look in the vicar's eyes carried a message, and if intuition meant anything at all, Rupert had a fairly good sense of it.

After supper, a bedtime story, and an early goodnight to Madeleine, he hurried to the fire watch station. When he returned, exhausted by tonight's sightings, a single piece of toast waited for him on the table. Madeleine—always thoughtful.

This bit of nourishment reminded him he'd not been forgotten, and biting into it, he realized the strength of his hunger. Not that this evening required heavy work, but three attacks had come in, with enough damage to warrant inspection.

Careful to avoid squeaky floorboards, he pulled back the heavy drapes. Madeleine shifted, and thankful she'd been able to reach the blessed state of sleep, Rupert eased into bed. The moon traced a design on the yellow flowered wallpaper she so painstakingly chosen after Mum died.

They'd lived here with her until she passed on, so this wallpaper proclaimed that Madeleine had become the woman of the house. Little by little, the dwelling filled up again, as it had when all his brothers were growing up. When Madeleine's father passed, Gran came to share the second floor with Anna. Then Junior married dear Kathryn, and Madeleine whispered yesterday of another grandchild on the way.

Houses had once seemed like characters in a book that grew and changed with their occupants, with either gloom or cheer settling over them. But seeing so many homes obliterated altered Rupert's perspective.

Bombing survivors shunted through those wrecked structures for something of value. Their loss went beyond reckoning—their place in this world vanished. What would he do if he returned home one night to find everything devastated beyond repair?

Such a fellow lived a few blocks away, and checking on him had become routine. Stopping by an abandoned automobile, that is, for the grief-stricken bloke had lost everything but his clothing. *All* included his wife, three children, and his mother... in one fateful day. With so many strikes since, some of the details had faded.

In the early mornings, that abandoned automobile glimmered in its alleyway, and Rupert cast up a prayer that the poor man still slept, but nearly always, he sat staring at nothing. How did he carry on his daily work at the docks?

The breeze changed direction, as often happened about this time of night. Beside him, Madeleine's quiet breathing brought intrinsic comfort. But now, back to his pressing question: what to do about Mr. Harwood's letter?

Madeleine's comment when he showed her the letter after the children slept showed her usual consideration. "That poor woman."

"Time in the country would be good for Cecil and Iris. What do you think?"

69

The mix of pain and hope in Madeleine's eyes tore him apart. Would she be relieved to have the children breathing fresh air, safe with the Harwoods, or would another separation be unmanageable?

He could scarcely imagine steady, stalwart Madeleine going 'off,' as some women had done. People said this of a grieving woman a few doors down, and the phrase described her dazed countenance as well as anything.

Two sons departed from this life—one in a sunken ship, the other during Dunkirk. So many made it back from that debacle that even Mr. Churchill pronounced the evacuation by ordinary citizens a miracle, but this mum would never forget. Like an empty flour sack with nothing to render it shape, she fulfilled her duties with five or six younger children.

Rolling over, Rupert retrained his mind. He ought to be able to read Madeleine better. Before the evacuation, he fancied himself quite adept at that, but all had changed. Finding designs in the moon's pattern, he sent forth a timid whisper.

"Show us what to do."

"Mornin' to y', constable."

Rupert tipped his cap to George Bridley, who woke long before dawn to drive his produce into Bethnal Green. Every Monday and Thursday, rain or shine, George's team clopped through the streets toward the market. Even with all the new Ministry of Food regulations due to black market activity, these trips must still be worth his while.

How easy for him to sell a few bushels of carrots or cabbage on the sly, or to smuggle a pig to a skiv waiting at the city's edge. Racketeers paid far more than the local grocer, and who would ever know? But George, a patriot through and through, would never stoop to this.

Besides, someone would find out and he might be fined, serve time in prison, or worse. What in normal times might reap a short prison sentence had escalated to treason. With prevention in mind, the Chief Constable often repeated this pronouncement.

Lifting an empty crate into his wagon, George wiped his wet brow, climbed aboard, and whistled to his team. Hopefully chores would not await him at home—perhaps some of the Women's Land Army cared for his stock.

As for his work, Rupert proceeded with cheer, for he knew what to write Mr. Harwood. Madeleine had clarified her desires as he left the house.

"I do hate to say no. What if the children go up to Whittlesea for only a week or two? Would that be sufficient to comfort Mrs. Harwood?"

Over the lunch she packed for him, Rupert penned his reply. Presumably, he would accompany Cecil and Iris. But another idea occurred to him—what if Gran managed the household and as a surprise, he took Madeleine along? A view of the countryside surely would uplift her.

The more he thought about the plan, the more he wanted to pursue if. He sealed the envelope, all the while recalling his wife's yawns as she mended. For two days, she could cast aside the thousand tasks she carried out without a whine or whimper.

Aware of her eyes on him that evening, he departed the back door for the fire station. Keeping this surprise bothered him a little, but the small gesture might hearten her greatly.

George's greeting this morning had reminded him of some local men who withheld their 'goo'days' since the tube station tragedy. At least one family intended to bring suit against the police force.

Why hadn't railings and better lighting been added to the stairwell earlier? Why hadn't an officer been stationed near the entrance on that fateful night? Fair questions, and Rupert sympathized.

But he missed exchanging greetings on his route, and eye contact revealing trust. If only the friendly atmosphere might be restored, but at least he could count on a welcome here. He loitered in the garden a few moments, recalling how Madeleine had waited for him on her parents' threshold when he'd returned from war.

The back gate creaked, and Anna slipped into the yard. Careful not to startle her, Rupert called, "Anna, is that you?"

"Oh." She paused beside the shed. "Da..." Such a weak tone. His pulse quickened.

"Are you well?"

She leaned on him and electricity coursed Rupert's chest. "What is it? Has someone..." Why had he allowed her to traverse the streets at this hour?

"I... I had a terrible toothache that worsened this afternoon, so the supervisor sent me to Mildmay Hospital for an extraction. A bit woozy still."

"Sit here." Rupert ran inside. "Madeleine—it's Anna. They sent her to Mildmay for a tooth extraction. She's very weak." She threw aside her darning and raced outside while he poured a glass of water.

Madeleine supported Anna's feeble efforts to sip. "They let you leave in this condition?" She hugged Anna's slender shoulders.

Blighted dentists—how could they let a girl walk home like this, and in the dark? Passing pub after pub, with so many foreign soldiers in town, Anna might have... He'd a mind to run by that hospital straightaway and give them what for.

But then he quieted himself. The Mildmay Mission Hospital offered free services, and being near the factory, it made sense to send Anna there.

"Let's get you inside." Madeleine stepped aside for Rupert to gather Anna in his arms.

Almost as light as Iris—she'd lost weight during these last three years. Bugger Adolph, anyway!

Madeleine drew down the coverlet Gran had stitched for their wedding. Safe on their bed, Anna opened her eyes.

"Thank you, Da."

Madeleine bustled into the kitchen—saucepan on stove, gas switching on, sulfur ignited. Balancing on his left knee at Anna's side, Rupert attempted to rein in his thoughts. Perhaps her supervisor might be reminded of her age, barely 19.

At the same time, gratitude edged in. Anna had prevailed through the dark byways behind Shoreditch Church tonight. Thankfully, the pubs served beer so watered down that soldiers and sailors maintained their senses. All-in-all, things had turned out well enough.

"The dentist's assistant told me to pray as he worked, but I could think of nothing..." Anna reached sticklike fingers to her forehead. "The mask was rubber..."

That anesthetizing mask certainly left its mark, but Madeleine had surely noticed. The medicine chest door squawked open—ought to oil that hinge. Rupert smoothed Anna's hand while picturing its conglomeration: Uncle Phil's Chillblain Ointment, Linctus, Wintergreen, Fry's Balsam, Germolene, Bella Donna plasters, Camphor oil, and others.

The old cabinet received frequent visits. Balsam for colds, camphor and White Horse oil for coughs and colds, a remedy for chapped hands and legs, arnica for bruises and soreness, and of course, ipecac for a baby's congestion.

Anna's breathing deepened. Another gift for which to give thanks—Madeleine's knowledge of first aid. The teapot whistled. Soon, she carried in a tray with her tools set in careful rows.

"I have everything in hand."

"You're certain? I might be able to—"

"No, no. The station needs you, and I've Gran or Kathryn if I need them." Madeleine applied a warm wet cloth to Anna's mouth, where dried blood formed rivulets. "Sending her off barely able to see straight—there ought to be a law."

"I shall speak with the magistrate straightaway." Rupert hoped his attempt to at lightness would bring a smile, and received his reward.

"Off with you then."

"I'll not be late, barring any massive bombing. Then I can spell you..."

Bent over their daughter, Madeleine tossed her head. She would not leave Anna's side this night.

The remembrance of dear Anna in their bed brought up such emotions. How quickly she had developed into a woman. How unseemly, even two years ago, for her to be out alone at this time of evening.

But now, girls even younger did their bit, and family members rarely saw them any more. Years ago, Junior and Anna slept in Iris and Cecil's room, and no day went by without interaction. How strange to have Anna home so little now, and the same with Junior. They saw more of Kathryn and spry Henry.

Approaching the fire station, alarm overtook Rupert. What if this episode originated in something more sinister than a painful tooth? What if one of those reckless Americans who behaved as if they owned England had hurt Anna?

"Surely not," Rupert whispered. Those traces of blood evidenced only a trip to the dentist. He must trust his daughter.

As if to shoo away such considerations, a blast reverberated from Hackney. Not another one—that area had taken such a beating already. Rupert scurried to the station just in time to catch the wagon to the scene.

Chapter Nine

November 1943 Mondello Beach, Sicily.

"At least we're close to a real live hospital—lucky ducks that got to set up there."

"Alongside Italian and German prisoners. I think I'd rather breathe this salt air."

Dorothy and Millie headed to what passed for a mess tent here on the beach. Every day, full transport planes landed with wounded from the Italian invasion. The nurses waited at the airfield, as some patients required immediate first aid. Most men had received minimum emergency care before boarding, but some developed complications on the way. Those who made it would be stabilized before being flown to better facilities in North Africa. One plus— the ordnance staff had begged, borrowed, or stolen some fine Navy equipment, far better than the Army's.

Everyone took great care to preserve these machines from the weather. Handling them proved far easier than the older Army models, and once Dorothy made a few adjustments for left-hand-edness, things went smoothly.

Waiting between flights created the biggest challenge. She'd caught up on answering letters, and where mine sweeps permitted, collected more shells than she could haul around.

Wally had set up a makeshift kitchen, and the cooking crew now served what they called miniature meals, an improvement over the MRE's they'd been eating.

At least this tent gave everyone a relatively warm place to congregate, and an extra buzz rose this morning when Dorothy went in for some toast.

Another nurse tugged at her arm. "Didja see that sign? Fairbanks is coming. *Douglas Fairbanks Junior!*" She primped her hair. "He's due next week. Can't hurt to look our best."

"Mmm... like we can do much about that." Imagining a thick slice of Woebbeking Bakery bread, Dorothy sank her teeth into a meager piece of toast. A couple of others joined them and began bantering about the famous Mr. Fairbanks.

"What a dreamboat—Eleanor's got a picture of him in his Navy blues. Show them, El."

A nurse from South Dakota held up her photograph. "Whadd'ya think, girls? Who wouldn't like a couple of hours with this dish?"

"Even more handsome than ever, if that could be."

"Yeah, and patriotic besides!"

"Aren't you excited, Dorothy? These Hollywood types didn't have to sign up for duty, and Douglas has been serving since the beginning."

"You mean they're immune to the draft?"

"Well, it sure looked that way at first. But then Clark Gable joined up as a private in the Air Corps OTC and became a gunner, even though he was 40. Pretty amazing."

"He'd just lost Carole Lombard—didn't know what else to do. But you're right, he started the ball rolling."

"Tyrone Power tried to enlist as a non-commissioned officer, but the Navy refused him—remember the brouhaha after that? So what'd he do?"

"Enlisted in the Marines, and Henry Fonda signed up as a Navy seaman. Then everybody hustled to get in."

"What about Humphrey Bogart and Bob Hope and—"

"I don't know, but did you hear Jimmy Stewart was rejected for being underweight, even though he'd already become a pilot? I read that he gorged on steak and pasta to gain enough pounds."

"Oh, I loved him in *You Can't Take It With You!*"

"Jackie Coogan's a glider pilot. Don't tell me those guys don't have guts!"

"You all sure do know your modern history." Several others shared Dorothy's chuckle.

"Anyway, back to Douglas Fairbanks, Jr."

"I suppose it would be fun to see him in person. Sure liked him in *Gunga Din*. But I can do without a bunch of starlets dancing around here saying how sad it is the troops haven't seen a woman in years. We may be dressed in seersucker and pants, but we're still women."

"You tell 'em, Moonbeam. Who's riveting airplanes together and threading bomb heads and packing parachutes back home?"

"Exactly. It's Rosie. My cousin and your sister, and—"

"Okay, okay. But how about Fairbanks in *That Lady in Ermine* with Ginger Rogers? Now that movie..." The South Dakota nurse seemed intent on making Douglas Fairbanks, Junior the center of this conversation.

Millie slid in beside Dorothy. "I liked him best with Joan Crawford. Can't imagine why they got divorced."

Abner joined them. "He was fooling around—isn't that what happens in Hollywood?"

"Now he's found true love. Mary What's-Her-Name must be keeping him happy."

Abner picked up his coffee cup. "Rumor has it that one lucky nurse gets picked to be his date for Saturday night."

"One of *our* nurses?"

"Of course."

"I thought officers couldn't consort with—"

Henrietta squashed that comment. "The winner's *eating* with him, not going to bed."

"What I wouldn't give to be the lucky girl. My friends back home would be so jealous." A blonde nurse with a great figure almost swooned on the spot.

"Maybe it'll be one of you at this table. Who knows? Whoever it is, I don't want them assisting in surgery the next day." Abner's declaration produced hoots and everyone jabbered at once.

Dorothy muttered to Millie, "I'd be scared to death. Besides, I've already met my quota of famous people—Josephine Baker did it for me."

"That's right, the Black Pearl—you met her at the officers' club in Cairo. Didn't you say she'd became a French citizen?"

"Yeah—in '37. Rick said she wouldn't perform for segregated audiences back in the States. Now, that's a star I can respect." Rick had also suspected Josephine was aiding the French Resistance, but Dorothy kept that to herself.

"Incoming! Hurry it up!"

Millie nearly knocked the table over as she leaped up, so Dorothy steadied it. As she followed Millie to the operating tent, Millie said, "You're the one with all the adventures, kiddo, but you also hold things together."

On Friday around noon, a private signaled Dorothy to the surgery entrance. "You're wanted in the admin tent. Pronto." He handed her a note, and the nurse working with her gave her a nod.

Dread niggled at her stomach as she carried a load of dirty laundry to a bin and washed her hands. Now what?

Surely her escapades with those pilots had been long forgotten. She'd made the trips on her leave, and in the daylight, anyhow. True, no other nurse had attempted such a thing, but that wasn't her fault. Until the note Rick dropped fell into the wrong hands, no one had known the difference.

His message, *Meet me next weekend,* brought those visits to a stop, and she'd been called to face one of Colonel Scott's officers. His questions still rang in her head.

"Private, was this note written to you?"

"Yes, sir."

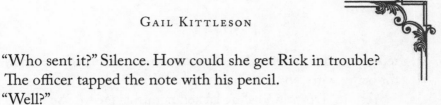
"Who sent it?" Silence. How could she get Rick in trouble?

The officer tapped the note with his pencil.

"Well?"

"I'm sorry, but I can't say, sir."

His flush deepened. "All right. I'll turn you over to Lieutenant Eilola."

But the head nurse had never addressed the issue. Not long afterward, Rick had sent papers arranging for Dorothy to transfer to his unit. But his letter read like an order. Thinking about that still made her grit her teeth. Of course, she'd never signed those papers, and hadn't answered Rick's letters. Finally, he stopped contacting her.

All water under the bridge, but what else had she done to cause this summons? She'd taken a few breaks with the smokers lately, but didn't non-smokers deserve time off, too? Besides, she'd already been called out on the loudspeaker for that. Ah well, the docs valued her skills, especially in surgery—what could the army do to her?

The admin tent was one she avoided whenever possible, but Lieutenant Eilola gave her a friendly smile and gestured her toward an office farther down a makeshift hallway. At the entrance, Dorothy knocked on a pole, and an officer rose from behind his desk.

"Thank you for coming." At her salute, he nodded. "At ease."

She might have reminded him she had no choice. But at least she wasn't facing Colonel Scott.

"We have a VIP visiting soon, and..." Most of what followed escaped her, because the gist was that she'd been chosen for the date with Fairbanks. Everyone would say, "Oh you lucky girl," but she didn't feel lucky.

"You seem less than pleased?"

"I'm... It's..." No possibility of mentioning she'd much rather hear some other nurse describe a date with Fairbanks.

The officer mistook her fumbling for insubordination. "Well, we're not going to choose again, I assure you. You come highly recommended. You're a looker, but have also acquired a reputation for being witty, so try to have a good time."

"Yes, sir." Dorothy's salute lacked her usual gusto. She turned to go and he added, "Wear your dress uniform."

Fortunately for him, the nurses had finally received such a thing. Somewhere in North Africa, an officer managed to find them green jump suits called fatigues. Before that, they'd worn World War I Army issue wool uniforms, or men's shirts, pants, and blouses. *Perfect for the miserable heat of an African day*, Hank quipped.

They'd joined up before anybody gave thought to a Women's Army Corps. But now, the Army had also issued shirts, smart woolen skirts and jackets called over-blouses. Maybe Colonel Scott's reassignment had something to do with this.

Returning to her patients, Dorothy wished she could somehow wriggle out of this assignment. Pairing her with Fairbanks had the hallmarks of a typical Army boo-boo. Somebody looked at the surface of things, made a decision, and sealed the deal.

Back in the recovery tent, she put her heart into her work. That evening, Millie asked if she'd heard who'd been chosen.

Might as well get this over with. "You'll never believe this. It's me."

"You're kidding."

"I wish I were. They called me in today."

Millie squealed, "Oh, it'll be fun, just you wait. If I had won, Delbert would've been so proud of me!"

"Maybe I can fake a bad sore throat or something. I'd much rather have you or Hank go." At this precise moment, Hank magically appeared.

"I'd be the last one they'd pick, that's for sure."

"Would you two please keep this quiet? I don't want to answer a million questions. In the meantime, I can pray Mr. Dreamboat cancels his visit, right?"

"And steal everybody's chance to glimpse *Doug*las *Fair*banks, *Junior*?"

"I'd far rather see Bob Hope—at least, he's funny. Maybe he'll end up somewhere along our path. Or Babe Ruth—remember that guy from the 355th?"

"You mean the Anti-Aircraft Artillery fella who met the Babe in California?"

"Yeah, his battalion was guarding the coastline at Santa Monica, right? The Bambino came down to visit the soldiers."

"Right. I'd much rather meet the Sultan of Swat than Douglas Fairbanks. My brothers would give anything to get his signature."

"I haven't heard of any baseball players coming over here. But in the meantime we've gotta get you ready for your big night."

"Okay, sure. How about you wave your magic wand and find me a bathtub?"

Hank cackled again. "I'll see what I can do, gorgeous."

"Mum! Come here. See that hay sticking out way up there? Mr. Harwood used to let me play with the kittens while he forked hay."

A laugh resounded from the muscular Mr. Harwood. Rupert liked his heartiness.

"Did he, now?" Madeleine let Cecil pull her toward the barn.

"We was safe, Mum. There's a big gate across, and…"

"Mr. Laudner, you've no idea what a gift you and your wife have given us. I had to write you, because Evelyn… It was so hard to watch her grieve."

"Nothing can be worse than losing a child, and we're grateful for this opportunity for Cecil and Iris."

"I expect Cecil will be a bit more on the brave side this time."

"Do some other boys live nearby?"

"Two swarthy lads just down the road—we'll invite them over soon. I wager Cecil might even remember them from school."

Nothing to do but climb to the barn loft—if Madeleine could manage, so could he. Rupert paid extra attention to the overhead rafter he might have thunked with his head, and found Madeleine nestled in the hay petting a weeks-old kitten. Her eyes glinted when his head appeared through the hole in the loft floor, but refocused her attention on Cecil and the kitten.

A growing lad ought to have moments when the world stopped—even a world at war. The backs of Rupert's eyes heated at a memory as sweet as the mounds of clover hay clumped here. Decades ago, his mother had come out onto the porch, holding the new baby. There'd been such a to-do with the birthing, but a few days later, everyone else left, and he'd ended up alone on the porch.

His mother sank down beside him. "Have you met your little brother yet? He looks just like you when you were born. Even his cry brings you to mind, son."

A huge lump wallowed in Rupert's throat as he touched the babe's cheek with a trembling finger. Mum asked if he'd like to hold the infant, but he hadn't time to reply before the warm bundle slid into his arms.

"You're the one he'll look to, his closest big brother. We've named him Shelby."

Hay dust sifted down, returning Rupert to the mow. Cecil spotted him and called, "Da, come see!"

A shaft of sunlight from the high cupola cast radiance over the scene. This was the right decision—two weeks for the children away from the city, and two precious days with the woman he had vowed to love and cherish.

"Captain Fairbanks, I'd like you to meet Dorothy Woebbeking, one of our nurses. Lieutenant Woebbeking, Captain Fairbanks."

Knowing Hank, Millie, and who-knew-how-many other nurses ogled from behind tent flaps, a hot flush razed Dorothy's neck. Thank heavens she wouldn't be alone with the white-gloved movie star offering her his hand.

An officer ushered him into the front of the jeep, and another squashed in beside her. No need to converse as they passed through the ruins of Palermo. Whew! Now she could save all the topics Hank and Millie suggested for dinner.

Bombed-out Palermo gave her a sick feeling. Ragged, dark-eyed children swarmed the streets, piled with bricks and debris where buildings once stood.

At one corner, a thin little girl about three years old shadowed another child pawing through debris. A large ulcer ravaged one child's leg. Chances were, their parents had been killed, and the streets had become home. At the airfield, the nurses sometimes offered care to locals, but that lay miles away. Would this child ever find help?

Along a bumpy beach road, the officers discussed the war. They'd expected to claim Tunis months earlier, before the rains came. But then Rommel reinforced, launched his surprise attack, and the monsoons created impossible muck out of sand and dirt.

The jeep stopped in front of a low, dimly lit building set back from the shoreline, Dorothy's seatmate jumped out, and she fell in line with him behind Fairbanks. Inside, the star motioned her to a chair, and a waiter brought water.

The Eleventh Evac officer studied a menu. "*Poulet* or beef. What's your pleasure?"

Easy... the memory of Mama's homemade noodles and chicken had taunted Dorothy for months. The war talk continued, so she relaxed. Officers began to drift in and stand near the bar—mostly RAF.

One red-haired pilot chatted with some others, and his sparkling eyes seemed familiar. Was she imagining he kept looking her way?

Holding Madeleine's hand on the train back to the East End amidst ordinary folks, sailors, and soldiers, Rupert basked in quiet wonder. Suitcases jarred his arm from the narrow aisle, but stole nothing from his enjoyment.

The view offered lovely countryside, horse carts on seemingly

endless byways, straw hatted drivers coaxing teams through var-
iegated shades of green, and workers stacking hay on wagons. The
nearest to heaven a man could come—perhaps when he retired, a
move might be possible.

Rupert had wakened to birdsong after a peaceful night in a wee
house on the farm's far side, with pre-dawn shadows rendering
Madeleine as lovely as on their wedding day. How good to simply
lie here and take in her profile.

Vicar Towsley had bade him goodbye the day before yesterday.
"A word to take along, my friend. R - E - S - T—Heaven knows
you and Madeleine have little enough. What a capitol idea, going
away for a night—surely the Lord's will."

Yet this train might meet with an accident, injuring them both,
and he would wish they'd never come. Would that be the Lord's
will, too? Dash that thought—enough trouble around without
dreaming up more.

When they arrived back in London, he made his way to the volunteer fire station, and Madeleine took up her mending. The next
morning after bidding her good day, he braced himself as Towsley
ran into him headlong at the corner and spat, "Melvin Williams...
due today... going to catch him before he sees anyone else..."

In faint early light, the vicar's face revealed something unfitting, a
mere flicker, but enough to sound an alarm. When Towsley caught
his breath, Rupert accompanied him at a slower-than-normal pace,
and waited for more.

"I thought perhaps... it seems right that... you see..."

Towsley, at a loss for words? The slight tremble of his mustache
became evident, and his hand on Rupert's sleeve made his desire
clear—would he come along?

Melvin knew his wife and child had suffered a freak accident,
but would now learn the details. Not a pleasant prospect, and this
had allowed the specter of fear a foothold. With Luftwaffe pilots
still using London for target practice, each week saw new families
to comfort in their distress.

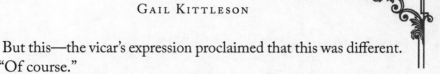

But this—the vicar's expression proclaimed that this was different. "Of course."

At Rupert's words, visible relief aligned Towsley's posture. "I shall bring him straightaway." The taut line creasing his forehead slackened, and a glimmer stoked his eyes. Friendship's unspoken gratitude.

"After my rounds, I shall be in the office." Rupert touched Towsley's hand, still poised on his coat sleeve. "Speaking with him cannot be easy."

The vicar backed away. "I baptized each of their children. This last baby, God's late gift..."

With no children of his own, did he form a bond with each infant he baptized? Clearly, the children loved him, for he always managed a smile. But not today.

Chapter Ten

"So, how was Douglas?"

"Come on, Moonbeam, give us the lowdown." Four other nurses crowded in with Millie and Hank when Dorothy arrived home.

"Handsome as all get-out, perfect."

"Tell us everything."

"You're all missing this chance to sleep?" She shed her sweater and yawned.

"What did he wear?"

"Impeccable blues—he must bring a valet when he goes to war."

"Well, he *is* a commander, for goodness' sake. Did he talk about his ship, his men?"

"Two officers rode with us, and we met some more at the club. They talked mostly about the war, but Fairbanks did mention his wife."

Sarcasm laced Hank's comments. "Can you *imagine*? Out with Douglas Fairbanks JUNIOR—my mind can hardly contain it."

"Oh, Hank, you're just jealous. Did he thank you for the evening, Webbie?"

"Sure. He played the perfect gentleman."

"So he gave you a salutary peck on the cheek?"

"Good grief, no—he has a *wife*."

"Yeah, but—this was special. Poor, isolated, faithful Army nurse dates the spectacular Mr. Fairbanks."

"Hate to disappoint you. The food was pretty good, but there's not much else to tell."

The others faded away and Dorothy changed into her jumpsuit, the safest thing to wear when she might be called out any time. She'd just burrowed into her pillow when Millie whispered, "You're sure he didn't kiss you?"

"No, but I did decide to get rid of my old uniform. Gonna bury that thing."

"Really?"

"Just watch me."

At last, silence. But sleep came only after Dorothy revisited the treasure she'd found tonight, nothing to do with Douglas Fairbanks, Junior. When he left with the officers for a while, that red-headed pilot slipped into the chair beside her.

"Houston Pinkstone here. Couldn't help noticing you in your uniform."

"The latest style. Attracts men like flies." Dorothy grinned at him, and two dimples marked his cheeks.

"Might I ask, are you with one of those officers?"

"Just for this evening. It's—I won a contest. The one sitting next to me is an American film actor."

"How did you win?"

Dorothy shrugged. "My bad luck at work."

"Ah—not a swimming competition?"

"That's where I met you—you tricked me into bothering a deposed king!"

"And you're with the Eleventh Evac. I jolly well like that group. It's good to be around blokes not so caught up in military guidelines."

The officers entered the restaurant again, so Pinky scooted back to his buddies.

Later, D.F.J. spoke with officers in the foyer, so Dorothy looked around for Pinky. Already gone.

Just outside the door, her date stopped again to chat with admirers while she waited, hands clasped behind her back. A few seconds later, something slipped into her palm and a whisper came from the shadows.

"Tomorrow morning on the beach. Unless we get called out, I'll be there early."

The officers turned to greet someone else, so she glimpsed Pinky's smile and the gleam of sparkling golden wings above his left pocket. His inviting eyes challenged her, as they had in Tunisia.

"Can't promise, but I'll try."

"Fair enough." He slipped away. Captain Fairbanks engaged in military talk with the officers on the ride home, so Dorothy leaned her head back to an ocean of stars and a nearly full moon. Against that backdrop, Pinky's contagious grin and those delightful dimples seemed so close she could almost touch them.

Millie groaned in her sleep, bringing Dorothy back to her own cot. Unless she curled up tight, either her head or her feet stuck out. But at least Hank and the rest of those nurses had tired of fishing for more information.

Weariness overwhelmed her and she faded into her own private swoon over that dreamy Scotsman.

"We should've taken Rome by now, but still haven't even gotten to Italy. Jerry's got us buffaloed, but when we break through, we'll scatter 'em across the Mediterranean."

A sergeant paused long enough for a bite of dinner and a corpsman asked, "Wouldn't you rather spend Christmas here instead of freezing in Italy?"

A medical officer added his two bits. "Not if freezing would shorten this war. I just hope we don't beat the troops to the beach again and give the Air Force another opportunity to shoot at us."

Everyone enjoyed the reduced patient load this evening, but Dorothy's thoughts strayed to Albert. Had he destroyed the wrong bridge yet, or had his crew targeted GIs instead of the enemy? And where was Vernon by now?

Someday they'd be able to exchange stories. Hopefully. With mail so slow, she'd heard nothing about Vernon for months. Elfrieda sent one of Albert's postcards in her last letter, but the censoring obscured his meaning.

At least Mama had her grandchildren nearby. Elfrieda described the four big stars Mama hung in the bakery window, one for each son and one for her stubborn daughter. Good thing she had three more sons too old to register.

"'Only two daughters,' Mama says, 'so why did one of them have to go?'"

Breaking the news to her had been so hard. Years earlier, Mama had declared she'd never let her become a nurse when a friend invited Dorothy to take training at a Catholic hospital in Indiana.

Of course she complied, but then their pastor said he supported her desire to go into nursing. What could Mama do?

"We need good nurses, Mrs. Woebbeking, and Dorothy is strong and dedicated. I will vouch for her at the Lutheran hospital in Sioux City."

So she'd left home a year younger than most of her school class, having skipped fifth grade after returning from Germany. After her hands-on training, the hard work in the hospital revealed the value of furthering her education. That motivated her to apply at Drake University.

Exchanging her services as school nurse for room and board at Drake suited her well, and another job paid for books. Then came the government offer to pay educational costs for Nurses Corps inductees. Why not accept?

After Pearl Harbor, there'd been no hiding her evacuation hospital assignment, but telling Mama had been no fun. At least she had crossed the Atlantic three times—in fact, all those trips might have planted Dorothy's adventurous bent.

"What do you think, Webbie?" The question from an officer sitting across the table startled Dorothy.

"About?"

"How far away were you?"

"Several thousand miles, in the heart of Iowa."

"Nice country?"

"Oh, yes. The Cedar River Valley spreads as far as you can see."

"It flows into the Mississippi?"

"Yes, about two hours away."

"Farmers raise corn and soybeans there?"

"Yep, plus hay, sorghum, and some wheat."

"Let me guess—your dad's a farmer."

"No, he's a baker in Waterloo."

Suddenly the whole table honed in and someone said, "Isn't that the Sullivan brothers' hometown?"

"Yes, they lived right down the street from us. Their dad worked for the railroad, and my brothers played with them."

"Can't imagine what their poor parents went through."

"It took a couple of months for them to get official word because of security issues with the *Juneau*. Their mother, Aletta, encouraged Tom to go to work that day as usual, since the trains were moving war materials."

"Did their daughter really join the *WAVES*?"

Dorothy nodded, but the sergeant reclaimed everyone's attention. "Brings us back to our topic. Our boys'll see to it that Hitler meets his Waterloo."

A couple of listeners chuckled, but Dorothy left a few minutes later. One of those at the table had been Colonel Scott's right-hand man. He might have been the one to send eight nurses and three administrative officers home for fraternizing.

She kept her distance and watched her Ps and Qs around him. Besides, speculations came a dime a dozen in the mess, while she hungered for facts.

A slight breeze wooed her to the camp's perimeter. Everything seemed brighter, since she'd finally slept a few hours in a row last night. She'd even taken a good spit bath and washed her hair and laundry in her helmet.

Interesting how one night's sleep allowed for beauty to show up, even though her Scottish friend failed to make an appearance early this morning. Disappointing, but pilots were at the mercy of their commanders.

A half-moon highlighted the horizon. Twilight made nondescript shadows of bombed-out Sicilian landscape, and she longed for home. Ahead lay the Italian boot, then France. How long would this war take?

Right now, Papa would be coming in from a long day of stirring and lifting, packing delivery boxes and supervising helpers. He would listen to the evening war report and fall asleep reading the newspaper, his enormous arms slack against his torso. Bread baking would begin at three a.m., a deadline he met six days a week.

What she wouldn't give to spend one evening discussing the headlines with him after the evening radio news. But a Mediterranean breeze reminded her that Iowa had become an idle dream.

Earlier today, one of the docs placed his bet that the Eleventh would be in Italy by early November. "In time for the worst of the autumn rains—I hear they're torrential."

Everyone groaned, and someone asked, "Like the ones in Tunisia?"

"Quite a bit colder, I'm afraid."

At least he'd picked a safe subject, the weather. Mama wrote that the Farmer's Almanac foretold record low temperatures this winter. But surely not as bad as in '36, Dorothy's last at Drake, when food and fuel had fallen short in Des Moines.

And then in '40, a November blizzard found farmers unprepared. Thousands of turkeys froze, and the storm destroyed the late apple harvest and killed seven Iowans. When someone at the hospital mentioned the origin of the word blizzard, she'd thought of Mama, and made the word the topic of her next letter.

Mama, I just learned that the English borrowed the word blizartig from the early German settlers. What a perfect way to describe a winter storm's sudden fury—like lightning.

"And perfect to describe the *blitzkrieg*, too." To the shifting breeze, Dorothy added, "A letter from home would sure give me a boost right now."

91

She missed Rick's letters from Cairo. He may have made decisions about the future without asking her opinion, but he'd been faithful to write. Maybe Pinky would be, too. Thinking of him, she held her arms out and turned a circle, and a doctor sauntered up.

"If we ever get up a dance team, I want you on my side."

He'd be giving her orders tomorrow, so Dorothy snuffed her retort.

Someone yelled, "No fraternizing with the nurses over there."

The doc gave the guy a stilted salute as he neared. "Especially not this one—she's my right hand man in surgery."

As they continued on, Dorothy lagged behind. Beyond the hospital tents, the strafed countryside welcomed darkness. In the distance, a bombed-out German truck made a grotesque bulge, but a gaggle of saplings spent from shelling produced a hopeful sign—birdsong.

A nightingale in that scraggly tree outlined against Mount Etna's continual orangey smoke? Yes, a brave little bird raised its voice in what was left of Sicily.

At the posted boundary, Dorothy turned back. Then an idea formed—no time like the present to get rid of that scratchy old skirt and heavy wool blouse from the last war. The white shirt, she might need.

"Hey—you're not really going to—" Millie set aside her knitting to follow along.

"Why should we lug these around?" The back of a truck produced a shovel, but finding a burial place proved a challenge. Finally, behind the sulfage pit the engineers dug before they set up camp, a likely spot appeared. Two feet down ought to do it. Plopping the outdated burden in, Dorothy covered the evidence.

After she returned the shovel, Millie stood arms akimbo. "You really did it. What if—"

"I can dream up any number of excuses, but ten pounds less in my duffel makes sense to me."

92

After Towsley left, Rupert continued to the tube station. In this spectral underworld, sleepy souls received their weak morning tea. Not like Madeleine's brew, strong enough to jar your nerves and sinews into functioning.

Ah well, at least these mole-like folks knew someone cared enough to help them greet the new day. Bravo to the faithful ladies who tended the canteen.

But seeing blanket-robed citizens still asleep beneath the platform, lined up like full cocoons in the deep depression under the tracks, brought a shudder. Ten years ago, who would have thought to spend a night here? How reduced the British people had become, how humiliated.

The great Imperial Navy had suffered so many defeats, and home after home in the East End bore sorrow, with dear sons, husbands, and grandsons buried somewhere in the high seas.

Who might ever have envisioned great sections of London in piles of rubble, tens of thousands displaced, yet still no relief from Adolph's mania? Who would have thought Bremen, Cologne, and many other German cities would lie ravished, the most recent conspirators against Herr Hitler hanged, their bodies presently dangling on meat hooks in Berlin?

Even three years ago, who could have foreseen the bombing of Rome, and throngs of American and British forces clawing their way onto the Italian Peninsula under fire? Daily reports caused listeners to quaver.

Returning to the office, Rupert no sooner set an inked seal to a couple of documents when voices sounded out in the hallway. He started up at Towsley's deep resonance, a voice worthy of a preacher.

Then the office door opened, and Rupert advanced toward Melvin, noting the storm cloud on his countenance. "Do have a chair, won't you?"

His hospitality met a frigid glare. Rupert dared not look at

Towsley, especially after what he'd seen in his eyes a few hours ago.

"My heartfelt sympathies, Mr. Williams." Like a fool, he blundered right in. "The tragedy occurred on—"

"I know when it happened, man. What I want to know is, *Why?*" Williams thrust his big nose so close to Rupet's face, he might have licked it.

"Perhaps we might go to the scene. Perhaps there—"

Towsley interjected, "Yes, let us be on our way." He turned, and Melvin, fists clenched and muscular shoulders as tense as iron, followed. Rupert followed.

This man's furious silence raised the hair on the back of Rupert's neck. He had nothing but sympathy—imagine coming home from the misery of war to face this.

At the same time, if the grey hovering in Melvin's eyes and the terse line of his lips were any indication, nothing good would come of this meeting. And those fists lined in ship's grease promised a dockworker's brute strength compounded by recent war experience.

At the station entrance, the vicar attempted to grasp Melvin's elbow, but Williams shook him off like a flea. His only comment rang untethered.

"I see they've installed a center handrail. A little late, don't you think?"

"Yes." Rupert stepped forward, for surely this was directed to him. His brief admission set Melvin off on a tirade.

"Never do your job... ought to have been watching out... might have warned the citizens... how could you stand by...?" The questions, not unlike the swirling accusations Rupert still warded off in the middle of the night, swirled like flaming dragons.

But then Melvin turned on Towsley, as if the vicar bore sole responsibility for the accident. "I'm away at sea, doing my bit. And what were *you* doing?" Could he not note the vicar's age? This man must be confused—entirely understandable.

A slender ridge of bubbly white rode the corner of Melvin's lower lip as he shoved the Vicar's chest with a broad finger. "You preach

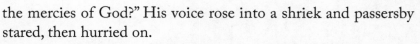

the mercies of God?" His voice rose into a shriek and passersby stared, then hurried on.

"But you let them kill my Marian... the baby. I only held her once!"

What happened next shocked all possible replies down Rupert's throat. Melvin swung at Towsley and winged his shoulder. Before Rupert could react, he swung again, with terrific force. Bone cracked on bone and the vicar swayed to the cold cement like a felled tree.

"Useless, the two of you! Damn you both!" Melvin's scream echoed up the cement walls. The stairs swam before Rupert.

Ought to cuff this bloke—show him the meaning of respect. But he stood stupefied. He thought he'd surely seen the worst of human nature, yet Melvin's fiery eyes left him breathless.

Expecting a blow as well, Rupert stooped to aid Towsley. Melvin fled up the stairs, and bystanders gathered. Rupert waved them back as he knelt.

"Are you all right?" Though Towsley's bloody jaw hung at an odd angle, he whispered back, his voice crackling like the first autumn leaves dotting the pavement.

"Yes, thank you." The Vicar might have been greeting his parishioners after Sunday services. Except for one thing—his words issued so slurred and broken, Rupert could barely sort them out.

"Towsley," he cried. "Towsley..."

Chapter Eleven

Swinging at the school playground, Dorothea giggled at a joke her classmate made about a stern instructor. Pumping harder, she gloried in the way her stomach dropped on the downward *whoosh*. This must be like flying in an airplane.

All of a sudden, Vernon called to her, "Dorte! Got a secret to tell you." En route home, he gave a furtive glance behind them. "We're going back to the United States."

"We are not!"

"Mama told Frau Toeter. She wrote to Papa that she wants to go back, something about trouble with her stepbrothers. But don't say a word—you know how she hates tale-telling."

Memories of life back in Waterloo centered around Dorothy's schoolmates, her teachers, and Tante Bremen and Nana, who had emigrated before Papa and Mama.

Tante Bremen, a podiatrist, had urged Papa to follow them. Years earlier, he had apprenticed to a baker and earned his certification. He decided to close his thriving Bremen bakery and start afresh, so it had been back and forth, and now back again.

Of course, when Dorothea returned to the big house on Admi-ralStrasse, Mama acted as if nothing had changed. How long would she wait to tell them the news? Another ship; another journey to New York City over the huge ocean.

Papa's letters said he missed them all dearly, but he'd sent them here so Mama could escape the strange land of America. So many foreigners, accents and challenges in Waterloo.

An Irish neighbor had tried to help her. "*Frau Woebbeking*, why sweat over the washtub in the house?" She leaned down and gathered a pile of dirty laundry in her arms.

"You can heat the water outside, I'm a-certain. Children, show us the way."

But Mama became even more homesick. Finally, though the bakery was flourishing, Papa sent them all back to Germany and saved for his own passage.

An urgent voice brought Dorothy back to her cot in the latest evac camp. "Moonbeam? Is that you thrashing around over there?"

Dorothy groaned and closed her eyes.

"Hey, wake up." Someone was shaking her shoulder. "They're bringing in more wounded. I would've let you sleep a little longer, but this came for you."

Millie thrust a brown paper package toward her, so Dorothy sat up. Even through the wrapping, the faint scent of home wafted—lemon peel, citron, anise, orange. Had Papa sent an early batch of pfeffernesse? Dorothy tore open the box and inhaled.

"Smells like your father outdid himself this time."

"We'll dine in style later."

A door slammed, making way for a spurt of profanity, and the sharpness of gasoline fumes invaded. Dorothy stashed the box under her cot and put on her shoes. There would be surgeries ahead for sure, and the docs had recently asked her to specialize in assisting.

Two days later, they loaded up for the next move, this time to Cefalu. "Our fifth station in Sicily. We've got this packing down to a science."

"The good thing is, we can see Mount Etna from anywhere. I'll miss our friendly volcano when we go to Italy."

Surely Hank was kidding—didn't everyone realize Mount Vesuvius was in Southern Italy? Captain Siemons had mentioned they'd likely be able to see it soon after arriving.

Next, Abner ventured a prediction. "I bet our next home will be a beach. Haven't you always wanted to spend Christmas beside the sea?"

"Give me a one-horse open sleigh and snow drifts ten feel high." Even though Hank plied him with questions, he refused to give any more details about his disclosure. Must've gotten some inside word.

He turned to Dorothy. "You seem chipper today—still thinking about Douglas?"

"Nope. But he's on your mind, obviously?"

"Beats thinking about what I'm missing at home. My son's championship little league game is this week. What I wouldn't give to be there." With a dejected look, he took a load of cots to a truck.

Millie spoke for all of them. "Makes me glad I don't have children yet."

Somebody said, "Wouldn't it be awful to leave them? I've got a friend who did, though. When her husband joined the Marines, she became a pilot and flies planes across the States now. Her folks are taking care of their two little ones."

The topic brought a twinkly-eyed Scottish pilot to mind. What had kept Pinky away the morning after her date with D.F.J.? Thinking positive was her only option, but would she ever see him again?

"Hey, look at this—our bakery's making Danish Rye bread for Black's Department Store now. It's featured in the Tuesday and Wednesday Specials."

"I take it Black's is Waterloo's biggest and best?" Hank munched a hunk of Papa's gingerbread that somehow crossed the Atlantic without molding.

"Definitely the best."

"Well, if everything tastes as good as this scrumptious stuff, the city's one lucky place."

"Amen to that. When this is all over, I'm making a trip to your dad's bakery, Moonbeam." Millie cut a slice of fruitcake.

"It's a deal. Depends on the season, but he concocts specialties all the time." She continued reading the *Courier* ad, thankful Mama had double wrapped everything in outdated newspapers.

"Listen to this: California grown golden Palm dates, California Sunkist Valencia oranges—five pounds for 55 cents, Red Malaga grapes, two pounds 29 cents, homegrown leaf lettuce, two bunches 19 cents. Ooh—how about Borden's wedge-cut cream cheese, your choice: relish, pimento, or chive, Iowa-made colored cheddar cheese 34 cents a pound, Wisconsin Open-eyed Swiss Cheese—"

"Stop, I can't take it. We're finally thinking about leaving this island, but I have a feeling the Germans will leave Italy—"

"Stripped bare. Word has it even farmers are starving to death there, thanks to the Nazis." Hank's gloomy outlook matched the downward turn of her lips.

"Yeah, but look at the progress we're making. Our guys'll soon be in Germany, and then we can all go home."

"Oh, Mil, you're such an optimist. We only have the whole length of Italy and France to conquer first, not to mention Germany. Hard to imagine old Adolph would leave his domain unprotected."

"Optimism is my breath of life. 'A pessimist sees the difficulty in every opportunity. An optimist sees the opportunity in every difficulty.'"

"Sounds like something Churchill would say." Hank shook her head. "That guy is all about words."

"Yes, and his words have brought the British through. How else are we ever going to make it?"

"You two think I always see the dark side, but the other day some docs were talking about why we're fighting here right now. They said we should've crossed the Channel right away and attacked Jerry head-on. Why does Churchill want to waste so much time in Africa and Sicily? If we'd smacked Hitler in the mouth right off, there'd have been lots less casualties."

"Something to think about," Dorothy conceded.

"But there's really nothing we can *do* about it. Who's going to move the whole army up to England?" Something to think about in Millie's counter argument, too.

"My point exactly. Everywhere we go, we get stuck in an impossible situation."

Dorothy set aside the weekly ads and started reading another section dated February 1933. Mama must be scraping the bottom of the pile.

Black Hawk County supervisors met at 1:30 p.m. pursuant to law, to the rules of said board and to adjournment... a motion all bills were allowed as read. Black Hawk Coffee and Spice, provisions $310.50 Rath Packing Co., provisions, $84.00, Swift and Company, provisions $84.00, Standard Biscuit Company, provisions $36.43.

Woebbeking Bakery appeared twice, for provisions at a cost of $24.00 each.

Moved by Rector, seconded by Miller, that the following be appointed official county workers for relief work in Black Hawk county: D.M. Kelly, C.G. Woodley, R.A. Doty, Zelma Warren. Motion Carried.

Probably Papa gave the county a reduced rate. Mama always said he worried about the state of things in Germany, but people had been hurting in Iowa, too. Still, the bakery kept them all in food and clothing.

Hank wiped a gingerbread smudge. "We ought to write a book called 'Signs of the End.' This had better be over in '44, or I'll be an old maid for sure."

Millie wrinkled her nose. "If Delbert still wants to get married when we get back, it'll be a wonder."

"We didn't christen you Daisy Mae for nothing—you're quite a prize, and he knows it."

"I'm going over to the pharmacy tent to do some organizing." Hank left, but her observation about Delbert took Dorothy back to Tunisia, when they were packing up the hospital once again. Outside the operating tent, the transportation crew grabbed boxes full of sheets, bandages, medicines, and equipment.

Hank wiped her brow. "Where are we again?"

"Ouchatata." Millie and Dorothy both answered at once. "The armpit of the world."

"You can say that again—enough heat to last a lifetime." For once, Millie admitted discomfort, and as usual, Hank ran a step ahead.

"We'll remind you of that next winter when we're freezing in Italy or France."

"But any place that has a name with O-u-c-h in it makes me leery—what kind of a name is Ouchatata, anyhow?" Dorothy emphasized the first syllable.

"How many times have I heard 'Ouch, a tater!' since we got here?"

"And we're headed to Mateur. They'll make mincemeat of that one, too."

From the corner of her eye, Dorothy noticed a soldier enter the tent—looked like Captain Siemons, so she walked over. "Hello, Captain—what're you up to?"

His brow furrowed and he drew her a few steps away from the others.

"Got some news?"

"Always. Just call me Eric Severeid. We've made an air raid on the Focke-Wulf factory in Bremen, where they make all the FW-190 fighters. They're the Messerschmitt Me-109's best buddies to knock out our heavy bomber formations."

"So this is good news."

"The fewer 190s in the sky, the better. But here's the other side— the Ninety-First flies out of Bassingbourn, England, under the British Eighth Air Force. Their raid was successful, but they took some losses. Some pilots had to bail out, and others crashed into... Anyway, wasn't Bremen where you said...?"

"When I was a kid, we lived there for nine months."

"Well, at least their factories won't be putting any Focke-Wulfs out anytime soon. Hey, you look a little pale—you still have family over there?"

"No. It's..." Dorothy glanced back at Millie and whispered. "Millie's boyfriend is a gunner with the Ninety-First. I don't want her to..."

"You think it's better for her not to know?"

"What do you think?"

"Maybe he's fine—why worry her?"

"I'd rather have her hear this from somebody we trust."

"If I knew his squadron, it would help—the 322nd, 23rd, 24th, or the 401st."

"I'm not sure."

"...and the name of his plane. Those guys pick the greatest names. *Delta Rebel, Hellsapoppin, Shoo Shoo Baby, Stormy Weather*—if we knew, maybe I could find out more."

Dorothy waved Millie over, and Captain Siemons took the cue.

"The Ninety-First has really been busy lately, and..." Millie turned white, and Dorothy grabbed her hand.

"Do you know the name of Delbert's plane? We might be able to find out something about him if—"

Millie blurted, "It has an O on the fuselage. I saw that in a picture, but the censors won't allow complete photos of the planes. Del started out in Louisiana and trained at MacDill Field in Florida and in Walla Walla, Washington, if that helps. His crew was one of the first to attack over Germany."

Captain Siemons touched her elbow. "The 323rd, I bet. And he's a gunner?"

"Yes."

"That helps a lot. I'll see what I can dig up."

When he left, Millie dropped onto a box of sheets, and Hank spewed her usual doubt. "Where does that guy get his news, anyhow?"

"Probably the same place he gets our mail—he has to do a lot of finagling to make sure we end up with letters in our hands." Dorothy handed Millie a glass of water. "So far, everything he's told me jives with something I hear later. If there's any way to find out more about Delbert, I have a feeling he'll manage."

"A feeling?"

"Yes. An intuition. I trust Captain Siemons, don't you? If he didn't care, why would he have offered to help?"

"Oh, you trust everybody."

Dorothy might have listed a couple of Colonel Scott's former henchmen that she definitely did not trust, but what was the use? With Hank, humor was about the only thing that worked. Sometimes, anyway.

"Anybody who loves Wrigley's spearmint as much as the Captain does has to be trustworthy."

"Phffw.! What *is* that with his gum chain, anyhow? It looks so silly."

Millie's chuckle quieted Hank. "You know what he told me? Mr. Wrigley has made our troops his priority for however long the war lasts. Captain Siemons' daughter spends her allowance stockpiling packs for him, and she's making a chain, too, back in Kansas. When he gets back, they'll connect the two. Isn't that a nifty idea?"

"Wow, that's great—when we were separated from Papa for a year, I really missed him, and this is way longer than that." An image of a little girl who looked a lot like Captain Siemons rose before Dorothy—so many children missing their fathers right now.

A yell from one of the transportation workers brought her back to the present. Five months had passed since that late April day, and soon after, Millie's frequent letters from Delbert had stopped. But in all this time, Captain Siemons had dredged up nothing to encourage Millie. Still, she carried on, and hardly ever complained.

Even when someone brought word of feats performed by the Ninety-First in raids over Germany, she said, "That's my Del, up there with the best of them."

Chapter Twelve

Vicar Towsley moaned as Rupert pulled him from the concrete.
"Careful there. Your jaw looks broken."

"Bro—?"

"Take it slow. We'll get you to the hospital."

"Please. I should rather—"

"No arguing. You're bleeding from your ear, too." Rupert half-carried him the three blocks to the infirmary and struggled up the stairs. As he approached the desk, panting, a scene from the Great War niggled him.

After he'd been wounded and was found concussed, someone had helped him to an aid station. Who had that fellow been? Had he survived the war?

But this was no time to revisit his experience on the other end of things. The ruby trickle from Towsley's ear unnerved him. A clerk pointed them to a chair in the waiting area, but the vicar waved him off.

"The doctor will patch me up and send me on my way shortly." After he sank into a chair and closed his eyes, Rupert disappeared around a corner and soon returned with a nurse.

"Reverend Towsley?"

The vicar's eyes flashed open, but he made no attempt to reply.

"Come with me, sir—we'll find you some help."

Supporting Towsley down the hall, Rupert pondered. So much for his own illusion—until now, he'd believed a divine hedge protected Towsley, even though the vicar had described the bombing deaths of two seminary chums.

If this is how you treat Your friends... If anyone was a friend of the Almighty, it was Towsley—and now look at him.

As the first visitor to ring at the hospital entrance the next morning, Rupert apologized to the night nurse. He had no idea how he would find the vicar, but in case his spirits were high, he had a word at the ready. *HEAL*—what could be more appropriate?

At the nurses' station, a bleary-eyed woman ready for her shift to end beckoned him to a male ward. "He's in here. Severe break that required emergency surgery last night. He's sedated, but still in great pain."

Ashen was the word for Towsley's face, hollowed-out and withered overnight. Rupert had no idea of his age, but a few years back, they'd celebrated his thirtieth anniversary of ordination.

As he neared, the patient spoke through gauze and tape. "I knew you would come."

"How're you feeling, old boy?"

Silence. Then, "How... does... the... other... fellow look?" He had to repeat this twice to clarify his meaning, and the effort made Rupert wince. But when he realized the joke, he relaxed.

"He should be incarcerated. Are you thinking of pressing—"

"No." The utterance, however thick, came out strong.

"But Melvin deliberately... He should never have struck out at you like—"

"Doing his work with God—nothing harder."

"With..." Rupert bit his tongue. Bugger that, why hadn't this Williams fellow been classified LMF—Low Moral Fibre—in the first place? And why hadn't his commander sent him home sooner after his wife died?

Doing his work with God. By taking his anger out on Towsley? Livertwittle! But Towsley's explanation made as much sense as anything. Still, a man should not be allowed to accost someone without—

With great effort, Towsley rolled his head. "Wounded in... the line... of duty..."

His humor, still intact, caused a burning behind Rupert's eyes. He clutched the bed's cold metal railing. As Vicar Towsley closed his eyes, a conversation they'd had at the onset of troops being called up came to mind.

"I would register myself if I weren't too old. They're going to need chaplains."

"And military police." Rupert kept quiet about his own attempts to enlist, which led to the Chief Constable calling him in.

"I shall never sign off on this, Laudner. You did your duty in the last war, as did I. This time, your duty lies right here in the Green. Believe me, I want to go, too. But with all the scalawags about, we shall have our hands full here."

When Junior had been called to serve, the urge haunted Rupert again. Surely the Navy could find work for men like him, especially trained policemen. But one night out in the garden as he put away his hoe and shut the shed door, Cecil had clung to him—at that time, the lad had been a mere six, possibly seven.

"You shan't have to go, shall you, Dadda?"

"No, son." With that, Rupert's desire faded.

A nurse rounded the corner and shooed Rupert away. "I daresay you will have plenty of chances to visit. He won't be going home for some time."

Returning to the station, Rupert bounced the day's word—*HEAL*—back and forth with Heaven. When Melvin's father stopped by later, he held his tongue. The sins of the sons ought not weigh upon a father.

"Before he left, Melvin said something about having hurt the vicar, officer."

"Where did he go?"

"Back to the fight."

"But I thought his ship was off the Indian coast."

"Aye, he was with the main fleet when the Japanese sank the *Dorsetshire* and the *Cornwall*. Served since '39, he has—knows ships' motors like these streets." Mr. Williams worked his lips.

"His commander released him, but now he's found another unit."

"They accepted him?"

"When they heard Melvin can fix anything, why..." The elder Williams shrugged. "Seeing the stairs and all and hearing about that night..." He scratched under his cap. "In due time, I expect Melvin's unit will be crossin' the Channel."

"Well, then."

Ruing his quick judgment of this man's son, Rupert shuffled some papers on his desk. "My sincere sympathies, Mr. Williams—so awful, indeed, what has befallen your family."

His words issued hollow and empty. "These things take time—"

Mr. Williams' pale eyes scanned him. "You'll not be pressing charges?"

"No. Vicar Towsley has chosen against it."

The old fellow drooped as he turned toward the door. "Takin' the high road—that would be the good vicar. Anything we can do for 'im?"

"He will stay in hospital for some time."

Williams shrank back "He will be all right?"

"With time, yes. And he sees this all as part of his job."

Mr. Williams scrunched his heavy white brows.

"I mean, this war touches us all in such peculiar ways. Vicar Towsley should soon be on the mend. You and your wife can pray to that end."

Cap in hand, Mr. Williams gave a half-nod that brushed his white whiskers against his collar. His shuffle almost reached the hallway when Rupert added, "I wager he prays for Melvin even now, and for you as well. He told me he performed Melvin and Marian's marriage ceremony and baptized their children. I am altogether certain he bears your son no ill will."

The door closed softly, leaving him to contemplate what just came from his mouth. The truth, no doubt, about Towsley's goodwill. But could he, R. E. Laudner, offer a sincere prayer for Melvin Williams? The answer rested in the passion still writhing at the pit of his stomach.

Days later, the question of Melvin still haunted Rupert. Some time after the elder Mr. Williams left his office, his eye fell on Marian's handkerchief, still on the corner of his desk. Why had he not thought to give it to the poor fellow? His wife would surely take comfort in this scrap from her daughter-in-law's hand. Since then, he'd meant to drop it by their home several times, but—

Ah well, back to Melvin. He had returned to the fight without needing to, offered his skills to the cause once again. This ignited respect.

But then, Vicar Towsley's scarred visage came to mind. Along with this consideration rose the memory of that gut-wrenching *craack* when Melvin slammed his fist into the innocent vicar's jaw. Rupert could proceed no further, at least not yet.

Not one to discuss upsetting things at home, he made an exception this time. It started when Vicar Towsley returned after a week in the hospital, and Madeleine stopped by the station one day.

Surprised and expecting some family upset, Rupert drew her to a back corner, away. "What is it? Has something gone wrong with Cecil or Gran?"

"No, I took Vicar Towsley some soup. Whatever happened to him?"

Feet apart, her basket overflowing with mending to deliver and a few purchases for supper, she stood as if determined to remain until he divulged all the particulars.

"It was that Williams, wasn't it? I heard rumors when one of the deacons took over last Sunday, but you never mentioned..."

The Chief Constable's door opened and he approached with a report in hand. "Burglary last night, probably black market connected." He noticed Madeleine in the shadows and nodded. "Do excuse me, Madame."

"I shall check with the proprietor right away, sir." The Chief continued down the hall and Madeleine bit her lip. "Forgive me. We can talk more at home—I just—"

Rupert touched her elbow. "I know—Towsley looks awful. I ought to have warned you."

How had he gotten so befuddled of late? Perhaps this had to do with the first V-2 rocket attack on London September 9th. As if they needed a new form of tyranny to worry about. Several informational meetings had sprung up, and inevitably, more haranguing questions.

With Adolph busy on the Eastern Front and in the Mediterranean, officials had thought most of the bombing at an end. Certain areas had even diminished the blackout to a dim-out as the threat of invasion seemed unlikely. Some breathing room at last—or so they thought.

But now this—ordinary citizens, women, old folk, and children struck down by the enemy in a new inventive way. When would the first V-2 hit their section of London? 'Twas only a matter of time.

Questions knocked about in Rupert's head like incendiaries ready to burst. How could the military not have foreseen this possibility, and if they had, why had they not warned the police force? But what could officers do in the way of prevention, when these new rockets originated not from a flying Messerschmidt that could be spotted and shot down, but from a lunatic launching them across the Channel?

Lastly, how should they go about informing the citizenry? These attacks left no time even to hurry to a back garden Anderson Shelter. What tactic might people employ to preserve the lives of their loved ones?

Considering how upset Madeleine had been about the vicar— she'd come to the station but once before in all their married years, when Junior or Anna had taken ill— Rupert accompanied her and the children to church the next Sunday. He had begun to do this when Cecil and Iris returned from the Harwoods. Now, he felt even more protective.

Not that they had suffered—by no means! Emerging from the train, they boasted ruddy cheeks and added weight. All the better for having been away, they swung right into the routine again.

Mr. Harwood had voiced his pleasure. "Wonderful children. We hated to say goodbye. Perhaps you and your wife would want to visit us again. Maybe during Christmas?"

Rupert replied that another visit certainly would do them all good. Mr. Harwood returned home then, but not before handing over a rather large suitcase, in addition to the one Cecil lugged on ahead with Iris and Madeleine.

At home, such treasures peeked from their carefully folded clothing—two small jars of precious preserves, cherry and apricot, along with some nicely washed and packaged vegetables. In addition, an assortment of apples, nuts, dried apricots, and cherries in cotton bags.

Seeing everyone's faces alight with wonder did the heart good. What if he had listened to his first fearful "intuition" and relegated Mr. Harwood's letter to the rubbish bin? What joy that rash act would have squelched!

"What's in the one you've got?" Cecil had sprinted over, so Rupert knelt to open it. Oh, the very best possible gift, a dried rump of beef! Weeks had passed with only a modicum of meat, so what a feast they enjoyed. If only he might share some with Towsley, but the altercation had cost him several teeth.

This heartwarming scene tweaked Rupert's fatherly instincts, so he simply could not bear to watch the children leave with Madeleine the next Sunday morning. But today, a shock awaited them all.

He recoiled at Towsley's first stumbling words. The determined fellow stood his post manfully enough, yet struggled with his delivery.

Part way through the sermon, Madeleine grew very still. Her face, already pale, turned almost translucent in the half-light through the high windows. So sensitive to others' pain, she was. But this went further. Pure tension radiated from her.

He edged his smallest finger toward hers, but she leaned more intently toward Vicar Towsley, as though deciphering his message required every ounce of strength.

"What's wrong with him, Da?" Cecil's question startled Rupert. "Later, son."

He had been visiting Towsley regularly and learned to understand his speech. Still, the other day, he urged the vicar to delay taking up his preaching duties. But if stubbornness were a virtue, this man was even more righteous than Rupert assumed.

Fiery-eyed, he rejoined, "*Better to obey God than man.*"

"From the book of Acts. I am somewhat educated, chum, Mum saw to that. But I daresay, this will bring hardship upon your parish. Do you not think it will be quite difficult for them to see you this way?"

"I am not ashamed, friend. And this wound," the vicar touched his jawline, "may yet bring healing to Melvin."

"You would put his parents through this? Everyone knows he attacked you."

"You told them?"

"*Everyone* told them, hospital workers, one of the witnesses. It's Bethnal Green. Word spreads."

Towsley appeared rather stricken, and Rupert bit his tongue. Still, he had merely spoken the truth. The vicar fingered the edge of his sleeve for long moments before speaking again.

"My heart instructs me in the night, though I thank you, and am grateful for your prayers through this ordeal." Towsley took a moment to rearrange his mouth. "I shall speak with Mr. and Mrs. Williams before Sunday, and perhaps they will stay at home. By the way, do inform dear Madeleine that the wonderful broth she keeps leaving in the kitchen has most likely saved my life."

This morning, the vicar had to utter so many words at once. Rupert grimaced. He had done his best, but one can do only so much for a friend.

Full midday light streamed into the sanctuary. Rather a small edifice compared to London's vast structures, yet safer from the bombs by virtue of this feature, its dark, homey architecture faded into the background as the vicar's face took on a glow.

Worn wooden pews and pulpit smelling of dusting powder from a recent cleaning, made a placid setting. Rupert sat rapt as Cecil grasped his hand.

The attentive silence became a living thing, a rule to be observed. As he neared the end of his pages, Towsley veered down the steps toward them, bringing several jagged red marks from his attack into full view.

"Our Lord said to Thomas, 'Behold my hands and side...' He did not hide his wounds, nor shut himself away from his loved ones. Just as he was, he met Thomas, and it was then that Thomas cried out, 'My Lord and my God!' What if our Savior had hidden his wounds?"

Towsley took a moment to clear his throat, but still, no one person so much as shifted from one foot to the other. Had a church mouse been present, it might have raced hither and yon without attracting attention.

"Throughout human history, our Maker reveals Himself over and over. Out of every disaster comes powerful change, and often spiritual growth. In the long tale of nations this terrible time has arisen, and our Maker sets before us opportunities to view Him anew. In broken limbs, absent eyes, cruel blows to human minds, alterations in emotions, He appears to us.

"Let us choose to look deeper. Let us search for the real person, and see beyond their bruises and scars to the spirit within."

Aware of innocent sleeping sounds from Iris, Rupert scarcely dared to breathe. Madeleine gripped his hand now, and Cecil leaned in under his left arm. Suddenly, as if called forth by some silent summons, the congregation rose in a great rustle of skirts and coats and walking sticks. En masse, they veered toward the vicar.

Two pews ahead of Rupert, a returned soldier with one empty sleeve sat bolt upright through it all. Beside Madeleine, Iris still lay unaware, her head cradled in her mother's lap.

Meanwhile, Towsley walked down the aisle among the congregants and threw up his arms. "Let us behold and embrace what we see. Let us not turn from our brave boys, but open our hearts and minds and eyes. May God grant us courage in so doing."

It seemed that Heaven observed, for a strong noontime light enveloped the gathering. People forged down the aisle with embraces all around, though to Rupert's knowledge, they had never before done such a thing. No one seemed in a hurry to leave, and as Madeleine turned to someone in the row behind theirs, he noticed that soldier still sitting, but his shoulders had begun to quake.

Quietly directing Cecil to wait, Rupert rounded the pews and drew near the poor fellow. He'd seen this young man of late on the street, coming out of an alley. Such details stayed with him—might come handy in a search one day. That day, he attempted a greeting, but the soldier turned away, seemingly drawn by the contents of a shop's side window.

Later, curiosity bade Rupert check that window. What had kept that fellow here so long? Faded remnants of fabric, bric-a-brac, and women's millinery?

Today, the reason could not have been clearer: along with his arm, the lower half of his nose had gone missing. The surgeon had begun some mending, but had sent this boy home from an estate-hospital for respite, and surely would have him return for more surgery.

At the sight of those trembling shoulders, something crumbled inside Rupert. His homecoming from the Great War flashed before him. He sank to the pew and wrapped his arm around the soldier. Oh, for the perfect words, but none presented themselves. And yet, a strange solace emerged.

In due time, Towsley spotted them and hurried over. Rupert relaxed his arm as Towsley settled in and the soldier began pouring forth his anguish.

Rupert lifted Iris to his shoulder and they started home, past the school, the bakery, the butcher's, Boots Pharmacy, the candy store and all the rest. Normally, Cecil would have pulled at Madeleine

113

to gander at windows where shopkeepers still made bold attempts to lure patrons. But today, another curiosity won out.

"What happened to the vicar, Da?"

"He suffered an injury, son."

"But how? Did he fall down?"

How best to answer? The blatant truth would do no good, and Madeleine offered no help at all. When Cecil tugged at his hand, Rupert finally brought forth. "He suffered an..." He had almost said *attack*. "Yes, you have guessed correctly. Vicar Towsley fell quite hard, on cement."

"Where?"

"Not far away, right here in the Green. Someone—ah—ran into him, someone quite beside himself." The puzzled lines in Cecil's forehead only deepened. Better shift the focus. "Fortunately, I was nearby at the time, and could help him to the hospital."

"But that soldier—he got shrapnel in his face, right?"

"Indeed he did."

"Like what we find after a bomb?"

"Yes, son. But have I not instructed you against collecting it?"

"We only take it to the metal collector, Da."

Rupert rumpled Cecil's hair. "Of course, but some may be quite sharp and could hurt you." Knowing that all the boys were on the lookout for the shrapnel, put a rather lame end to the discussion.

"All of this—Vicar Towsley's injury and so much else that troubles us is due to the war, Cecil. We can only pray it will soon end."

The weight of this truth cloaked him afresh—no getting away from this violence, no matter where you lived. The West Side received as many hits during the Blitz as the East, and that held true today. Wealthier inhabitants, finer buildings and better public facilities ensured no safety.

While Officer Fletcher kept track of the hits with straight pins on a large city map posted in the briefing room, the Chief had blustered at one newspaper report calling Bethnal Green a slum.

"Poor we may be, but for Adolph, we make as valuable a booty as the richest side of London."

Just as they neared their corner, Anna came running to join them. At church, she most often sat with her girlfriend, who worked with her at the factory. As she scooped Iris up, another comment from Cecil drew Rupert up short.

"I bet that soldier needs a job. Could he work down at the station, Da? Would he need his arm so much to keep the records?"

Madeleine touched Cecil's shoulder. Oh, the eternal hope in those eyes. Rupert dredged for a fitting reply.

"What a quick mind you have, son." Emotion forced him to pause. "And a good heart, as well, after your mother. One never knows—perhaps such a thing might be possible."

Later, on his way to the volunteer fire station, Rupert stopped by the church, but first, he fetched something from the police station, wrapped the item carefully in brown paper and carried it like a sacred object.

Coming from the back, he spied Towsley resting in an armchair. Without knocking, he called, "Towsley? Laudner here."

"Ah, do come in."

"I have brought you something, my old chum. Perhaps you may make use of this, or give it to the Williams family." He held out Marian's handkerchief, and Towsley unwrapped the fabric.

Noting the initials, he fingered the thin cotton. "Marian Williams'—How did you...?"

"It lay balled up in a corner of the landing. I thought perhaps you might—"

"Give it to Mr. and Mrs. Williams?"

Rupert nodded.

"How fitting. I shall do so tomorrow."

Handing off that stained white piece brought consolation. No words arose for the feeling, but the hankie would finally be where it belonged. Rupert went on his way, thankful that Towsley had probed no deeper.

115

Chapter Thirteen

Drying her hands on her trousers, Dorothy headed out into the promise of daylight after her night shift. Thankfully, the powers that be had banished 18 hours of duty. Twelve at a time, seven days a week—this was manageable.

Doubtless, some man devised the original schedule, and Lieutenant Eilola had allowed it to stand, knowing that soon, nurses would be dropping like flies. When that occurred, she offered the voice of reason.

All around, crews readied the Eleventh for the move to a staging area before proceeding to Italy. Trucks piled high with boxes and wooden crates waited to be loaded onto LSTs. Jeeps and other vehicles bulged with supplies.

In the midst of all this activity, Captain Siemons hailed her. "Hey—what do you think of all this? We're headed for a place called Bagrano."

"And they'll drive all of these onto landing craft, right?"

"Yep. Already waiting in the harbor. Kind of hate to leave Mondello Beach, don't you?"

"I won't miss the smell."

Without dwelling on the stench of decomposing civilian bodies piled high along city streets and throughout the countryside, the Captain nodded. "The streets are as sobering as the operating theater. So many innocent islanders caught between gunfire from both sides."

"What a spectacle we create for the civilians—the immensity

of this operation never ceases to amaze me. Reminds me I'm an Iowa girl. Not what I ever imagined."

"Me neither. I expect by now you'd be married, with little ones tugging at your apron strings."

"Maybe. Definitely not camping out. How is your little girl, and your wife?"

"As well as can be expected—working hard. Doing their best." Something about his demeanor stopped other questions Dorothy might have posed.

"You've probably heard things will change once we're in country?"

"We're being put up in Italian hotels?"

The Captain laughed out loud. "The Eleventh will be attached to the Fifth Army now. General Patton's worn the Seventh out and has to stay here. His old friend Ike chastised him for losing control with those shell-shocked soldiers and forced him to apologize."

"He's a showman, right? So he managed."

"Yeah, but after taking the city of Palermo and saving Montgomery's hide, he even beat the British to the city. After such wild success, this has to be quite the downfall. Where are you headed?"

"I think I'll go into town to do some shopping. Maybe I'll get my hair done, but first, I need to wake Millie and get some breakfast."

"All right if I walk you to your tent? It's on my way."

"You're bringing mail?"

"I wish. I just sent two of my men to figure out what's holding it up. Maybe something to do with Patton's goings-on."

"That could affect the mail?"

Captain Siemons shrugged. "Just about anything can interfere. Things intertwined in ways so complicated, it gives me headaches. We're at the mercy of weather, commanders, torpedoes, artillery, laziness, stupidity—you name it."

This officer always seemed to have insider information, and as they walked, he returned to General Patton. "He's fussing and fuming, but I doubt it'll do him much good. He went too far this time. The British press got ahold of the story, and no matter that

117

Patton fought under General Pershing against Pancho Villa—even his friendship with Ike couldn't save him."

"We really need him, don't we?"

"Sure do, but I doubt he'll see action in Italy. Too bad for the overall picture, because when it comes to tactics, he's head and shoulders above the rest. Did you hear that even one of the guys he slapped says he respects him? Says Old Blood and Guts has been under heavy stress too, and perhaps has battle fatigue himself—no hard feelings."

"Wow, that's loyalty!"

"Yeah, toward the commander who forced you on to Messina in spite of how many casualties the Germans inflicted, then threw you across the recovery tent for admitting you had the shakes. Those units went from hill to hill, literally, against two panzer grenadier divisions blowing bridges and laying mines the whole way."

"Too bad the General couldn't show a little compassion, but he's a tough guy. For him, it's all or nothing."

A seagull swooped to the waters' edge for scraps as the captain gave something between a sigh and a groan. "The Germans even booby-trapped dead soldiers, did you know that? The guy Patton slapped had seen plenty of his buddies die, I'm betting."

A shudder took Dorothy. "I don't know how they do it, do you?"

"There's only one way. Gut it out. But then they're left with all those scenes to deal with. That might be the worst part."

"Sure would've liked to be a mouse in the corner to hear the general's apology."

"Yeah. That might be the hardest punishment Ike could have given him. Apologizing comes hard enough for folks like you and me, but he's a big shot. Bet he did a few practice runs with his staff."

"How did you learn all these details? The GI that got slapped—did you know him from somewhere?"

"Nope, I've got short wave." The captain grinned and pointed to his temples as if claiming superior perception.

"So, how long do your short waves tell you it'll take to get us to the staging area in Italy?"

"It's near Naples, and the Fifth is already having its challenges there. Unfortunately, while the Seventh focused on Messina, we let over 100,000 enemy troops evacuate from here, and they headed straight for Italy. Once Mussolini fell, they took Rome, and their fortifications around Salerno are what's killing us as we speak. Pardon the pun.

"General Clark's getting his comeuppance. His men are trapped in peach and apple orchards or tobacco fields, with incoming fire from German positions on the high ground."

"So that's it! I thought I smelled peaches!"

"On the wounded?"

"I swear it—I've been baffled. But now I know why."

Captain Siemons shook his head. "I'm glad they found something left to eat—the Germans usually destroy everything edible. At least the Eighty-second succeeded in claiming the Chiunzi Pass—now they can guide our naval guns to enemy supply lines. We'll get them, but it's going to take longer than most people thought."

"Where have I heard that before?" At the nurses' area, Dorothy stopped. "You're a walking encyclopedia. But you still didn't answer my question—how long will it be until we load up?"

The captain lifted his palms to vast blue sky. "No guessing allowed when the US Army's involved."

Bit by bit, this morning's heavy mist gave way to sunlight. As Rupert proceeded past Kelly's Pie and Mash Shop, the best spot to eat mash, meat pies, and stewed eels, the rich aroma of baking pies enticed him. A bit further, a spectacle appeared. Half a block away, a collision of sunshine and mist created an ethereal aura over the street.

He slowed his pace to study the effect and then hurried to

stand at that exact location, between two lampposts and in front of a butcher's shop. Inside the ray, he turned, but saw nothing out of the ordinary. Baffled, he hurried back to where he'd first spied the radiance.

It was still there, an intersection of mist and sunlight, but the radiance could be viewed only from afar. Interesting. You might be standing in the midst of something glorious without realizing it.

A few blocks along, someone hailed him in a familiar, determined female voice. He squinted into the sun. Ah, Mrs. Evans.

"I'd hoped to find you along here, off'cer." She shifted her youngest child to her other arm and continued. "I'd just come out of the infirmary, and down the street a ways, Avery Ritter stood right across the street, sure as I live and breathe, and he was talking with somebody.

"I hid in a doorway, to be sure it was him. You know his crooked stance, almost as if his body shows the state of his mind, wouldn't you say, Off'cer?"

"I never thought of it that way, but that makes sense." Rupert called on his patience, for Mrs. Evans never took the direct route to a story's end. "Did you recognize the bloke speaking with him?"

"Looked som'at like Mrs. Perkins' cousin from Cardiff—she's our neighbor, you know. But not enough to *be* him."

"Tall or short?"

"Shorter than you, but taller than me. Dark hair and a short beard."

"They spoke at length, then?"

"They did." She brushed a downfall from her eyes. "Probably all of five minutes, sir. And—"

Rupert jumped back in. "Quite valuable information, Mrs. Evans. Could you please describe the gentleman for me?"

"He was flustered-looking, as though he might have just had a domestic."

"Did he wear a hat, carry a walking stick or have any distinguishing features?"

"He had a beret. Brown, I believe, and he sported a tweed jacket.

Had a walking stick, rather fancy at that, and everything else he wore was dark. Eyes, hair, even 'is skin. Maybe an Italian—maybe one of them prisoners." Her eyes grew large at the possibility.

"Excellent work, ma'am. Did this man and Ritter exchange anything?"

"They did indeed. Oh—did I say Ritter had a small leather case that he opened and the stranger drew near to look inside? When Ritter shut it up again, the stranger nodded and said something.

"Then he waited while Ritter passed through a door into a building. 'Twas painted green, a double affair like as if you might pull the two sides apart at the middle to drive a lorry through. The paint looked awful bad, though. Yes, Avery Ritter went in there while the man waited outside, and came out with two packages, one about the size of my husband's duffel bag, and the other—"

"Did he give them to this man and receive money in exchange?"

"I warrant he did. Couldn't see exactly, but something spilled on the sidewalk, and jingled as though he'd dropped a half crown and some farthings. Rather nerve-wracking, but I couldn't say for sure, as a lorry rolled up about that time, and—"

"A lorry? Did the driver park in front of the two men?"

"Why, how could you know? Truth be told, he did. After that, there was nothing more to be seen of those two. I might've stayed longer, but my work at home called me. I left my middle child in charge, and 'e's trustworthy, but things can happen—"

"Mrs. Evans, thank you so very much. Now, as to this building. It is situated down from the infirmary, between here and there, am I correct?"

"Exactly. Not half a minute's walk from the doors."

"Had it a sign above the door?"

"No sign that I recall, but a dist... one of those marks. A big black smudge ran all the way across on the low side, like as if somebody backed a lorry there regular and cared nothing about the consequences. Near scraped the wood in two. I would imagine that door might not be so sturdy as it once—"

Rupert pulled out his watch. "The afternoon wanes and you must get back to your children. I simply cannot thank you enough for your fine investigative work. We may have to take you onto the force."

A chuckle lighted Mrs. Evans' eyes and she blew at a wayward swatch of hair. "Like as I would assist the Prime Minister, eh?"

"Or I. Thank you again."

Thoughts churned in Rupert's head. This required immediate action. Better inform the Chief. As he neared the station, he outlined his report. But crossing the noisy main entryway where officers booked criminals and citizens made inquiries, second thoughts troubled him. Had he jumped to conclusions?

Given Ritter's previous crimes, he doubted that. Best get straight to the Chief's office, trusting he would surmise the necessary action. As an officer, his own task was to accept that determination. Through the window in the Chief's door, Rupert noted his superior at his desk, hard at work.

His bowed head evidenced a great loss of hair. Rupert touched his own topknot. With all the responsibility the Chief Constable carried, reasons for balding were legion. And first on the list, the tube station tragedy. Still unthinkable.

At his knock, the Chief looked up. "Do come in, Laudner. What have you for me?"

Rupert summarized his interpretation of Mrs. Evans' report.

"You believe something might be afoot presently?"

"I do, sir."

The Chief rubbed his finger over his forehead, creating an ink stain. "What say you check the premises straightaway and send me news by the phone box? Hopefully we can bring his dealings to a sudden end."

Invigorated, Rupert hurried on his way. Half an hour later, after scouting about the alley in question, he formulated his case. From what he could see through a painted over but badly chipped window, the place held a large amount of goods, all in boxes or crates stacked nearly to the rafters.

His height often proved a hindrance with London's low doorways and ceilings—difficult to race about a structure with small rooms in pursuit of a man half your size. But in this case, his height provided a definite advantage. Minus six inches, how would he have gained a view through a rather large chip towards the top of a window?

Forced to take off his helmet, the top of his head compacted against the eave works. But the reward was noting pile after pile of articles—merchandise, most likely—carefully boxed and stored inside. No doubt, a variety of supplies that might be provisioning British troops in dire straits all around this weary world.

Heavy iron locks on both doors hinted at the high value someone placed on this building's contents. Put together, the entire scene smelled of black market.

And that deep scrape gouged all along the wooden doors portended numerous backings-into. In addition, the pavement bore black tire marks coming and going both left and right. Back and forth, back and forth. Perhaps this locale supplied scurrilous exchanges all over the East End—or over London at large.

Viable rubber tires revealed someone with access to ready cash. These days, hardly any commodity was more prized than rubber. Scientists had been researching synthetic substitutes for shipbuilding and other manufacturing.

Balancing these facts with the money exchange left little doubt about how this owner acquired the funds for upkeep on his truck. Not for a moment did Rupert think Avery Ritter owned the vehicle. No, he performed the dirty work at the low end, the heavy lifting that provided a truck—and who knew what else—for someone higher on the ladder.

In her own way, Mrs. Evans had pinpointed Ritter's standing, but something besides his gait captured Rupert's attention.

Mum used to say, "Your father told me how a shifty eye helped him read people's intentions, and that nine times out of ten, this characteristic foretold trouble. He often declared he'd rather not shave a customer with a shifty eye."

His father never admitted to a secret longing to officially uphold the law. But the offer to join the police force, brought forth the very day after Rupert's return from the war, made him wonder if his father hadn't played a role. Mr. Laudner, Senior knew many influential men, such as the local magistrate. These public figures trusted him to hold a razor to their throats.

By the time a troop ship belched Rupert out on the docks after his time in the trenches, the elder Laudner had passed from this world. En route home, he visited the grave. Then his mother informed him of his inheritance. She fed him and he begged for an early bedtime. But the next noon, a courier from the precinct called.

Rupert followed the messenger to the police station and was ushered into an office, where the Chief at the time offered him a detective position. Quite the unexpected shock, yet he could think of no reason to say anything but "yes."

That evening, his Mum went tight-lipped when he inquired about the offer. That increased his theory's reliability, for when had he known her to lack an insight? He let it go at that, since the offer set well and he was too exhausted to investigate further. But it wouldn't surprise him to discover that Da heard about an opening and lobbied on his behalf.

Since the Chief asked him to call in, Rupert strapped his helmet under his chin and veered toward the closest police telephone box, a distance of two blocks. What would he suggest if asked his opinion?

Station two or three other officers here and catch him red-handed, for skivs might upend their networks and vanish of a night. But he was not the Chief. That honor would fall to Chief Derby's son, slated to rejoin the force when he returned from the front. A chipper fellow, his experience as an infantry officer would serve him well and he would step into his father's shoes naturally.

Approaching the blue box, formerly fashioned of teak but now of sturdier concrete except for the door, Rupert organized his thoughts. This box stood like a monument, about as tall as him. The electric light atop was blinking—perhaps the Chief had tried to reach him.

Reaching inside to retrieve the receiver, he felt something squishy. The day's fading sunshine fought against his search. Nothing left but to pull out whatever had been thrust in.

"Blimey!" Rupert tossed a putrid mound of raw turnips to the pavement and surveyed the area. The citizenry showed respect for these devices installed by the Metropolitan Police about 12 years after he joined the force. The authorities realized how instrumental they had been in squelching crime in other areas.

Local citizens also might call to report an emergency, and during this war, had often done so. Imagine a distraught mother calling to report a burglary and coming up with this mush!

No bombed out building languished nearby to shelter young toughs or provide a playground for small boys' soldier games. He had passed just such a building, though, in the next block, and determined to check the premises.

Lifting the receiver, he glanced around once more. He had taken the usual precautions, but one could not be too careful. No shadows flitted from corner to corner when he turned, but Ritter might still have observed him from a doorway or a second or third story.

"Chief Constable, please." As he waited, something seemed amiss. He wished the administration had upgraded these calling boxes to tiny offices where an officer might shut the door and make notes at a small desk. As it was, Rupert stood and waited as the phone rang.

"Is that you, Laudner?"

"Yes, sir."

"Your findings?"

"I believe an evening raid would be called for." He detailed the evidence, and could hear the chief tapping something on his desk.

"I shall draw up the needed papers. Tonight?"

"The sooner, the better."

"There might be no time to lose, if we are to catch them." Scribbling sounds emanated from the receiver, so Rupert held it away from his ear.

"Knowing your heavy schedule, I hesitate to ask, but would you be able to supervise the raid? We've fallen dreadfully short of men."

"I shall be there. Nine o'clock?"

"Good—full dark. The others have far less experience."

"Righto. To be honest, I would hate to miss out on this, sir."

"Fine. Report to me in the morning. I shall expect you."

Hanging up, Rupert's sigh reverberated. He had no reason to believe the Chief might not take his word, but even so, 'twas good to know. He hoped with all his heart that Ritter would show up with enough evidence to be arrested. He'd like to have this thing done with and get on to other pressing matters.

So much to sort these days. Yes, like the continuing wreckage and deaths from those blighted V-2 Rockets.

Recalling that bombed out house en route, he decided to check the rubble-filled basement, and found only boys playing in its vacant lot. Chatting with them for a while, he observed no rotten vegetable essence or stained hands, and they ran off, shouting, "Let's play Leap Frog."

"Everyone form a queue." The first boy squatted, the next jumped over him and squatted, too. The third did the same, and so on until the last lad had to leap over a line of six. He and his chums once played the same game without incident.

If grown men tried this, someone would surely break the fifth squatter's neck, or fall headlong into the pavement. But boys suffered only scuffed shoes, bloody knees and hands.

The shelled-out house contained telltale signs of the boys' game of *war*. Makeshift guns from sections of old broomsticks or small branches broken over a knee, were scattered here and there. Did boys of all cultures, even those that never made war, play this game?

In a corner, a tight-cinched cotton bag held marbles, Rupert surmised, and leaning down to pick it up, noticed a mother's careful stitching. One shake revealed the contents—glass scraping on glass. One of the boys must have dropped this when the lookout spied him coming and yelled, "Copper!"

126

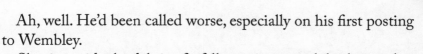

Ah, well. He'd been called worse, especially on his first posting to Wembley.

Shoving aside the debris of a fallen stairway with his boot, what had occurred here became obvious. He'd bet his whistle the bomb had left the banister intact, so these boys had 'ridden the rail,' and their weight had crashed the structure into oblivion.

Yes, even the gritty cement dust still riding the air smelled of a recent origin. Thank heavens the wall had not come down on them—more broken bodies to pull from rubble.

Farther on, a few dark brown conkers had rolled to one side of a second brick wall still standing. The sight of those horse chestnuts set Rupert's heart aflame. Such a simple thing, millions of them all 'round in the parks or wherever the trees grew, but these particular ones transported him straight back to 1916.

Though tempted to collapse against the wall, he gathered himself. Much remained to be accomplished. With ample time, he might address those young fellows and serve them a warning. But instead, he hurried across the front yard and made his way toward home.

Chapter Fourteen

Staging area, Sicily

After supper on December 24th, a nurse named Sharon approached Dorothy and Millie. "I noticed Henrietta's birthday's a week from today. Since we have extra time now, why not have a party? I hinted around, and she said her family never celebrated birthdays—can you imagine?"

"She'd never agree to it."

"So we won't tell her."

The contagious twinkle in Sharon's eyes did its work, and her Georgia accent provoked a chuckle from Millie, whose face lighted up like a—well, not a Christmas tree exactly—not on this Sicilian beach.

"Wally told me he's cooking up a little something special tomorrow, even without his kitchen. Maybe I can put a bug in his ear about a cake on the 31st—that's Hank's birthday, isn't it?"

"Yes. New Year's Eve."

"So she won't expect a thing. By then, we should be about to ship out, and after supper, I'll lure her somewhere. When we get back; lights, camera... action!"

Millie clapped her hands. "I love surprise parties. We'd better come up with some entertainment."

Dorothy waylaid Captain Siemons. "We need your help on New Years Eve, a surprise for Hank's birthday—she's never had a party before. You're so up-to-date with the news, would you play a news anchor spewing forth wisdom? The girls and I—maybe we'll sing an advertisement or something."

"Sure, why not? We have heavy duty coming in Italy, so why not have a little fun?"

"Whoo boy—you're usually right. You can think of some jokes, right?"

"I'm on it." He gave her the victory sign and cracked his gum. "Have you heard somebody's going to read FDR's Christmas address tomorrow morning?"

"No—what time?"

"0700 hours."

"I'll be there."

Millie had been awfully quiet lately, but this idea returned the color to her cheeks. "Let's get started right away. We need a song and some ads."

The next morning, someone set up a speaker, and most of the hospital staff gathered to listen.

"December 25, 1943, a message from the President to the men of the American Merchant Marine. As we celebrate this Christmas we must all extend our greetings to the peoples of the united nations. In their leaders I met open-minded men of great vision forecasting a lasting peace and a future of peace and good will toward men. Today we have overseas almost twice the number of armed men that we had a year ago.

"Peace and goodwill, right." Hank's ineloquent interruption raised a call for quiet. Her eyebrows did a dance intended only for Dorothy and Millie, but from the chuckles that rose, others must have been watching.

"We have handed the men of the Merchant Marine the great job of furnishing these men with supplies, with food and munitions, with planes and tanks, with guns, and more men to bring closer our victory. As fighting men you of the Merchant Marine are scattered throughout the world far from families and friends on this Christmas Day. The great plans made at the recent conferences will speed the day when you can again be with them. I bring to the people of our nation and

to its proud sons in the Merchant Marine the purposeful intentions of Churchill, Stalin, Chiang Kai Shek, and the nations they represent that we will fight together until ultimate victory.

"The pressure of our united attack is constantly increasing on every front. That pressure will engulf our common enemy. The steel walls of Hitler's and Hirohito's brutal empires will draw tight about their throats. Our plans are made and we are united. Hitler is listening and he would like to know when we are launching the attack that will seal his doom. So I cannot tell you, but those plans are set and they will be carried out. A truly great American will lead that attack, our own General Eisenhower, and back of him in a powerful united effort are the full resources of all our nations combined to render a crushing defeat to those who gained what they have through force. We will defeat them.

"Those who have been enslaved will be freed, even those who have through force been brought under the grinding heel of their own leaders. Three fourths of all the peoples of the earth are joined in a common cause of freedom loving people. We will be strong, united strength for freedom, not for enslavement. There will be no slaves in our free world nor will the aggressor arise again to enslave his fellow men. It will be peace even if we must resort to force to maintain that peace on earth and good will toward men.

"On behalf of your friends, your loved ones, and the people of the United States, yes, and of the united nations, I send you this greeting. Our hearts are with you as you travel the wide deep oceans. May God's blessing and comfort guide you and keep us strong in our faith that we fight for a better day for all mankind."

Sharon started clapping. "Merry Christmas, everyone. I guess our upcoming transport is our Christmas present. Did you hear that even the President is using the plain boxes his wife's gifts came in this year? It's all about the paper drive, my mother wrote."

"What a sacrifice." Hank could multiply an ounce of sarcasm into ten. Meanwhile, others added their comments.

"Yeah, my sis said there's no paper to be had in the stores. Our hometown newspaper published an article about wrapping with waste paper, and then donating it to the paper drive."

"Good thing my mom hoards stuff in the attic—that's her main source this Christmas. But I bet my little brother won't even know the difference. A baseball bat is a baseball bat, whether or not it has some nicks in it, right?"

"See you later, can't wait to taste what Wally's cooking up for us."

Before they went their separate ways, Hank added one more jab. "Thanks to the Merchant Marine, we've had no mail since Thanksgiving, Mr. President."

With Hank often in their tent, finding a time to work on the party created the biggest challenge. But one day she watched over the last patients bound for North African hospitals, so Dorothy tried out her first draft on Millie near the makeshift kitchen while Wally rolled out dough.

"I borrowed the tune from the Marines," Dorothy put her hand over her heart and plunged in:

From the sands of No-rth A...fri...ca, to the shores of Sicily
We will stand with the Ele..he...venth, over land and over sea.
First to welcome the in...COM...ing, first to diagnose a spleen,
We will clean and dress our patients as fast as a Marine.

Millie's chuckle and a grin from Wally encouraged her.

"We need to get some folks to memorize the words and work up a few chorus line kicks."

"Perfect. Maybe we can find a doc to dance with us. I'll go spread the word. Practice tomorrow night, same time, right here—is that all right with you, Wally?"

His nod sufficed—definitely a man of few words.

What a hoot that next practice was—a couple of spontaneous acts found their way into the line-up, and Abner showed up for the dancing. Chorus girl kicks and harmonizing, a quick run-down by Captain Siemons, and so much laughter, even Wally wiped his eyes.

Sharon turned out to have real performing talent, and her drawl lent itself to dramatizing almost anything. Dorothy and Millie gladly let her take the lead.

The night of the gala, everything went better than they'd hoped. Sharon disappeared with Hank right after the meal.

As soon as they left, everyone set to work transforming a small area near Wally's table into a stage. Somebody backed up a couple of trucks, and a few nurses created a banner from a stray swatch of canvas. In big letters, "Happy Birthday, Hank" made a splash when some corpsmen hung it from truck to truck.

Wally produced a cake complete with boiled frosting and candles, to astonished "oohs" and "aahs." Someone asked, "How'd you come up with them candles?"

Wally pursed his lips. "Gotta give credit where credit is due." He pulled forth a supply sergeant, who took a bow.

"Tell us how you got them."

"It's a company secret."

"Okay, okay. Sharon and Hank just rounded the corner by the nurses' tents."

Someone ran for a cloth and recruited two corpsmen to hold it in front of the cake. Wally uncovered several bottles of champagne. A corpsman stationed himself along the path, ready to spread the red carpet—his long coat—for the guest of honor.

"Quiet, now. Everyone simmer down."

A hush fell over the group. Outside, Sharon was leading Hank along. "It's New Year's Eve—don't you wish we could be in New York or somewhere for a celebration?"

"Right. That would be my style, for sure."

When Sharon came abreast of the waiting group, Dorothy gave her the high sign and Sharon started singing "Happy birthday to you."

Sharon kept Hank in a firm grip, though Hank tried to wriggle away. The corpsman grabbed her other elbow, and for a half-second, Dorothy was afraid she might cry.

Sharon called for quiet. "Welcome to your special night, Hank. We'll rip raaaght into the entertainment. Hope you enjoy." She plopped Henrietta's hand on the corpsman's forearm, and he escorted her to the place of honor, a wiggly chair confiscated from who-knows-where.

Hank looked so flushed she might boil over, but once she sat down, she took a deep breath and composed herself. Millie sighed in tandem with Dorothy as Sharon took it from there and introduced Captain Siemons, seated behind a curtain.

Earphones made of socks and a metal mixing spoon for a microphone brought gales of laughter.

"Good evening, listeners. We bring you greetings from WCLX, all the way from...." He glanced over at Hank and Dorothy. "Where was that we're broadcasting from again?"

"Little Town, Wisconsin."

"Ah, yes. Right from the belly button of the heartland, folks. Out here where corn grows as tall as your horse's tail, the wind brings storms from NORD Dakota, and the snow finally melts in May."

During strong applause, he adjusted his headphones and rubbed his lips as if to warm them to their task. "So then. What would you say to our friend Herr Hitler if you were stuck together in a rain storm?"

No answer.

"Come on, I know it's been a long week, but wake up, y'all! You'd say 'Hail!'"

"Boo...boo!"

"Yes, well. Just warming up here. Did you know Bob Hope said at one stop in North Africa, "The California Chamber of Commerce is calling this my victory tour—it gets me out of the state!"

More boos, and a "Yeah, so why didn't we get to see him? We were there long enough, that's for sure."

Quick on the draw, the Captain declared, "He was afraid to get near us. We smelled too bad." He raised his eyebrows at the nurses. "I do believe it's time for our sponsors to break in."

Posing like the Andrews sisters, Mildred, Dorothy, and Sharon leaned together.

133

"Fels Naptha, the best soap that you're afta...
Use it in the shower, use it by the hour,
The best soap in the U...S...A..."

That rated wolf whistles and cries of "More! More!"

Sharon held up her finger. "We do have more. Moonbeam, display our next product, please."

Dorothy held up a bar of Lifebuoy soap still in its wrapper, and Millie started them off.

"I ain't Betty Crocker,
and you're way, way off your rocker
if you think you can find
a soap better than mine."

They sidestepped from the center and Captain Siemons took over again—he really ought to be on the radio. In a pause, he nodded to a tall, thin corpsman who hurried to the mic with his mouth organ and sped through *I'm A Yankee Doodle Dandy*, raising another cheer.

"Now, back to your favorite: Bob Hope often mentions going to the New Year celebration in Times Square one year. 'Boy, was it crowded! It was so crowded that the pickpockets wouldn't take your watch unless it was gift-wrapped.'"

A few chuckles.

"One of 'em had his hand in my pocket, so Bob asked, 'What's the idea?' The pickpocket answered, 'Don't get excited; I'm just making change.'"

Without slowing down, Captain Siemons added another Army joke: "Who tells a four-star general what for?"

The whole crowd yelled, "His wife."

"You're all way too smart for this poor excuse for an announcer. One more local color story, and then we have a real treat coming. Why did we only bivouac overnight at St. Amour?"

"Because our commander said it was only a one-night stand."

Hoots and applause.

"All right, then. We have one more act from three of our illustrious nurses, and then a last bit of cheer for you tonight. You will have the amazing treat of watching Doc Abner dance."

Cheers broke out, and Captain Siemons finally regained everyone's attention. "After the dance, Commander, you're on."

Standing so close their faces touched, the trio crooned,
"We've called you together,
To wish Hank all the best
And have a laugh or two,
So good for me and you.
We're off to Italy, so
As we pack up and go
Thanks for coming here,
This will have to last all year!"

Doing high kicks, they exited stage left to wild applause. Sharon grabbed Abner and the corpsman played "Yankee Doodle Dandy." Dorothy and Millie had their chance to dance with him, too, and then Sharon pulled Hank up and turned to the crowd.

"Wally has outdone himself tonight, so let's have a round of applause for him."

After clapping and Wally bowing, she gestured toward the refreshments.

"Now, enjoy a sip of champagne to welcome in 1944, and here's to our boys preceding us to Italy!"

Horse chestnuts. As long as Rupert could remember, they fell every autumn from hundreds of trees across England. On any given day, one could hear them *plop plop* into the leaves. After all these years, how could the sight of them in that bombed-out row house have caused such a violent reaction? Halfway home, he stepped into a quiet alley and leaned against the wall until his heart calmed down.

Just last week, Cecil had come running into the kitchen late on Sunday afternoon with a handful of the smooth maroon globes.

"Mum, could I borrow your meat skewer?"

"Whatever for?" Madeleine seemed surprised—could she have forgotten how Junior used to ask the same thing?

"To make conker holes. Then if I could use a little vinegar from the larder—"

Her frown deepened. "Vinegar?"

These days, it took courage to ask for anything from the larder. "Only a little, to soak them in until tomorrow. And then would you bake them for me, please? Anthony says the longer, the better. One of them might even be a twenty-oner!"

When Madeleine caught his eye, Rupert smiled, so she consented. After Cecil went outside with the skewer, she worried, "What if he cuts his finger, or worse?"

"I shall help him, love." That afternoon, handling the horse chestnuts hadn't bothered him at all. In fact, he'd enjoyed their smoothness under his fingers. Sharing this changeless boyhood tradition created a warm sensation.

Then why this reaction, today of all days, with the raid scheduled in a few hours? His pulse slowed gradually from galloping horses to its regular steady plod. During that interlude, his old teacher, Mr. Purling, appeared before his mind's eye, in a scene he had long forgotten. One day, Mr. Purling entered the schoolroom wiping his brow, a bit late for the younger forms in the next room. Even the date was clear, because Rupert had written it down in Purling's ledger.

"Please record that we've just sent four bushels of horse chestnuts to the Minister of Munitions, Laudner. Our students gathered each and every one for the war drive as our patriotic duty."

"Sir, do you know how these are used?"

Mr. Purling's salt-and-pepper eyebrows rose and fell. "Stop by later," he whispered, "and I'll tell you what I surmise."

The rest of the afternoon, Rupert pondered, to the point of received a chiding for daydreaming. Finally, he knocked on the professor's door, was invited in, and took a seat in the front row.

"Because you're likely to go off to war soon, you deserve to know the facts. My friend working in munitions says they've asked children of all the parishes for as many chestnuts as they can send, and rather many of the schools make time for this occupation. Like you, most boys belong to the scout troop, and like as not, you've also collected chestnuts there?"

Rupert nodded and Mr. Purling continued. "And you removed the green shells, leaving just the nuts before bagging them in sacks?"

"Yes. Then we wheeled them off to the station for transport."

"Did your scout master explain about their secret destinations?"

"No, sir."

"From your studies, you will be familiar with cordite, often used as a propellant for shells and other arms. A necessary component of cordite is acetone. Throughout the land, hidden factories have been set up to extract this substance. I am aware of two, one in Dorset and another in Norfolk.

"At one time, American maize supplied all the acetone required, but with German U-boats striking down American ships in the Atlantic, munitions factories began to run short, for they require 90,000 gallons per year. Someone discovered that the starch in conkers could substitute for that in maize, so we began collecting them, and even receive a little pay.

"I entrust this information to you, knowing your character. Not a word to a living soul—heaven help us if the Germans discover our ingenious production method." Purling paced the length of the room and back. "Spies lurk about. Therefore we cannot be too careful."

Aware of the grainy brick wall against his back, Rupert shuddered back to the present—spies still lurked about. Barely a year after his talk with Purling, his platoon endured blasts as they sent projectiles sailing toward the enemy, thanks to the lowly horse chestnut.

All of those wounds and amputations—so many ended in death, including Rupert's best friend who had signed up with him. He might have entertained memories of his comrade's horrifying last minutes, but the urgency of his mission precluded that choice.

Filling his chest with air, he stepped out into the alley and perused behind and before him. Failing light receded under the horizon, lending mystery to his official deed.

Spies about... cannot be too careful...

"Almost 25 years later, here we are, again at war, with skivs taking advantage at every turn."

The rest of the way home, Rupert considered his state when he had staggered along this same street, just home from the Great War. Shell-shocked, filthy, and starving for a decent porridge, he'd become a different young man from when he left. Along the way from the railway station, boys had shouted and pushed at each other in their annual matches, their horse chestnuts threaded carefully onto the ends of strings.

The peaceful scene struck him as a sign. He and his local comrades had waged a gruesome war. Several had perished, along with so many others across the island. Those thousands would never have the opportunity to greet their families as he soon would. He breathed deep of the Green's air.

Truly, this had been the War to End All Wars, but it had finally ended. He picked up his pace with hope in his heart. From now on, the nations would live in harmony.

"Ah, if only..."

He must gather his wits, for he was about to engage a thief, a man without honor, to whom this all-encompassing war meant nothing more than an occasion to fill his own pockets. Loathing flooded Rupert at the thought of Avery Ritter. His fist tightened around his baton. They would capture Avery Ritter, he felt it in his bones.

Towsley's words attended him... *HOPE... BEHOLD.*

Chapter Fifteen

Even though the evac hospital had shut down, local citizens still showed up for care, along with some soldiers. This morning, a GI with a leg wound waited near the pile of boxes that used to be the hospital tent.

"Could you change my bandage?" He pulled up his pant leg to reveal a questionable wrap on his ankle.

"Sure." It took a while and asking a corpsman for help, but Dorothy found sulfur powder, tape, and gauze. Whistling *Mersey Dotes*, she changed the bandage. As she applied ointment, the soldier started a conversation.

"Pretty happy, aren't you?"

"Yep."

"Gimme one reason."

"I could give you ten. We're not being shot, that's a plus. I've got some good friends in my unit, and just heard my three brothers are all right, and—"

"Got it. Bet you have a fella, too." He leaned back against a box and she ignored his comment, but heat crept up her neck.

"How about lighting a cigarette for me?"

"Is something wrong with your hands?"

"No, miss, but you're a nurse, aren't you?"

"Sure am, but there are plenty of other patients waiting. Hmm, your wound needs debriding, so this is going to hurt."

"Aw, come on—light one for me."

"I'd rather not—I don't like to breathe smoke."

139

"Sister, I'm dyin'—for a *Lucky Strike*. You know how the ad goes, 'Lucky Strike Green has gone to war.' I heard it on *Information Please*, didn't you?"

"Yes, I was one of those listeners that it annoyed. Who wants to have the announcers stick in an ad during the program? Whoever did that had a really bad idea."

"They was just advertising—"

"Well, it had the opposite effect. My friends and I were in training, and tuned in NBC every Friday night at 8:50 we weren't on call. But for a while, we stopped because of that monotonous interruption."

"You did?"

"Yup. Did they really believe all that repetition would convince listeners the company was patriotic? Who would fall for the claim that they changed their packages to white because of a green paint shortage?"

The soldier moaned as she finished cutting away proud flesh. "Makes sense, don't it? What ain't green here? No green left when the army got done paintin' everything."

"My friends and I took bets on it—ten to one the company planned to change the color anyhow. The war just happened to come at the perfect time. They're trying for a bigger name than *Camel*."

"Anyway—how about that light?" He grabbed a smoke and leaned closer.

"Private, I don't think smoking's good for you, and I want you healthy."

"I'll just get somebody else—"

Dorothy picked up her bandage tray. "All right."

A wave of chagrin hit her en route to a thrown-together supply box. No reason to be so snappy. That GI had survived a lot so far, and one nurse's opinion wasn't going to change anything. Besides, the Red Cross kept the soldiers supplied with cigarettes to quiet their nerves. Time to give herself a talking to.

140

"You're in fine form today, Moonbeam, but you'd better watch your tongue."

Sunlight undulated on the beach, creating sparkles on reflective particles. She'd had to fight worry ever since Pinky said he'd be bombing enemy positions in Italy, and soon be making raids on Germany from Adriatic air bases recently claimed as the Allies began their advance north.

He and his buddies—she grinned, recalling how he called them chums—were "softening up" the Rhine for tank and infantry units. Once they chased the Germans out of Italy and Southern France, that final challenge remained. The dangers made Dorothy tremble. So many planes and lives had already been lost to anti-aircraft fire. Millie still hadn't heard from Del—he might be one of them.

But one of Pinky's statements stuck with her. "What I wouldn't give to be back home with my feet in a river, fly-fishing. I'd take you to meet my family. I've already written them about you."

When she'd returned from her walk that morning, Hank had quizzed her. "Where've you been?"

"Out walking again."

"You take more walks than a centipede. Did Douglas Fairbanks decide to leave his wife, after all?"

"That doesn't even deserve an answer."

"You're head over heels for somebody, I'd bet money on it."

"You've already figured that out—it's Paul, right?"

"Yeah, but you're two-timing him. This is somebody else."

"A girl can't even take a walk without getting the what-for."

"You haven't heard the last about this from old Hank, hon."

"Hey, listen. If it *were* true, I wouldn't want you to say anything to Millie. She hasn't heard from Del for so long—"

"Of course not."

At dinner, a corpsman asked, "Has anyone heard when we're leaving?"

"I don't mind waiting. We don't want a repeat of the Sicily landing, right?"

Her mind still on Pinky, Dorothy pondered his description of the RAF's next assignment. *Softening up the Alps...* That reminded her of Bremen, and for the hundredth time, she pictured the beautiful old home at 149 Admiralstrasse. Could it still be standing?

And were her brothers still safe? Once, she and Albert had been skating on a frozen pond and he veered too close to the edge. She'd been the one to rescue him, and how many times had she shielded little Ewald from disaster? Now she could only pray for them and Vernon. That was all she could do for Pinky, too. That, and knit up a storm.

January 12, 1944

"We'll be crossing the Tyrrhenian Sea—see how it's sheltered by these islands?" Colonel Tabor pointed to a large map someone had drawn. "That should guarantee smooth sailing, but one never knows." He glanced around at the gaggle of corpsmen, doctors, and nurses.

"One thing I *can* guarantee: we will not be fired on when we land. Our infantry and marines went through that already. You know how to prepare—fill your canteens, and go easy on breakfast. Any questions?"

"Can you tell us what's happened so far with the Seventh?"

"I'm sure you've heard the Germans were ready for them at Salerno, and we made some tactical errors. Jerry had no intention of mounting a counterattack at the toe of Italy—too much territory to retreat over. But we still mounted Operation Husky, so the British Eighth had to traipse 300 miles north over land mines and bombed-out bridges to meet up with our units."

"So that was our main mistake?"

"In retrospect, the landing on September 11th should have been preceded by naval or aerial bombardment. There was no surprise to the enemy at all. I'm going to level with you. I can hardly believe our first wave was accompanied by a loudspeaker message to give

142

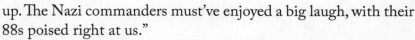

up. The Nazi commanders must've enjoyed a big laugh, with their 88s poised right at us."

In the silence, Eric struggled in Hank's hands and Dorothy reached for him.

"We've been dealing with the aftermath in surgery. The enemy nearly broke the beachhead—some of our pilots were so sure they'd have to return to Sicily, they slept under their planes' wings that night.

"But when all was said and done, neither side gained the initiative. The fighting has moved northward, and more information will be forthcoming once we set up at Vairano, toward the middle of the boot. I trust our forces will make adjustments based on what they've learned.

"We're tasked with replacing the Ninety-fifth Evac, which is moving forward to a place called Anzio. We open on 14 January, so enjoy your last few hours of leisure."

"We're seasick and headed where nobody wants to go. So what else is new?" Hank spoke for everyone as their LST approached Italy's coast.

"At least the new commander told us the truth."

"Oh, you are such a romantic."

"And you see the dark side of everything."

Dorothy threw a comment into Millie and Hank's back-and-forth. "I'm about as nauseated as I've been since we left the States."

"That's really saying something. Your stomach's made of iron."

"Why can't they pick calm days to send us out on the Mediterranean?" Millie's color resembled a pale green tablecloth Mama used in the dining room back home.

Captain Siemons pointed off the bow. "We're not really on the Mediterranean."

"I thought I smelled Wrigley's Spearmint. How did we end up with *you*?"

"Search me, Hank. Must be random good fortune."

"You're way too smart for us peons."

"I bet somebody can name the small island at the top of this sea. Any takers?"

Long-ago geography classes passed through Dorothy's mind, but no answer surfaced.

"It has to do with a famous Frenchman from the last century."

"Elba!" She couldn't tell who came up with the answer.

"There you go. We're privileged, living history right here and now."

"Privileged? Are you out of your mind?"

Hank's barb incited Captain Siemons' chuckle—he expected this stuff from her "Absolutely. Say, does anybody know what's between *ship* and *tanks* in LST?"

"A space?"

"Nope, a comma. Technically, it's landing ship, *comma*, tank."

"I think it should be a slash."

"They're not asking you."

Having the Captain on board gave Dorothy something to focus on besides her rolling stomach. Usually she managed, but this heaving vehicle seemed intent on producing its own casualties.

"Speaking of LSTs, imagine how tough it'd be to unload one under fire. A Navy radioman told me his vessel tried to land in Operation Husky, but Jerry disabled one of their engines. The Germans kept hitting their mark while he called for help.

"His commander waited in the bay until our planes bombed the German positions. Then they tried again, but still had to turn back. At one point, he really thought all was lost. When they finally received orders to reverse course and approach the other end of Green Beach, he requested a smoke screen. Even so, artillery fire killed several of their sailors."

A doc spoke up. "The Sixteenth Panzers?"

"Yes. Our units beat them off and made progress throughout that first day, but failed to link up with each other until the next evening. The Germans knew the Eighth was advancing from the south, so they battered us. We were spread way too thin, so the commanders reduced the perimeter—a good move. That was the beginning of it."

"The pilots really slept out under their wings?"

"So I hear. The situation must've looked pretty bad. But the Eighty-Second paratroopers and Gavin's 505th chuted in to reinforce the lines until the British Seventh Armored could land. The Fifth Army finally advanced toward Naples on the 19th. It took until October sixth to reach the Volturno River line, and from there, they secured Naples. Meanwhile, the Eighth advanced to the Adriatic coast."

"At least this time, they waited until things settled down to bring us in."

"Amen to that." Hank spoke up again.

"Our former commander, emphasis on *former*, thought combat nurses really meant *combat* nurses. It's a miracle you made it through that one—even Eric survived. Who's got that little fella, by the way?"

Dorothy spoke up. "Millie just took him down below."

"Anyway, in spite of screw-ups, we got our foothold, and the fighting's bound to be intense now. You've probably heard that the Fifth Army has a new commander, General Lucas."

Shouts broke out from the forward deck—maybe they were nearing land.

One thing Dorothy counted on. This landing would be far safer than the one in Sicily. Whether the nurses took a train, trucks, or even horse carts to Vairano made little difference.

The noise on deck quieted down, and she found a corner to nod off. Her dreams took her back three days, to the morning when Pinky once again appeared and renewed her hopes.

A northerly wind off the Mediterranean had whispered in her ear before dawn, "This day starts a new chapter." The moon still cast silver shadows on the shore from the west when she left the tent, with Millie in a sound sleep.

In this lull as the Eleventh awaited the order to load up, early morning solitude had become a luxury. Today, she and the other nurses would continue packing the final supplies and their own belongings, but right now, silence reigned.

Even at that hour, ragged black-eyed children scavenged for scraps. Captain Siemons warned that the population fared even worse in Italy, since the Germans had taken over after Mussolini's downfall. Impoverished Italian mothers sold their bodies to save their children from starvation, since the country's cattle and swine had been slaughtered to feed the German army and navy.

People raided animal salt licks for otherwise unobtainable salt. But dwelling on those stories did no good.

Along the dock, massive loads of supplies lay piled to kingdom come. At an open spot, Dorothy scanned the shoreline, a gorgeous silvery thread hugging the island.

And there stood Pinky. The sight took her breath away.

"Houston Pinkstone here." His first simple words had enticed her. Since that morning, she'd been analyzing his brogue. *Book* sounded like *boot. Monk* rhymed with *honk*, and a double *t* back in his throat made *Scottish* sound more like Sco...ish. The differences intrigued her, forced her brain to keep working.

But that morning, he might have spoken an African tribal tongue, for all she knew. His brilliant eyes beckoned her, but her feet failed to move. When he waved her closer, she obeyed. His tanker pants blew in the wind, his pilot's jacket and warm smile convinced her he was real, and feeling his welcoming embrace settled all doubts.

"Aat for a walk s'eerly?" His voice quickened her pulse.

"Yes, and such a worthwhile one."

"Ready for your crossing?"

"As ready as possible."

"We heard about your adventure in Sicily. Such lovely targets in those days—Catania, Gerbini, Sciacca, Comiso, and Milo. I cannot imagine how the natives will ever restore their coastline after the wreck we made of it."

"But where would our infantry and marines have been without you?"

"True—we lost only 13 planes to the enemy's 44, a good percentage, what say?" Pinky looked at his watch. "Enough about the war. Tell me about your trip here."

"You mean across the Atlantic?"

"And any other trips. I want to learn about them all."

"We sailed on the USS Monterey, a transformed cruise ship, in a convoy of 600 ships, and landed in Casablanca on November 18th at midnight. We'd been warned to take great care on the gangplank. Another troop ship had landed before us, and General Patton met them.

"They got their introduction to war right away—an infantrymen lost his balance on the plank between the ship and the dock. He was so loaded down, he sank and drowned before anyone could rescue him."

"Whew."

"Your *whew* sounds just like an American one."

"Glad I've got it right. Such a horrible death for that fellow. So after you went ashore—"

"We were taken to Rabat, to the Sultan's racetrack, where the Eleventh had set up surgery under the grandstand. Most of our patients at that time were accidents, or—"Dorothy's pause created a glimmer in Pinky's eyes.

"Let me guess—diseases of the private parts?"

"That's a good way to put it. One infantryman told me that before we came, he and some others had volunteered—at the commander's request—to bare themselves before all the troops to serve as a warning. Said he hoped he kept at least one GI from consorting with the local women, especially in some parts of Casablanca."

"Aha—the age-old temptation. If it's any comfort, some of my mates have had outbreaks, as well—visits to the Casbah got them in touch with more than one sort of thief. Hopefully, their suffering has deterred others. But do go on. Did you cross Algeria by train?"

"No, by truck—lorry. Those long days gave new meaning to the word *sore*. But the first battles were the worst. I still have nightmares about one. North Africa taught us what to expect, at least. One of the nurses says if Africa was all she'd experienced, it would be plenty."

"Did your training not prepare you?"

"We had no basic training. I barely knew how to salute. But how could they prepare us for Africa, when none of the instructors had ever left the States?"

"No basic. Who taught you the ropes?"

"Our mistakes, but at least none of us have gotten killed."

"And glad I am of that." Pinky climbed a rise and sat looking out to sea, so Dorothy joined him.

"Our good fortune to have met, and re-met." He draped his arm around her shoulders, and nothing ever felt so good. "War is chaotic, but also gives us opportunities we'd never have experienced."

"That's how I feel. I'd never have seen all these places or met so many great people. Your turn. Tell me about your home."

"Wigtownshire, in the southwest of Scotland, borders the Irish Sea on the west, the Solway Firth to the south, Ayrshire to the north, and the Stewartry of Kirkcudbright to the east. You have heard of Galloway, perhaps?"

"Maybe."

"Wigtownshire and Stewartry together make up Galloway. In the western section of Wigtownshire, the Rhinns of Galloway, when I was far too young to realize it was the best place to be born, I came into this world." His dimples seemed even deeper than she remembered.

"Do you have a big family?"

"No, much to mother's chagrin. She could have managed lots, but as she says, was blessed with only a daughter and a son. Where were you born?"

"In Iowa—have you heard of it?"

Pinky shook his head. "Not to my remembrance. Is it in the east?"

"No, the Midwest. My older sister and two brothers were born in Germany, but my grandfather's sister convinced our father to move to the States in 1914. On our mantel at home, we have a picture taken with the ship's captain.

"Mama used to tell us that my oldest brother Karl had injured his leg before they boarded. During the trip, the leg worsened and he felt sickly.

"The ship's doctor wanted to amputate and tried to convince Mama to allow the surgery. She refused, and by the time they docked, Karl was still having trouble walking. So Mama devised a story for everybody to repeat when they went through port entry.

"She gave Karl an empty suitcase to carry, so it looked like he was too small for such a heavy load. That disguised his limp, since regulations didn't allow sick or unfit people to enter."

"What a quick mind your mother has."

"Yes, but she had lots of trouble adjusting, and when I was about eight, she wanted to move back to Germany. We all did, but Papa stayed in Iowa to close up the bakery. In the meantime Mama changed her mind, so he saved enough to bring us back again. We re-crossed the Atlantic when I was ten. Nothing like the troop ship this time, zigzagging to avoid the mines."

"Do you recall the name of the ship you took from Germany?"

"Oh, yes. The *Lloyd Bremen*."

"Quite possibly, that vessel now transports German troops. We may even have targeted it. Now, tell me about your county."

"It must be harder to hit a ship than a city?"

"Requires more of a bird's-eye view, one might say. Now, about your county?"

"Counties don't mean so much in the States. Ours is called Black Hawk, after an Iowa Indian tribal chief."

"Do Indians still live there?"

"Yes, but on a reservation, land the government set aside."

"And your county? Tell me more."

"There's not a lot to tell. Our county system is simpler than yours."

"We've had lots of extra centuries to complicate things." Pinky's grin brightened his whole face, and the rising sun set his red hair aflame. "But I should like to visit yours one day, and take you to mine." In a gust of sea breeze, he threaded his fingers through hers.

"Yes." That seemed enough to say as they watched the sun rise. Half an hour later, they walked toward the tents, and Pinky stopped shy of the workmen in full bore at the docks.

"Against the morning sky, you have a halo."

"Believe me, that's a mirage—I doubt anybody in camp would accuse me of being an angel."

"Perhaps not—you seem quite spirited, which can be mistaken for disobedient. And sometimes we fail to see ourselves as we are." He sounded so earnest and thoughtful. "Do you know which ship you'll be boarding?"

"The *USS General G. O. Squire,* they tell me. The one they're loading right now won't have room for the nurses."

"And ye're leaving...?"

"In a few days, but you know how unreliable military predictions can be."

"We shall soon be blowin' the *Jayrmans* apart in the Andes. So glad you won the date with that movie star, Daaroothy. I had been thinking of you ever since we met in Tunisia."

"I didn't want to go that night, but now I'm so glad I did."

"And we have some time. Whatever we have we shall enjoy, righto?" Pinky held out his arms. "Do give a poor pilot a prop'r goodbye, will ye? I expect the next time we meet might be in Italy, or farther north, if good fortune shines upon us."

Obliging him seemed so natural, and when he kissed her, time stopped in Sicily. Then his voice became a whisper.

"No more words. This is what I want to remember. Tomorrow I shall be gone, but your tents are easy to spot—I hope to find you somewhere along the way." With that, he turned and walked south.

If feelings could be trusted at all, she and this man belonged together, but when would they see each other again?

Salt spray launched overhead and the spray wakened Dorothy from her nap. Shouts overwhelmed the swell of waves along the

Italian coast, and she opened her eyes. Eric was licking her hand and Millie shaking her shoulder.

"We're here, kiddo. Italy's right over there."

Chapter Sixteen

Knowing the Chief Constable trusted him infused new energy into Rupert as he tucked in Iris and Cecil. With their meager holidays past, the routine of daily life immersed them all once again. But at least the entire family had been together, eating Madeleine and Gran's best offerings between V-2 blasts and attending Christmas Eve service.

Little Henry became the star of the show when he tore open the package Cecil carefully wrapped in brown butcher paper he'd earned by sweeping the butcher's floor. Seeing the string-and-rag ball Cecil had made for him, Henry tossed it right into Cecil's face and giggled up a storm. The applause incited more laughter, and even Anna, rather drawn at the beginning of the festivities, brightened.

Before she went upstairs, Rupert hugged her and whispered, "Are you feeling well? I fear you work far too many hours."

"Doing my bit, that's all. Don't worry about me, Da." Her reassuring smile quieted his concern. But later, Madeleine voiced her own worry.

"So many girls work double shifts or triple jobs these days. At least she's not out in the middle of the night like some of her friends, driving dignitaries from meeting to meeting across London. Without headlights, too."

Ah, the woes of war. Rupert turned his attention back to tonight's raid on Avery Ritter. This time of evening, warm and secure in their tidy surrounds, brought a particular sense of ease, in spite of

GAIL KITTLESON

anticipating what was to come. He'd stopped in at the volunteer fire station after work and notified them of his absence tonight. Good thing they'd formed a list of replacements for times like these.

As he rounded the corner to the kitchen, Madeleine gave him that look he'd come to cherish. She needed him—even a short chat would do.

Pulling out his watch, he noted about an hour and a quarter until the raid. But since this had been his idea, he needed to arrive before the other officers, to foresee any possible obstacles.

The homey aroma of the children's toast still lingered in this small room. Absent the essence of melting butter, thanks to the rationing. He tucked a stray hair behind Madeleine's ear and pulled her to a chair. "Did you have to stand in line extra long today?"

"No. I thought I might see you, though, since I delivered some shirts close to the station."

Rupert cleared his throat. "I had some business down by the infirmary, dear. You know that black market thief I've mentioned?"

"Yes—Ritter?"

"Some recent discoveries have led to a development tonight. The Chief has conscripted a police wagon to go after that rogue, and has asked me to be present."

"So late?" That concern in her voice, no doubt about his duty, only thought for his safety.

"I shall be back as soon as I possibly can."

She angled her head. "You will be so tired."

Remembering their precious days alone a few weeks ago, Rupert reached for his helmet. Before he buckled the strap, he pulled Madeleine close and whispered in her ear, "Not that tired, my love."

Out in the brisk fall air, he noodled the evening BBC report—the Allied landings in Central Italy, hailed by many as the Prime Minister's brilliant idea, now saw thousands of American GIs mired down on a beachhead, when everyone expected they would be proudly marching toward Rome by this time. Those dastardly Huns, flooding lowland that Mussolini had drained for crops.

153

German vengeance popped out everywhere, especially in their treatment of occupied citizens. Burning and pillaging like the Vikings of old—what sparked such brutality? The Italians would rue the day they'd collaborated with Adolph. No one would be spared as the Wehrmacht eventually retreated before the Allies.

According to the Chief, the Prime Minister still remained in the Mediterranean after his bout with pneumonia, and perhaps even maintained a hand in planning the invasion of the Italian mainland. That thought provoked mixed emotions, since Rupert recalled his fiasco at Gallipoli back in the Great War.

What a tragedy when the Ottoman Empire squelched the Allied attack and killed over 350,000 good men. Hopefully the P.M. had learned his lesson and would accept the decisions of the Chiefs of Staff.

But at the same time, several military commanders had descended on headquarters here to plan something else, perhaps the war's most significant invasion. Since General Eisenhower had been named head of the Allied forces, *headquarters* took on new meaning. The central nerve of this vast military conglomeration in London spread its tentacles far and wide.

No one on the streets mentioned a word, but invading the Normandy coast surely must be in the offing. The Chief Constable shared Rupert's belief that only this invasion would bring Adolph's minions to their knees. To that end, the city and its surrounds fairly burst with troops from all nations and origins. This too, brought back the Great War, when Turks, Germans, British, Australians, New Zealanders, French, Indians, Senegalese, Arabs, Austrians, Gurkhas, and others had fought in the Gallipoli campaign.

These gathered troops troubled Rupert—perhaps it was, precisely, another Gallipoli. That campaign had nurtured such hopes in its day, all to be dashed. For Churchill to have ascended as Prime Minister with that humiliating defeat in his past was nothing short of a wonder.

About the present abysmal progress in Italy, Towsley had

something to say, for his jaw had come a long way toward healing. Just this morning, they'd met and discussed the war.

"I cannot understand why the Americans went to the Mediterranean—why not across the Channel? But greater minds than mine are at work. When I doubt, I recall Dunkirk. We must never forget that hopeless time leading up to the miracle."

With each new bit of bad news, Towsley intoned, "Lord, have mercy." Recently, he had reinstated the word-a-day project. Not surprisingly, *MERCY* had been his first choice. Rupert had little to say on that, with his own darker instinct toward Melvin Williams in such contrast to the vicar's generosity.

Their word for today was *PLUCK*. At this point, Rupert turned over the choosing entirely to the vicar. His mind had enough trouble as it was.

PLUCK fit this operation perfectly, a time to show no mercy whatsoever. Situations arose when justice alone must reign—Towsley believed this, too. How had he put it? "Our faith points to mercy through the working out of justice."

Of late, they had both been too occupied with the consequences of incendiary attacks to discuss much at all, and their words came less regularly. Comforting survivors and burying the dead engaged Towsley, while providing order at the scenes, writing reports and attending to nightly calls consumed Rupert.

Approaching the south side of the building in question, he collected his thoughts. He must keep to the shadows unless, perchance, Ritter already engaged in his underhanded dealings. In that case, he must hold tight and wait for the promised reinforcements.

But what if the deal went down and the marketeer made to leave before that? No, this was where *PLUCK* entered in, for what was it if not spirited and determined courage. The deal would not go down—the skivs would not leave.

He would have to make a split-second decision. But skulking down the alley in the still of late evening, when most families had tucked in their children, he startled at a sudden bark. Then came a squeal—could there still be a living pig in London? His reaction made more noise than he wished.

Even a flagrant intake of breath might give away his presence, so he froze. A few minutes later, quiet returned, and he moved on Then, about two rods from Ritter's warehouse, a faint hum issued from the south. Scarcely a bit of unnatural light reached this alley, so sound became all.

Soon an older lorry braked, circled 'round in the empty street, and backed to the exact spot he hoped it would, all with its lights blacked out. Seconds later, someone fumbled with a latch and a door slid open, *squeak squeaking* against rusty hinges.

Flattened against the alley wall, Rupert sidestepped closer. These fellows were making so much noise, he might throw caution to the wind if he'd a mind. But wait. Amidst the scuffling, shoving, panting, and profanity, was that another hum he heard?

Soon, after turning the corner directly ahead, a black wagon with room enough for two criminals proceeded down the street and parked behind the lorry. Wonder of wonders, the skivs, thoroughly engrossed, paid no notice.

To Rupert's surprise, another police wagon parked behind the lorry—the Chief meant business. Two officers exited the first vehicle, checked before and aft, saw him wave from the shadows and hurried over. Thankfully, the Chief had passed over Officer Fletcher.

"These are the men?"

"I do believe so." Rupert addressed Sergeant Young. "Alert the other officers to stand by." The Sergeant saluted and raced off.

Meanwhile, the skivs still carried out their business, unaware of being watched.

Remember the miracle of Dunkirk...

Like the Prime Minister, Rupert issued his command, "Shine your lights in their faces. Take them down."

In all his years as a policeman, he recalled nothing quite so thrilling as noting Avery Ritter's shock. The felon's bugged-out eyes and animal squeal delighted the other officers, as well.

The lorry driver might have wished for a nearby public WC. His face turned ghostly, and when the officers produced a wad of paper bills and coins from a not-so-well-hidden cashbox, their gleam of triumph stood in stark contrast to his groan. For a moment, Rupert expected the man to fall to his knees and beg pardon.

Seeking further instructions, the two officers delivered the confiscated treasure to Rupert. "Check again for trap doors, hidden exits and passageways, large trunks—anything suspicious. Then secure this location for further search in the morning." They saluted and hurried off, leaving him to watch the captives.

To his credit, Ritter spoke no word in his own defense.

This hour made police work's miserable assignments and monotonous duties worthwhile. This, the officers' eyes declared, brought the sort of earthly glory allowed to mankind. Reporting the initial search complete, pride—the rightful sort—aligned their shoulders.

This moment would bind these men together like nothing else. The satisfied expression on Sergeant Young's countenance said more than words..

All for one, one for all. Rupert's own sigh concurred.

They locked one skiv in the paddy, the other in the second wagon. Crowds might have heralded them, for all the wonder that emanated within their small parade. Rupert calculated six years of duty for the man beside him, and barely one for Sergeant Young. When their spirits sagged, they had this victory to call up and cherish.

Ahh... *GLORY.* The day they'd focused on this word, Towsley quoted a passage, "...made him a little lower than the angels... crowned him with...glory." A man might still play his part in thwarting the evil rampant in this land.

So much might have gone wrong—timing, the explosion of a V-2 near the warehouse, word slipping out concerning the raid. But everything had come together as though—as though part of a divine plan.

Quietly, Rupert treasured these thoughts on the walk home after seeing Ritter and the downcast lorry driver into seclusion. In the morning he would make his report, and—oh, my! How roundly the Chief would interrogate these prisoners.

The Green seemed illogically placid. What if this marked the first night with no rocket attacks? Halfway home, a military officer with a woman beside him slipped down an alley. The woman's gait seemed similar to Anna's, but Rupert shook himself—hadn't Madeleine said extra quotas would force her to spend tonight at the factory?

Returning his thoughts to the raid, he reconsidered the multiple meanings of *PLUCK*. The force had shown great pluck, the Chief might say. They had *PLUCKED* two bad actors from their wicked realm. And for some time ahead, they'd be eating *PLUCK* in prison.

Entering through the back, he halted. There in the parlor, her hands buried in eternal mending, sat the most beautiful woman. Her smooth forehead and translucent closed eyelids touched a deep place, and without a sound, Rupert removed his helmet and coat, pulled off his boots and tiptoed to check on the children.

Angels asleep in their beds.

He returned to Madeleine and bent to gather her in his arms. A few steps down the hallway, her eyes fluttered open. The promise he saw there, as true as their wedding vows, never faltered.

Light on his feet, he placed her in bed before peeking at the children one more time. One local evil had been thwarted, and who knew the extent of their affiliations? Perhaps this raid had thwarted many more all across the island.

Beside him, Madeleine's breathing deepened, and upstairs, a wee cry sounded, followed by footsteps—Kathryn caring for Henry. Her midsection swelled with a second child now, making Junior proud as could be. In spite of this war, another generation blossomed in this roof.

Chapter Seventeen

March 1944 Vairano, Italy

Six weeks earlier, the Eleventh replaced the Ninety-fifth Evacuation Hospital, now in Anzio to support the hard-hit Ninety-third. Passing through Naples on the way, Dorothy had watched for Pinky in vain. Now, endless truckloads of wounded evidenced the fierce struggle at the beachhead.

Once again, things were not going well. From the surrounding hills, the Germans seized the advantage and kept firing down at General Clark's Fifth Army.

As usual, Captain Siemons had the complete story. When Dorothy and Millie asked him for details after mail call one night, he hesitated. "You're sure you want to know? The Ninety-fifth has taken some mighty hard hits."

Millie insisted. "Tell us. I have a friend with them—we graduated from high school together."

"All right. The beachhead is only about 15 miles wide and seven miles deep, so it's impossible to relocate the medical units out of range of sporadic enemy fire. The Thirty-sixth Engineer Regiment has dug in the hospital tents and reinforced them with protective earthworks, wooden beams, and sandbag walls to protect patients and staff from flying shrapnel and incoming shells.

"In short, they're stuck in the line of fire, with rough seas behind them. There's no possible retreat. Little wonder they've nicknamed the area 'Hell's Half Acre.'"

An MP passed by, and the Captain engaged him. "Any news from Anzio?"

"They buried a nurse with the Fifty-sixth."

"Oh wow—what was her name?"

"Ellen something..."

"Ainsworth? Ellen Ainsworth?"

"Yeah, that's it. With the Army Nurse Corps, wounded on the tenth, shrapnel to the chest..."

"Oh my." Millie's grasped Dorothy's arm. "She's from Glenwood."

"What state?"

"Wisconsin."

"Yup, I'm afraid she's the one. The nurses helped the patients crawl under their cots when Jerry started heavy artillery shelling. Ellen and some others evacuated 42 of them under fire, but it's tough to survive a chest wound."

Captain Siemons rubbed his forehead. "The situation couldn't be much worse, then."

"That's what I'd say, sir."

Hank and a chaplain Dorothy had never met joined them. Strange to see her walking with a chaplain, but then, war turned everything upside down.

"We've been discussing the situation at Anzio, Padre. Give us your take."

"Such a small parcel of land, but so much agony."

"Do they have enough docs?"

"I'm not sure what would *be* enough. They're working around the clock."

"What about beds?" Hank asked what Dorothy and Millie were both wondering.

"The troop list calls for 9,500 mobile and 7,000 fixed beds to be phased in after 45 days. They need them all, and then some."

The three nurses shared a groan as Captain Siemons spoke.

"That's a lot of hospitals. The Ninety-fourth and fifth, Thirty-second, Eighth, and Fifty-sixth are all fixed in the theater, right?"

"Yes, plus the Fourth, Tenth, and yours as field hospitals. There's talk of bringing in two more units directly from the States, too."

Uneasy quiet spread over the group. The incoming casualty count was already hard to maintain.

"The North Africa and Sicily invasion convoys taught the command some lessons, so they sent in only field hospital platoons with attached surgical teams this time. That included nine teams of the Second Auxiliary Surgical Group in the assault wave, attached to the divisional clearing platoons.

"Field hospitals were scheduled for later convoys, to open after the troops secured the beachhead, but two evacuation hospitals, the Ninety-fifth with 400 beds and the Sixteenth with 750, went in on the first convoy. That's without nurses—they followed on D-day plus 2."

Hank snorted. "At least they got *that* right."

"Taking into account previous campaign delays and deficiencies in bed strength, the planners doubled the number of 750-bed hospitals assigned to Fifth Army, one for each two divisions."

The captain rubbed his forehead. "Good thing General Blesse changed his mind, eh? After the Southern Tunisia campaign, he was willing to abandon the larger hospitals. You were there, weren't you?"

"Yes. You know your history. Thankfully, the General saw their value after the Sicily campaign, so four field hospitals and a fifth, minus one platoon, were scheduled for Italy."

Quite the crowd was gathering, so the chaplain held up his hands. "Mind you, I'm certainly not in on every decision."

"Yeah, but you've been down there. What about the Fourth Medical Supply? Weren't they headed to the beachhead, too?"

"Right. They supported the combat medical units in the assault, and carried extra necessities from the LSTs—plasma, atabrine, plaster of Paris, dressings, and biologicals. Combat troops hauled medical supplies ashore in specially designed containers, too."

"You were there from day one?"

The chaplain nodded. "The Fifth Army Invasion Training Center has proven its worth on this beachhead. Their floatable containers made from empty mortar shell cases did the trick—American ingenuity at work."

"That's one bright spot, I guess." Captain Siemons touched his Wrigley's chain.

"And we secured the beachhead right off, but that sure didn't produce safety. Our units are still stuck in that box, and obviously, the Germans don't care whether their bombs strike infantry troops or a hospital—there's wounded everywhere. To save space, some cots are placed so men's heads stay inside the hospital tent, with the rest of their bodies outside."

"You don't really mean that?" Hank almost spat.

"I'm afraid so. Some casualties even sleep on litters between hospital tents."

"Oh man."

"If you want to hear more, come to tonight's chapel—1900 hours." Weariness etched the chaplain's countenance, "But if you can't, here's the basic message. Pray for everyone trapped there." He took a step and turned back. "And then pray again."

A corpsman commented. "How did he get here? Hasn't Jerry blocked all the roads up through the Alban hills?"

"Yeah, that's what I've heard." Captain Siemons scratched his head. "Maybe an LST took him out to sea and some other vessel brought him farther north. Or maybe he walked on air."

Hank chortled, and Millie added, "Sure looks like he could use some rest."

"Yeah. The poor guy's been run ragged down on the beachhead. Everybody wants a chaplain right before battle and when they're hurt." The captain glanced at Dorothy. "You're sure quiet today."

"Just trying to grasp what's going on. You and the chaplain know so much about it all."

"Well, I've always been a learner—can't go long without hearing some news."

"Just like Moonbeam here. Did you know she even hauled along a radio? And it's heavy!"

The Captain raised his eyebrows. "Really? What kind?"

"Oh, just a regular one. I rarely can get anything in on it."

"Hmm—at least you try."

"I'm beginning to think you have things rigged somehow, to get the inside scoop. Are you a reporter in disguise?"

Captain Siemons hooted. "Nope, but it sure would be an interesting occupation."

"Rigged...Wrigley's... Hey! We ought to call you Rig."

"What a great idea, Millie! Rig it is." Dorothy broke a pretend bottle over the Captain's head. "I hereby christen you Rig for the duration."

"I think I'll head to the chapel service." Dorothy set her knitting aside, and just then, Hank arrived with Eric in tow.

"Not me. That chaplain only has bad news."

"I'll go with you, Moonbeam. I could use something new to think about. Besides, we haven't had one of these in forever—when was it, anyway?"

"I don't remember." Hank let out a chuckle. "Probably because I didn't go."

"It was December 24th, back in Sicily. Remember that one little candle, Millie? The service brought back so many memories. Didn't you go to Christmas Eve service when you were growing up, Hank?"

"Off and on. Mostly off—not real high on my family's priority list."

"Mmm—one of my friends grew up like that, so she started going with us. We went every year, and when I was in high school, I had a part."

"Up front?"

"Yes—each member of our youth group carried in a large lighted candle and we formed a human cross at the front of the church. Everything else was dark. Then our pastor explained how the candlelight service originated, and we lighted the small candles the congregation had picked up on their way in. I always loved how the sanctuary brightened little by little."

"Oh, me too! Each face glowed above a candle. My little brothers thought it was a big thing when they could have one all to themselves—they were all agog."

"They really liked it?"

"Every year. Probably our German heritage—but I sat with my whole family, not up front like Millie."

"I'm Scandinavian, so the candles can't be only a German idea, although maybe putting lights on the tree started with them."

"Hmppf!" Hank was about to make a declaration. "So how did the Germans end up so rotten, with all those years of candlelight behind them?"

"I don't think they're *all* rotten—I'm pretty sure whole bunches of them wish they'd never heard of Hitler. At least, our neighbors there were wonderful folks. The mob is ruling their country."

Hank gave another *Hmppf.* "Germans—I've had enough of them, and most of the whole world would agree."

Millie patted her arm. "I'd say we're not going to settle this tonight. Come on Moonbeam, let's get going."

"Today's scripture comes from Isaiah 41:10. 'Fear thou not, for I am with thee. Be not dismayed; for I am thy God: I will strengthen thee; yea, I will help thee; yea, I will uphold thee with the right hand of my righteousness.'

"People have always sacrificed in the fight against evil. We have only to go back to the Great War, when so many millions died, or to our own Civil War.

"At Gettysburg alone, more American soldiers died than in the Revolutionary War, the War of 1812, and the Mexican War combined. All told, the deaths from Vicksburg—over 19,000, through Gettysburg—51,000, shocked our population. It's likely even more died, if we take into account reporting inaccuracies.

"But both sides believed in their cause. In this war, many have already paid the ultimate price to defeat Nazism, set to destroy everything in its way. Thousands have died at this great evil's hands and little by little, the true nature of Hitler's hatred becomes unveiled.

"We came to this conflict late, many would say, but there's no pulling back. We must win—we will.

"I've just come from the fighting, and cannot bring good news, except that our forces are holding, and that more troops will ensure final victory. In the meantime, things look grim.

"One thing I can say with assurance. No matter what, our God is with us, and He's saying 'Fear not.'

"His 'I am with you' provides comfort, His promise to strengthen us gives hope, and the assurance of eventual victory raises our heads. To face this great trial without divine aid would stymie us. So many men ask for prayer—a foxhole knows no atheists."

"No matter how frightening the odds or how vicious the enemy, we will prevail, with the Almighty's help. Some battles are worth fighting for the sake of future generations."

Millie stirred in her chair—probably thinking of Del.

"When our Lord walked this earth, He knew the slings and arrows of a ruthless enemy. He knew what it was to be attacked and hunted down, to suffer great physical and mental anguish, to fight battles with eternal consequences.

"In this lies our hope, that He is with us. Emmanuel comes not just in the Christmas season as an infant, but this very moment. He's here when our hearts break, and when courage fails us.

"He offers us his presence anew right now. Come and taste His goodness, for He has promised never to leave or forsake us."

A line formed and Millie led the way. After all the others left, she stayed in her seat and wiped away tears.

"Do you want to be alone?" As the chaplain chatted outside with some corpsmen and doctors, Dorothy's whisper seemed loud in her own ears.

"It's—it's just—why would I still have such a strong sense that Del is alive? I mean, after all this time?"

"I don't know. But if he's captured and in prison somewhere, maybe he can feel your faith."

"Do you think so?"

"Yeah. Shall we ask the chaplain?"

Millie shrugged. "It can't hurt."

"Here we go again." A friendly young corpsman launched a winning smile toward Dorothy. "Hi-ho, hi-ho, it's off to work we go!" A mid-April breeze wisped in, still smelling of salt though they were a distance inland.

Another worker took up the chant from the *Seven Dwarfs* movie, and soon the tune popped up everywhere. Moving again—what else was new? But this transition to Anzio sobered everyone. Whoever started the singing and whistling knew what this group needed.

In this confusion, Pinky had found her again. She'd begun to wonder if she'd dreamed up his visits. But last night she, Millie, and Henrietta walked toward the nurses' tents, and there he stood, about a rod away.

When she gave a little gasp, Hank caught on immediately. "Aha! So we finally get to meet Mr. Wonderful!"

Dorothy raced off, losing a shoe in the process, but landing solidly in her Scotsman's arms. The sheepskin lining of his leather jacket brushed her face, and the steadiness of his stance felt like home. She'd forgotten how bright his eyes shone.

"Hello to you, too." His jaunty grin set her afire. "I take it these must be your comrades in arms?" He gave a smart salute to Hank and Millie. "Greetings, ladies!"

Hank never missed a beat. "Nice to meet you. We've been waiting a long time for this." Millie shook Pinky's hand and handed Dorothy her shoe.

"I remember you from the beach—Millie, right? You nurses do

166

get around. Finding you this time was quite a feat. In Naples, they said you were still en route."

He looked around the compound and shook his head. "I spotted you from on high today, but it looks as though you're changing locations again. How do you keep track of each other?"

"Oh, that's not hard—we're sisters." Millie's explanation made Dorothy smile. "Moonbeam's the hardest one to keep track of. She's always finding—"

"Moonbeam?"

Dorothy leaped in. "We all have nicknames. I'll explain later."

"Jolly good—we do, too. A pilot without a nickname is an airplane without air."

"Wherever we go, Dorothy always finds something new and exciting. All the way across the Strait of Sicily, you should've heard her go on about how we'd be on a Greek island soon—until she fell asleep. But when we got there, she was such a trooper."

"You don't say. I heard your commander got sacked for sending nurses in so early. What a rogue. It's one thing to dislike having women in war, but quite another to try to kill them."

"You heard about that?"

"Word gets around—we're all family, you know." Pinky caught Dorothy's eye. "Pleasant to meet you two, but my time is short. You will excuse us if we venture for a walk?" He took her hand and started off.

They shared little more than an hour, but wonder filled every second. Hardly aware of trucks passing, men sputtering as they loaded supplies, and plenty of other activity, Dorothy recalled only the sensation of Pinky holding her hand, his kiss, and instructions to watch for him in France.

"We'll be transferring north. Troops are building at the Channel. I'll watch for you, too, and until then, I'll be wreaking havoc on the mother country." As twilight fell, a sliver of moon rose. "They nicknamed you Moonbeam?"

"Yes. What's yours?"

"Skedaddle. I tripped once when we were doing a practice scramble, and somebody said that. You know how things stick—so, what about Moonbeam?"

"Do you know the L'il Abner comic strip?"

"Abner is a man?"

"Yes, he's the handsome main character, and all the girls swoon over him. His girlfriend is Daisy Mae, but another girl lives out in the country. Her clothes have patches and she's always muddy, so they call her Moonbeam McSwine."

"As in real swine?"

"That's right. Don't Scottish pigs like to wallow in the mud?"

He grinned. "No, ours stay as clean as kittens."

"Oh, I believe you." Dorothy chuckled.

"But how did you become Moonbeam?"

"Well, I've fallen in the mud a lot on our campaigns."

"You? You're so well-coordinated!"

"When we take long trips, I get so antsy in our trucks, I can't wait to get out and usually leap before I look. Sometimes I've wished I hadn't been in such a hurry."

"You Americans, always finding humor."

"We try."

"Not a bad characteristic. So who has the Eleventh christened *Abner*?"

"A surgeon. I think you met him on the beach—he's always the life of the party."

"Ah, I remember that chipper fellow. Doesn't he specialize in setting broken bones?"

"Yes, along with splintered, shattered, and crushed ones."

"What would we all do without miracle workers like him?"

Pinky's sigh brought the war back full-force. He edged Dorothy's chin up with two fingers and kissed her. Then he held her close and whispered, "Pray for me, my dearest moonbeam."

"You can believe I will, Houston Pinkstone."

Just like that, he was gone again, into the night. She took her

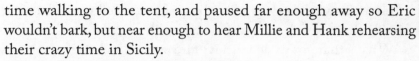
time walking to the tent, and paused far enough away so Eric wouldn't bark, but near enough to hear Millie and Hank rehearsing their crazy time in Sicily.

"It was Licata where we set up first."

"Northwest of there, because the Tenth Field Hospital operated in town."

"Right. Then to Agrigento and Nicosia. Leapfrogged all over that island, didn't we? What was that last place?"

"You skipped a few. Santa Agatha—we were there about a week, and at Cefalu from August through late November. How could you forget that, or Mondello Beach from Thanksgiving 'til January third? Then it was Messina and Bagrana, and after that, Praia A. Maria."

"You've got quite the memory for details. But did you say Cesaro and Randazzo?"

"Too many places to remember all at once. I'm just glad Dorothy's writing them all down—she's covering for the rest of us."

Good thing she'd told Millie about Pinky a couple of weeks ago. Still waiting for word from Delbert, Millie had seemed sincerely happy. Now, she and Hank would exclaim over "her pilot." Maybe this would finally convince Hank that Paul was truly just a friend.

When she stuck her head in, Hank had taken over her cot, and immediately started the interrogation. "Now I can see why Douglas Fairbanks was no big deal. You already had a pilot with eyes only for you."

"But I didn't. Not until that night."

"What do you mean?"

"Remember how badly I wanted to get out of that date? But there was something good waiting for me. I still marvel over that—what if I'd dreamed up some excuse not to go?"

"You're sure you're not two-timing Paul?" Hank's squint measured Dorothy's reaction.

"Honestly—you can be so frustrating!"

Hank broke into a grin—just the reaction she'd hoped for.

"How many times does Moonbeam have to tell you he's only a friend? Besides, he's too old for her, and has become a Catholic."

"What's that got to do with it? He's a man, isn't he?"

"Where Moonbeam and I are from, never the twain shall meet. My mother told me if I ever brought home a Catholic boy, she'd send him packing, and if I didn't cooperate, she'd cut me off." Millie cast a knowing glance at Dorothy.

"That's the way it is back home, too. Paul's been a real friend to me—I learned so much in his classes, and talking things over with him always helps."

"Things?"

"Come on, Hank. You know how Dorothy rolls everything around in her head until it makes some kind of sense. Can't you imagine how much it'd mean to have a professor around who liked to discuss life's deep questions?"

"Ha! Like how deep was that water those gazelles were drinking in North Africa when we crossed. What river was that?"

"All right, you asked for this." Arms akimbo, Millie stuck her finger in Hank's face. "I've noticed you getting pretty chummy with a certain fellow, yourself. He spends most of his time in the mess, and you've been there with him quite a bit lately—"

Hank's flush told the tale, along with her sputter. "Not fair—we're talking about Dorothy, not me." She turned to Dorothy. "Give us the lowdown on this Pinky fella. It's not every day we have a genuine Scottish pilot around here. What kind of a name is Pinkstone. anyhow?"

"Scottish."

Hank growled, "Come on—"

For a second, Dorothy considered pursuing her new friendship with Wally, the cook, but decided against it. She'd much rather talk about Pinky, anyway.

"He joined the RAF three years ago and flies with the mission action division."

"Which means?"

Millie took over. "The bomb squadrons—they fly everything from Spitfires to Whitleys to Bristol Blenheims. Del would say 'He's still alive, that should tell you something.'"

"You know far more about the particulars than I do—Pinky talks mostly about his home and family." As Dorothy continued, the three of them almost forgot they were headed to Anzio.

Chapter Eighteen

The April 15th briefing filled an area between two loaded trucks, with some corpsmen straddling boxes and cots on either side. Dorothy sat with some nurses on rocky Italian earth. Sunset flamed in the west as the commander outlined the scene at Anzio, using a large map strung from the trucks' mirrors.

"If you can't see, move closer—this map shows us everything we need to know. But first, I'm sure you've heard about President Roosevelt's death. Power has passed without incident in our democracy, and the war continues. Now then, the Alban Hills surround the beachhead. They're otherwise known as the Coli Laziali, and Highway Seven, the ancient Appian Way, skirts the hills' southern shoulder through Albano and Velletri. Then it runs southeast to Terracina on the coast, about halfway between Rome and Naples.

"Resort towns Anzio and Nettuno sit about 30 miles south of Rome, here and here. Ten miles east, the Mussolini Canal separates the Anzio plain from the reclaimed Pontine Marshes, with partially wooded farmlands cut by deep gullies to the northwest. Rolling country extends 25 miles to the Tiber.

"Highway Six, the direct route from Cassino to Rome, runs along the northern slopes of the Alban Hills, within 30 miles of Anzio. VI Corps' original mission was to seize the hills and cut both highways, the German Tenth Army's supply lines and escape routes. But the command foresaw a difficult landing, so General Lucas received final orders to seize and secure the beachhead, with no mention of timing or how far to advance.

"The Sixth was assigned to envelop Campoleone, 18 miles north on the Albano road, and Cisterna, beside Highway Seven, about the same distance northeast. On January 22, General Truscott's Third Division landed three regiments here." He tapped another dot on the map. "At the same time, British commandos proceeded north. The 509th Parachute Infantry Battalion took Nettuno as quickly as Colonel Darby's Rangers took Anzio.

"Because they faced only sporadic enemy fire from long-range guns, the assault body unloaded by midnight. Battle-aid stations went ashore with the combat units, and the 52nd Medical Battalion accompanied the Third Division, Rangers, and Paratroopers. In the assault's early hours, casualties were carried directly to equipped LSTs or held at battle aid stations.

"By six p.m., one platoon of the Thirty-third Field Hospital south of Nettuno was ready to accept patients. For the first two days, this field hospital functioned alone on the beachhead, but soon filled to capacity, with three operating tables being used at all times and a backlog of 20 to 30 casualties."

Rows of wounded men waiting for care—Dorothy could visualize them. Eric wiggled away from Henrietta and bounded over to her, so she set aside her knitting. In the midst of bad news, cuddling him soothed her.

"Shell fragments and debris pierced their tents without producing casualties. However, in spite of General Martin and Colonel Huddleston's planning—he's been a surgeon since Salerno—artillery fire killed Colonel Huddleston as he exited corps headquarters on February ninth. Colonel Bauchspies, commanding officer of the Sixteenth Evac, succeeded him in directing medical services on the beachhead."

Hank jabbed her sharp elbow into Millie's ribs and spouted, "Good grief."

"Long-range shelling soon rendered no spot safe back on January 28, so Col. Huddleston chose an open field about two miles west of Nettuno for the Fifty-sixth Evac to set up. Two miles north of Anzio on the road to Rome, the British set up their medical installations.

"Hospital ships offshore made easy targets, and could be reached only through very rough water, but the air raids endangered the casualties already on the beach. Displaying the Geneva cross on the tents did little good—the enemy deliberately bombed three British hospital ships on January 24, and sank the *St. David*."

"Lousy Germans!"

The commander located the source and nodded. "Well said. As to the military advance, we may find fault, but what's done is done. What matters now is our boys down there in the direct line of fire." He surveyed docs, nurses, and corpsmen. "We all know the army makes mistakes, right?"

Someone whistled, and Eric threw in a bark.

"We'll figure out how to deal with the aftermath—not that different from life back home. By noon of day one, all military objectives had been reached, including securing the canal bridges, but the key towns of Campoleone and Cisterna had not been taken, nor the Alban Hills. By January 24, not much had changed. The Sixth Army occupied the original beachhead, with the advantage of surprise long gone as General Lucas decided to await reinforcements.

"The Germans trained huge railway guns called "Whistling Willies" and the "Anzio Express" on the beachhead from concealed positions they changed nightly. All along our 26-mile perimeter, opposition stiffened as Jerry rushed in new units.

"The Forty-fifth Infantry Division, half of the First Armored, and the First Special Service Force from Naples launched an attack on 30 January. Unfortunately, fresh German divisions from northern Italy, southern France, and elsewhere had already been situated to repel.

"At present, our hospitals sit only six miles from the fight, with overflowing medical stations and little progress. Now into the fourth month, the Ninety-third hospital, replacing the Ninety-fifth, has suffered grievous losses."

The commander looked at his watch. "On February 7, after approximately a full week near the coastline, hospitals were functioning in spite of drainage and disposal difficulties, and being unable to dig in as deeply as prescribed.

"Even heavy smoke screens made little difference in German marksmanship, and no one believed this amount of damage could be done accidentally. On February 7, an enemy plane pursued by Allied fighters jettisoned its load over the hospital area, and five antipersonnel bombs exploded on 400 patients in the Ninety-fifth. At the time, some freshly wounded were being carried in from an ambulance.

"With a crowded x-ray tent and surgeries working to capacity, those bombs killed 26 people and wounded 64. Three nurses, two medical officers, a Red Cross worker, 14 enlisted men, and six patients died. The wounded included the hospital commander."

The commander turned a page in his notebook, and in the palpable hush, even Hank held her tongue.

"The blasts destroyed 29 ward tents, x-ray equipment, and damaged many other small pieces. But within an hour, surgery cases had been transferred to other installations, while doctors and nurses continued their work. However, personnel and equipment losses were so great that commanders ordered the Ninety-fifth to change places with the Fifteenth Evac from Cassino's quiet front.

"The Fifteenth moved by rail to Naples and on two LSTs to Anzio. Bringing only necessities to replace what had been destroyed, they began operating before the end of February tenth. Again in February, the enemy bombed U.S. and British hospital areas, with some casualties resulting in each instance.

"The German counterattack continued on through March. On the 17th, the British 141st Field Ambulance suffered three direct hits, with 14 killed and 75 wounded. On the 22nd, 88-mm shells blanketed the Fifteenth Evac, killing five and wounding 14."

Colonel Tabor took a long breath. "From the reports, troops felt safer in foxholes at the front than in the hospital.

"General Truscott was convinced the 22 March shelling was deliberate, but no safe place existed, and going underground was not an option, although the installations could be dug in somewhat. After a conference with Fifth Army and VI Corps medical officers, he ordered the engineers to reconstruct the British and American hospital areas for maximum protection.

"By then, the rains had let up and the ground dried enough to excavate tent sites three or four feet down. The engineers pitched two ward tents in each excavation end to end, with earth revetments three and a half feet thick at the base and two feet at the top. Then they built up three to five-foot barricades around the tent walls. Steel stakes and chicken wire now hold these in place.

"Inside, sandbag baffles divide the double tent into four compartments of ten beds each, providing security against anything but a direct hit. Sandbags also cover two-inch plank roofs."

"Late last month, the Thirty-fourth Division arrived, along with the Ninety-fourth and 402nd Collecting Company of the 161st Medical Battalion. The unit opened on 29 March to manage the bulk of new casualties for the next five days while the other hospitals dug in.

"That night, only a few hours after General Clarke's inspection, the enemy again bombed the hospital area, killing eight and wounding 68 from the Ninety-third and Fifty-sixth Evacuation Hospitals. On April 3rd, 4th, and 6th, the Fifty-sixth suffered further damage from long-range German guns. On the 8th, too badly damaged to continue, the Fifty-sixth exchanged installations with the Thirty-eighth Evac at Carinola on the southern front.

"This background leads us to today. We're set to change places with the Ninety-third, and the British hospitals also rotate with those in the Cassino area. We expect the shelling and bombing to continue, but casualties and damage should be considerably reduced, thanks to VI Corps engineers."

The Colonel took his time making eye contact with everyone. "This most likely constitutes the longest briefing you will ever attend, but I felt it necessary—it's only fair to know what we face. Any questions?"

Someone asked one, and Hank muttered, "Chicken wire? We'll be sitting ducks."

Late April 1944

"With such severe damage to his throat and jaw, I want you to keep this tube in place. Whoever applied sulfa powder and the first bandage secured the bone and soft tissue pulled down into the airway. They had plasma on hand and got him to us in time to clamp off the artery, so he's still got a chance."

Cornflower sky met with Cerulean waves around the flat-topped hospital ship as the doc chewed a pencil. "He needs reconstructive surgery and will have to be moved by ship to a hospital on land. But at least he's survived so far."

His sigh fused hope and misery. "You'll need to keep him intubated in the transport to the hospital ship and stay with him until someone else can take over."

Assigned to this patient since his emergency surgery, Dorothy looked out over the army ship as the doc resumed his rounds. Though the water stayed relatively calm today, her stomach threatened to act up. They'd been able to save this GI's life, but with so much of his jaw blown away and a severe chest wound, his prospects still looked dire.

Nothing to do but wait. At least it wasn't raining. As she surveyed row upon row of wounded lined up on deck, the Florence Nightingale pledge she'd taken at her capping back in '38 came to mind. She'd rehearsed them again at Fort Leonard Wood when she was inducted into the nurse corps. By then, she'd worked at the Drake University women's dormitory for two years and had plenty of opportunities to put these vows into practice.

I solemnly pledge myself before God and in the presence of this assembly to pass my life in purity and to practice my profession faithfully. I shall abstain from whatever is deleterious and mischievous, and shall not take or knowingly administer any harmful drug. I shall do all in my power to maintain and elevate the standard of my profession and will hold in confidence all personal matters committed to my keeping and all family affairs coming to my knowledge in the practice of my calling. I shall be loyal to my work and devoted towards the welfare of those committed to my care.

"*Deleterious and mischievous*—" A scene from a few months back recurred—on the day when Second Lieutenant Eilola had evaluated each nurse.

"You've certainly seen a lot of action, and have excelled at your work. Being designated a surgical nurse is impressive. Do you have any concerns?"

"No, ma'am."

"That's the spirit you've shown all along." The Lieutenant thumbed through some papers before looking up with a slight smile. "I'm impressed with your gusto for life. When this is all over, you can certainly say you made the most of it."

"I hope so—we only get one go-around."

"So true, but some folks live as though they have all the time in the world. You seem to know the secret of embracing each moment with whatever it brings."

How much had the head nurse left unsaid? Surely that file contained a note about the incident with Rick's note. Maybe Lieutenant Eilola saw people like Papa, always with a positive slant. On the other hand, a promotion seemed awfully long in coming.

A corpsman passed by and murmured. "Pretty day, ain't it?"

"Sure is—gotta be thankful for this sea air and sunshine." These past few weeks had overflowed with horror. So many casualties with no hope of survival, but they'd saved as many as they could.

Like Millie said back in the desert, they had to take what comfort they could. *"...loyal to my work and devoted towards the welfare of those committed to my care..."* Her family would be proud of her, and yes, she was proud of herself.

Some time later, the doc returned. "All right, here you go—no matter what, maintain this patient's airway during the transfer. You'll move along through our hatch, and when the transfer ship gets close enough, two corpsmen will jump over with you and the gurney. If anybody can accomplish this, it's you."

Exactly what the C-47 pilot said in North Africa when she'd acted as his assistant co-pilot. But she felt far safer then than now—the doc was asking her to suspend herself over the open sea between two ships.

The corpsmen hoisted her patient into the hatch, with two more transports in front of them. *Bang!* The vessels bumped together, and two corpsmen leaped with the first patient. Dorothy timed the next jump—*one thousand, two thousand, three thousand.* Then her group huddled at the edge.

One of the corpsmen muttered, "Only one way to do this—without looking back."

Bang! The three of them leaped as one. Midair, Dorothy still listened for her patient's breathing. Finally feeling the deck under her feet, she took a breath herself.

"Success, gentlemen—the tube wasn't even jarred."

They grinned and set the litter down.

"You're really good, nurse." The younger of the two saluted Dorothy.

"Thanks—so are you."

He followed his partner to the edge and leaped back over.

With the patient's airway intact, Dorothy hunched close to reassess his vitals. A little mucous in the tube, so she pulled out her bulb syringe.

He must have felt the suction, but barely moved. She hated to leave him. When a nurse passed by, Dorothy hailed her.

"Could I borrow some paper?"

The nurse handed her a notebook and tore out a sheet while Dorothy marveled at the first crisp white uniform she'd seen in months.

Here she sat in her spattered, stained fatigues—how many days had it been since she washed them? Too many to calculate. In a way, that nurse's outfit seemed out of place in this sea of woebegone wounded. But to the troops, she surely presented a welcome picture.

Ah well—this war had a place for everyone. Dorothy pulled out her pencil and wrote, *Please write me in care of the Eleventh Evacuation Hospital. Let us know how you're doing when you get to where they are taking you. All my best, Dorothy Woebbeking.*

She folded the paper and tucked it into his pants pocket, thankful she could stay with him so long. Who knew? Maybe he would enter the same British reconstructive hospital where her nursing school friend Bev worked.

Back aboard the Eleventh's flat topped barge-ship, it was days before she returned to the beachhead. So much took place onboard—impossibly long days and nights of surgery to save mangled GIs. But even when she finally stood on solid sand again, the soldier she'd accompanied to the hospital ship stayed with her.

She knew nothing about him except that he'd fought at Anzio, but sitting with a man fighting for his life develops a connection. His breathing still echoed in her ears when she found her tent and tried to sleep. For weeks, she watched for word, but her fervent prayers brought no return note.

Late May 1944

Rig never sought the limelight, but his quick knowledge of history and geography attracted a following. Today in the mess, confused corpsmen and nurses chorused their questions.

"I don't get it. Why is the Fifth Army turning toward Rome instead of destroying the German Tenth and Fourteenth? Isn't that Operation Diadem's objective?"

"I'm afraid General Clark wants to say he liberated Rome." Everyone gawked as if Rig had lost his mind.

"After all of this, he would forego knocking out the German Tenth? Wasn't General Alexander's plan to drive east from the beachhead, cut off Kesselring's escape route and trap the Germans?"

"Exactly."

"He's the Field Marshall—didn't he order Clark to lead the Fifth Army after the enemy?"

"Isn't this insubordination?"

"Now what'll happen?"

"Yes, Clark received a direct order, but disobeyed. We'll still have a fight on our hands here in Italy, even though HQ is moving the Seventh Army up to France."

"Won't that stretch our resources?"

Rig fingered his ever-present wrapper chain, doubled in size since Dorothy first noticed it. "Sure will. Hitler would never put up with insubordination like this. At Frosinone, we were only six kilometers from closing on Jerry when Clark redirected the Fifth north towards Rome. Now, we're leaving the trap we've set wide open. Kesselring's probably drinking champagne to celebrate our stupidity."

"So we'll follow the Fifth—"

"The order hasn't come down yet, but it will, and I imagine Clark will have us all troop through the city, maybe even get in on his moment of glory. All bets are on he'll hold a press conference somewhere in Rome, and back home, folks'll see him in tomorrow's newspapers as a conqueror."

"Oh man. Everyone will think the war's about to end, but this'll mean lots more fighting on Italian soil." Abner's sigh floated over the group.

Imagining Mama deceived that everyone would soon be coming home left a bad taste in Dorothy's mouth. Only a good walk would ease her tension. Hurrying away, she followed a truck path.

Soon, Millie caught up and fell in step. "A penny for your thoughts."

"Jumbled. I can't understand this at all."

"I'm with you, hon. How can Clark get away with this?"

"He's a General, I guess. It's probably about outshining the British. These guys are so childish. Like Rig says, nobody that close to the top wants to take orders, especially from somebody foreign."

"Makes me sick." Millie lit a Chesterfield, inhaled and let out a stream of smoke—away from Dorothy.

"Me, too—actually, *furious* is more like it." At the edge of camp they stared out over row after row of breastworks dug in by the engineers. "So many have been killed here in January and so many nurses and docs. You want this suffering to count for something, at least."

"Yeah. An officer said the British Eighth has lost more than 40,000 men on this front alone. I sure hate to think they died in vain, but..." Millie turned away to exhale, and her smoke dissolved over the sand. "I want to find General Clark and talk some sense into him."

"It's too late. The Fifth has already turned toward Rome. The commanders have no choice but to obey or be court-martialed." Dorothy kicked at a stone. "Can you imagine what it must be like for those guys out there eating C rations and getting shot at?"

"Remember when we looked forward to Italy last winter?"

"Most of us thought things couldn't be as bad as they had been. Shows you what we knew. And in Africa, we knew far less. Those were the days, huh?"

"Do you ever think of Rick?"

"Once in a while. Meeting him was pretty exciting. But remember that day in Algeria when Abner said how much he appreciated us?"

"That was the first time anybody mentioned the difference we made. So—would you do all it over again with Rick?"

"You mean fly to Cairo on my off days? I know you and Hank must've thought I was crazy, but the pilots told me they covered the extra miles by saying they'd gotten lost coming back from their last raid."

"But then that note fell out of the sky."

Dorothy had to smile. "I'm glad now that somebody else found it. Really, why would he have believed it would fall straight to me?"

"He had to know he was putting you at risk. So—*would* you do it again?"

"Mmm—I'm not sure. Probably not, if I'd known more about him. I had no idea how controlling he was."

"How could you? That's why I'm glad Delbert and I have known each other forever. There's no way he can sneak anything over on me."

"You still think he's all right?"

"Maybe not all right, but alive. Someday we'll look back at all this and shake our heads, won't we?"

"Yep. That rough time, though—you and Henrietta kept my secret, and made me feel like we were in it together."

"We were, although we thought the scheme audacious. We also thought Rick bore most of the responsibility. He's a VIP. He could've said, 'You know I love to see you, but we'd better not involve pilots.' Did he ever voice any misgivings?"

"No, he encouraged me to do whatever I could to get to Cairo, and since he was a pilot, he suggested flying. I had to hitch a ride cross-country one time. That probably could have been dangerous."

"If you weren't so vivacious, kiddo, the whole thing would never have happened. He fell for you at first glance, and you stick your neck out more than we do. Who else in our unit found a way to take flying lessons?"

"Nobody that I know of, but they could have if they'd wanted to."

"Exactly. You're not scared."

"Is that what you think? Of course I was afraid, but when those guys offered to give me lessons, I couldn't see a good reason not to accept. That's the only way to conquer my fears."

"And you did?"

"Yes. It wasn't as if I was the pilot. First they let me be the navigator, then the assistant co-pilot. The first flight was 3,000 miles, and the second a little over a thousand—gave me time to get used to my job."

"Can you count those hours if you ever take lessons again?"

"I hope so—20 and one-quarter altogether. I've got notes from the pilot of the Douglas C47 and the Wells Fargo we flew."

"Good thing you took the opportunity—we've been way too busy since then. The bottom line is, you've got more gumption than anybody I know, Moonbeam. You've kept things lively for Hank and me, that's for sure."

"A three-fold cord is not easily broken."

Millie crushed her butt with her heel. "Hank and I have had a couple of escapades, too, but you didn't snitch on us."

"You mean checking out the cheap side of town in Algiers? You had lots of male company, with guns."

"But I was still terrified. Something about GIs with sheets over their heads gave me the willies. Any minute I expected someone to trip and set off their gun."

"Now I suppose we'll start looking forward to France. Do you think things could possibly get worse there?" Millie started back toward the tents.

"Good thing we don't know what *worse* might mean, huh? Maybe that's part of war in general—your idea of *worse* keeps expanding."

"Maybe so."

"At least the Red Cross keeps us in cigarettes. Without 'em, I'd be lost."

"We all need something to keep us from going over the edge. Rig has his gum and his wife's letters."

"What about you?"

"If I didn't know my life was in God's hands, I'd be in big trouble. Keeping busy helps, too. That reminds me, I'd better do some knitting before I try to sleep—my fingers are itching."

"I'm so glad for this warm weather. Maybe everything will change fast once the Allies cross the English Channel. Isn't that what Rig thinks?"

"Yeah—Hitler will divert so many units in that invasion, the fighting everywhere else will quiet down. Except in the Pacific—sure wish I'd hear something from Albert and Vernon."

"In my opinion, that crossing can't happen too soon. Something's got to give. How long do you think it'll be before we head to France?"

With a shrug, Dorothy chuckled. "Ask Rig. He's the expert."

June 10, 1944 Santa Marinella, Italy

Another pre-move briefing. Hungry for news of Operation Overlord, everyone except a skeleton crew in the recovery tent gave the Colonel their attention.

"The Normandy Invasion commenced four days ago, putting hospital units under immense stress. Yesterday, American P-51 Mustangs repulsed German Bf 109 bombers near Lion-sur-Mer. Meanwhile, Seventh Corps continues attacking at Montebourg in the Cotentin.

"Other units have silenced the German battery at Azeville, which has fired on Utah Beach since D-Day. On Omaha Beach, the 1st American Infantry Division disembarked on June 6 and launched an offensive west of Bayeux, freeing the villages of Tour-en-Bessin, Etreham and Blay.

"The Twenty-ninth Infantry Division seized Isigny-sur-Mer, and southwest of there, the Second American Infantry command post settled in the village of Formigny, advancing toward Rubercy.

"Sixth Corps and the French Expeditionary Corps have been transferred to Seventh Army. Personnel will be borrowed from several front lines this summer, including the Ninety-third and Ninety-fifth Evacuation Hospitals—and us."

"In spite of command mistakes, we keep at our job under extreme adverse conditions. The Eleventh has made an enormous difference in the lives of thousands, and that, my friends, is what we're all about." The commander raised his fist.

"Onward to France!" The whole crew raised a loud hurrah.

185

Chapter Nineteen

O n the radio show *Monday Night at Eight o'clock*, Sid Walker had just begun his evening chorus. Cecil and Iris sat rapt as the opening tune led into his intriguing weekly story. But the beastly radio speaker sputtered, coughed and went silent.

"Oh no, Mummy!"

Startled by this whimper from Iris—he had expected Cecil's dismay—Rupert twisted and turned knobs. His efforts failed to wring obedience from the contraption. He'd been looking forward to the story as well.

"Come." He lifted Iris from Madeleine's lap and held a hand out to Cecil, whose be-smudged face needed a good scrub.

"Mrs. Harwood's jam was wonderful, wasn't it? Bring the wet washrag near the copper, Cecil." Madeleine must be worn out tonight, making this request.

So as not to miss a speck of the glorious sweetness, Cecil continued licking as she applied the rag, and squirmed at her ministrations. "Ouch, that hurts!"

"Young man, apologize to your mother and get into your bed." Rupert gestured with his chin toward the children's bedroom. Once inside, he closed the door, deposited Iris in bed, and scowled at his son.

"You will *not* speak in that tone to your Mum. Do you hear me?"

Cecil hung his head.

"Now then. If it were you alone, I would forego your story, but Iris should not have to suffer. So this will be a short one, as I must get along to the fire station." Rupert perched at the end of the bed, his knees up to his chest, crowding his supper.

"This tale takes us back to my childhood, when my departed parents made ends meet as best they could. After his barbering day, your grandfather sometimes took a second job. One evening early in winter, thick yellow fog had rolled in over the Green as he hurried along to his tasks as a night watchman for an industry.

"Working from six until midnight, he always grew hungry, and made use of the *brassiere* the company provided to cook his sausages. Often, rag men or seafarers would happen along, and he would offer them a sausage if he'd extra."

Iris closed her eyes, but still clung to his hand. Cecil stared at the ceiling.

"On this particular night, the fog obscured the red lanterns placed at several points around the worksite. After checking on everything, your grandfather settled down to cook his supper. As the sausages sizzled, their savory smell—"

"Only sausages? Could he not afford faggots or saveloys, or pease pudding?"

"As you well know, faggots require gravy. Besides, being globular, they might slip off one's fork. Times were stringent, and wasting a faggot most unbearable."

Cecil laced his fingers over his chest.

"Your grandfather prepared to enjoy his feast. But just then, a hungry hound sauntered out of the fog, and a man's voice called, "Reggie.Reggie, come back here.""

"Do you think he bought his sausages at the Home and Colonial?"

"I daresay not. At that time, a German butchers was located on Mape Street, and was known for the finest meats. He also cooked and sold them outside his shop, but I expect Father bought his raw."

"So he ate with your Mum and you, but later cooked for himself?"

"Correct. He traipsed nearly a half-mile to this industrial site in the dark and cold, made his rounds on the hour, and then had to return home again in the middle of the night. So you see how hungry he would have become."

"Did he ever buy you a sweet?"

"By times, he would bring home a packet of wine gums after his regular day of barbering. Now, close your eyes."

The trembling slits Cecil maintained did not escape Rupert's notice.

"On this particular night, you recall, the fog had closed in like a..." He almost said *shroud,* but thought better. "Like an impenetrable blanket, and as that dog straggled through, your grandfather tightened his hold on his poker and picked up a good-sized rock."

Cecil opened his mouth and shut it again. Iris wriggled in her sleep.

"*Thunk!* My father's aim caught the hound on the backside. The animal raced off with nary a growl. With one sausage in his mouth, Da settled into consuming his supper, but through the dense air, that call resounded. He downed another of his sausages. And then..."

Not a movement on Cecil's part.

"From the wall-like fog burst a man dressed in uniform—a guard of King Edward the Seventh, who reigned from 1901 until 1910. 'Have you seen the King's dog? The fool ran off, and for over an hour I have chased him.'"

"The *King's* dog?"

"Indeed. Your grandfather, somewhat shaken realized the fellow's desperation. 'Here, have a swig of water and a sausage, sir. And take care of the deep excavation up ahead.'

"The fellow downed a fat sausage and some water, said a proper thank-you, and hurried off. And that, children, is a tale from your very own grandfather."

"Umm..."

Pulling the coverlet up to Cecil's neck, Rupert whispered, "Good night, my son." He kissed Iris and left the room.

Out in the parlor, Madeleine bade him a sleepy goodbye, and he started on his way, remembering to dislodge the accumulator batteries from the radio before he left. He placed them by the door so as not to forget them in the morning, when the shop in Hackney Road would be open for recharging.

A few steps into the fog, someone ran right into him—a man about his height, but slighter built.

"Is that you, Da?"

"Why Junior—are you just now getting home?"

"Yes, the fog caused several delays in shipments, and—" Rupert could barely make out Junior's facial features. "They're waiting at the fire station, no doubt, but—"

A worried edge tinged his voice. "What is it?"

"I stayed a bit later for another reason. I have been concerned about Anna. Finding her has become a challenge in recent weeks."

"Finding her? Does she not come to work?"

"Oh yes, but then—I may as well say it right out. I believe she might be involved with a soldier."

"Involved? A soldier?" Fire shot through Rupert's belly, and he nearly added, 'British?'

"From Canada, I think."

Rupert let out a relieved breath. Anything but one of those cock-sure Americans, though he had his doubts about the Poles, as well, not to mention others now swarming the city.

"The other thing is—"

Rupert held his breath. Junior lowered his voice.

"Anna might be—" Belabored by emotion, Junior stalled. "She might possibly be carrying a child."

Rupert's pulse pummeled inside his ear. "Why would you think—"

"One of the women on my line has hinted this, although Anna has no idea she let her secret slip." Junior grasped Rupert's forearm. "Are you all right?"

"Quite a shock, indeed. Please—refrain from telling your mother yet."

"Yes. I haven't even mentioned this to Kathryn, with her—"

Her expectant state.

189

"Yes. Well, then. Thank you, son."

Leaping from his story of yesteryear into this vast unknown threw Rupert into a state. At the station, several volunteers looked up as he entered.

"Evening, Officer."

"Yes. Ah, sorry to be on the late side."

"At least you refrained from knocking your head on a lamppost on the way, as one of our number did."

An older air warden gestured to a woman lying on a pallet up against the wall.

"Oh, no—Mrs. Ogilvie?"

"Perhaps you might take a look at her. Doctor Adams begged off tonight due to an emergency near his home."

Without removing his coat, Rupert knelt beside the woman, whose face had been obscured by a cold cloth.

"Mrs. Ogilvie? Begging your pardon, I should like to see your—" Removing the cloth, he stared at a grand swelling on the woman's forehead, the makings of a deep bruise. "You did indeed wonk yourself a good one."

She made no sound, so he followed his instinct to check her wrist—almost no pulse. "Mrs. Ogilvie? Mrs. Ogilvie, can you hear me?"

Nothing.

All thoughts of Anna faded. "Warden, do come here. This woman needs aid."

But just then the siren went off. He couldn't very well leave Mrs. O here—she'd suffered quite a blow and might even die. Oh, where was the doctor when they needed him?

"Warden—do you know of a doctor in this area? We have no way of getting Mrs. Ogilvie to a hospital, and her pulse is quite weak."

The warden, one who relished his authority—perhaps 'twas he who had accosted Rupert the day of Melvin's attack on the vicar—squinted in response. Meanwhile, volunteers dashed to the emergency wagon destined for the bombsite.

"See here, warden. I've no choice but to leave her. Find her a doctor, and now!"

Without looking back, he hurried to the wagon just before the driver took off. *Help Mrs. Ogilvie. Help her.* He sent up his silent request. Only then did he remember what Junior had said about Anna.

He must have groaned out loud, because the volunteer next to him peered over. "Beastly day, Officer?"

"Rather, thank you." Rupert stared out the window at the darkened city. *And help Anna. Please help Anna.* Then a memory flashed before him. The night of the raid, he'd had an intuition about that girl out so late with a military officer.

Perhaps that had been Anna, after all.

191

Chapter Twenty

September 1 Aspremont, France

"We camped at Dramont, then at Le Muy, and now we're at Aspremont. Dum dum diddy dum, dum dum diddy dum..." Sitting beside Dorothy and Millie's tent, Hank sang off-tune with Eric nearby, snapping at flies.

"And all this progress because of a successful Allied landing. It took four times, but our boys got it right at last, and here we are in France."

Hank's tone, while still cynical, had altered. Dorothy felt sure she and Millie weren't the only ones who noticed a new softness in her. Even her fiercest expressions seemed milder. What was going on?

A few days ago, Millie said she'd seen Hank with Wally, and the light dawned.

"Our Wally?"

"Yes. He's almost 35, you know."

"How did he get in?"

"He got so angry at the way some rich boys got off in his county, he decided to offer his cooking skills. The army leaped at the chance."

Seeing Hank and Wally chatting a few times, they seemed a likely couple. Both were tall, Hank angular as a monkey wrench, Wally as portly as one could be and still pass muster.

Millie, who was washing some clothes in her helmet, responded to Hank's comment. "With all the smoke and mirrors our troops used this time, it's a miracle we can even find ourselves. Pretty nifty how they landed all those paradummies so far from the actual landing beaches, huh?"

"Yeah, and whoever blew all that smoke inland as cover was a wizard. Six thousand tons, somebody said. Did you hear they used airplane propellers to spread the stuff? That's something that would really interest your brother Albert, right?"

"That's for sure. Did you see the drawing my sis sent me of his airplane? Don't know how the censors let it through, but maybe it helped that she put it in a food package."

"Wally has mentioned that one—ts wings dip up, and the Japs call it *Whistling Death*. Does Albert fly in the Black Sheep Squadron?"

"I don't know. We don't hear much from him."

"I'm so glad that smoke trick confused the Germans. One of our patients told me the Bougnon Bay defenders were mostly older men and gave up quickly. You think Hitler's finally getting desperate? I've always wondered how one country could produce so many soldiers."

Hank got up to tighten the sagging clothesline. "But then, I know a girl from a German family who has so many brothers, she—"

"Hey—careful what you say." Dorothy wrinkled her nose. "My sister's married to a prize fighter, and he'll come after you."

"Seriously?"

"Yeah. Elfrieda's built like my father, big-boned and tall, and Blackie's her match."

"The guy's really a prize fighter?"

"Sure is, and he was working on our parents' porch when Elfrieda met him. I don't remember all the details, but Papa had to lay the law down about the way he treated her. Anyway, he works for the John Deere Foundry now and they have two daughters." By the time Dorothy put the finishing touches on a letter and sealed the envelope, Hank moved to another subject.

"You know that GI in the sickbay with malaria? He said this landing was the best yet, but he had to sit it out. He oughta thank his lucky stars. Besides, there'll be plenty more battles."

Millie agreed. "That's for sure, At least they secured this port, and here we are on the Riviera. But this is just the beginning. So many wounded, and we know there'll be more."

"Hey, that's my line." Hank chuckled. "You always see the bright side."

"Yeah. Well, anybody can change." Millie wrung out her shirt. "There now, those spots came out after all. I'm going for a smoke before I do another thing. Remember, you two, meeting in the mess at 14:00."

"Yes, sir!" Hank saluted. Then she looked at Dorothy's letter. "Another one to Paul? I thought that Scotsman was your boyfriend now."

Ignoring her became easier and easier. Finally, Hank stood up. "Come on, Eric, let's go do our own washing over where they appreciate us."

Oh, the luxury of a few minutes alone to enjoy the sunshine and fresh breeze northeast of Toulon—Dorothy stretched her arms and turned a circle. Even better, the Fifth Army was making steady progress and the Germans had fled, leaving behind the usual ravished countryside.

What a joy to do the everyday essentials she'd neglected recently. Too bad German minefields made the shoreline off-limits, but she had only a couple more letters to write. One to Pinky—her tenth, with only one reply.

When a nurse yelled it was time for the briefing, Dorothy was ready. The Eleventh now had another new commander, and she'd barely seen him. Besides, all, what could possibly be worse than Anzio?

"We'll travel to Beaumont, almost 300 miles beyond Marseille, up the Rhone River Valley." Colonel Ward gave a few more details and said goodnight.

The next day, getting to Beaumont created new records for discomfort. Road builders had to cut through rocky Alp foothills, and all the German tanks that rolled this way hadn't helped.

"Once we get home, give me a nice new Chevy on a smooth highway." Hank rubbed her hip while somebody pulled out a canteen and argued with her about car makes.

The word *home* set Dorothy thinking of fireflies in Papa's cousin's field and a full load of corn to husk. If they hadn't come back from Germany, where only swine ate corn, she'd have missed out on so much. That made her think of Grandma's house again. If she got the chance before she went home, she'd find a way to visit Bremen.

When the truck jerked to a halt at last, she flew up and over the back. No use spending one extra second in here—if mud awaited, so be it.

This time, Adolph's new message came from a V-2 rocket propelled by a liquid fuel engine and hit much closer. The explosion woke Rupert from the first solid sleep he'd had in ages. He bounded out of bed and realized that somehow, Madeleine still slept.

Through the kitchen and out into the garden, he stared west at ominous flaming sky. The military's jamming devices proved to have little effect on these new vengeance weapons, so the government was installing anti-aircraft guns in Hyde Park.

After the first London strike on September 8 killed three people, Chief Derbe held an informational meeting—instructive, except in matters of prevention. In the meantime, hundreds more died. Rupert punched the side of the shed.

"Bugger Hitler!" He felt a little foolish, as though someone might be watching. Such unrelenting viciousness from the Fuhrer bedeviled the entire island.

This afternoon, the Chief had scheduled a visit from a scientist to explain the workings of this weapon. But these facts did nothing for those poor people west of here, or those still to be hit.

A wave of despair enveloped Rupert, and he hardly fought it. Better now than later, when he must appear calm and collected before the world at large. Distant cries wafted as sirens wailed, a scene replayed throughout London. Police wagon doors would slam, ambulances roll on cobblestone, lights flash, flakes of burning cinder flavor the air as they floated free and unattended—a general melee.

"Thanks be—this one fell away from the Green." Guilt trapped him at this thought, but here in the garden, he could be honest.

"Interesting how I can tell the location, even from this distance. We've been spared again, but this cannot last forever." With a shudder, he glanced back at the house, especially noting Rupert Jr. and Kathryn's window directly above Iris and Cecil's.

Appreciation for the blackout engulfed him as his heart gradually quieted. Hadn't it been rather lovely, having almost full darkness in the city these years? True, the ever-active searchlights destroyed all sense of the placid countryside, but between their swoops, one might view the stars unhindered.

A deep breath later, with the all-too-familiar clutch of smoke in his throat, Rupert passed what was left of his vegetable patch, a few die-hard squash and tomato vines ready for the burn pile. A foretaste of winter's cold—but always, spring returned.

Re-entering the house, he filled the kettle so Madeleine might be surprised he'd already made tea. Good to scoop porridge into a pan and light the burner, pour milk from the cooling shelf into the white pitcher her hands touched each morning.

Smoothing his rough fingers over its smoothness created a burning behind Rupert's eyes. Home and family—how could he place enough meaning here? But without doubt, this was what truly mattered. His children asleep in their beds, his grandchild safe between his parents, Gran and Anna stirring, about to begin their respective duties.

If Junior's hunch proved true, he would have to tell Madeleine. Realizing how people put off accepting uncomfortable truths, he stirred the porridge and pondered. If only he could whisk that conversation with Junior into the dustbin and pretend it never occurred.

Another part of him wanted to lie in wait as that Canadian

soldier trekked through some dark alley towards his base. How he longed to pulverize that young fellow!

How could Anna have stooped to such shame? If only she would tell him and Madeleine of her own accord after the children had gone to sleep, on a night the fire station had not scheduled him, and pour out her misery. On the other hand, she stayed away more and more.

What a befuddlement, being a parent.

By dawn when he left the house, his nose told him the flames had died out, leaving only a grey tinge and a vast swath of rubble. So it went, from disaster to disaster, and in-between, hoping for less of the same. Ah, *hope*.

An hour later, Towsley chose that very word for their day's attention. Rupert refrained from mentioning the coincidence, but how did one take these happenings that seemed connected, especially when other occurrences reflected no universal plan?

"I'll be seeing you later, for the meeting."

"Ah, yes. Later, then."

After a full morning, Rupert stopped at home for some corned beef hash left over from last night. Madeleine was still in the queues, Gran said as she heated his food, adding a spoonful of fresh mince. My, that spritely taste stayed with a person.

Then he made for the station. The Chief invited Towsley to these new meetings, along with other community leaders. Having been in the thick of the attacks, the clergy often shared statistics as vital as any police report. Soon the scientist began in earnest.

"Our intelligence, aware of a V-2 rocket crossing the Karman Line with the vertical launch of MW18014 on the 20th of June, still had no idea when or where these attacks would launch. These vengeance weapons, produced to revenge our air attacks on German cities, travel at 3,500 miles per hour, and can be launched at targets 200 miles away, fueled by ethanol and oxygen."

He tapped his pointer on a drawing of the V-2 on its launching device. His sigh met with absolute silence in the packed room.

"Unfortunately, we had no idea how to prevent the launching or prepare our citizenry. The V-2's trajectory and speed make it virtually impossible to shoot down with anti-aircraft guns and fighters.

"The rocket—did I mention this bomb is 14 feet long and drops from approximately one mile above the earth and at three times the speed of sound at sea level? Quite the beast. We have nicknamed this new killer *Big Ben* and formed the Crossbow Committee to develop countermeasures.

"We have been attempting to jam the bomb's radio system with both ground and air-based jammers flying over our territory, thus far, to no clear effect. Meanwhile, our Anti-aircraft Command analyzed the evidence falling from our skies, and are working toward a successful deterrent.

"At the same time, our ground and air forces across the Channel seek to reach and disable the mobile launch sites in an ongoing, brutal battle. Unlike the V-1's buzzing sound which alerts us to its location, the V-2 unfortunately gives absolutely no warning before impact. The only sound comes after it has landed.

"Thus far, strikes have been mostly in London, but cities to the east have also taken hits. So what can we tell our citizens?

"Those of you who lent aid in Cheswick on September 8 or have visited the west side since, recall the severe damage on Stavely Road, near the Thames. An entire block blown to bits, hardly a wall left standing, a crater 60 feet wide and 20 feet deep marking the impact, three dead and 17 injured."

A murmur passed through the gathering—nearly everyone had hurried to this scene. Towsley had stood and gaped with Rupert after the worst casualties were rushed to the hospital.

"Eleven houses demolished, 15 more beyond repair, and an estimated 3,000 tons of debris to be hauled away. So you see the vast capability of the V-2. Another Big Ben struck only minutes after the one in Cheswick, but near Parndon Wood, leaving wreckage yet to be cleared.

"Since then we have endured more loss of life, although some V-2s have landed north, in unpopulated areas. Oh, that the Germans would make more errors." The scientist swiped his forehead with his kerchief. "I must add that publicly, our government makes no acknowledgement of this new threat, due to concerns that the enemy will take heart.

"Rather, the incidents have been charged to gas line failure." A general stir in the room caused the speaker to address the Chief. "I wonder if this might be the appropriate time for local reporting?"

"Yes. We cannot express how much we appreciate those of you at the scene immediately after an attack. We welcome your insights and concerns." He nodded toward Vicar Towsley, Rabbi Stein, and several others present, and one-by-one, they chipped in, with the vicar starting it off.

One after another, the others made statements:

"Lacking the *putt... putt... putt* warning of the Doodlebug, what can we do but clean up afterward?"

"No strikes in our vicinity yet, but we remain on the alert. Some of our local air wardens voice frustration with so little information."

"This latest challenge has only increased my flock's determination to conquer fear. As usual, our British humor shines through, and we make do the best we can. Several of our members hold a 'Sally Ann' canteen in readiness and appear at bombsites with hot drinks as soon as possible after a local attack."

With commendations for everyone's work, the Chief closed the meeting. The Rabbi, a potent conversationalist whom Rupert met often, walked out with him. He nearly always had a story at hand, and today was no exception.

"It's the children I worry about most."

"I agree. They seem so resilient, but one has to wonder about the long-range consequences of all this upheaval."

"Indeed. I can attest to the worry and to the resilience. The other day, a family had sent their children off to school, including a two-year old that the older children saw to her daycare center. They proceeded to their own school, only to have a rocket explode along the way, on Heathway.

"Later that morning I heard about the bomb and hurried there. Gas line failures, my eye! Witnesses were still mulling the tremendous explosion. Rubble filled the whole area—a direct hit on the pre-school playground, sending large objects straight up into the air. Miraculously, all school occupants were indoors at the time.

"The children's mother, having found her youngest safe, was in a state. We searched and searched, and finally located the older two at a casualty center where an ambulance had taken them. Who knows what scenes remain in their tender minds?"

Approaching a corner, with visions of little Iris and her clear-eyed trust, Rupert dared a question. "Do you ever doubt, Rabbi? I mean, does hope ever fail you?"

"Hope has a way of returning, despite our circumstances. To hope is to be human." He paused and stroked his beard.

"Have you heard that they're launching Big Bens from Holland—our troops in Antwerp are suffering their blows, as well. See, I have added one more worry, but at the same time, I believe we may soon gain the upper hand."

After a dramatic pause, he caught Rupert's sleeve. "We have it on good authority that many of our own people work in terrible labor camps where these monster bombs are created."

"You—you are certain?"

"Of the camps? Absolutely, my friend—many of them. But now we have received even more dire reports that some exist deep underground in Germany, hidden like mines, and out of them come these detestable machines. Darkness and light—we balance these two each day."

Rabbi Stein went his way, and Rupert began his late afternoon rounds.

More fodder for thought...a bit too much. Captives trapped underground, forced to create instruments of death that might even kill their own loved ones—how could one accept such things?

Still, Rabbi Stein maintained hope. Rupert hurried home. Perhaps today, he would roust Cecil and Iris for another trip to the sweet shop.

Chapter Twenty-one

"*P*rivate Woebbeking, for outstanding service in the line of duty, you are being promoted to Captain.*"

The ensuing applause woke Dorothy from her pleasant dream. "Captain, hah!" Making sure to keep her mutter quiet lest she wake Millie, she eased from her cot. "I'll be lucky if I ever make First Lieutenant."

Out in the encampment, a faint light radiated from the mess hall entrance—the cooks at work already. The air, warm for this time of night, carried that unique sweetness they'd smelled at—where? Keeping track of all their locations became a challenge. But tonight, such a rich aroma enveloped the Eleventh—like milk coming into the kernels of Iowa sweet corn.

Summer had long passed. Even with the longer growing season here at St. Amour, supposing any farmers remained, the time for kernels to fill would be over. Besides, the Germans had trampled every inch of cropland. Still, the essence tantalized Dorothy.

They'd moved from Aspremont to Assey, where she'd first treated German PWs. From then on, their number increased. At Conflans, nearly a thousand American wounded came in, along with 150 PWs. Before setting up here, an hour and a half northeast of Lyon, they'd had to borrow trucks and drivers from the Seventh Army to evacuate the wounded.

Good thing the engineers had built ambulance drives and a drainage system before the Eleventh arrived. Constant traffic raised big dust clouds, and the roar of truck motors rarely ceased.

French troops required aid, also, plus a smattering of other nationalities. When her German or English failed, hand signals and facial expressions communicated as well as anything.

Tracing the route to the recovery tent, she skulked like a phantom—she'd gone to sleep early last evening, and this solitary time seemed a special gift. Her duty would not begin for hours yet, so maybe she could go back to sleep after breathing fresh mountain air.

A sentry nodded as she passed—tough duty to stay awake all night, especially with the constant moving as the Eleventh followed the Allies' unexpected quick success securing a port. Soldiers ended up doing everything from pushing trucks out of muddy ruts on mountain roads to digging hasty latrines. Pulling guard duty when you were already exhausted must be a trial.

At the hospital tent, the night nurse gave Dorothy a smile as though she understood nighttime wanderings. Walking down the rows of sleeping patients brought a sense of calm.

Here, the difference the Eleventh was making became obvious in sleeping rows of GIs. Passing between the cots, hearing their breathing, Dorothy stopped here and there to pull up a blanket or tuck in a protruding foot. Yesterday, many of these men had needed emergency surgery, without which they would have died.

Now bones were mending, wounds closing, and sleep was renewing aching bodies. Many of these fellows would require rehabilitation or more surgeries, but at least they'd survived. Now and then, one of them lay wakeful and held out a hand. Touching them, giving one a shoulder massage in the middle of this long night, or listening to a whispered request, she kept on.

Since the Eleventh kept most patients no more than three days before shipping them to more secure field hospitals, new rows of wounded would take their places by tomorrow night. But this moment offered the opportunity to provide a little extra care.

Now that she'd been dubbed a full-time surgical nurse, seeing these fellows on the way to healing did Dorothy's heart good. Under this canvas roof lay so much potential, along with myriad possibilities for things to go awry. But all-in-all, hope filled this space.

Three of the men's uncovered feet bore balls of cotton between each toe. This outbreak of trench foot raised her ire—surely the U.S. Army could afford decent wool socks for men risking their lives. Hadn't the Great War taught them that lesson?

Years ago in Sioux City, an instructor had emphasized this malady brought on by too much moisture for too long. The suppliers had better hurry their orders before winter set in—this miserable affliction could keep a man from the fight for weeks, or even send him home with circulation problems for life.

Just yesterday, Hank spouted, "I swear, I'll learn to knit yet—a change of socks would've kept these guys walking." Millie shot Dorothy a look—they'd believe the knitting part when they saw it. But so far, the two of them had produced 30 pairs of socks. As long as someone back home sent yarn, they'd stay in business.

One of these GIs, healed enough from rest and having his feet elevated, seemed likely to make it back into the fight. She paused for a closer look—the skin took on a glow in the dim light. Daily olive oil massage would bring him through, and right now he slept in peace.

The other two—time would tell. One fellow's feet still hadn't regained normal color, since he'd come in with severe swelling. If only everyone would realize the futility of trying to tough out this ailment. To someone ducking German bullets, their feet might seem trivial, but healthy feet could win the war.

Back outside, the walkway back to the nurses' area appeared like a long country road, with the engineers' drainage channels on either side. Slogging through flooded beaches in Italy taught them this necessity.

When someone approached with a flashlight, Dorothy swung aside.

"Is that you wandering around out here, Moonbeam?"

Good. Rig. He always had a positive word.

203

"I couldn't sleep, and thought a little walk might help. How about you?"

He passed on that one. "Thinking about your Scot? Weren't you supposed to meet up in France?"

"Yeah. But things happen."

"Isn't that for sure? If it's any comfort, I heard yesterday that the command diverted a lot of RAF pilots farther north last week."

"Really?"

"Yeah, so—"

A silent moment passed. In the Midwest, a steady hum of cicadas and crickets would be creating incessant background music right now. Maybe this ravaged countryside had nothing to offer even insects.

"Headed back to your tent? Better get some shut-eye. We've got a mountain of work ahead of us."

Rig often mentioned his wife and two children back in Kansas. Once, his wife included some yarn for the nurses in one of his care packages.

"Work? Who would have thought—" But her light comment fell short as Rig lowered his voice.

"I mean work like at Anzio."

In spite of her wool cape, a chill ran the length of Dorothy's spine.

"There's bound to be a major conflict before we cross the Rhine. That's why they diverted the RAF—never underestimate soldiers defending their homeland. The Germans have faced this before, not that long ago, either."

"You don't think—"

He anticipated her question. "Hitler's not about to surrender. Add that to generals intent on glory, and you know this'll be a fight to the death."

"Generals—like Monty?"

"Yeah. Commanders' egos play way too big a role."

"Mmm—I suppose we ought to dwell on the bright spots. My latest letter said my little brother Ewald is here now, in Patton's army."

"A medic, right? Good thing new recruits keep coming. And we've had some bright spots, like our welcome to Lyon."

"Do you wish you'd been one of the infantry guys, with French women hanging all over them, singing them songs?"

"Hardly. I was glad when they attached us to the Evac. I knew then we'd never get the glory, just the guts—pardon the pun. Riding ahead in those jeeps—that's more General Clark's forte.

"Those women jumping on the trucks for a ride, with the FFI Resistance there in plain sight gave me the jeebies. You can never be too careful."

"I felt that way in Rome—how could we drive right through its heart in daylight? Seemed like there could be an attack any minute."

"But you got to meet the Pope."

"Yeah, and show my ignorance. When those guards pulled me front and center, I had no idea I was supposed to kiss his ring when he held out his hand."

Rig's chuckle floated around them. "Us Lutherans ought to stick together."

"You're Lutheran? How did you know I am, too?"

"Don't you remember? When they asked why you didn't kiss his ring, you said so."

"Mmm—I was so flustered. Say, I've been wanting to ask you, what does your wife do?"

"She works for the military in Kansas City."

"A secretary?"

"No.—well, sort of." He bit his lip.

"Top secret?"

"Not exactly." He fiddled with his gum wrapper chain. "Better get some shut-eye."

"I'll give it my best shot."

His reply set Dorothy to wondering. At the same time, her questions about Pinky returned. His upbeat tone from their last talk surged back in full force.

"We'll meet again, probably somewhere around Lyon. I'm betting you'll go through there, so let's make it a date. Watch for me on the south side before your unit drives through."

"Doesn't a date require a *date*?"

He'd flashed his winning smile. "Not a date of the heart."

But things must not have worked out for him. Perhaps by the time the Eleventh made their stop-and-start way through the city, the RAF had already begun barreling down on the Germans in the Netherlands.

As they set up in St. Amour, Dorothy's sigh joined many others over the past few days. Didn't *amour* mean love? Here she was, closing in on 30 with no promise of marriage.

Back in Cairo, Rick had been that serious, but he'd gone a step too far. If she had allowed him to take control of her future, she wouldn't have met Pinky.

Back at the tent, the idea of sleep loomed impossible, so she headed for the mess instead. Might as well get some coffee.

There, an officer was already spreading new orders. "We're packing up again tomorrow, bound for Aissey. The trip'll take a week or more, so we should be setting up again by the 18th."

"September or October?"

"September."

The cooks groaned at the news, but edging toward Germany had to be a good thing.

Dorothy gave two corpsmen at her table a grin. "Whoohoo— good news! When the girls wake up, I get to tell them we're on the move again."

"He's been here. Melvin has been here."

Vicar Towsley practically pulled Rupert into his office. Truth be told, he had hoped Williams might stay away longer.

"His commander sent him home for a respite. It seems they're making up for lost time. From the sounds of it, he's been putting his rage to good use, and his commander waited for a break in the action."

Visions circled in Rupert's head. The last time he saw Melvin, he'd heard the *crack* of bone on bone and watched Towsley double over on the pavement.

But this image led to one even worse, the same one that haunted Melvin. Surely he saw his wife and child, sacrificial lambs under a lunging heap of humanity.

"Did he? How was—"

"He has come closer to reconciling himself. He will never be the same, of course."

"So he visited you?"

"Yes, last evening. Knocked on the vicarage door and stood there turning his cap in his hands.

"He could not bring himself to step inside, but burst forth with apologies. I'm certain his father gave him guidance. His speech strung out like the phrases in a hymn, but he received the forgiveness he sought."

"You forg—"

"Exactly. Succumbing to memories of that dark time hurts only me, don't you see? Why not be free of them once and for all?"

"Mmm."

"Thus, you can probably guess today's word."

"Wrath?"

The Vicar snorted. "Yes, eternal, unending, perpetual wrath, my friend, like Herr Hitler's, resulting in this impossible war."

Towsley shook his finger. "No, of course not! Our word is forgiveness. I sent Melvin away with a little note: Let us forgive one another—only then will we live in peace."

"Tolstoy."

"Indeed. How many here would recognize—"

"Thanks to Mum, Vicar. I'll be off then. Today takes me to the other side of the Green."

"An errand for the Chief Constable?"

"Of sorts. Until tomorrow."

Rupert let himself out, but half a minute later, Towsley followed him, holding something small in his hand. "Wait—" How lovely to see him able to move about without pain.

"Melvin left this with me. He said his mother has kept all of Marian's hankies, so he brought one along, as a sort of remembrance between us." This hankie, another simple square, boasted dainty hand stitching around the edges.

"He told me his father gave him the one you found—the one Marian had with her when she died, and that it has become a source of comfort. Quite the admission from such a rough and tumble sort."

Towsley's somber black-brown eyes appealed to Rupert. No need to clarify today's word—*FORGIVE* enveloped his entire posture. Rupert opened his mouth as a sunny shaft highlighted a jagged mark along the vicar's jawline.

"You have healed well, my friend. Your speech is nearly normal."

Two vertical lines etched between Towsley's eyes. Rupert felt he should affirm his forgiveness of Melvin, too, but how could he? Realizing his smallness anew, he blurted, "Until tomorrow, then."

Chapter Twenty-two

September 27 Aissey, France

"American troops have liberated Nancy and the Sixteenth Corps has arrived in Europe. That's the good news. But with tons of explosives lobbed at them from of the new V-2 rockets, the Brits are pullin' out of Arnhem in the Netherlands. That's the Thirtieth Corps.

"They thought it'd be an easy sweep, but the German defenses have squelched Monty's Operation Market Garden. The worst is, the First Airborne parachuted in a raft of infantrymen, but the Thirtieth couldn't meet up with them."

"Another failure?" A truck driver asked the question in the mess. As usual, he was digging gunk from under his fingernails with his knife and wiping it on his pants. Even Hank had stopped telling him to do this outside.

He always replied, "No law against cleanin' my nails—you've got your smokes."

Rig shook his head. "I'm afraid so. On paper, the plan looked brilliant. The idea was to establish the northern end of a pincer that would eventually project into Germany, but the last bridge over the Rhine at Arnhem was one too many."

"So how did they choose the name this time?"

"Market was for the airborne assault to seize the bridges, our largest operation so far, and Garden referred to the ground attack. If we'd managed to claim that last bridge, speculations were that the war would be over by Christmas."

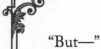

"But—"

"Our forces lost about 15,000 men. The British First took heavy losses, not to mention over 80 tanks and way over 100 planes."

Someone moaned, "Oh man—how can they ever recover?"

"So we chalk another one up to learning? Why didn't they put Patton in there?"

"Yeah."

"Sometimes I'm sorry your news is always so reliable, Rig." Millie's dejected tone reminded everyone she'd still had no word from Delbert.

"This operation turned into a real mess. Maybe the worst of it is that the Brits left 6,000 paratroopers behind."

"Six thousand—"

"Yeah, and Jerry's flooded out the Netherlands—people are starving to death there. But we're making progress at Calais, where he'll soon be forced to surrender."

"Soon—what does that mean? They've held out for so long, and that city has cost us so much, it's—"

"Right. On another note, the Canadians are about ready to go to the rescue in the Netherlands, and our boys are poised to attack the West Wall. Across the Rhine, where the Siegfried Line runs through the city of Aachen, the sides are lining up."

"That's not an industrial city—" Heads turned at Dorothy's outburst. Mama had taken them to visit beautiful old medieval Aachen when they lived in Bremen.

"That's right." Rig raised his eyebrows. "You've probably studied how Charlemagne spent Christmas and Easter in Aachen back in the late 700's."

With so many eyes on her, Dorothy held her tongue.

"Anyway. At first, General Hodges wanted to bypass the city altogether, but the Nazi generals ran the Siegfried Line through the city center—the narrow streets can interfere with our tanks and trucks passing through. Until now, we haven't bombed it, but a win there would be symbolic to the Germans."

Hank spoke up. "So if Aachen gets destroyed, it's their own fault."

"You could say that. It doesn't help that they string barbed wire everywhere and build strategic pillboxes and bunkers all along the Line. You can imagine how many spires and tall buildings give cover to enemy snipers. It's said that in some places, the Line extends over ten feet deep, and I'm betting it's the same in Aachen.

"We've made a mighty slow advance, and right now, with half of the city circled, supply problems have the First Infantry Division bogged down. This'll be a big win, our first on German soil, and giving up Charlemagne's ancient capitol will devastate Jerry."

From across the mess, a corpsman yelled, "What'd you do back in the States, anyhow? Sure weren't no mail carrier."

Rig ignored him, but his expression suggested something clandestine. To the others at this table, he zipped his lips with his forefinger and thumb.

One of the docs spoke up. "Heaven knows we need all the news we can get—don't lose touch with your source." Those left around the table fell to discussing the situation at Calais and the Market Garden disaster, while Dorothy headed to the surgical tent.

Late September brought cooler breezes, and the nights had grown downright chilly. Her wool sweater added just the right touch over her fatigues.

Apparently those orders of wool socks had not yet arrived. Seven cases of trench foot and other symptoms of exposure already took up recovery cots, so what would the numbers be when winter bore down?

Getting irritated with whoever was in charge of unloading full American supply ships stuck in docks did no good—they probably did the best they could. If military inefficiency angered her, how must the guys charged with all of the unloading feel? Not to mention those at the front enduring ever-lowering temperatures.

And this was only autumn.

Two days later, word came that the Eleventh would be moving to Bayon, straight south of Luxembourg and west of Strasbourg.

At the same time, a report heralded the German surrender at Calais. Excited voices filled the mess hall, and a private tacked up an announcement.

Briefing tonight: 20:00

Right on time, Colonel Ward made his way forward to stand on wooden crate.

"Having been through two months with you, I can attest to this unit's hard work, both in the hospital and on moving days.

"On September 9, when we closed our location south of Aspremont, our two echelons borrowed 12 two-and-a-half trucks from the 93rd and 95th Evacuation Hospitals for our move on September 11th. Two hundred sixty-five miles later, after an overnight at St. Amour, we opened again.

"The first echelon transported 300 cots, all surgical nurses, and half of our medical and surgical officers. The rest of us traveled in the second echelon, and we admitted over 150 patients during our first five hours. I call that high efficiency. Give yourselves a hand."

He started clapping, and everyone joined in.

"On September 17, we closed that facility to evacuate by 1700 hours, September 19. On September 20, we transported the hospital one mile east of Conflans, a distance of 62 miles. Within three hours from arrival, we received patients.

"During these past two weeks, continuous rain and cold has hampered our operations." To a loud murmur, he nodded. "We've lost some tents and faced difficulties in keeping patients warm. As you well know, trench foot has again reared its ugly head, but at least we're here to aid these men.

"Between August 15 and September 29, Seventh US Army medical installations have admitted and treated over 28,000 patients. Some 13,000 we evacuated to ComZ facilities, and nearly 10,000 have returned to duty. That's quite a feat. I'll be proud of this unit's accomplishments to my dying day." He paused for cheers.

"Now for some good news, somewhat premature perhaps. But

I have it on good word that we may set up operations in heated buildings as winter comes upon us."

The whole audience whistled and clapped. Finally, the colonel held up his hand.

"Thank you for your faithful service, ladies and gentlemen, and now, to the refreshments, brought to you by our ever-resourceful cook and his staff." He gestured toward the kitchen, where privates in khaki aprons took a bow, but Wally stayed out of sight.

After joining in the cheers, Dorothy quizzed Rig. "Do you know anything about those warm buildings he mentioned?"

"You might be surprised." He changed the subject. "Any word for Millie yet?"

"Nothing."

"And nothing from Pinky either, I assume?"

She shook her head.

"I like that Scottish guy a lot."

"You and me both."

On a late winter afternoon of mixed light, sunlight dappled the street between buildings, creating intrigue in alleys and byways. Trees had forfeited their leaves to the cold wind, except for a couple of pines along the way. Rupert hastened his steps when the bells of St. Mary le Bow signaled half past five.

With fire warden duty later, he looked forward to this family interlude. A pram outside the door reminded him that little Henry would be in their care while Rupert Jr. and Kathryn took in an American film at the cinema.

What little time they had alone, since Junior worked such long hours at the factory. What was it about today that instigated this rare outing? Oh yes, something about a delay in the supply of a substance necessary for production of the ammunition in Junior's area.

Even before Rupert opened the door, Henry's burbles soothed

his ears, after a day full of shouting and wrenching and cussing as cranes moved through to clean up last night's devastation over in Stepney. With so many missing buildings and bomb craters making movement almost impossible, small wonder the monstrous machinery could make progress at all.

Clanks and cranks and screeches grated on Rupert's ears as he made his rounds, but what would the populace do without them to clean up after another of Adolph's rampages? In the Great War, rubble had been cleared by hand across the Channel and somehow, people managed to recreate order out of chaos.

"Bapa—Bapa!" Henry lurched toward Rupert as Iris plied him with a spoonful of mash.

"We've got bangers tonight, Pa, bangers and mash." Cecil swung a paper bag from a local establishment, and rubbed his midsection.

"Oh my—nothing better. So you were the chum who provisioned the family this evening?"

Cecil's satisfied expression said he'd struck just the right note, and Madeleine, bustling about the kitchen, topped Cecil's proud look with her smile. Ah, the tender sentiment that awaited him here, the joy inherent in these simple, mellow activities.

So many ate down in the tube stations this evening, or at a canteen in their bombed-out neighborhoods, or trooped to their volunteer bomb-watching duties early for a spot of tea and human company. His throat filled as Iris gave up her quest to chuck food into his grandson, and Cecil unbuckled Henry from his chair so Bapa could lift him out.

Kissing the tyke on his fair head, Rupert took his seat and settled Henry into the crook of his arm. The softness of the child's warm skin entranced him.

"It's bangers and mash, then—our lucky Thursday fare. I could scarcely wait to get home." The tasty sausages had been ordered far in advance from Mr. Feacey's butcher shop on Dale Road. His cousin owned a farm, so he could predict within a week when a butchering would take place.

On that day, a hoard of takers descended for bangers and mash, along with a little pot of tasty vinegar liquor to tantalize the taste buds. After years of patronage, Mr. Feacey always held enough back for the Laudners and often tapped Cecil's shoulder on his way home from school with a reminder to return.

Madeleine sent Gran's plate upstairs with Cecil and reached for Henry. "Here, let me take him while you eat."

Rupert shook his head. "Enjoy your meal, my dear. We're settled in perfectly." Henry proceeded to grab a slippery sausage that slithered to the floor. The children giggled, and Iris retrieved the wandering meat. Rupert directed it to his plate.

"No need to wash it—every human body needs its share of floor dirt."

Madeleine scrunched her nose, but only looked more enticing. With every plate roundly cleared, she cleansed small hands of grease and Iris toddled over to Rupert, now retired to his armchair.

"Tell us a story, Papa?"

"A bonnie idea. Let's go out to the garden for some fresh air, shall we?"

The evening took on a loveliness he had foregone for too long. When Madeleine joined them, he'd launched far into the story of his father as a young barber, snipping a spot out of a public figure's ear as he shaved the man one morning.

'Blimey!' cried the rather important personage, 'You've nicked me.'

'Begging your pardon, sir. 'Twon't happen again.'

'There, you've spoken truth, for I shall never visit this shop again.'

"Father took heart at a slight glint in his apprentice master's eye. The customer wiped his face with his cape, threw it down and stormed out without paying."

"Did Grandfather lose his position?" Cecil's rounded eyes took in every nuance of embellishment Rupert could muster.

"Not at all. His master boasted a kind heart and a sense of humor. Besides that, he understood this customer thoroughly. He simply said, 'Pick up the apron, son. That fellow has fat ears, just like the rest of 'im. I've nicked 'em a time or two myself. Don't fret, for he'll be back rather than risk the long walk to the next barber. Besides, he comes here for our prices—he'd pay a shilling more on the West End.'"

Cecil giggled, and overhead, dusky evening sky produced a singular star. Iris spotted it first, cried out and pointed. Madeleine startled and grasped the railing.

"One of Adolph's rockets?" Her quaver touched a nerve, and Rupert recalled how in the trenches, the most innocent fog incited fears of another gas attack.

"Not at all, my dear." He held the children close before shooing them all back into the house before he left.

Night after night, Junior left for the air raid shelter, having barely kissed his young wife. But this evening, Rupert had notified the organizer that he would be covering for Junior. He deserved time with Kathryn, quite near to giving birth again.

In the station, women donned metal hats and took calls from citizen volunteers who'd spotted an incendiary. The buggered V-1s, or doodlebugs, gave off a warning noise, and sometimes lay unexploded upon landing. As they had when spotting a Messerschmidt during the Blitz, people rang up the local fire station when this occurred. Unfortunately with the new V-2s, the explosion had already taken place, so the calls led to an ambulance and a debris team dispatched to the given address.

At his normal station, Rupert lent a hand wherever he was needed, but this evening he would do the same in Junior's stead. Often, area fire warden volunteers had already snuffed out V-1 fuses with their sand buckets by the time officials arrived, but keeping up with the calls had become harder of late.

Since September, the Nazi's had added V-2 rockets to their arsenal, and hundreds to the death toll.

Bidding his loved ones goodnight, Rupert hurried to the dug-in entrance of a cellar transformed into an emergency station. Sandbags surrounded the stairs, and above, telephone lines crossed over the pavement like black latticework against a rising moon's promise. Down inside, the musty aroma of the cellar's former occupants—burlap bags of potatoes, carrots, and turnips—still triumphed.

Hardly a deep breath later, Rupert made close acquaintance with Hitler's new vengeance weapon. The impact blew him against an inner wall.

Coughing and sputtering, he felt for his helmet—blown from his head, buckled strap and all, but within reach. He'd been chatting with Rosamund Pliney, had just asked after her three young ones and her husband across the Channel.

Rosamund had set down her teacup—that was the last Rupert remembered. As he scuffled to get up, glass shards tore his palm. He recalled Junior saying that a small window fitted into the brickwork on the south wall had been closed up with boards at the beginning of the blackout.

So how had this glass found its way here? This was his first question. The next, *Where is Rosamund?* drove Rupert to search—easier said than done with bricks and timbers spattered willy-nilly, a table leg protruding from one pile, and over to his right, the shimmer of the metal teapot someone had donated.

Shaking his head, he aimed to concentrate. Rosamund had been wearing—mmm—perhaps a yellow sweater? Yes, a pullover, hand-knitted, like most in the Green.

Hanging from a ceiling board, an electric bulb still shed its sickly light. What troubled him most was the eerie silence, but through a film of cinder dust, people had begun moving about. Kenneth from the fire brigade held his hands to his mouth and strained forward. Someone else pulled at a fire hose.

Then reality dawned on him. The blast must have affected his hearing. In that understanding, he stumbled around objects recently launched into chaos. Reach Kenneth—he could think only that far. The next thing he knew, someone grabbed his elbow from behind and pulled. Turning, he noticed tear tracks through the dust and mire on a man's face—a young man about his height.

217

The fellow brought his lips together again and again. Rupert finally gathered his meaning.

"Da," he was repeating. And then "Oh, that wretched Adolph! Most likely a concussion. Can you hear me at all?"

"We'll take you to Bethnal Green Hospital straightaway. Steady as you go." He motioned for Rupert to follow, and the act of placing one foot after another on crushed teacups, mangled coats, and shattered bricks brought a sense of calm.

Somewhere along the way he realized it was Junior who preceded him. But hadn't he gone to—where had he gone? Perhaps down to the library? No, the cinema. They wouldn't let out for another—Rupert reached for his watch, but the chain dangled solo from his waist.

Between Madeleine and Junior, the message came through at about noon. Kathryn had just delivered another fine boy into this world. The warmth of Madeleine's fingers on Rupert's forearm had sustained him for—he had no idea how long. Now, her voice touched him as well, although the words arrived wrapped in thick gauze, and he could make out her meaning only by watching her lips move.

"Bugger Hitler for your injuries, but this way, you can see little Ernest sooner."

Ernest. They'd gone back to his mother's choice some 40 years ago. A namesake, although Henry was already Henry Rupert—two boys to carry on the Laudner heritage.

Rupert brushed his eyes and Madeleine squeezed his hand. "There now, love," she whispered.

For a while he faded, and when he awoke, evening shadows fell over the room, yet the window, situated behind Madeleine, asleep on a stark wooden chair near his bed, let in faint light. In that subdued radiance, her form appeared ethereal.

Gaping at her, head uncomfortably aside, he could not get

enough of the sight. Other sickbeds rowed this long room, but he and his beloved might have been alone in the silence.

He continued taking her in, this woman who'd told the children as he was leaving last night—was it last night?—"Papa's going out again now to keep us safe."

Had his vocal cords cooperated, he might have chortled aloud, for nothing could be further from the truth. On the contrary, he lacked even the ability to protect himself. These hours of passing in and out of some nether world solidified his vulnerability.

Somewhere along the timespan, he'd mustered the sense to check all his limbs—present and accounted for, mostly by pain. But his mind; ah, entirely another matter, not to mention his heart. His emotions jerked between cheer at Madeleine's presence to despair at his befuddlement.

But then the door to the ward opened and someone approached. Two individuals—or was he seeing doubt? Ah, yes, two—and one of them held something. Closer, he realized Rupert Junior and Kathryn had come to present their newborn infant. Madeleine wakened and stood beside him as Junior ever so gently slipped the tiny bundle onto Rupert's chest.

Instinctively, he circled the warmth with his arm, grazed near the wrist and bandaged above the elbow—he hadn't noticed until now. At a mewling sound, something like a baby puppy's, he startled, and Junior locked eyes with him.

"You hear him crying? A good sign, Da. Meet your grandson, Ernest Rupert."

The mewling grew louder and sent Rupert's heart to his throat. Such a moment, such enthrallment. He tipped the infant's thin blanket and beheld a perfect countenance—an image of Rupert Junior 25 years ago.

"He has your nose, son." The effort took a great toll, and he dropped his head back. Rupert Junior retrieved little Ernest.

"Oh my, his first words since the accident—his very first words." Madeleine grasped his shoulder, leaned over him.

"Visits must end." A rather severe nurse made her pronounce-ment before proceeding down the way to repeat her words.

Junior held the baby near again, and Rupert breathed in his scent.

Junior tapped his forearm. "You're going to be right again, Da, and very soon. Don't worry now, we'll skuttle old Adolph for you."

Last to leave, Madeleine kissed Rupert's forehead. "Righto, my love. Steady as you go. All will be well."

Chapter Twenty-three

Between the occasion of holding wee Ernest and the day of his dismissal, something overcame Rupert. Lying there in that lumpy bed, an image taunted him: Madeleine and the children when he'd left them the night of the blast, trusting that he would keep them safe.

What a sorry lot for an officer of the law! What a mean example of strength and authority was he, what a lout. In truth, his own weakness frightened him.

The arm of a greater force had defined a law unto itself. A bullying schoolboy, that law proclaimed the victory of strong over weak regardless of right or wrong. In this ward of invalids, it mocked him through long wakeful hours and set him wandering over territory he'd rather not revisit. Infrequent as they were, one childhood moment stood out—he'd slumped toward home with a bloodied nose.

Since he had dragged out his painful journey as long as possible, his father met him after a long day of barbering.

"Rupert, is that you?" His father squatted before him and touched his cheek. "What is it? You met with an accident?"

"No, Pa. Gordon Berry's fist done it."

"And I assume that fist was attached to Master Berry's arm?"

Rupert barely held back a sniffle. Until now, he'd been quite brave, but was only in first form.

"This was a playground affair?"

Rupert nodded.

"After school, perhaps?"

Again, he nodded. His father pulled out his handkerchief and commanded him to blow his nose.

"I can expect no visit from your schoolmaster?"

"No, sir."

"Did the other chap go home with any marks?"

Rupert shook his head.

"He said something to you?"

"He said I ought to be in second form, not first."

"Aha. A common error. He has yet to realize that people come in many sizes, and you have grown tall long before your classmates. To those unsure of themselves, your size poses a threat, even though you think quite kindly of them."

A long, shuddery breath granted Rupert relief. His father drew him into his arms then, and upon releasing him, provided direction.

"Well, then. Let us spare your mother any anxiety, shall we?" They stopped by a pub, where he wet an extra kerchief and wiped Rupert's face before continuing home.

Outside the doorway, he squatted again to study Rupert. "Tomorrow begins a new day. Perhaps this boy, Gordon, will now feel equal to you, having delivered his blow. But if he comes at you again, you may strike him. Only after school, you understand, and only to show him you are no weakling."

The next afternoon proved that young Gordon still suffered from his misconception, but a good slug to the left jaw taught him well. From that time on, Rupert felt as though he could manage his affairs. Except, of course, in the last war, for how does one manage bullets and deadly gas?

That sense of helplessness had passed when he came home to the good news of the police station opening. However, this recent blast left him impotent, exposed, perhaps even unable to carry out the tasks that fell to him.

This heaviness of spirit still attended him when Vicar Towsley paid him a visit. No one he would rather see, yet no one he dreaded seeing more.

The nurse had gotten him up to walk and returned him to bed as weak as water. At the Vicar's greeting, Rupert turned his head away.

"I've heard that blighter Hitler gave you a roughing up."

What was he to say?

"My friend, I am overjoyed to see you alive. I doubt anyone has brought you word of—the others. Kenneth's sister-in-law, Edith Worsley, Rosamund Stanley and..."

Rupert maneuvered up against the wall and faced Towsley. "No, I—I have heard nothing." Then he remembered. He'd been speaking with Rosamund. "I was searching for Ros..."

"I heard that you made every effort. But it seems they still have not found her, nor Edith—that is, found their..." The Vicar swallowed his last word, but Rupert's soul took it up.

Bodies.

"Most of the cellar collapsed under the weight of the building next door."

The quiet nearly suffocated Rupert. Towsley glanced down the ward for a moment and drew a deep breath.

"Mmm—we held joint services for them, six altogether, on Wednesday past."

Sickness washed over Rupert, so that he hardly digested the rest. How did the Vicar manage?

Aware that Towsley saluted him and passed on through the ward, Rupert lay there nauseous. The Vicar stopped back later, but feigning sleep seemed more honest than pretending to be on the mend.

Later, the ward quieted, and Rupert must have dozed off. He came to with one clear remembrance: *overjoyed to see you alive.*

Gathering his official nightshirt, he angled his legs out of bed and tottered to the door. Panting, he waited a full minute before starting down the hall. Yes, past the nurses' station and back again, all the way on his own power.

No one accosted him, and falling onto the bed, he buried his perspiring face in the covers. Even so, determination grew like a fledgling tomato plant. He must get out of here, must regain his strength.

The ward closed in on him. He must breathe fresh air, and soon. Urgent work remained to be done.

Arriving home in the middle of the day, Rupert passed through the kitchen, where scents of porridge and cream still wafted. In the children's room, he touched their coverlet. Holding a pillow to his nose, he visualized Iris asleep here, with Cecil beside her.

Then he went straight to the garden. The Vicar dropped him off en route to another appointment requiring the church vehicle, so that Madeleine could catch up on her mending deliveries this morning.

On this rather misty late autumn day, no draft of cold air through the grape arbor could shake his serenity. Tomorrow, come what may, he would return to work. He barely restrained himself from going in today, but the Chief had paid him a visit and instructed him to take his time.

In another breath, he expressed how everyone—even Fletcher—had asked after him. That produced a smile shared by the Chief. If anyone at the station came close to harboring a neurosis, it would be Fletcher, whose constant nitpicking drove some officers to outbursts. In normal times, his carrying on might have induced a firing.

Viewing Chief Derby's bloodshot eyes, a clear message came through. He would be greatly relieved to have Rupert back—his absence had badly stretched the already thin force.

One afternoon lounging about would suffice. Taking particular pleasure in the feel of his garden tools against his palm, Rupert snipped here, slashed there, and dug somewhere else. All the while, he thought of next spring when the growing would begin again. Maybe next year he would plant an extra row of carrots and beets over there near the wall.

So many would be planting nothing at all next spring because a V-2 had made a crater out of their house and garden, or they had decided to depart to the country for good, or... they were dead.

Regret filled him to think he could not attend the burial for Edith, Rosamund, and the other workers.

On the drive home, around partially filled craters that threatened to swallow their vehicle, the Vicar had described the location of the new grave. On his round, he must pay his respects.

A sprightly sun came forth from behind the clouds and rested its rays on Rupert's nearly healed arm. The warmth reminded him he had been granted another chance at this earthly life. And his hearing had returned, just as before the attack.

Filling his hand with earth made fertile through vegetable cuttings and scraps from Madeleine's cooking, he sifted the moist soil through his fingers.

BEHOLD. He had now beheld his new grandson, and his weakness as well. In this afternoon's light, he knew he could manage.

At this very second, another marvel lay right in his hand. *RENEWAL.* Food scraps turned into soil, he knew not how, and not just any soil, but that rich and desirable for growing things.

With renewed vigor, he vowed to fulfill his duties to the utmost of his ability. Earnestly. Going inside to wash, he thought of Anna. He'd put off considering her situation far too long.

Only something wrong with the wiring, a broken windowpane, or bats in the attic drew Rupert upstairs. But this afternoon, the stairs beckoned him. Finding Gran's door closed, he turned toward Anna's room. The door hung ajar, so he peeked in.

Bed made, clothes neatly arranged on their hangers, dresser rather well organized with a silver brush, comb and mirror, lamp, and... On the floor near her bed, something stuck out. The corner of a book—of course, she shared his love of reading. Rupert peered closer, stooped a bit to read the title.

Diary. Alarm ran through him. He turned to check the hallway and heat flamed up into his cheeks. No, this would never do—he'd no right to read her private thoughts. He would speak with her directly, at the first possibly opportunity. He hurried downstairs and back outside.

The sun lanced its cheer, and he basked in its warmth. By the time Cecil swung through the garden gate with Gran, Iris in tow, Rupert's heart fairly burst. They raced into his arms shouting, "Da, Da! You're home—you're home!"

"To the candy shop, then?"

"Oh, yes. Yes!"

With a mute touch on his arm, Madeleine's mother saw them off. Her eyes declared a silent welcome.

So off they went, the children's excitement entering into Rupert. It was as if a vast inner reservoir opened up, stretching his ability to see, to feel, and most of all, to hear. Every utterance from Cecil and Iris struck him as pure gold, refined and lustrous.

Passersby, their umbrellas, yes, even the sparse vehicles on the roads appeared through the eyes of his children. Everything seemed fresh and new, even the *Bugger Hilters* shouted by a group of older youths on their way to an evening of volunteer work.

In a word, this world, his Bethnal Green, despite its sunken craters and rubble and blown-up houses with lurching walls exposing kitchen cupboards and bedrooms split down the middle, displayed beauty unsurpassable. Several citizens stopped their progress to exclaim over his return and patted the children's heads.

And the shopkeeper—oh, my. His greeting overwhelmed Rupert, for he rushed around the counter with arms widespread.

"Oh children, you have received your Papa back. What a day to celebrate." He embraced Rupert, sticky apron and all, before leaning down to Iris and Cecil. "So, what will you have? Choose for yourselves, no shyness allowed, whatever you wish. Your father has come home!"

He guided them toward the jars of hard candy, then to the chocolates—a wonder, that, with such a shortage—while Rupert regained his composure. He'd not expected such a salutation, and standing there at eye level with the topmost shelf of sugary sweets, a lemon drop suddenly appealed to him.

When the children had made their choices, the shopkeeper

glanced his way. "And you, sir? What would you have this fine day?"

"A lemon drop, to be sure, and thank you kindly."

The keeper, whose hair seemed whiter than Rupert recalled, dragged his stepstool over and counted out six, which he placed in a small bag. Then he reached for another.

"Seven, the best number. Will that be enough for your household, Constable? Oh, what a day to be sure. We have cursed that blighter across the Channel a hundred times on your account."

"Indeed. Sounds like a blessing to me."

"Off you go then, children. What good fortune to have your Papa back again." The shopkeeper opened the door for them and patted Rupert's shoulder as he passed through. "A top drawer evening to you all, then."

With his throat thoroughly blocked, Rupert could only give a grateful nod.

He let Cecil choose their homeward route past the new library. "You still come here in the evenings?"

Cecil scrunched his face. Holding back his impulse to hurry up the steps, since sudden weariness over took him, Rupert leaned down to look Cecil in the eye. "Kathryn has been bringing you when Mum cannot?"

"No, Gran. But it's not the same as with Mum."

"Remember when we had to go into the tube station to find a book, Cecil? Thankfully, the librarians were able to save some after the bombing and have added more to spite old Adolph."

Cecil angled his head just a bit.

"What is it?"

"You think the library is so important?"

"Indeed. Your grand-mum taught me the value of reading, and in all these years, that has not changed. Some things never do."

Chapter Twenty-four

"Yet another camp. Well, at least we haven't lost any of our wall tents," a nurse commented while they set up cots.

Hank launched a reply. "And somebody figured out the engineers ought to do their building *before* we get here and unload. Brilliant, eh? By the time the war's over, everybody'll have their job figured out."

"Plus, we didn't come so far this time. It was starting to get pretty chilly on the way, though. Where are we, anyhow?"

"Le Muy, France."

Millie joined in. "My question is, where are those buildings the commander hinted at?"

"Promised, you mean." Dorothy centered a cot in its row. "He didn't say they'd be *here*, just *somewhere*. The main thing is, we're within driving range of the troops. Somebody told me they might be in for quite a fight."

"Where do you get your info?"

"It's top secret."

"Don't tell me you're consorting with an officer?"

Hank arched her brows and opened her mouth to come down on the other nurse who'd asked, but Dorothy realized the girl had no idea how she watched and waited for her Scotsman.

"Yep, that's it, hon." Dorothy stretched her shoulders. "I sure won't miss riding in those trucks, how about you?"

Everyone commiserated, and someone said, "Any more details about what's going on with the Seventh?"

Just then Abner joined them. "They're headed east, between Strasbourg and the Swiss border—that's how close we are to the mother country. But Jerry's waiting, we can count on that. He's holding out in a pocket."

Somebody chirped up, "Another pocket? How do we keep getting into these things?"

Abner scratched his head. "Seems the German's like them, and this will be a tough one, I'm afraid. A little town called Colmar borders the Rhine, and word has it we've got two French generals at the front. One of them refuses to fight with the other because he served under the Vichy government during the occupation.

"Can't say I blame him, but right now we need to attack. What a conundrum. Can't be easy for those Frenchies to take orders from American commanders."

Hank fussed, "We came over here to save their hides, and they can't take an order? Peace on earth, good will to men."

"This place won't be home for long. Anyway, I'd rather be here than in the midst of all that wrangling, with Jerry breathing down their necks."

Dorothy grabbed her jacket and went after the syringes. The air had turned crisp, but she'd been expecting it. They were practically in Germany, where heavy snow bowed huge pine branches to the earth during her childhood. After a storm, she and her playmates used to brush off nearly a foot of white and the boughs would snap up, swishing against their cheeks like brushes.

The closer they came to the Rhine, the more she thought about Bremen, with all the talk about the Air Force pounding German cities. Rig said the RAF commandeered all daytime raids out of England now, with our Air Force taking over at night.

Pinky's crew may have released some of these latest bombs. She pictured him in his flying jacket, ear-flapped hat and oxygen mask, teeth chattering high over the Channel. The alternative—she refused to think about it. Losing one boyfriend on this tour was more than enough.

"Moonbeam?"

"Jeremy, is that you?" A young private she met a few weeks back jogged up with a chuckle.

"Better learn to call me Scab, or I won't know who you mean."

"I see way too many scabs as it is. How'd you get that nickname, anyway?"

"The guys always take the low road. During our training, a recruit got the chicken pox, so I told him my mother warned me not to scratch when I had it.

"Of course I couldn't stop, and was sure I'd have terrible marks on my face. Somebody said, 'you mean scabs,' or something like that, and they've called me Scab ever since."

"You don't mind?"

"When this is all over, we take back our real names, and if it makes the guys happy— Hey, do you have time to listen tonight?"

"Sure, I'll be over in a while. Heard anything interesting?"

"You bet."

He took off, so Dorothy found her helmet to brush her teeth. As she walked to Rig's tent, where Jeremy set up his short wave radio, she recalled meeting this private in France. Rig had just delivered some more battle info, and ended with:

"Since you've asked how I get my information, I've decided to introduce you to my vital source." He motioned for her to follow, stopped at a truck, and climbed in. Another much younger GI appeared.

"Come on up." Rig offered his hand. "All right, show her, Private."

The young soldier looked about 14 as he uncovered a short wave radio stashed in the back.

"Oh, wow—my father's friend has one just like this."

"Made by Hallicrafters. Government issue, ma'am." The young soldier sat down before the instrument and turned a dial.

"But how do you—I mean, it's so big. Doesn't the commander—"

"At first I had to hide this, but everybody helped me." He glanced at the floor bed. "Well, mostly the Captain, and he felt Colonel Tabor out little by little."

Rig took a bow. "He knew he could run things a little looser here than in an infantry unit and realized we'd never receive this kind of info down the chain of command. Sometimes it's made a big difference—may even have saved a few lives."

"And Colonel Ward?"

"He understands, too. Even asks us to listen for certain info at times."

"So you brought me here to—"

"We'll be right back, Scab." Rig led Dorothy to the tailgate and lowered his voice. "This'll give you someplace to go when you've got a spare minute. When we set up, I always put Scab in my official mail tent, so you'll know where to find him."

"Somewhere to go?"

"You're always watching for that Scotsman, just like me with my wife's letters. It can drive a person nuts, and the short wave really helps."

He pulled her back to the radio. "You'll see what I mean. Puts you in another world for a little while—does you good."

"Why, I—thank you."

The private reminded her of Edgar, so she felt comfortable with him right away. But first, she made something clear.

"Private, I'll be schnookered if I'll call you by your nickname. What's your real one?"

"Jeremy, ma'am."

"Well, then, Jeremy. Teach me what I need to know."

Later, Rig jumped back into the truck, and Dorothy emerged from that "other world."

"How's it going?"

"Great. What time is it?"

"Way past your bedtime. Millie just asked if anybody'd seen you. I'll walk you back." He waited while she thanked Jeremy.

"You think I'm safe with this guy?"

"As safe as you'll ever be over here. I mean, for a girl who's taken secret airplane trips to Cairo."

She punched him in the arm and he pretended to be hurt. "Besides, I remember how you volunteered to stay with the doc and that sick native when we were crossing the desert. I forget exactly what was wrong with him, but he would've died if we'd left him alone."

"Wow. What a memory! I'd almost forgotten that myself."

"Anyway, there's no doubt you can take care of yourself." They turned a corner and he added, "I'm betting you won't have time to visit Jeremy again for a while. General Patton's keeping the Germans busy around here, or maybe it's the other way around."

"If he'd only had enough gasoline, he could have performed his usual rapid advance and taken Metz and Nancy by now. He's waiting for fuel, so the Wehrmacht can reinforce the Fifth Panzer Army and make a fortress out of Metz. It'll be a month before Patton takes the city."

"Late November—bet the General's about to spit nails."

"You've got it. When he finally can move again, the Germans will be ready. In the meantime, they're leaving their mark every step of the way, and their dirty work comes straight to our operating room."

The next morning, Lieutenant Eilola signaled Dorothy to stop by her tent and introduced a visitor. "I want you to meet Dorothy Sutherland, a war correspondent and the editor of the *RN Journal*. Miss Sutherland, this is Dorothy Woebbeking, one of our surgical nurses."

They exchanged greetings and Miss Sutherland pulled out a few pages of her work. "If you have a minute, would you mind looking this over? I wrote it while everything was fresh from the move you just made, but want to be sure I caught everything."

Lieutenant Eilola nodded. "I'll make sure somebody covers until you get to the surgery."

The article, in Miss Sutherland's handwriting, complete with cross-outs and erasures, started simply.

With the Seventh Army—France
Evacuation hospitals in France are moving.

They have to—fast—to keep up with the Seventh Army. The Eleventh Evac moved a 500–bed hospital in a jump of 140 miles from the Riviera to the Alps.

It was fast and beautiful.

The evac originally landed D-day. It moved directly inland to a field where paratroopers landed that morning. Patients were coming into the shock ward while the first tents were still being set up. They were paratroopers. Even more were Germans. The surprise airborne landings at Le Muy had captured two German field hospitals. For a while, the Eleventh had these around its wings, along with new Run casualties.

In one week, the hospital was already 140 miles behind the front.

It was no surprise to the commanding officer, Col. Charles F. Ward.

All night long, from the tents in nurses' row, we could hear the enlisted men pounding, packing, working.

By 6 the next morning the vast Armada of tents had disappeared. All that stood were the nurses' tents, a few of the doctors,' a couple of office tents, and a ward. Somehow in the miracle of packing, 500 patients were transported to evacuation points on the Gulf of San Tropes. Most of the trucks left that morning. They roared 140 miles by convoy into the Dauphine Alps. Our divisions were laying the trap for the now famous packet in the Drome and Rhone rivers. The Germans were fighting back. So again, while tents were going up, patients poured in. Men who had worked all the previous day and night, again worked through the night.

Back at the field where the nurses waited, a number of things were happening. Some like Lt. Diane Crosson, of Westchester, Pa, who had worked all night, were catching up on sleep. Pert Betty Cook, of Bryn Mawr, Pa, followed the average trend, washing and packing.

One girl, Lt. Dorothy Woebbeking, of Waterloo, IA, was fringing a red silk parachute scarf.

The bugle sounded at 5 a.m. the next morning. You ate breakfast a la mess kit, serving it yourself from the open kitchen. Then the last thing was packed.

The fields were quiet when they left. The hospital, like the army it followed, had vanished. The brief occupation of the Americans was already a memory to the villagers in the hills behind the Riviera.

"Any changes you'd suggest? Any errors?"

"Only one that I can see. I believe the word is Pocket, not Packet, ma'am. And one question: you're going to tell the whole world about my scarf?"

Miss Sutherland gave her a grin. "Why not? You were keeping yourself occupied—doing something constructive. Wish I could sew like you do."

"Mama gets the credit there, Ma'am."

Captain Siemon's forecast proved accurate—two weeks passed before things let up enough to pay Jeremy another visit. With nonstop surgeries for days in a row, broken limbs to set, abdominal wounds, and even brain surgeries back-to-back for hours on end, this was her first stretch of a few free hours.

More than ready to hear far-away voices from exotic locations, Dorothy hurried to the mail tent. From the depths, Jeremy's eyes glinted.

"What—something exciting?"

"In about ten minutes, there'll be a regular out of Germany."

While they waited, he told her how he'd learned to work his dad's ham radio and gotten hooked on the nightly process.

"Have you ever tuned in someone from back home—your dad, maybe?"

"Plenty of Americans, but not Daddy. Not yet, anyway. But that's part of the fun. You never know who you might hear—operators from all over the world listen in.

"Back home, something about sitting there in the dark with Daddy after everybody else went to bed—well, I can't explain it. He has a globe made by Cram, I think the company's called, with call letters from all around the world written on it. Before I left home, he made sure I wrote them all down."

"But how did you get this machine?"

Jeremy's grin hinted at intrigue. "Well, that's another story. Our quartermaster unit—they just lent a few of us out to the Eleventh, y'know and sometimes we really have to scramble to fill requisitions. The Army's like a giant snake—what you need may be stuck in a port or even still out on the Atlantic, way, way back at the tail."

"Mmm, makes sense."

"Works all right if that snake keeps movin', but that ain't always the case. Even if it stops, we know the docs need supplies, and quick. Some GI may need a certain medicine, and if we don't get it..." He flushed and looked away. "Anyway, this is pretty urgent stuff."

"It sure is. Without our supplies, we'd be hamstrung."

"During training, we practiced how to find stuff and the Sarge here has taught me a whole lot more. He took me along on midnight trips to other units in North Africa and Sicily. No place was too far if he thought they might have what we needed.

"We did the same thing up the boot and everywhere else. Sometimes, that's how we get battle info. Anyway, our job's about getting the word out, Sarge says. Let everybody know what you gotta have, then go find it. Best horse trader I ever saw."

He patted the radio's wooden case. "That's how I found my friend here."

"What did you trade for it?"

"Don't remember, but it was around that time we ran out of sheets. Maybe we traded—mmm, a jeep battery for sheets, but the battery was worth a lot more to the other guys, so they threw in the shortwave set."

"But where—"

"Oh, ma'am, I shouldn't be sayin'." Jeremy glanced over his shoulder. "But Cap'n Siemons trusts you. You promise to keep it quiet?"

"Cross my heart."

Jeremy slipped into a whisper, "A German unit left this behind, so the town mayor confiscated it and hid it in a back room of his office. When we drove in, he pointed us to the local doc, who had what we needed. Some of it, anyhow."

"What did they want in return?"

"That battery, cigarettes, rations, chocolate. They were starving—would've traded for black market if we'd had any. So we made a deal, but Sarge could see we were getting the raw end. He asked if they had a short wave, since I'd told him I'm an operator, and voila!"

The phrase seemed so out of place in Jeremy's lingo, Dorothy laughed.

"That's French, y'know."

"Yes. So the mayor spoke up then?"

"Yeah. That taught me to talk to locals, too, not just the town doctor. You just don't know what you'll find in any given place, or how much."

"Makes sense."

"Anyhow, we high-tailed it back to the hospital, delivered the meds, and took a truck back to the town to load up this baby." He patted the radio again.

"Where did you say this was?"

"I forget, but the doctor spoke French."

"In Morocco, then?"

"Maybe. I think so."

"Way back then? And there was a doctor?"

"Mmm... We've made so many deals I get them all mixed up."

"So you brought back the radio and hid it. How did you manage to get it to Sicily?"

"When Colonel Scott was around, mum was the word. But you do what you gotta do, right? The Cap'n was so excited to have a short wave, he found a way. I mean, when you girls need—mmm—certain stuff, you do the same thing, don't you?"

Did they ever. More than once, they'd run out of sanitary napkins, but she'd never disclose their remedies to a living soul, much less this kid. She could easily swap stories with him—sometimes you needed to see your boyfriend in Cairo, so you— But hopefully Jeremy hadn't heard about that.

"You're right, we always do." Dorothy pulled a chair up. "Okay, Jeremy—" She scrunched her nose at his puzzled look. "Sorry, I just can't call you Scab. You're far too good-looking."

That sent a flush over his face and multiplied the wrinkles on his forehead, so she added a little explanation.

"You remind me of my little brother—he's a medic here somewhere. Another brother's flying a plane for the Marines, and another one's busting tanks in the Pacific."

"So's mine. Signed up right after I did, got sent to the Pacific, and broke our Mama's heart."

"I understand that. Where are you from?"

"North Carolina, kinda in the sticks."

"In the mountains?"

"The foothills, not far west of a little place called Shelby."

"I'm from Iowa, plain old farmland." Dorothy rubbed her hands together. "Well, there's only one thing to do, right? Get this war over with."

His slow blink marked agreement, and just then, a voice came on *auf Deutsch*, but just as quickly became garbled.

"Rats—I was sure hopin'—"

"That's all right. I only have about an hour, so let's find another station."

"Can't promise, but I'll sure try, ma'am." He turned knobs and checked his list. Someone spoke in a Scandinavian language. The next station was in English, someone reading from a book.

Jeremy continued, and when a clear male voice rang out, he turned to Dorothy. "Hey, it's CBS. November 12th, that's today. This is Edward R. Murrow from London, I betcha."

"Really?"

Jeremy held up his forefinger and leaned in. "Too fuzzy tonight."

"Have you—do you recall ever hearing anything from Bremen, Germany?"

"That's way up north, ain't it?"

"Right. My mother still has family there. Back in '40, they sent us some leaflets the RAF dropped, warning them about the Nazis."

"Yeah, and then in June, they bombed the daylights out of them cities. Back then plenty of broadcasts came from there. 'Course, I couldn't understand most of it."

"But now?"

"Once in a while, something still comes through. The trouble is, I can only understand a little each time. Know anybody who speaks German?"

Thinking she'd be wiser to keep her mouth shut, Dorothy gave a half-hearted croak. "I do—but keep it to yourself."

He gave her the thumbs up sign, sat back in his chair and stared at her as if she'd pronounced the war over. "Wow! You and me can make beautiful music together now, Miss Dorothy."

Just like the last time, all of a sudden, Pinky appeared. The day before Hallowe'en when Dorothy emerged from surgery duty, there he stood. He caught her when she nearly fainted.

"Didn't mean to scare you. I caught a ride down here in a truck—"

"How long?"

"I've got a two-day leave—lucky me."

"And me. Tomorrow night we're having a Hallowe'en party."

They walked and talked for hours, and she stayed up sewing chaps and finagling makeshift cowboy hats, thanks to Jeremy's ingenuity—or his sergeant's. Strange, she still hadn't met him, but Jeremy said he left camp a lot and slept as much as possible when he came back.

The party, simple as it was, provided a few hours to laugh again. Pinky put on a cheery face, but looked awfully pale. Who knew how much he'd sacrificed to get here? Midway through the evening, he had to get back to his squadron, and was almost too exhausted to talk.

What Dorothy remembered were his final words when she walked him toward his ride—this time in an airplane. Rumbles to the east reminded her of the war they'd put aside for this evening, and she held his hand tighter.

"You Americans, making yourself a party out here in spite of all this." He waved his hand toward the rumbles. "I'll be seeing that little black cowboy hat on your head in my dreams now. Where did you get it?"

"A professional sleuth—a sergeant who deserves to be a procurement officer."

"Sometimes being enlisted gives you better cover than being an officer." Pinky brushed at bits of black silk clinging to him. "My flight suit may never be the same."

"It's only pin holes. They'll wash out."

His smile melted her heart. "Oh, Pinky, thank you for coming."

"And thank you for being here. Just think, if you hadn't joined the nurse corps, we would never have met each other." His sigh slipped away on an evening breeze. "The troops are pressing toward the Rhineland, so our next mission's—"

She could have finished for him—flying into the heart of Germany would be even more risky. But keeping positive meant everything.

"Maybe the next time we get together, the war will be over."

"Maybe." His voice came out husky, and the cloudy night emphasized the puffy skin under his eyes. "Yes."

He drew her close and his kiss smelled like the apple cider someone had managed to find for the party—probably Jeremy's sergeant. The promise in Pinky's embrace set Dorothy afire, and his eyes communicated what his words could not. But this was no time for spoken pledges.

As always, he vanished in silence, and so quickly she could hardly tell which way he went. Walking to her tent, the inevitable letdown came. But through her tears, she whispered thanks that he'd made the effort to come, and prayed again for his safety.

Chapter Twenty-five

A misty, early morning in late November, with clouds cloaking the sun. It might have been two o'clock rather than six. The fog had London so socked in that even the pavement below Rupert's feet hid.

All the way to the station, he ruminated over the note Chief Constable Derby sent yesterday. Over all these years, he could count summonses from the Chief on two fingers. Those meetings occurred so long ago he had forgotten the reason for them. The Chief's manner of operation had impressed him early on.

Each man in the force carried out his responsibilities, and in that sense, all the officers worked together. Camaraderie with other members worked out naturally, and at any given time over the years, Rupert maintained good rapport by taking each personality into account.

For example, he'd accepted that Officer Brannigan's penchant for being late was unalterable, and adjusted his expectations accordingly. At first, this habit troubled him more than he voiced. How could an officer fail to notice the time, especially when another waited for him?

But gradually, considering Brannigan's many other strengths, his lack of timeliness shriveled in importance. No need to label him, as did Officer Fletcher, selfish and unobservant of others' needs. Not at all the case—Brannigan simply had trouble saying goodbye to anyone he met.

Furthermore, no one boasted a more observant eye than Brannigan. Not even himself, Rupert admitted, though he constantly watched for things amiss in the quarter.

He had been the one to initiate the demise of Avery Ritter, 'twas true, but Brannigan could claim a far longer list of triumphs. He had been key in squelching the alarming affair on St. Peter Street—what a service to the community and the Crown!

Far beyond black marketeering, this involved leading the youth of Bethnal Green astray. To be sure, Rupert had noticed small gatherings of boys around a certain lounger in the vicinity of the candy shop, but felt no alarm.

Brannigan, though, had cozied up to those young fellows, kept a watchful ear, and uncovered a plot. The unscrupulous—nay, traitorous—nature of that older fellow led these young louts to avoid military service. Even thinking of such a venture brought a sour taste. Intent on nothing but lining his pockets, this deceiver convinced young gents approaching registration age of another channel to serve their country.

And what would that be? The boys never knew, for no other way existed—either you served in the forces or if deemed incapable, here at home. How down-in-the-mouth Junior had been when told he could not be a soldier—the difference was *HONOR*.

Towsley had expounded upon this just the other day. Five simple letters, but without this quality denoting integrity and patriotism, where would we all be?

In these street gatherings, Brannigan had smelled the opposite. When he brought his findings forward, the Chief took instant action. They had stalked this dishonorable sort until he had shown his hand. Soon, he found himself in bonds, awaiting a court hearing.

That was the last Rupert heard, but imagined that criminal executed by now, or imprisoned for life. And his following? All had been channeled into the military force.

Then there was the terrified fellow who went AWOL. Who had fished him out of the alleys? Officer Brannigan, but this time, he showed such obvious compassion, the soldier's commander gave the soldier another chance to serve.

A true expert, that was Brannigan. Late to a fault perhaps, but always about his business, cracking on, as Officer Young would say.

Seeing a light in the butcher shop but noting no copper smell in the air, Rupert proceeded around to the back. There ought to be some bloodletting by this time.

Covered by his grimy apron, a long knife in hand, Thackery met him. "Ho there, Officer. M' gout has me a bit behind this mornin', but I'm about it."

"Good. Just checking, sir."

"'preciate it, I do."

Back to the street, and to the note in his box announcing a brief meeting at ten. Hopefully nothing dire, though nearly everything fit that description lately. Daily V-2 launches that took out whole sections of blocks, debris teams beyond exhaustion, two fires breaking out hours after a strike, a crane crashing into an office building and injuring workers…

Ah well. For now, remember last night's report: French forces liberated Strasbourg, so close to the Rhine. In addition, American troops freed prisoners in a German concentration camp set up on French soil—the Natzweiler-Struthof camp.

The rabbi would have a word about that. Since he and so many other Green residents had escaped Russian pogroms, he kept his ear to the ground.

The news also reported that the Canadian government had now released 16,000 conscripts for overseas duty. Why wouldn't they, for Heaven's sake?

The commentator had gone into a rant. "What was this marching in the streets—these shouts of "Down With Conscription," and bedeviled Zombies deserting the ranks? Why should they not fight like so many other Canadians? Do these rebels not remember Dieppe?"

What could those chaps be thinking? Were they not Canadian citizens aligned with the Crown? And who were these so-called Zombies? Was not the United States deeply embroiled in the fight? Was this not a *world* war?

242

If Britain went down, so would the rest of them. What would have become of the free world had the British army's doom been sealed at Dunkirk? Without the Prime Minister, although imperfect, that surely would have been the case.

Adolph would have gained the upper hand early on. Free men everywhere would have trembled.

Rupert's heart raced. He checked his watch—just time enough for a spot of tea before meeting the Chief. Another note awaited him, and unfolding it in the break room, Rupert shook his head.

Officer Fletcher again—an observant fellow, but so weak in his communications.

"Heads up," neat handwriting read. "The citizenry seeks positive demeanor."

He included a notice from the *Gazette* concerning the need to keep a stiff upper lip, muddle through, and any number of other suitable phrases, as if the War Ministry's posters plastered everywhere were not up to their task. Down in the bowels of the W.M., someone had been given the task of printing up rousing posters, and the one they plastered all around the city during the Blitz had long ago done its duty:

YOUR COURAGE
YOUR CHEERFULNESS
YOUR RESOLUTION
WILL BRING US VICTORY

True, the Germans had not invaded the island, as many expected. But what if they had? Would any amount of courage, cheerfulness, or determination—the "stiff upper lip" British-born citizens supposedly possessed—have done much good?

Someone walked in. Rupert went on about heating the tea water, not even glancing up until he heard a rather loud, "Some blistering soul must think—"

Ah, Sergeant Young.

"Good day, Sergeant."

"What is this about?" The chap's face had turned peachy-red.

"Nothing of great concern. One of the officers considers it his duty to remind us of ours."

The nerve in the younger man's cheek still did a spritely dance, so Rupert offered more assurance. "The Chief has nothing to do with these notes. In fact, I would wager he received one himself."

"Chief Derby? So, someone thinks—"

"He knows better than the Chief Constable what we are about? Exactly."

"But no one can access this room except members of the force, correct?"

"Indeed—one of our own takes it upon himself to cheer us on."

"Cheer? I take this as the opposite. Perhaps he needs more assignments."

Mum always maintained that some things were better left unsaid, and her pronouncement instructed Rupert as he strained an extra cup of tea. What good could come of discussing Fletcher's nervous outlook? Instead, he held out a steaming cup.

"Here you go, Sergeant."

Towsley would remark on the humor inherent in this rookie's name. "And honestly—"

"Thank you, sir." Young's flush flamed brighter. "But I'll not be badgered. I do my work as well as—"

"As I witnessed on the night of our recent raid." Rupert sought how he might communicate his confidence in the new officer.

"Let us drink to the force!" When he lifted his cup, Sergeant Young hesitated, but then joined in the toast.

"And a fine force, at that."

But the sergeant's fingers trembled and Rupert looked away as his cup clattered against his saucer. This new officer had been wounded in the North African campaign. Who knew what memories lurked under his topcoat?

Downing his tea in a hurry, he gave Sergeant Young a nod. "A good day to you, then. I must be off."

No reply, but Rupert barely noticed as he approached whatever awaited him in the Chief's office.

"Hey, you got here just in time. I may have found Edward R. Murrow again."

"Oh, I hope you can keep him tuned in this time."

Jeremy held up his forefinger, so Dorothy sat back to wait. Sure enough, from across the Channel came a voice as American as a baseball game. Easy to lose oneself in Murrow's rich tones, but she had more interest in discovering facts.

November 12th, 1944

I shall try to say something about V-2, the German rockets that have fallen on several widely scattered points in England. The Germans, as usual, made the first announcement and used it to blanket the fact that Hitler failed to make his annual appearance at the Munich beer cellar. The German announcement was exaggerated and inaccurate in some details, but not in all. For some weeks those of us who had known what was happening had been referring to these explosions, clearly audible over a distance of 15 miles, as "those exploding gas mains." It is impossible to give you any reliable report on the accuracy of this weapon because we don't know what the Germans have been shooting at. They have scored some lucky and tragic hits, but as Mr. Churchill told the House of Commons, the scale and the effects of the attack have not hitherto been significant.

That is, of course, no guarantee that they will not become so. This weapon carries an explosive charge of approximately one ton. It arrives without warning of any kind. The sound of the explosion is not like the crump of the old-fashioned bomb, or the flat crack of the flying bomb; the sound is perhaps heavier and more menacing because it comes without warning. Most people who have experienced war have been saved repeatedly by either seeing or hearing; neither sense provides warning or protection against this new weapon.

These are days when a vivid imagination is a definite liability. There is nothing pleasant in contemplating the possibility, however remote, that a ton of high explosive may come through the roof with absolutely no warning of any kind. The penetration of these rockets is considerably greater than that of the flying bomb, but the lateral blast effect is less.

There are good reasons for believing that the Germans are developing a rocket which may contain as much as eight tons of explosives. That would be eight times the size of the present rocket, and, in the opinion of most people over here, definitely unpleasant. These rockets have not been arriving in any considerable quantity, and they have not noticeably affected the nerves or the determination of British civilians. But it would be a mistake to make light of this new form of bombardment. Its potentialities are largely unknown.

German science has again demonstrated a malignant ingenuity which is not likely to be forgotten when it comes time to establish controls over German scientific and industrial research. For the time being, those of you who may have family or friends in these "widely scattered spots in England" need not be greatly alarmed about the risks to which they are exposed.

"Well, I suppose that might make some American mothers sleep a little easier if they've got someone in London. Mr. Murrow is usually right. But still, I'd like to hear from some Londoners who've been hit by those V-2's, wouldn't you?"

"Sure would, ma'am. To tell y' the truth, anybody can be used to spread government propaganda these days. You've heard about the carrots, haven't you?"

"Carrots?"

"The British War Office put out the word that eating carrots increases a person's night vision. Captain Siemons says that's about as likely as Hitler surrendering tomorrow. The truth is the Ministry's blowin' smoke to cover the way their new range and direction finding invention hones in on German bombers. Pinpoints 'em so the anti-aircraft fellas like John Cunningham, an ace, can shoot 'em down."

"What do carrots have to do—"

"They've got the A-1 vitamin, see. And A-1 is short for the RAF's On board Airborne Interception Radar, too. So the Ministry put posters all over the place saying the A-1 in carrots helps their aces shoot down German planes. *Eat Carrots...they'll increase your night vision, just like our aces.*"

"Wow. You're like the Captain—you know a lot."

"Helps to listen to this baby so often." Jeremy tapped the radio. "But like my Daddy always says, we gotta take what we hear with a big grain of salt."

"Carrots—A1 and radar. That's pretty nifty."

"Yeah. The captain says, 'Leave it to the British to play with words.' But no matter what, ain't nobody with a smoother voice than Mr. Murrow."

Chapter Twenty-six

"Ah, Laudner. Do come in, old boy."

Old boy, was it? Rupert had noticed considerable hair loss on his head recently—not far off the mark there.

"Sit down. Sorry to take your time in the middle of the morning."

"I don't mind, sir. Gave me a chance for a cup of tea, which is always worth the while."

Behind the Chief's desk and on the west wall rose tall bookshelves. Lovely old cherry grain, aged rich, and mostly covered with dusty civil record books.

"Fine job on the Ritter case, Officer."

The compliment took him by surprise. "Why, we all worked on that, sir."

"Just so, but you stood at the helm." The Chief eyed him before drawing a protracted breath, and Rupert held his breath.

"We may—that is, I'm fairly certain—" Not like him to diggle-daggle around a point.

"I've a suspicion, not wholly backed up yet." Chief Derby drummed his fingers on the blackened edge of his desk, which, like his shelves, could use a good cleaning. "And so I called you in—you alone, you understand, since this may involve some of our own. You are aware that in soldiering on, as in the Great War, we may grow so exhausted that we tend to neglect—ah—common, everyday protocol?"

An uneasy niggling began under Rupert's last rib.

"Have you heard reports of unrest concerning the constabulary?"

"Unrest?"

"Then you have not. Good. After that officer being shot down in West Sussex a couple of years ago—"

Everyone knew about the tragic death of Officer William Avis, winner of the Distinguished Conduct Medal. His shooting took place in February of '42 in the West Sussex Constabulary. But what did that have to do with...

"And the Hyde Park incident in July of '40 with War Reserve Sergeant Avery, one cannot be too careful. The amalgamation of the police forces to the south has made me wonder how we might better coordinate our efforts within the city, especially considering the state of the docks."

Sergeant Avery's unfortunate stabbing death came at a homeless laborer's hands. The docks had always presented challenges, but what exactly could the Chief be getting at?

"Thus, I have decided to send you into the West End to represent our station at a meeting on Monday next, Laudner. I would go myself, but..."

"Whatever you wish, sir."

"Take this folder along, in case they ask for a list of our men."

"Certainly." As Rupert rose, the Chief Constable ran his hand through his hair stood, and rounded his desk. "We must trust each other in these dire times, righto?"

He held his hand up, signaling Rupert to remain. By now, they faced each other, and the Chief's worrisome squint set Rupert's mind racing. Perhaps he was suffering something personal?

"Is your family well, sir?"

"Thank you for asking. Yes, as far as one can tell with our two sons deployed. And now our youngest, Bonnie, has become a Wren. Gertie holds up as well as possible and takes her air raid warden duties as seriously as—" He caught himself. "And your family?"

"Doing well, sir. A new grandson has arrived in the midst of it all."

"Oh my, congratulations. A rigorous time, this. The news from overseas troubled me last night. Perhaps you missed it, being duty-bound in the evenings?"

Rupert pulled on his upper lip with his teeth—he must mean the BBC report he'd caught down at the air-raid station—the present Canadian conscription crisis.

"You refer to our western cousins?"

The Chief's forceful *Arghh* sufficed.

"I did hear that report, and mulled the situation on my way here, sir. Dreadful—unconscionable in such a time. Have those rebellious Canadians no idea how many of their forces perished at Dieppe?"

The Chief sputtered, "The very thing! With the entire world going up in smoke, I fail to conceive how they allow for purely political considerations. Dieppe, that nightmare, exactly so, Laudner. How could they possibly refuse to honor the sacrifice of their countrymen?" His voice rose with every sentence.

"I'm sure I don't know. Strange goings-on. All I can think is that I must keep my shoulder to the plow right here, sir. At times, though, the news seems nearly too much, especially after—"

"Yes." The Chief Constable voiced shared sentiments as though he could see into Rupert's mind. "The tube station. Such an utterly devastating travesty. How could such a thing possibly have happened, and on our watch? I fear we shall never live that down, should we attain to a hundred years."

So the colossal failure still riveted him, as well. Thinking it unwise until now to speak of the officially hushed circumstance, something in Rupert's chest crumbled as the Chief went on. Finally, someone risked saying what no one could.

His outburst over, the Chief leaned his hands on his desk and let his shoulders slump for a full minute, the wall clock marking time's passage. Finally he reclaimed his normal posture.

"Laudner, this talk has been much too long in coming. Perhaps I called you in because—because such things cannot be held in forever. I *knew* this burdened you, also, weighed you down more than some others."

"I cannot go an hour without seeing those poor—"

"Especially that one child. How could the crush have been so strong as to obliterate her completely?"

"You mean the little girl? The one whose shoes—"

The Chief nodded. "How could it be that only her shoes were recognizable for identification purposes?"

The fire behind Rupert's eyes nearly overwhelmed him, calling up the sickening taste that had plagued him for days after the event—that still kept him wide-eyed at night. The clock's regular ticking, at times unnerving, brought an odd comfort today. At least one thing remained stable.

"What bothers me most..."

"What is it, Laudner? Indeed, you witnessed the very—er—pile-up."

"Yes. But even worse—the survivors, sir. We have just relieved our minds by speaking of the horror, but they cannot. Must not."

Chief Derby shook his head. "I know. Unthinkable. I see them some of them on the street now and then. I cannot imagine." His groan burned the backs of Rupert's eyes.

"Even our Allied military leaders have noted this need in those who serve. They require some—some extra attention." He puffed his cheeks and blew out a stream of air. "Still, what are we to do?"

Another long, silent pause ensued, and Melvin Williams' face appeared before Rupert. *FORGIVE*. He shook away the image.

"Surely you noted that at long last, the Daily Herald has admitted the falsehood in the War Ministry's report of 'ruptured gas veins.'"

"Yes sir. Even though they still refer to the bombs as comets. Do they think ordinary folk fools, with these rockets leaving behind metal shards as long as three meters?"

The Chief caught Rupert's eye. "I do thank you for your fidelity through all of this. We have served together for so long—"

An idea flashed through Rupert's mind, wholly out of context.

"Sir, what would you think of— The thought just now occurred to me that with the holiday approaching, we as a force might help the Green make merry a bit. Might create something of a celebration for the families. We might invite all the children for a—"

The Chief's mouth dropped, as did his shoulders. "Why, what a capital idea, Laudner! Let us—" He stared at the clock. "Oh my, we have gone on far too long, but what say we put our minds to this very thing? Do take this in hand on my authority, my man. A bit of cheer would do us all good—a small way of showing our concern for the survivors."

With the Chief's crisp handshake and hearty pats on his shoulder, Rupert prepared to re-enter his world. But just as he started out, the Chief drew him back with a hand to his sleeve. In *sotto* voice, he asked, "Did you perchance receive one of those damnable notes in your box this morning?"

Hardly giving Rupert time to nod, he rushed on. "None of my doing, to be sure—you know as well as I who set them out. I must say, keeping Fletcher about his own business tries me to kingdom come."

"Mmm. Did I hear that his wife moved to—"

"Left him, that's what, and I cannot say I blame her. Imagine living with a sort like that. His overbearing ways would drive anyone to distraction."

Struck by yet another brilliant idea, Rupert plunged in. "Sir, what if you put Fletcher in charge of the Christmas party? Wouldn't all the details give him something to—"

The Chief struck his back with such force that Rupert nearly vaulted forward—not an easy blow to administer, considering their difference in height. Then he fairly bubbled over with enthusiasm.

"Another smashing idea. I say, Laudner, you must be due for a promotion. I shall get right on this, summon Fletcher this very day. Yes, I shall make a list of things to accomplish and present it to him. His kind likes nothing better than a list to be followed, eh?

Through the hallway back to his office, Rupert could not snuff out a grin. A Christmas party—indeed a capitol idea. Cecil and Iris, Madeleine, Grand, and Kathryn, too, would be delighted.

Securing his helmet, he advanced to his midday rounds. But as he did, an aggrieved countenance accompanied him. A countenance bereft, a man stunned by sorrow at the loss of his wife and youngest child.

"*Warnung* seems pretty clear. That means *warning*, right?"

"Yes." Dorothy giggled at Jeremy's pursed lips. Such an amiable young man, and not shy at all after several meetings.

"Remember those leaflets the RAF dropped on Bremen? I could never translate them, since except for *Warnung!*, they're written in Hebrew."

Jeremy's puzzled expression drove her to explain.

"We're Protestants, but my father kept abreast of what was happening as Hitler came to power. He especially worried about some actions of the police against the Jewish community.

"In some places, Jewish children already had to stitch a yellow star to their sleeves. That was one reason he sighed with relief when we came back to Iowa."

"You might've been stuck there."

"Yes, if we had stayed long enough. But we only lived there for nine months, because Mama's stepbrothers gave her trouble and she decided she wanted to live in the United States, after all."

Jeremy looked even more at a loss.

"She had a rough time adjusting to the States when they came over in '14 with my two older brothers and my sister. I was born in 1916 after we came back to Iowa, and my younger brothers came along in '22 and '24. But Mama had such trouble learning English, and my father saw how miserable she was.

"When he'd saved enough money, he booked passage for her and my brothers and sisters. It was all a surprise, but once we were in Germany—well, after some months—Mama changed her mind, so Papa saved enough to bring us all back. I still remember seeing the Statue of Liberty in New York Harbor when we returned—"

"You've crossed the ocean three times already?"

"But those two other times weren't anywhere near as scary as on the troop ship. No mines to watch out for back then."

The whole time, Jeremy kept tuning the radio. "Here. I just found something from Germany. Can you understand what they're saying?"

For a full minute they listened. "They're going to give American prisoners of war a chance to send messages to their families. Do you believe they really will?"

Jeremy's shrug answered for him, and he made some adjustments. Then someone spoke in English, giving his name, rank, serial number, and saying a short hello to his parents.

Jeremy scribbled it all down. Then another one gave his information, and another, followed by a German moderator explaining.

"So you see how we are treating these prisoners, according to the Geneva Convention. Christmas is coming soon, and to all these men's families, this is our gift."

Sitting here with Jeremy furiously writing notes seemed surreal. What if Ewald had been captured and his guards allowed him to speak over the air? What if someone heard this broadcast and wrote a letter to her parents to say they had heard him tonight?

A whole new world opened up, full of "What ifs." What if Delbert had been taken prisoner and someone tuned in at just the right time to hear him say he was still alive?

Millions of stars speckled the night sky. Somebody in an army tent in southeastern France could hear American GIs speaking from Germany. And that meant that someone in the States might hear the same voices.

Halfway to her tent, Dorothy turned and hurried back. Still hunched over the radio, Jeremy glanced up and stared at her as if he inhabited another planet.

"Jeremy—what if I wanted to send a message to Waterloo, Iowa?"

"Don't see why not, but somebody there would have to pick it up. Does anybody near your folks have a radio set?"

"Sure. My father's friend, and there must be quite a few more in town."

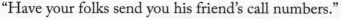

"Have your folks send you his friend's call numbers."

"Do you have orders to listen for anything about a pilot?"

"That I couldn't say, ma'am. Some orders are top secret."

"I mean a certain American pilot. His name is Delbert. I was there when the Captain said he'd see what he could find out about him."

"In that case, yes. But nothin's come across about him yet."

Back at the tent, Millie was in a dither. "Hank came by with Eric. He's acting really strange, and she's beside herself."

"What do you mean by *strange*?"

"He keeps falling over when he tries to walk. Hank wouldn't even put him down. She's afraid he's had a stroke."

"Whoo boy, just what she needs. But doesn't that sound like something vestibular? Was he tilting his head or walking in circles?"

"No, but like I said, Hank won't let him out of her arms."

"Did she say whether he's vomited?"

Millie shook her head. "I hailed one of the docs to look at the little sweetie, but had to get back to my shift before he made a diagnosis. Now I can't find either of them anywhere."

"I have 15 minutes before duty. I'll see if I can scare them up."

Since Wally and Hank had become a permanent item, it made sense to start at the mess. Sure enough, there sat Hank stroking Eric's trembling body, with Wally down on one knee beside them. Hank's tear-stained cheeks glowed in a single hanging light bulb's glare.

Dorothy stalled in the doorway, thinking she looked almost radiant, but what Wally said stopped her cold.

"Honey, I'm so sorry—I know Eric's been with you from day one. You don't think that doc could be wrong, do you?"

"He knows his stuff. If he said there's nothing we can do, that's that. I'm enough of a realist to know—"

"But docs can make mistakes."

"Not with a heart that's racing as fast as Eric's. All we can do is keep him warm and stay with him. At least it shouldn't take long."

Dorothy backed out of the tent and smacked into someone. Turning around, she realized it was Jeremy, and drew him a distance away.

"What's wrong?"

"It's Eric. He might be dying."

"What happened?"

"I don't know, but maybe you can offer some comfort. I need to get to my shift."

Jeremy pressed his lips together. "I said goodbye to my Buster before I left. Had him since before I was born, so he probably won't make it 'til I get home."

"Mmm. You're just the guy Wally and Hank need."

The docs tackled the worst cases right away and whittled down those needing less surgery to just four. Meanwhile, corpsmen moved several of yesterday's cases to the recovery tent.

Dorothy came on duty at the same time as a fresh doc. "Looks like we might have a slow night?"

He glanced around the surgery. "Right now, but an ambulance and a truck have been stuck up in the hills somewhere. The Fourth Armored under Major General John Woods is hurting Jerry a lot right now. Someone said the Germans call the Fourth 'Roosevelt's Butchers,' and our own men call them 'Patton's Best.' I'm not sure what happened with these vehicles, but we just had word that they're on their way down. Should be here within the hour, so might get pretty busy."

"That's all right, I'm ready."

"You always are."

"That's why I'm here."

She kept Eric's condition to herself. Seemed crazy that one little dog's suffering would affect her so, with human beings fighting for their lives and so many dying every day. But that precocious little mutt's suffering broke her heart.

During their training, Hank had found Eric in an alley, a mere puppy whining for his mother's milk. Against all odds, Lieutenant

GAIL KITTLESON

Eilola allowed her to keep him, and eventually dubbed him their mascot. She won everyone's loyalty when she let Hank bring him on the transatlantic voyage.

He'd been with them through so much, and no matter how bleak things became, he still brought joy. No one in the unit had anything but a pat or a kind word for him.

While she helped the doc wash up for surgery, the thought of Hank holding Eric kept troubling Dorothy. She'd be inconsolable. Good thing she had Wally now.

Chapter Twenty-seven

Urgent events after his meeting with the Chief Constable gave Rupert little leisure to reflect on their discussion. A German V-2 rocket struck the intersection of High Holborn and Chancery La Bane in Holborn, killing six people and wounding almost 300.

The Chief Constable sent three younger officers and two police vehicles to lend aid, so everyone else on the force took on extra work. Rupert had followed this extended beat in his earlier years, and found it pleasant to renew old acquaintances.

At the same time, the extent of the bomb damage in this part of the Green struck him anew. Back in his home area, he'd gotten used to gaping holes in row houses and cratered streets—interesting how destruction wormed its way into your existence and became the norm.

Not long after the Holborn hit, in the most disastrous attack thus far, another V-2 landed across from the Woolworth's department store in New Cross Road, Deptford, South London. South of Bethnal Green about five miles, the New Cross bombing caused such rage, Rupert could feel its palpable essence as an ambulance delivered him and other emergency workers to the scene.

How could anyone begin to describe this disaster? The mild weather and the Allied push towards Berlin had put people in good spirits, and Woolworth's recent receipt of a shipment of new tin saucepans had figured in the outcome. With pans so scarce these days, they'd declared a sale. Nearly 150 of the saucepans, word had it, so the public had a good chance of purchasing one. Thus, a long queue formed—mums, grannies, and also some soldiers.

On this busiest of days, Woolworth's called in all their full time workers, including a group of Saturday boys and girls who welcomed the opportunity to increase their regular earnings. Besides the crowd of shoppers, noontime saw manual workers collecting their week's wages from the Deptford Town Hall directly opposite the store.

Of course, many of them decided to shop now rather than return later.

When the second break for Woolworth's workers began, a new group of staff headed upstairs for a cooked lunch. The Woolies Tea bar offered hot Bovril to sip, so the New Cross Station Southern Railway cleaners hurried to Woolies to eat their noonday meal, as well.

At 12:26, a V-2 rocket, the 251st to land in England, hit the rear of Woolworth's flat roof. Residents told Rupert they experienced a moment of silence before the walls bowed. Then the building collapsed and exploded, creating a massive inferno that incinerated even the Royal Arsenal Co-operative Society store next door.

Bystanders recalled another queue waiting for a tram out in the street. The conflagration engulfed the tram and the entire queue.

Half a mile away, the ambulance driver said he must stop, since shattered glass filled the street. At New Cross Station, Rupert emerged with the others to make his way onward through ankle-deep glass. The crunching beneath his boots gave him pause—so much like his sensation in the volunteer fire station bombing, yet at that time, he could hear nothing.

When his contingent arrived at the scene, emergency workers and locals were already lifting heavy beams and cement blocks from the rubble. They hoped to find someone—anyone—still alive.

In addition to memories from the fire station bombing, the taste of the tube station tragedy filled Rupert's throat. Willing these vestiges away, he plunged in to do what he could. Not that lifting and shoving obstacles to make way for those with machines would do much—even those machines could not alter what lay under this wreckage. Nothing could.

At one point, Rupert clawed toward a snatch of rose fabric, perhaps the dress of a mum who came for a saucepan, or a young female worker delighted with this extra day to earn a bit more money. A girl like Anna.

Less than an hour ago, such excitement had filled this place. Looking forward to Christmas, when perhaps their lad would return on a short leave, customers gathered in anticipation. With a new saucepan, they would cook up something special despite the rationing.

The fabric in his hand, though shredded and burned, represented a blouse or scarf, clothing bought or carefully stitched by hand, and bespoke its wearer's taste for the bright and beautiful. The scrap floated from his fingers into this vast sea of rubble as he stared into the distance.

Not far away, Vicar Towsley bent to offer someone aid, and from another direction, Chief Constable Derby gave instructions. He's missed those morning times with the vicar of late, and must again make them a priority.

In this sea of sorrow, each worker kept to himself. Looking into another's eyes would be too much to ask.

Hours later, when they had done all they could to rescue survivors before the cranes rolled in, a local debris supervisor reported that to date, this attack had killed over a 150 people. And the injured? No accurate accounting as yet.

Dazed by the body count that doubtless would rise, Rupert crunched toward the police wagon and accompanied the other officers back to the station. Everyone rode mute with shock, although shock had become normal. For Rupert, the same thing happened during the Great War.

At some point, after so many merciless struggles with the enemy in the trenches, he succumbed to numbness. How could one compare one battle with another? Back then, he had no idea of the casualties, but would those figures have made a difference? From siege to siege, battle to battle, he set one foot in front of the other like an automaton.

So it was presently. Except for one battle he'd been putting off far too long. Since she had not come forward on her own initiative, how might he speak with her? How did one express disappointment—yes, even fury—while love for her still filled his heart?

With heavy feet, he trod home, dropping by the fire station, rehabilitated two blocks from its former location. The warden in charge sent him home. With each step, he determined to discuss Anna with Madeleine. Tonight.

At the fire station, the warden had eyed him with consternation. "We shall find a replacement for you tomorrow night, as well, officer. A person can manage only so much in this increasing cold weather without developing a fever. Clearly, you would benefit from some time off."

Why argue? Two nights at home. Lovely. But on this one, he dreaded what he must do.

As soon as Cecil and Iris had been tucked in, he sat near Madeleine. She gave her fingers a different occupation this evening—knitting. The *click* of her needles vied with the *tick tock* of the hallway clock.

"I saw the vicar this morning. He seemed quite well."

"Good—we had no opportunity to speak today." No need to tell her how ensconced Towsley had been in the attack's grisly aftermath.

"It must have been horrendous for him today, and for you."

So, she had heard, or read his mind.

"A perfect choice of words, my dear." Rupert leaned his head back against the back of the armchair that fit him to a T. "I say, I have been meaning to ask you about Anna. I have seen her so rarely since her tooth extraction—"

"Of course. Both of you are quite busy on your own accounts. But I keep up with her."

Relief surged through his chest. "Good—that pleases me no end. These are such hard times for young women." He must go a step further, but how to formulate the question? Finally he blurted, "Junior has spoken with me about some concerns—"

Her slow blink revealed that she knew more than he, as often happened. So Junior had gone to her, after all—or perhaps Anna had confided. His own fault, for putting this off so long.

"Yes?"

"Our Anna has learned a harsh lesson in recent weeks. Perhaps you noticed the signs, as I did."

"Signs?"

Madeleine's sigh struck him like a loud wind. What had he missed?

"She appeared even more weary than normal, and she'd foregone eating breakfast for a while. There were other—" Not even the minutest lag in Madeleine's attack on some dark blue yarn. "—symptoms."

Gulping down a vast swatch of fear, Rupert's voice issued scratchy. "Symptoms?"

"At times I forget you're a man." She gave him a forlorn smile. "Symptoms of being with child."

He choked on his reply, then let it dissipate completely. So it was true. A vice ringed his chest.

"But this has now passed."

"P—passed?"

"Yes, but not before Anna confided her situation."

"Her sit—"

Foregoing her knitting, Madeleine grasped his hands. "Anna has been seeing a Canadian soldier for some time, it seems. As things often go these days, she—she gave in to her desires. For a time, Rupert, she was expecting a baby."

"For a—"

"Yes. Anna miscarried last Sunday."

A whirlwind tore through his head. Last Sunday? He made an attempt to remember. Yes, Madeleine had seemed preoccupied after church. On the way home, she'd had no comments on the Vicar's sermon, not his best ever.

After dinner, he thought she looked pale, and offered to take the

GAIL KITTLESON

children to a park. She accepted without argument and insisted on packing the three of them a picnic. Thus, he had not seen her again until early evening.

And then, another V-2 attack called him out. Arriving home quite late, he tiptoed to bed, with Madeleine fast asleep. Or so he thought.

His head swam with what had occurred right here under his roof. "She—here?"

"I did fetch the nurse, since…" Madeleine bit her lip. "It seemed wise to make sure all was well."

"Well?" He wanted to shout, "How can all be well when she has—" But the softness in his wife's eyes halted the explosion. Her mix of apology and tenderness—what was he to do with it?

"I never intended to deceive you, but things have been so—disrupted, especially since your injury. And then that attack after you brought the children home. I could see how these new horrid bombs were affecting you, and decided Anna and I could work this out."

"Mmm." He strengthened his grip on her hands. "And the soldier. What of him?"

"He vowed to stand by her. They planned to marry. Now, I believe Anna will give their plans more thought."

"Did you—meet him?"

"No. She wants us both to meet him at once. I…" Madeleine tossed her head. "Bugger this hateful war! We had to let her go far too young. Things would be so different, if only she could have—"

In silence, Rupert finished her sentence. —maintained a normal young woman's life. If only Hitler had died of influenza a decade ago, or stepped on a rusty nail far from medical help, or if only someone else had risen to power in Germany, someone with a heart—a soul.

"I hope you—" Madeleine's forehead erupted in furrows.

Could she possibly think he would be upset with her? Oh, some men might claim she had usurped his rightful place as head of this

263

household. But what constituted his rightful place? Did he not need every conceivable aid in carrying out his duties?

After all that had happened this past year, and Madeleine's devotion to this family, to Anna—to him, how could he find fault?

What if Anna's child, however conceived, had not been lost? Would the doctor have suggested Anna live in South London at a home for unwed mums and their babies established by the evangelical Mission of Hope? A foundling home? Or perhaps Mr. and Mrs. Harwood would have welcomed her?

Or would Madeleine insist on Anna living at home, regardless of the stares she would endure? In fact, he could not imagine her sending Anna away, no matter how difficult things became—no matter the effect on Cecil and Iris, yes, and Junior and Kathryn's sons.

Those images of walking Anna down the church aisle in white— he had said goodbye to them right off. He had also neglected to speak with Vicar Towsley about this.

Dear Anna. His little girl. These days, far too many of his friends and neighbors faced this situation, bugger the influx of foreign troops. Such goings-on—dances for the soldiers, movies for the soldiers—everything focused on *their* needs.

But were the daughters of the Green still not as precious as ever?

Since Junior had alerted him, he'd held back, all the while lamenting his cowardice. Not long ago, he witnessed a father down the street pack his expectant daughter's things in a brown paper parcel, call her a disgrace, and send her away. The pain of that parting stayed with him.

"Right is right." The father muttered this as his daughter tearfully made her way down the street. When it came to it, Rupert feared being too harsh with Anna. Along with that, a sense of things being far, far out of his control descended.

But now, things had turned out far better than his bumbling attempts might have. He would never know, for the problem vanished without him lifting a hand. He gave himself no pardon for his inaction, but at the same time, accepted this new reality.

As for Anna—what ought he to say to her? When he saw her next, she would know that Madeleine had told him. Why, he would walk that path when necessary.

Across the two feet separating them, Rupert gently pulled Madeleine from her chair, and she sank against him with a heartfelt sigh. Her head lay flux with his heartbeat, her body wrapped in his arms. Washed in Sunshine soap, the warm scent of her hair wafted, and her closeness filled his senses.

His whisper floated over the crown of her head and echoed back. "Thank you, my love."

Chapter Twenty-eight

"Load 'em up." How many times had that order rung out since North Africa? Dorothy threw her backpack over a tailgate and scampered in, with Hank close behind. And Eric. Somehow, the little dog experienced a miraculous healing—nobody could explain it. In the aftermath, Hank's eyes had softened even more.

So weary that even the uncomfortable steel truck bed felt welcoming, Dorothy closed her eyes right away. Why stare out at what the enemy did to landscapes when they retreated? She'd seen more than plenty. Besides, the surrounding chatter would describe everything, anyway.

"Wow, look at that. The Huns left nothing behind this time."

"Yeah—generous as usual. Hey! Look at that overturned tank. I suppose they checked to make sure—"

"Of course they did, but wouldn't it be something if a Jerry popped out?"

"If I had all the money these wrecked vehicles were worth, I'd—"

"What would you do?"

"Bribe Bing Crosby for a date."

"He's married with children, you know."

"Well, so is Douglas Fairbanks, Junior, and Dorothy still— Hey, Webbie! Tell us again about your night out, will you? I bet you left a lot out."

With the truck engine roaring and bolts scraping against their fittings, it was easy to pretend deep sleep. Besides, everyone expected this of her. It wasn't long until the steady roar and the movement secured her that blessed state.

A dream took her back to last summer with this same bunch of nurses, but on the wharf in Bizerte, Tunisia. Colonel Scott was briefing them on the Allied strategy to take Sicily.

"As you know, our troops captured the island of Pantelleria on June 11th, after severe bombing by our air and naval forces. Allied naval parties took other islands, including Linosa on June 13th and 14th, preparing the way for our joint Allied assault in which British and Canadian troops will join our men. We have every reason to expect success. Now load up the LCI."

Short for Landing Craft Infantry, and manufactured for the Navy, the LCI differed little from an Army LST. With waves splashing up over the side, Dorothy tried going down below. But with 40 infantrymen, four medical officers, and 40 nurses on board, the heat became so intense that she soon sought fresh air on deck.

What a relief from such close quarters, with each passenger carrying their duffel, a backpack, canteen, and bedroll. Cramped soldiers had no place to put their guns, so their rifle butts jammed into hips without mercy. And to make matters worse, some of their comments threatened to get under Dorothy's skin.

"What're these nurses doin' here? Isn't this an attack?"

"Dunno. Makes no sense to me, either."

"Nice to know we'll have first-aid when the shooting starts."

The nurses certainly hadn't begged to come along—orders were orders. For a while she bit her tongue, but eventually, she knew she would let loose. Months in North Africa had taught her that.

The lowness of the ship allowed her to dangle her feet over the side as it plowed toward Sicily—what a marvelous cooling effect! But when the spray started to soak her, she explored the gun turret and found it a perfect place for protection. She crawled in, and after a while, fell asleep.

Wild yells and *pings* against the steel LCI awakened her. What was going on? Before she could look over the side, something hit her in the ribs. Someone's boot. A soldier had jumped right on top of her.

Wide-eyed, he hollered, "What the—?" She rolled to the edge. "Get outta here! Gotta return fire."

Heart pounding, Dorothy grabbed her helmet. *Pwapp-pwap-pwap*. She skittered across the wet floor as the gunner peppered the beach with shells. Her breath came hard as she crawled below. Lieutenant Eilola pushed toward her through the mass of nurses and corpsmen.

At that point in the dream, or nightmare, Dorothy realized her eyes were still closed, but try as she might, they refused to open. Someone clamped firm fingers around her shoulder and shook her.

"Webbie. Moonbeam! Wake up. You're dreaming again."

Forcing her eyes open, she looked into Hank's long, calm face. "Let me guess. Dreaming about the Sicily landing again?"

"Yeah."

"How many times are you going to fall asleep in that gun turret?"

"Who knows? I can't seem to stop."

"A moment to remember, for sure." Hank's sarcasm could have sliced a cement block. "Cotton-pickin' Colonel Scott—I really think he was trying to get us killed."

Somebody else dove in. "Me too. He always wanted to get rid of us."

"Amazing we survived, but at least the army finally got the picture and replaced him. Thank heavens for those engineers on the beach. Remember how their eyes popped? If they hadn't seen us, we'd have been goners."

Someone else chuckled. "Never was so glad to see soldiers in my life. And I never saw anybody run so fast. They had us in their trucks in seconds, and the wheels sprayed sand like 60. If they hadn't loaded us up and dug foxholes for us, who knows what might have happened?"

"*Who knows* is right. At least the Sicilians let us glean from their gardens when things calmed down, or we'd have starved."

Hank harrumphed. "Which brings us back to Colonel Scott—when he realized that, he took our food away. What a jerk!"

"That was low of him. But didn't Rig say he got sent to the Pentagon to recruit nurses?"

"Ha! How ironic is *that*?"

As usual, Millie summarized the discussion. "After what he put us through, and Anzio, what do we have to fear?"

"At least Colonel Tabor was fair. And smart, since they transferred him to Seventh Army Headquarters."

"Colonel Ward keeps things moving as smoothly as possible, considering the circumstances."

A nurse named Loretta touched a ring on a chain around her neck. "Through it all, I've still got my lucky charm. It's been with me all the way from Montana." Her fiancé hadn't written for so long, Dorothy felt sorry for her. Hopefully his next letter wouldn't be a "dear Jane."

That reminded her of Pinky's long silence, even though the mail caught up with them three times in France so far. The thought of never hearing from him again gave her a chill. Folded into her duffel bag with Mama's hankie, his last note carried a faint reminder of the sparkle in his eyes.

If he were American, she could ask Elfrieda to contact his parents, but Scotland—What could a person do?

Wait, that's all.

But then, one simple phrase went through her mind. *Short wave.* Why not ask Jeremy to broadcast Pinky's name and his county? What could that hurt?

Pinching herself to keep down her excitement, she tucked away the idea. In the meantime, she'd been receiving as many letters at mail call as anyone else. Her family and Paul wrote faithfully, and a couple of her girlfriends from nursing school. Best of all, on the last delivery, a package came from Mama, with four balls of Red Cross yarn.

Hopefully, Papa would pack more of his specialties to arrive around Christmas. Her stomach growled just thinking about the last one. Small joys meant a lot right now, and picturing him laboring over his delectable creations spread warmth through her, even in this chilly truck box.

Rumors of a real live building for the Eleventh swirled as the truck came to a halt. Dorothy was first to jump into a paved driveway.

"Here we are, folks." A corpsman started pulling boxes from a truck. "Might as well start carrying stuff in."

In? The nurses looked around in wonder. A huge lawn spread to their left, and on the right stood a massive stone building with a sign engraved above the door: *L'hopital Psiquiátrico.*

Hank hooted, "A French psychiatric hospital—I knew we'd end up in one sooner or later. Just what we need. Maybe Colonel Scott passed this way."

"Any old building would do right now." Wally hurried by with a huge load of boxes. "Maybe I'll have a real kitchen now! Come on girls, roll up your flaps and grab your stuff."

Any other time, Dorothy might have reacted, but not today. Instead, she simply stared at the building. Sleeping inside again, no longer fighting to keep the patients warm and dry—the concept seemed too good to be true. No more battling mosquitoes and flies, no more latrines. The truth was almost too much to absorb.

Whoever built this place believed in plenty of stone stairways, outside and in, and whoever had just vacated left things relatively clean. A stream of excited nurses led Dorothy to the third floor and turned left down a long hallway.

Someone cried. "We've finally got a home."

Finding a bed—who cared which one—Dorothy dropped her heavy load. A bed with a mattress. Sheets and a pillow. White. Clean with the scent of soap. Solid wood flooring underfoot, and nearby, a chest of drawers. Windows a few feet away, and doors— she got up and danced around, slid a couple of the drawers in and out, fell back on the bed.

"Come on, Moonbeam. It's really true—unpack your duffel."
Hank, noticing her trancelike state, felt compelled to give orders.
"On second thought, watch Eric while I find the bathroom."

Sequestering Eric in a corner of her bed, Dorothy unlatched her
pack. A bathroom—they could wash everything, wash themselves.

In a bathtub!

She hardly dared say the word until Sharon shrieked, "Come
in here, y'all. It's a *tub*! A great big ol' bathtub. The French may
not believe in normal toilets, but have we ever got ourselves a tub!"

When everybody else had taken a look, Dorothy touched the
cool porcelain and smoothed her fingers over the iron faucets. How
could one object make such a difference? Even a single bath in this
beautiful creation would be nothing short of heavenly.

Considering what hot running water would mean to the hospital
operation almost brought tears. This was a time for the hankie
Mama gave her—actually, Grandma had hand stitched and embroidered it years ago in Germany. No irony there.

This white porcelain felt so smooth. Maybe they could stay here
through Christmas. Wouldn't that be something? Unless it meant
more suffering for the troops, she hoped the Eleventh wouldn't
have to move again for a long, long time.

A few nights later, with the hospital all set up on one floor, Hank
swept into the nurses' area with her hands behind her back. With a
silly grin, she looked back and forth between Dorothy and Millie,
who had just settled the final bobby pin into her curls.

"I know I look pretty scary. Don't worry, everything'll be normal
by morning."

"I wasn't thinking about that. I've got a surprise for you both.
Come close. You can smell it." Mischief laced her invitation. "Hurry
up—it's still warm."

One whiff was all it took... "Fresh bread?"

"Yeah. Dripping with butter."

"Oh wow. This reminds me of—"

"We know. Your dad's bakery."

With her mouth full, Dorothy burbled, "This is delish. Sure am glad you've gotten so friendly with the cook."

Hank squinted at her, but failed to hide a grin. "Tonight he let me help with measuring. Never made a bread recipe for a hundred people before. Fifteen pounds of flour, a pound of sugar, seven mess spoons of salt. Poor guy—still has three more batches to make before morning."

"After this long on field rations, all I can say is, 'Don't stop.'"

"You said it. Gotta take advantage of *fresh*. On my way over here, some guys were following their noses to the kitchen, too. It's gonna be tough not to gain weight here, since the smells will drift right up the stairs."

Hank plunked down on Millie's bed. "Right now, Wally's really browned off about one of the MPs. Boy, did he let loose.

"I was thumbing through the *Baking Manual for the Army Cook* when he started letting off steam. Ten minutes later, he'd turned the air blue, and I still didn't know which MP he meant."

"He's got kind of an isolated job. I've never thought about it."

"Yeah, he catches two naps a day, a long one after he's finished cleaning up after supper and a shorter one after breakfast. That alone would make me cranky, not to mention all the bubble dancing he has to do."

"You're really starting to sound like a soldier. Bubble dancing, huh? Who ever dreamed up that phrase for washing pots and pans?" Hank's cheeks reddened at Millie's good-natured ribbing "Are you sure you're not spending too much time around the kitchen? What do you think, Moonbeam?"

But Dorothy's mind had already slipped back onto its favorite track. Tonight, Jeremy agreed to send out a short wave message requesting information about Pinky—and one for Delbert, too. The mailroom, set up on the top floor, made the perfect spot for good reception. Hope—that described the state of things right now.

"Our officers share hearty Christmas wishes to you for a most—. er—pleasant holiday." Sergeant Fletcher cleared his throat. "And to that end, our Chief Constable has allotted funding for the goodies of which you will now partake, and our American friends have extended their generosity, as well."

Along one side of a long table, Iris squeezed next to Cecil, all agog at the festive scene. Seeing their eyes alight gave Rupert's heart a turn. In a moment, Iris would be Anna's age, and Cecil, Junior's—best take advantage of these youthful years.

Fletcher had arranged three tables in the station's basement, normally a repository for ancient records and equipment. Officers rarely came down here unless the Chief sent them on a search. But now, the gloom had turned into a cheerful space, thanks to Fletcher's exertions. He'd even spent evenings whitewashing the walls, and had decorated the tables with long streamers.

"Now for some cake and chocolate cream. Enjoy every single morsel." A cheer went up from the crowd, and Fletcher's stiff posture loosened a tinge. He raised his voice again. "Hear me, children—later, you shall have more beside."

"Smashing idea, this." The Chief elbowed Rupert in the ribs. "And it was all yours. If Fletcher keeps on this way, he may even smile before day's end. Such a splendid day for the children. Jolly good idea, old chap."

After a moment he added, "It has been weeks since Fletcher has bothered any of the officers."

"Indeed?"

"Indeed. What a relief this has been for the force, Laudner."

"I couldn't be more pleased, sir. Would you like me to think up more community tasks for him?"

The Chief chuckled, and Rupert took a deep breath. How wonderful to witness this gathering, much like the outdoor parties the women of the Green set up for him and his playmates in days long past. Peaceful days.

Mothers looked a bit less weary as they helped their children to the cake, baked by a church ladies' auxiliary as a fundraiser for the war effort. Hearing their exclamations over the gifts provided warmed the heart.

"Take special care with this new cap, dear. Winter will only get colder," coaxed a mother at the nearest table. "And I wouldn't doubt we'll find some mittens here, too—without holes, at that." Her cheery glance fell upon Rupert and the Chief, and she stepped over.

"Seems awfully good, sir, to have the—well, you know—so far behind us. Was it your idea to invite the children here? Rumor had it that the party might be held in the school?"

"Mmm—we considered that, madame, but decided it would be safer down here. Those V-2s have hit more than one school in the last weeks." The Chief surveyed the room.

"Laudner, we had best greet them all. I can hardly wait to see their reaction to what happens next."

He proceeded to the far table, where he stooped to whisper in children's ears. Rupert said to himself, "Drumming up excitement, he is. A good example, so I shall do my part."

In the doorway with his arms akimbo, Fletcher beamed. Had his face ever borne such a look? Not that Rupert recalled, especially with so much loss of late.

The latest report sickened him—deaths from this so-called Baby Blitz had climbed over 10,000. Hard to accept, yet the figures could not lie.

These mums and children roused such tenderness, especially in light of all who had perished in the attacks and on the tube station stairs. Little girls and boys trusting they were on their way to safety—they ought to be here today. Glancing around the room, it was clear that each family had lost someone, if not a blood relative, then a neighbor or friend.

Moving through the rows, Rupert maintained a smile, and when he passed by Madeleine, she whispered. "Fine work, love. This day is making the children so happy—they will never forget it."

Her understanding meant the world. She also shared his

disappointment at having to write the Harwoods that they'd be making no excursion north during the holidays. With the V-2s added to continuing V-1 attacks, leaving his post was out of the question.

Once, the fleeting idea of sending Madeleine, Gran, and the children off to the countryside had occurred, but how could he ever forgive himself if something went wrong on the trip north? A V-2 might hit a train as well as any other object, and the Germans seemed bent on sending them far and wide.

His injuries and recovery had taught him he could control nothing, but still, a man must make an effort.

Touching youngsters' heads scrubbed recently with Sunshine soap, soft hair carefully picked through for lice, Rupert's heart filled, in spite of everything. How he wished Vicar Towsley had been able to attend, but he'd been called home—something about an ailing relative, someone said.

In fact, the vicar had confided that his mother was dying. Towsley had been approached about playing Father Christmas today, and had accepted, but with a finger poised in the air. "Unless Mum takes a turn for the worse and I must go to sort things, I shall be on hand. Best to find a back-up, though."

That had not been easy, so Fletcher doled the task to Rupert. "You might do it yourself, old boy, except with your height, we could never find a costume to fit."

Beset with a cold and sniffles that day, Fletcher had looked so miserable that Rupert agreed to find Father Christmas for him. He also supplied Fletcher a bottle of Madeleine's honey and lemon syrup.

Finding Father Christmas—several brainstorms passed through his mind, but none met with a *yes*. Finally, Madeleine proposed what became the solution. One of the GIs brought his uniform to her repeatedly, and she discovered that he worked in administration. Clearly, his adequate diet kept his buttons popping.

Stories circulated that the Americans enjoyed better rations than the British boys. Not to mention the parties for the flyboys when they returned from bombarding German cities—that is, if they made it back. It took only a few tales of British girls being driven in American jeeps to these festivities to turn his stomach.

On the other hand—always an *other hand*—what would the Empire have done if the Americans had not entered the war? Awfully late, to be sure, but their involvement was absolutely essential, so Rupert refused to join in conversations blighting the Yankees for their uppity ways.

Yes, they acted like they owned the Isles, dated British girls and committed all manner of other offenses. If Anna were to take up with one of them— He pushed the thought aside—no use borrowing trouble.

So many ironies to hold in balance. But in the end, Madeleine's customer used his connections with a procurement officer who produced a velvety red suit. At about the same time, the rather ample figure of a grocer with access to richer food than the rest of the populace came to mind.

He agreed to play the part for the party, and that was that. Fletcher's shocked look had been worth a great deal, and Rupert had to admit, he rubbed it in a bit.

"Did you think I would fail? Ah, Fletcher, you must believe!"

Thus, American ingenuity fused with a Londoner's need. This was the way of war. Rupert reached the final table and his ponderings came to an abrupt halt as a horn sounded.

Surely not today—an air raid?

No, that would be Fletcher's foghorn, alerting the children to look his way. Chins scrubbed of cake and cream, they all startled at the blaring noise, and one girl younger than Iris burst into tears. Heaven knew, these precious little ones needed no more upsetting signals. But that was Fletcher, and nothing to do about it.

"Now, children, we have a very special surprise—something we've not seen in the Green for some time. If you all gather 'round me here." He continued with precise instructions, but before he finished, the older boys, including Cecil, broke out like rats scurrying through tunnels, and of course, everyone else followed.

Fletcher, besieged by the young mob, forewent his horn and gestured helplessly at the other officers. Thank goodness he hadn't brought his whistle.

Helped by the mums, Rupert and the others restored calm within the ranks, so Fletcher could make his announcement. He went to pick up his horn again, but the Chief held down his arm and whispered something.

"So then. The time has come for—" Fletcher took out his watch. "Ah, yes, 'tis time to listen very carefully."

Just as he uttered the final syllable, something sounded outside, a rumbling of wheels on cobblestone. The children aimed their sights for the windows, where a big U.S. Army truck lurched to a stop. The side door opened with a cranky screech.

Boots pounded the stairs, and escorted by Officer Young, someone rather rotund, dressed in red velvet with white trim, entered the room. Fletcher kept his head and stepped aside.

A few steps farther, this rendition of Father Christmas set down a large bag. He swished his fake white beard and gestured someone forward. No less than three young American privates came forth, dragging more large khaki bags with bulges at every angle.

A hush fell over the children of the Green.

"Ho, ho ho!" The soldier in red puffed like a storm, and universal delight broke out. Unfettered joy—he must call it that, for Towsley would—entered into Rupert as well, and in the ensuing few minutes, even into Fletcher.

No matter how heavy your load, to see children's eyes sparkle at the simple gifts handed out—oh my. Fletcher's tight jaw dropped a little and warmed Rupert's heart.

He breathed a thank-you for the Americans, for this bounty clearly extended far beyond the station's paltry funds. Balls and tops and dollies, miniature pocketknives, paper cutout kits, and books, sweaters and apples—for heaven's sake—apples!

Indeed, the Americans somehow supplied a luscious red specimen for each child, along with hankies and hard candy and chocolates. And all of this not just for the children, but their mums as well.

No matter their "step-right-in-and-take-over" attitudes, these blokes had come to England's aid. Thank God they had, or what would have become of this isle? Now, the young GIs' eyes glittered with excitement, too. Perhaps some of them had left little ones at home, from whom they would be separated for who knew how long?

When the festivities wound down and the Americans prepared to leave, Rupert shook hands with each of them, and Madeleine greeted them, too. Then she shocked Rupert to his toes.

"I'm sure you will be missing your families on Christmas Eve. Would you like to spend the evening with us?"

Heat fired his neck and he stood there dumbfounded at her proposal. But then he could scarcely gather in his breath, for all of the Americans accepted. Blimey!

Madeleine gave him a knowing look—she was reading his mind again. Where on earth would they scrounge enough to feed three grown men?

But he could read her mind as well. Calm and collected, she was thinking, "We shall find enough somewhere. All will be well."

The War Ministry ought to place his wife's serene face on a poster beside each of those instructing the populace to "Keep Calm and Carry On."

Chapter Twenty-nine

As the last of the children and their mums passed through the police station doors toward home, reminders of the war troubled Rupert. What a dastardly holiday this would be in the Hurtgen Forest.

In those dark, forbidding woods, the battle had begun in September and raged on in winter's bitter cold. Those poor soldiers out there fought the elements as well as Adolph—the thought made him sick at his stomach. With each news report, all promise of the war ending this year joined so many others from the War Ministry, and even from General Eisenhower himself.

A cry from Iris shook Rupert back to the moment where mums and children frolicked at the same time as this gruesome war. Iris gave him that look that called him from whatever else that might engage him.

"Da!" His daughter's excited cry saved him from memory's pit—from falling back to that other war. Without doubt, he had survived by sheer mercy.

Iris clung to his knee and Cecil to his waist. "Da, look, look! See what Father Christmas brought. Thank you, thank you." Cecil held an apple, a new sweater, and a set of coloring pencils. Iris cradled a store-bought baby doll complete with a bright yellow blanket and matching hat.

Invigorated, Madeleine accompanied the two youngsters. A simple celebration, but worth every effort. Around them, the Green itself seemed somehow brighter this afternoon.

Soon they would honor their own quiet Christmas traditions. Last year, they'd retreated to the Anderson shelter for a good share of the day, as Adolph made their holiday a cozy one.

No tree again this year, but he and Madeleine would take Iris and Cecil on a walk one day soon to view the one erected in the tube station. There, children from families without an Anderson shelter—many with no home at all—would share cakes and goodies to honor the birth of this world's Savior.

Oh, the irony of that phrase. Without the Vicar, Rupert could scarcely consider its context. No, this was no time for pondering. At such a time, one carried out traditions regardless of the mire riding one's soul.

On their visit to the tube station last winter, Cecil had spied a schoolmate and begged to stay. His plaintive request still rang.

"Why can't we live down here, too?" Madeleine tried to explain, but Rupert forsook all attempts. Some things, a youngster like Cecil would not understand until much later.

Tears swelled behind his eyes as he paused just outside the door. Oh that his children might grow to embrace Truth and goodness. Seeing them lead the way brought Anna to mind. Last night, she'd been waiting up for him when he came home from his volunteer duties.

Sitting there at the kitchen table, a book in hand—*Jane Eyre*, to be exact—she attended his return. Minutes before he caught sight of her, he'd been dragging his weary body home, longing for the relief of sleep.

But seeing Anna, all else flitted away. Nothing mattered but his firstborn daughter, clever and lovely, the pride of her teachers, and long the joy of this family.

The years paraded before him—Anna at her birth, pink and chubby in a miniature cap and sweater knitted by Gran. Anna as a two-year-old cherub, dimpled and delightful, Anna with her hand tightly in Junior's, headed off for her first day of school, Anna parading with the dolly carriage he'd made her for Christmas.

The retinue might have continued, but for the very real 19-year-old young woman before him.

"Da…" Anna's voice broke, along with any resolve Rupert had made. Before he could gather appropriate words, she fell against him. "I—I never meant to…"

Rupert could only envelope her against his damp wool coat. Anna's sniffling and the hurt in her eyes undid him.

What had she expected him to say? He could barely imagine, for his emotions overcame all rationality.

This afternoon in such jovial company, figments of their conversation had returned, but last night, snuffles, trembling lips, sighs and tortured looks inundated their words. One sensation remained quite vivid; Anna so near—the trust in her eyes.

Yes, and the strength in her voice when she vowed to be more circumspect, and named the father of her child—Marcus. His unit had now crossed the Channel to slug its way into enemy territory. When he returned—if he did—they would rethink their so-called "stepping out."

He must have responded in an appropriate way, because she thanked him and kissed his forehead before retiring. How long had he lingered afterward, bewitched by her essence?

Now, at the close of this festive day, sweet Iris had touched his cheek in much the same way as Anna. He gave her another hug, and then Cecil broke out, trembling with excitement.

"Soldiers are coming for Christmas, Iris, did you hear?"

Oh, the energy of this lad! With a satisfied smile, Madeleine set them on the course for home. Just then, someone poked Rupert on the shoulder.

Fletcher, in need of human connection. "What do you think? The affair went jolly well?"

"Oh, indeed—you have done yourself proud."

Fletcher looked almost happy, but for the perennial downturn of his lips. Yet his eyes exhibited a new fierceness.

The Chief Constable approached and thumped him on the back.

"Good work, Fletcher. Absolutely capitol!" Fletcher beamed, if only for a moment, and started to clean up.

How alone that poor man must be, how terribly echoing his flat, how devoid of warmth and cheer, for he and his wife had never been blessed with children. And now, she had left him. Perhaps he ought to invite him over on Christmas as well.

He shook himself as the Chief turned to him. Oh, my goodness, no—three American soldiers would be quite enough. They'd be stretched accommodating them. Against his better judgment, Rupert might add. But Madeleine had her heart set on welcoming the strangers.

"No room in the inn—" Rupert determined to comply with her wishes, though his heart went cold at the thought of Anna helping Madeleine serve those brash fellows. Perhaps he might— No, no. Cecil would never let him hear the end of a turn-about.

"What a day this has been, Laudner. I hear 'twas your wife who linked us to the Americans. My, my, what generosity they showed—perhaps they possess some redeeming qualities, after all."

"Mmm. Quite."

Snow-laden pine branches dipped into three-feet-high drifts as truck drivers rubbed their gloved hands between runs. Through a partially frosted window, Dorothy viewed a pile of litters awaiting transport in the hospital yard, and closer, several corpsmen hurrying up the sidewalk.

After 12 hours of surgeries, she dropped into a chair and sipped hot coffee. Where would they be without this wonderful black liquid? Nearby, two off-duty doctors discussed life on this December 21st, 1944.

"Still in our fancy hotel—Luneville, France and it's almost 1945. Never dreamed we'd still be at this."

"We could be out in a field hospital, trying to make things work in this cold."

"I can't imagine. Guess I really believed the predictions that this would all be over by Christmas." The speaker held up a cinnamon-sprinkled donut. "But I have to give it to Wally—how does he manage to bake stuff this good?"

The other doc threw up his hands. "Like those Red Cross girls with their traveling donut-mobiles, I guess. Saw one of them the other day when I went to—"

"Yeah." Obviously, he'd rather not hear details about trips to the front to haul in the wounded. So many medics had perished in the line of duty that some doctors volunteered to help during their down time.

Oh, Ewald, do be careful. Keep your head down, little brother.

"It's hellacious out there, but there's a little mobile canteen with two bright-eyed young women, one from Indiana, one from Pennsylvania. Talk about courage. They're parked way closer to the fighting than I'd want my daughter or my wife."

"No kidding? Out in this winter weather?"

"Absolutely, and I had a chance to speak with one of them. She was frying donuts by the dozen—should've asked how they keep supplied with ingredients."

"Who knows?"

"That would be a good motto for this whole confounded war right now. Who knows? What will we do when a certain medicine runs out, why hasn't the mail caught up with us, and what is keeping that last shipment of wool socks ordered months ago?"

The doc rubbed his forehead. "But mostly, will this new Ardennes offensive work better than the one in that treacherous Hurtgen Forest?"

"An awful place to launch an attack, yet they say it was the only way to get to Aachen. I sure am tired of hearing about the Siegfried Line."

"So many casualties this late in the fighting. After the reports we heard about Normandy, I thought things would slow down."

"Underestimating the enemy's resolve seems as epidemic as trench foot."

283

Silently, Dorothy concurred. If there were one thing she could do to change things, she'd get better clothing for the troops, extra sweaters, earmuffs, scarves, and especially socks.

The wool socks that could have prevented this awful outbreak must be stalled somewhere—if only those in power could see the misery she saw daily. Trench foot had run rampant, and kept so many men from their posts.

She wanted to march into some General's office and scream, "Where are those socks?" She and Millie knitted as many as they could, and had recruited several other nurses to help. Mama and Elfrieda sent yarn and their own finished pairs, but it all amounted to a mere drop in a massive empty bucket.

"Hey, there. I thought I'd find you here." Millie pulled up a chair. "You'll never guess what Lieutenant Eilola told me."

"The war's over?"

"No, silly. A Big Shot is coming. Her name's Lieutenant Colonel Florence Blanchfield from Washington, D.C. She's flying in to inspect us. Lieutenant Eilola told me you and I are in charge of making sure she has special food while she's here."

"Wow—what does she mean by special?"

"Maybe we could dredge up a little more meat and—I don't know, maybe some dessert and wine?"

"Right. I know exactly who to ask."

"I figured. So that's all taken care of. Glad we're not in charge of her accommodations—some of the girls are busy decking out a private room for her."

"I'd far rather work on the food. Don't know how I'd come up with any more parachute silk around this place."

"Now that you mention it, that might work for the tablecloth and napkins."

"Hmm. Let me put my thinking cap on."

"Great—when you start thinking, I know something good's going to happen."

Millie started away, but something in her voice was off. Dorothy caught her hand. "What's up, Mil?" That touch was all it took. Her face crumbled.

"Oh, Moonbeam—"

"Here, sit down. I'll get you some coffee."

Finally, Millie allowed some tears to flow. In fits and starts, her message came through—Loretta's boyfriend hadn't sent her a dear Jane letter, he had died.

"He'd been wounded and was recovering, they thought, but—"

Dorothy handed her hankie over, and Millie made good use of it. "If he can die in a hospital back in the States where they can really care for him, then Del—"

Patting her back was all Dorothy could think to do.

"The thing is, I've been—" Millie started over. "You know that feeling I had that Del is still alive?"

Dorothy nodded, dreading what was coming.

"It's gone, Dorothy." Fresh tears broke out, and the two of them sat staring through the frost at all the activity out in the yard.

Two days before Colonel Blanchfield arrived, Jeremy said he and his sergeant would be gone for the night—something to do with the upcoming visit. With so many surgeries, Dorothy had no time to help with the table, but several nurses jumped at the chance. What a *happening* this would be!

On the big day, Dorothy checked in the kitchen, and Wally gave her a pleased smile. "Too bad the guys out in the foxholes can't enjoy what Jeremy found. You won't believe it, but he brought in a goose. Don't ask me how—he wasn't sayin'. I'm about to butcher the old girl. Goose ala orange sauce, coming up."

"And this cake's for the Colonel, too?"

"Yeah. I'm gonna slice it and put whipped cream between the layers."

"You're outdoing yourself. I feel like I'm back home in my father's bakery. Thanks so much."

"Hey. Hank told me to hustle. When she commands, I obey." He made a formal bow, difficult with a dripping spatula in his hand.

A few hours later, the red carpet treatment went into high gear, and that evening the nurses sat listening to Colonel Blanchfield. Even Hank lent her full attention.

"I'm pleased to view your facility here, and commend you for your labors. But I must say, you all look a bit tawdry. I expected uniforms and caps in good order, at least." She tightened her lips.

"I hate to say it, but I'm a bit ashamed. Most of you have not even cleaned your shoes properly, and some of them have not been polished in weeks. I expected better of nurses with such a long record of service."

Hank's cheeks appeared even more sunken than normal—she was biting the insides of her mouth to maintain control. She'd worked all night, and now this? She had every reason to lash out at this high and mighty fool. A retort sat on the edge of Dorothy's tongue, too, but she saved her fury for later, up in the nurses' quarters, where they would tear this pompous desk-sitter limb from limb.

"In addition, not one of you is wearing a tie. I find it difficult to believe you have let yourselves go, and this distresses me."

When Lieutenant Eilola dismissed them, Hank stormed behind Dorothy. "To hell with her! How dare she—"

"Shhh."

"Why're we going to the kitchen?"

"To change the menu for tomorrow. Pronto."

The sparks in Hank's eyes agreed, and she managed to contain herself while Dorothy spoke with Wally.

"You know that goose Jeremy found? Can you save it for after the Colonel leaves?"

"I—sure, if you want me to."

"I do. Make something so everybody gets at least a little bit. And the cake, too. This old bat doesn't deserve all we've done for her—let her eat exactly what we do every day. We'll eat all that great food tomorrow night for supper."

Wally was looking at Hank, not her. What was going on here? "What did she say to you?"

Hank dove in. "I wouldn't waste my breath repeating it. She can eat worms, for all I care. I regret every minute I spent helping clean her room. I might even sneak in and put snakes in her bed." She turned to Dorothy. "Think Jeremy could round some up?"

"It's possible—he can do almost anything. Anyway, we're *not* treating her like royalty any more."

Hank almost spat her clincher. "And that's *that*!"

Wally gave her a salute. From the corner of her eye, Dorothy thought she noticed a wink pass between the two of them. But what mattered now was undoing all the preparations they'd been making for tomorrow's noon meal honoring the Colonel.

That hard-earned tablecloth would make a hankie for every nurse here—yes, for Christmas presents. And why not take someone else's place in the recovery ward during the meal tomorrow? Instead of scrambling to finish hemming the cloth, Dorothy checked the schedule and offered to take Sharon's place. Then she settled in for a much-needed nap.

The next day, seeing Hank on duty too brought a smile. They'd have to be careful not to talk—the patients didn't need to hear them grousing about the Colonel. Ah, well. Soon, she'd be gone.

Hank did whisper an aside when she brushed against Dorothy. "You know, I think I'd like the Army, if it weren't for big-shot officers who think they're so brilliant but have no idea what they're doing."

"My sentiments exactly."

A little later, Jeremy signaled to Dorothy from the entrance. Things were quiet, so she stepped out for a moment.

"What's up?"

"The Captain says to let you know he'll be gone for a couple of days." When she nodded, he asked, "What happened with the Colonel?"

"Let's just say she showed us what she really thinks of us, and it's not much."

"Why that—" Jeremy huffed out his next statement. "If she had half a brain, she'd realize the work you nurses have done for this outfit. Think of all the men you've saved."

"Yeah. Well, good riddance to her. Thanks for the great food you found for us. We're going to have a fabulous feast tonight after she's gone. "

"Good. The goose was, umm, an interesting find, and she don't deserve what it took to get it. But you do."

"I'll be done in ten more minutes, if you can wait for me."

"Sure thing."

True to his word, Jeremy loitered outside the room when Dorothy walked out, and they talked some more.

"Been thinking about that cotton-pickin' colonel. Somebody oughta tell her all you girls been through."

"She must've made no effort to find out, but I imagine Lieutenant Eilola has filled her in. Hopefully we'll never run into her again."

"I got a peek at her. Reminds me of a pet peacock we had once. A fox got into our coop one night, and the peacock barely got away with his life. Lost a big chunk of his tail feathers, though, but when mating time came, he still strutted around big as you please. But the womenfolk realized he had a whole lot less to offer than he realized. Just like that ol' battle-axe."

"Jeremy, thanks. You're a true friend."

"Hey, got somethin' in on the radio last night from New York, a guy listening on the 41 and 49 meter band. Somebody chimed in from Iowa, a place called Dubuque. Have you been there?"

"Sure. It's not that far from Waterloo."

"So people there are listening in, even though it's banned."

"They're breaking the law?"

"Looks like it. But my Daddy wrote that some lady in, I think it's Ohio. She's organizin' folks to let people know when they hear somethin' from Axis Sally or Lord He Haw about their kin in German prisons."

"Lord He Haw?"

"Don't know how that fella got his name, but he's a traitor. Betcha he'll hang when this is all over." He looked at his watch. "Gotta get back—might be missin' somethin' good."

"All right. I'm going to sleep better, just thinking about that peacock of yours."

The huge onslaught of casualties continued right through Christmas. Finally, they had a spot for a tree, but who had time to find one? Besides, thinking of home might not be a good thing in the midst of all this misery.

On Christmas Eve, though, a surprise waited when Dorothy left the operating room. In the foyer near the building's entrance, a small pine complete with twinkling lights graced a corner. The sight nearly brought her to tears and she sank into a chair. Somebody bustled around, fiddling with the pail of sand holding the tree.

Finally a figure stepped out of the shadows. Jeremy—no surprise. As soon as he spied Dorothy, he grinned, but then he sobered. "Whoa, you look way too tired."

"You found us a tree—and lights. How did you—"

"Sarge here's a genius. You never know where he'll come up with things."

Behind him, some scraping and grunting ensued, but only the sergeant's boots showed as he finished whatever he was doing and faded back into the shadows. Typical—he rarely appeared in the mess, where people got to know each other, or anywhere else. No one had any clue how much he'd accomplished for the cause.

Jeremy wound a few more lights around the top of the tree and picked up a small wooden crate of tools. "Come and see me when you get time."

She had no energy to answer. The way casualties were mounting, she might never enjoy another evening glued to the shortwave.

But staring at the scraggly little pine gave her pause, and a sense of wonder stole in. Such a seemingly insignificant object, yet it took her back to childhood Christmas Eves that Mama made memorable. Real candles on a tree hewn by Papa only hours before, and always a practical gift for her and everyone else—new ice skates if they'd outgrown their old ones, sturdy boots, a book, or school supplies.

Footsteps from the hallway marked a man's approach. Before he spoke a word, Rig's spearmint breath gave him away. He stopped nearby.

"Pretty awful day, huh? You look as though you could hardly stand up straight."

"You've got that right."

He shook his head. "They came up with a tree—how about that?" His eyes glinted. "Three Christmases away from home is three too many.

"My wife says my daughter's wrapper chain reaches around the tree six times now, top to bottom. Too bad she had to start with the Orbit brand last summer, but I've still got quite a stash of spearmint she sent me.

"Guess the company lost their source of one ingredient, and instead of lowering the quality of his gum, Mr. Wrigley decided to create a new one. That's what'll be available until after the war."

"What's your little girl's name?"

"Rosanna." His voice grew heavy. "We never expected this to last so long, but the way it looks right now—"

His pause suggested she might not want to hear what he'd learned on his private grapevine.

"Don't you hate thinking about what our patients have gone through?"

"That's an understatement. Even knowing the Army, I can hardly believe it. Bastogne, the 101st Airborne jumped in wearing their summer uniforms."

"Yeah, some of them have made it here. The frostbite cases make me sick."

"The command made transporting fuel and ammunition the priority, but that means no coats or winter boots are to be had. So those guys tramp through slush and mud by day and ice by night.

Can't even light fires to keep warm, with the Fifth Panzers so close.

"Every time I shave, I think how impossible it is for them to even wash their faces. Even if they have a change of socks in their pack, think what an effort it would be to untie their boots and make the switch." His groan spoke for them both.

"It's such a shame the Hurtgen Forest was the only direct way to get to the Rur Dam. At first, this front was all about preventing Jerry from reinforcing their troops at Aachen, but we also wanted control of the dam.

"Of course, the generals wrangled again, so we started out in the dead of winter, and with too few men."

"So here we are." Dorothy leaned back against the wall. The high ceilings seemed to tower as far away as victory. "And we lost 22 good young men in the surgery today."

"Mmm. But how many did you save?"

"All I can see is the ones gone from this world."

"Think about those who made it through surgery—they'd have died otherwise. Wound after wound, you're tending them, doing your best. They'll live through the night because of you and the docs."

Too weary to push back the cries of the wounded, the blood, and the helpless feeling when some died waiting in line, Dorothy allowed them to crowd in. Always, that one set of crystal blue eyes from way back in North Africa, that fellow who'd lost everything but his head and torso, haunted her.

"You have to look at it this way, because—"

"—if we didn't, we'd all give up right now."

"Exactly. Even guys like me who only deliver the mail have to believe we're making a difference."

Make a difference. Yes, that's all she'd ever wanted to do. The last light of day filtered through a tall window to their left, and Rig's quiet breathing brought a sense of calm. In spite of everything, gratitude claimed her heart.

So far, her brothers were all still safe. Her last letter from Elfrieda included one from Vernon—amazingly, the censors let a little logistical info slip through.

Moving again. Heat oppressive. Crossed 180th meridian at 1 a.m. Task forces contacted enemy somewhere around Salmon Islands, two aircraft carriers and oil tanker. Will be glad for earth beneath my feet again, not meant to be a sailor. Even in a tank, you can see land.

So he was on the move too. A sudden recollection of a younger Vernon bent over a ship's railing rose, and Dorothy debated—that was on the second trip to Germany, but was it going or coming back? The figment was too vague for her to decide, but seeing her big brother retching had scared her. Anyway, it was good to read words in Vernon's own handwriting.

With Millie and Hank, Rig and Abner, plus so many others who really cared, however long this war took would be manageable. Sometimes surgery seemed like a forced assembly line, but just today she'd watched a surgeon rumple a sedated GI's hair after amputating his foot.

"Awful surgery, but I'm pretty sure he's gonna make it."

Rig meandered over to the tree. When he returned to sit opposite her, he dropped his head into his hands.

"What is it? Bad news from home?"

"Just more of the war. My wife—"

Maybe finally, he would say what she did for the war effort.

"It's terrible, what she has to do. She works at the Army Effects Bureau in Kansas City, on the tenth floor, where they send all the deceased soldiers' effects. They hired her as one of the first employees in '42 when the office opened. Now, they've had to expand to over a thousand workers."

The tree lights outlined his profile as he stared off into the distance. "There's no end to it—the stuff comes from all over; here, the Pacific—thousands of shipments every month. Workers go though it all piece by piece. They read each letter, study each picture."

Dorothy's gulp sounded loud in the silence. How many people even knew about this sort of work going on?

"Betty supervises a room full of workers, each at their station

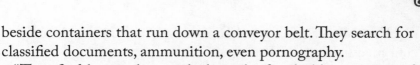

beside containers that run down a conveyor belt. They search for classified documents, ammunition, even pornography.

"They find letters that might hurt the family, like a picture of another woman, or correspondence with a married soldier who picked up a girlfriend overseas. Before they send the effects to his next of kin, they remove anything that would cause more pain. They're supposed to think like the soldier—what would he want his family to see?"

"Oh man." Half a world away, stuck in a building all day long, these people dealt with this grim task.

"They use grinding stones and dentist's drills to clean up blood from helmets and gear, and scrub stains out of uniforms. In another room, typists write letters to the family, to find out where they should send the possessions."

"I knew somebody had to do this, but—" The clock ticked away a full minute.

"And then today I heard how many of our guys were taken prisoner a couple days ago—thousands of them. This whole war makes me sick to my stomach."

Finally, Rig got to his feet. "Sorry. Didn't mean to—"

"It's all right."

"We'll make it through, I know we will. We just have to keep putting one foot in front of the other."

"Yes."

As his footsteps echoed up the stairway, Dorothy focused on the tree again. She might have sat there all night, thinking about all those soldiers in enemy hands. It seemed incredible that so far, Vernon, Albert, and Ewald were all still alive and free—but what had they endured in this horrible fight?

Some time later, Hank swept in. "Well, lookee there, a Christmas tree." She strode over. "You look way beyond beat, Moonbeam. Come one, let's get you up to bed."

On Christmas Day, the Colonel posted a note in the mess.

"A few days ago, General Eisenhower said this in his order to our men fighting for Bastogne:

"By rushing out from his fixed defenses the enemy may give us the chance to turn his great gamble into his worst defeat. So I call upon every man, of all the Allies, to rise now to new heights of courage ... with unshakable faith in the cause for which we fight, we will, with God's help, go forward to our greatest victory."

"These are our orders, as well. I am happy to report that the weather finally cleared enough for our Air Force to attack German positions on the 23rd—cause for rejoicing, since it also allowed for reinforcements and supplies to reach our trapped troops.

"And for those of you unable to hear President Roosevelt's Christmas Eve address, we have typed it here in part.

"It is not easy to say, 'Merry Christmas,' to you, my fellow Americans, in this time of destructive war ... *We will celebrate this Christmas Day in our traditional American way ... because the teachings of Christ are fundamental in our lives ... the story of the coming of the immortal Prince of Peace.*

"Rather than issue a hollow, "Merry Christmas," let me say that your efforts on behalf of our brave men in uniform do not go unnoticed. Strength to each one of you.

In the midst of today's nightmarish influx of wounded, somehow the Colonel made sure that everyone at least tasted the dinner Wally and his men worked so hard to prepare. When Dorothy's turn came, she stood in line reading the Colonel's note and wishing for even the shortest possible chapel service to mark the holiday.

But the chaplains were all out with the troops, where they should be. Her thoughts centered on her brothers. Was Vernon still aboard ship, or on some other Pacific island by now? Was Albert dropping bombs on Japanese defenses? And Ewald, out in the bitter cold aiding GIs somewhere in the Bulge—would he eat at all today?

"Merry Christmas, Ewald. Stay safe, and the same to you, Vernon and Albert. Maybe next year we'll all be together again, back in Waterloo."

Chapter Thirty

After the horrific Christmas bombing of Manchester and other northern industrial cities, January weather came in like a lamb. The second week brought cold, sleet, and snow. Last night freezing fog and wind gusts of 60 knots assaulted the island.

On the 21st, Rupert flipped up his collar as he trudged home. What exactly did *freezing fog* mean? If the stuff touched you, did you develop a slippery sheen?

In spite of the weather, the glow of Christmastide stayed with him longer than normal. His family had done right by those American soldiers, nor could he fault the soldiers. Not at all, especially considering their beleaguered colleagues holed up in the Bulge. No Brit could deny their fortitude in standing up to Adolph's blighted hoards.

How could so many Germans have amassed with such fierce resistance? If only the world could go back to Versailles—yes, he believed, along with Towsley, that a bit of kindness back then might have changed the state of nations today.

Ah, but one only saw such things in hindsight. At least, the Americans finally took Bastogne, and were making great strides toward final victory. One sign in particular heartened the people of Bethnal Green—on January 15th, for the first time in five years, commercial shipping resumed in the Channel.

But back to the Americans. What a surprise when one of them knocked on the door the evening before the holiday, bearing two large feathery chickens. Madeleine actually shrieked and the children came running.

295

Rupert rose from his chair in time to see the young fellow blush. "My mother's family still lives north of London. I went to see them today and told them about your invitation. My uncle insisted on sending these for our dinner—he chopped off their heads only two hours ago."

Madeleine's thanks was lost as Rupert shook the soldier's hand and ascertained details about his uncle. When the young fellow left, wonder laced Madeleine's voice.

"How long has it been since I cooked a chicken? How shall we—" The fowl, now at rest on the table, tantalized Rupert even in their undressed condition, while Cecil stood awestruck. For once, Iris took the lead and began to stroke the soft breasts.

"I do hope I can do them justice. I put in an order at the butcher's, but had no idea what would come forth."

"Righto. Do them justice? So you shall, my dear. Now then, Cecil, let us tackle the plucking out in the garden—we've only a short time before the service at church."

The best of it was witnessing Cecil's boundless delight. Later, his gleeful chortles replayed in Rupert's head as he lay in bed. Madeleine's sighs matched his own—what generous provision!

The next morning when Cecil spied the chickens in Madeleine's roaster, stuffed and prepared for baking, he simply could not contain his delight.

"How long will they take to bake, Mum?" His questions continued until Rupert took him outdoors to hunt down wayward feathers before their guests arrived.

Later, one of the GIs presented Cecil a jackknife, not to mention a box of fudge sent from his family in faraway Oklahoma. The friendly American pulled out a notebook and drew a map of the United States. He explained where his state lay on the map, west of the Mississippi and north of the Gulf of Mexico.

Of course, Cecil's interest lay with the fudge. "Could I eat some right now, Mum?"

Madeleine indulged him, and soon he and Iris had sticky brown goo running down their chins. Apart from one of the Americans entrenched with Anna in a corner, involved in a deep discussion, the day left nothing to be desired. And Junior had seen to the situation with Anna by joining in on their conversation.

Hopefully by next Christmas, all the foreigners would be back in their homes. That would still be preferable, gifts and luscious chickens notwithstanding.

But when one of their guests pulled out a mouth organ and launched into "Hark the Herald Angels Sing," and "God Rest Ye Merry, Gentlemen," how could he restrain himself from joining in with Madeleine and the others? One of the GIs boasted such a lovely tenor—how could Rupert not admit that some of these fellows' parents had reared them honorably, after all.

As of today, the BBC broke the spell that had lingered from that lovely day. The foreign service reported so much negativity on several fronts that Rupert left the break room. Better the drudgery of reports than being peppered by that string of disheartening events.

Who wanted to hear about Operation Nordwind in northern Alsace, on the west bank of the upper Rhine? During the Great War, Rupert had had Alsace and Lorraine up to his hairline. Everyone knew how badly France, having lost this area to Germany in the Franco-Prussian War forty-some years earlier, coveted the territory.

Their obsession formed a study in revenge as the French spent more than a year back and forth along the border to win their objective. The Germans would win, the French would soon defeat them in another battle. Then the Germans would recover what they'd lost, somewhat like a game of badminton. Except thousands perished in these attempts.

All of those deaths over a few yards of real estate. Although those in the know declared the present push against the Allies to be Adolph's final major air offensive in the West, how could they know whether or not his Jagdgeschwadern, or fighter wings, might resurrect? In fact, that had occurred in the Colmar Pocket, where in the fall, the tide had seemed to turn in the Allies' favor.

But in an effort to retake Strasbourg from the American forces, the Germans broke out in the north and headed east to the motherland. Besides that, the SS had killed many American prisoners in cold blood at Malmedy.

That December atrocity, like a bad egg's stench, spawned more viciousness. Now, the Americans had killed dozens of German prisoners at Chenogne, and such retaliations would surely continue.

On the plus side, the American Air Force was bombing Formosa and India—but the Japanese had introduced kamikaze pilots to wipe out American ships. Such devotion. These men went to their missions welcoming death.

Such a gloomy prospect, the war dragging on through 1945. This dreary outlook hung like a pall over London. Why hadn't the Americans, with military leaders like Patton, closed the pincers with their tanks east of the Bulge when the opportunity arose? It was almost as if someone wanted the war to continue.

Since before Christmas, Vicar Towsley had been occupied with matters concerning his mother. But the last time they spoke, he assured Rupert that *someone* was not the Almighty.

"Then why—" Rupert might have completed that inquiry in so many ways. Why didn't one of the attempts on Hitler's life *work*? Was that too much to ask? How many times had people tried to blast that maniac off the planet, only to lose their own lives as a result? And why had such a load of sorrow fallen on the Williams family and so many others?

The house, his refuge in more ways than one, provided a steamy welcome. Madeleine had heated the copper for Saturday night baths, and Cecil's complaints rose as she scrubbed his head. Merciless about preventing scabies and lice and all other manner of infestations, she paid his screeching no mind.

This meant that dear Iris had already received her scrub without argument. Her constitution resembled her mother's—take what comes in stride. Do your best and move on to the next challenge.

Quietly backing out into the garden, Rupert detested the rise of cowardice in his heart. Is this what a man does—returns to the cold to avoid chastising his son?

His sigh carried the weight of the world. Such a long day it had been. On top of all the rest, Melvin Williams, home for a night, had stopped by the station. Someone pointed him to where Rupert sat filling in government records.

Answering the knock, he looked up into a countenance shadowed by grief and marred by war. It was all he could do to keep faces like this from the Great War at bay, and seeing one in the flesh agitated something in the pit of his stomach.

"Beggin' y'r pardon, off'cer, but—"

"Do come in, Melvin."

But Williams stayed in the hallway. "That day with the Vicar. What came over me, I canno' say—"

"Well—"

"I have come to say m' apologies, off'cer. You'd ev'ry right to cuff me on the spot. Yet you—" He took a deep breath. "Beggin' y'r pardon, but I must say thank you."

Dark pools of misery hovered under Melvin's heavy brows, and Rupert thought how he favored his father to a T. Now he waited, poised in the threshold as if expecting something.

"I appreciate you coming. Perhaps in the future you will find a way to—at some point, you may be able to clear yourself in your own mind."

Had that made any sense at all? Melvin seemed satisfied enough and jerked away, cap in hand. Rupert crossed the room just as Melvin touched something in his breast pocket—something white. Oh my—

As surely as he knew his own name, Rupert recognized that swatch of white—Marian Williams' hankie. The one she'd been carrying when she descended the tube station stairs, the one that flew from her hand in the crush. The very one he had found in the corner, dried and shrunken into a bloodstained ball.

That bit of cloth walloped him in the chest and he failed to send Williams off with a better word. But in retrospect, his critical thoughts about the man dissipated during that encounter, though he'd expressed none of his sentiments and made no attempt to follow Melvin through the station's front door. Relief flooded Rupert and also rendered him speechless.

Quite a day, indeed. And now, the drenched garden glistened like a head of slicked-back hair. *Freezing fog*, the weatherman called this ghastly downfall. That phrase might describe what had occurred inside his head during Melvin's attack—a freezing fog locked him in shock, unsatisfactory behavior for a namesake of Sir Ernest Shackleton.

But truth was truth—this circumstance had revealed his own weakness. At the same time, it brought forth his strength. Yes, strength. For this afternoon, no trace of hatred toward Melvin had marred his spirit. If Towsley were here, the word would be *VICTORY*. And in these dark days, nothing warmed the heart like a victory, however small.

From the lack of sound inside the house, Cecil's battle with Madeleine had subsided. Rupert turned the doorknob and pretended to walk in for the first time this evening. Iris ran to him, and he put his heart into bringing cheer to his household.

Not since the day Towsley faced the congregants with his wretched jaw had Rupert been so moved by a sermon. Not that the vicar's style had improved—in fact, his haggardness led to some errors in reading.

But the message—oh, how this one sliced into the soul. Strangely enough, the deepest crevasse opened on the walk home with Madeleine

Watching the children slide along on the glazed pavement, she set the lesson before Rupert. "That man with the crippled hand— the Pharisees were *doing* something to him, weren't they?"

"Doing?"

"I mean, by not allowing him to be healed on the Sabbath, they were leaving him helpless. That was, in effect, *doing* something."

"I suppose so, if you look at it that way."

"So many people need help. I wonder how I can possibly do enough, and whether things will ever be normal again."

"As do I." This was all he could say at the moment, for her words brought that trembling soldier to mind, the one whose face was slowly being reconstructed. Did his absence today mean he was back in hospital? He could do more to help that fellow.

Cecil had run on ahead, sliding as far as he could at a time, and called, "Hurry, Iris—it's even slicker up here."

Something about the moment summoned Rupert. He handed Madeleine the umbrella and tore off like a madman, hollering as he gained steam and cracked down the pavement like a lad once more. He swooped Iris up and she giggled so profusely, he giggled, too.

Nearing Cecil, he crashed headlong, and they all fell in a heap of arms and legs. When Madeleine drew close, he pulled her down, too, for the simple fun of it. That afternoon they played games, and later, Junior and Kathryn joined in.

By then, Anna had returned from her friend's house, and she made over Henry and the baby. Christmas seemed to have tiptoed back, though it would be impossible to reinvent the intimacy this family experienced just after the GIs left.

The air raid siren blew, so in the Anderson shelter, they bequeathed each other a few handmade gifts. When the "All safe" siren sounded, Junior voiced the perfect sentiment.

"All together again—the way it should be."

And so it was once again on this January day. After Rupert returned early from volunteering, Madeleine's yawns grew vigorous. Then Vicar Towsley happened by, with apologies for the late hour.

"Tomorrow after school, would you have Cecil bring a couple of his chums by? I promised to help one of our elder parishioners who lives partway to Poplar."

"Certainly, but see that he comes home by half past five."

"Ah, yes. I shall bring him myself."

Bless Towsley—so good to have him back. And tomorrow, Rupert could rest easy, knowing Cecil and his chums had not ventured into one of the derelict buildings so prevalent in the Green.

Quite the dreary Monday at the station, what with ongoing bad weather—but hot tea waited in the break room, and relative safety, unlike so many enjoyed this afternoon. Looking back through the reports and newspapers piled on his desk, one stuck out to Rupert.

The Daily Mail's reporter Eric Lindel, who had witnessed the tube station tragedy had turned in his story, he stated, but the article that ran the next day described a large German bomb striking the tube station. Staring at the out-of-date record brought Melvin Williams to mind. Had he read this?

The tale fit well with the visiting bomb scientist's explanation, since the Nazis had labeled Bethnal Green *Target Area A*. But every word of the article rang with falsehood.

He'd half a notion to discuss the matter with the Chief, but what good would that do? Nearly a year had passed, and nothing could change what had occurred. The rest of the pile before Rupert contained no truth about the disaster's cause, either.

The scene through the window brought no relief from his dark thoughts. But just then, as he began looking forward to going home, the floor vibrated. Then came a rumble.

Again, louder.

Scrambling up, he saw that people had halted in the center of the street and stared southward. Another rumble, and smoke ascended—not that far away. Rupert collided with the Chief in the hallway.

"Come, we shall take the car."

Down St. Peters Street, Rupert's throat stopped up in flumes of smoke. Worse, he noted their direction—toward where Towsley had taken the boys. When the car failed them due to debris in the street, Rupert leaped out and raced ahead toward the rise of grey-blue smoke and flame.

That widow—if he were not mistaken, she lived down the next street. Hacking at the dreadful filth in the air and stumbling over massive dirt clods, he lunged on.

Great metal shards splattered like weeds over a gigantic crater. Rupert rummaged among the glass and splintered wood, bricks and cement and— He held his breath at an impossible sight. A human arm, still in its sleeve. A workman's hand, thick with muscle and hairy.

If Towsley and the boys had started back home, where could they have gotten by now? How would he ever find them?

In a sudden gust, a portion of spire appeared—St. Matthews. No, more like— In another insistent shower of ashes and dust, he lost his bearings.

And then another gust. He rubbed his gritty eyes, covered a few more yards, and viewed what he had hoped not to.

Sprawled gracelessly over the street, Vicar Towsley's unmistakable form brought a terrified gasp. In a stupor, Rupert stared. What was that underneath the vicar's long coat? Something brown and of leather.

Shoes. Unmistakably. Boys' shoes.

Cecil had only one pair, quite scuffed.

From the frayed hemline of a pant leg spewed a length of homemade undergarment. Had Cecil not fought Madeleine of late at having to wear just such a piece?

Near Towsley's hand fell a black forelock, cloyed with blood. Below it, fair skin showed. The skin of a youth, with a protrusion—even as Rupert recognized little Peter Abrams' nose, his mind denied the possibility.

Peter, the spritely Jewish boy who often played with Cecil, lying silent and still in the midst of this wreckage? *No!*

Now the Chief arrived and leaned down. He attempted to ease Towsley over—what a heavy-boned fellow. Then the situation clarified. Some terrific weight had caught him at the knee and pinned him down.

The Chief took a haggard breath, gave up the effort and touched the vicar's throat. "No pulse." He half-turned.

Then his breath seized, and he cried, "Oh, dear God, Laudner."

Superhuman strength surged through Rupert, and he heaved against a fallen rafter, allowing the Chief to turn over Towsley's body. And there, underneath, lay three youths, their clothing still colorful due to the Vicar's body protecting them from the constant grey downfall.

No movement, not even a tremble in any of them. One could scarcely take in their serene posture, all together but placid.

Cecil's ruddy cheeks had turned ashen. In the roiling dust, Rupert knelt beside the lad, raised his head into his lap. Scarred by the blast, his cheek felt warm. Hope flitted as the Chief checked for pulses. His face showed no emotion as he bent to seek the breath of life, though the boys' caved-in torsos declared the truth.

Then the Chief eased back. He removed his hat and turned completely. In that moment, the reality etched on his face shattered Rupert's soul.

Shouting ensued as volunteers invaded, hoping to pull survivors from death's grip. Sloughing through debris, stretcher-bearers skittered behind crew chiefs. Rupert felt he should do something, yet could not move.

The Chief now stood staring at Towsley and the boys. Finally, he covered the vicar's face with his handkerchief and bowed his head.

Time stood still as he came 'round and placed his hand on Rupert's back. That touch, through several layers of clothing, loosed an inner torrent, and a great wail ascended.

"Oh, Cecil—dear God, no! No! My little boy—my boy." Clinging to Cecil, Rupert crumbled, and then he felt himself gathered in.

The Chief crushed him against his chest and sobbed with him.

Chapter Thirty-one

Early January 1945

"*Eh, mein leibchin, dein Papa schickt dir Küsse und Umarmungen...* Your papa sends you kisses and hugs."
A short nap took Dorothy back to her childhood year in Bremen. Awakening, she mulled the effort Papa had made on Mama's behalf.

On March 30, 1927, their names appeared on the ship's manifest as "Alien passengers for the United States: Therese and Elfriede, Otto, Karl, Werner, Albert, Dorothea, and Ewald. Therese was Mama's mother. She'd always used her middle name instead of her hated given name, Rudolphine."

The journey remained vivid—Mama had charged Dorothy with little Ewald's safety. Toting him until her arms ached, she allowed him down when he wiggled and chased him here and there. When he finally fell asleep at night, she did, too.

At age 40, Mama undertook this trip on a violent Atlantic with gigantic waves bursting over the ship's sides and sailors yelling for all passengers to hurry below deck. At ten, Dorothy experienced success—Ewald experienced no harm.

They'd made it to Ellis Island, as the family had in '14, two years before Dorothy's birth. After the inspection, her older brothers arranged for travel inland by train. What a long trek, but Elfrieda told story after story to lull the little ones to sleep.

Soon after they arrived in Iowa, Papa respelled their names. From then on, the children spoke in English except with Mama.

At the bakery, Papa used English, but back in the kitchen with the older boys, only German would do for the finer points of a complicated recipe, and at home, he and Mama spoke German. But they wanted their children to become as American as possible.

After all these years, though, she still recalled Mama in Bremen, crooning loving messages from Papa. *Eh, mein leibchin...* Those rich tones brought comfort in this war's absurdities.

From the hall wafted the smell of something wonderful for dinner—Wally was still doing himself proud. Dorothy tied her shoes and headed that direction, but just inside the mess, the Colonel had posted the results of some recent air raids over Germany.

Yesterday, everyone took heart at the news that on January 1st, the Luftwaffe had lost half of their fleet attacking Allied bases in the Netherlands, Belgium, and France. Rig trumpeted this report, and everyone within hearing distance cheered.

"Now, we need a couple more major victories to convince 'em of our air superiority."

A crowd gathered around the posting—if it were accurate, the latest bombing raids ought to do the trick.

On Jan 2–3, over 500 Lancasters and a number of Mosquitoes from Nos 1, 3, 6 and 8 Groups attacked the city of Nuremberg, with negligible Allied losses. Repeated attacks of this city in the past had not produced the desired effect and resulted in great RAF losses, but this time, clear visibility and the aid of a full moon made all the difference.

Pathfinders created accurate ground marking, and the raids destroyed the center of the city, including the castle, the Rathaus, and almost all the churches. RAF raiders also hit more modern northeastern and southern areas. The MAN and Siemens factories and southeastern and industrial areas sustained severe damage.

This area bombing destroyed 415 separate industrial buildings. The loss of this city, including much of its medieval treasure, strikes at the very heart of German culture.

In addition, nearly 400 bombers of 4, 6, and 8 groups attacked Ludwigshafen's chemical factories. 500 HE bombs and 10,000 incendiaries fell inside these factories, and complete production failure resulted from loss of power.

In all, RAF Bomber Command flew over 1,000 sorties to begin 1945 and suffered only a small percentage of losses. Munitions and fuel support for the Reich will no longer be forthcoming from these vital locations.

"Finally!" An officer spoke for several gathered around the posted memo. "It's about time—this ought to convince the populace that Jerry can't win."

"Sure wish the Bulge defenders would get the message."

"It's only a matter of time."

Most of those reading the notice went on to get their food, but Dorothy stayed to go over it again. *Negligible losses.* How many times had she said, 'anything to hurry the end of the war.'

But the group numbers niggled at her. Had Pinky told her his? A cold shiver traced her shoulders. A few minutes ago she'd been ravenous, but her desire to eat disappeared.

Soon the Nazi war machine would die out. Peace would come again, and Europe would rebuild. But would Pinky live to see it?

In Bastogne, the 101st Airborne held on with elements of the Tenth Armored Division, until the fighting finally ceased late in the month. Such a hoard of casualties, though. Through gruesome days in the surgery tent, memories, memorized songs and verses renewed Dorothy for the next surge.

Through the hallways, a growing murmur portended victory. Everywhere she went, snitches of conversation caught her attention.

"We've lost over a thousand bombers and thousands of crew-members in raids over Berlin during the last year. Seeing the Luftwaffe falling apart is the best news we've had for a long time."

Rig summarized things without much ado. "The Nuremburg strike was a psychological blow—such a shame that ancient city had to be destroyed to prove our point." He shook his head. "Now, if we could just persuade the Japs that we're going to win."

But in spite of the air strikes, German defenders fought on at the Bulge. Throughout February a steady stream of litters reached the Eleventh. In between the waves, Dorothy sterilized instruments, mixed doses of the new miracle drug called penicillin, boiled water, removed hopelessly soiled bandages, and tidied up the operating room.

Always, the needle tips needed attention—running sterilized cotton along them revealed barbs that had developed. This task provided a certain satisfaction. Far be it from the Eleventh to let a barbed needle cause extra pain to these suffering men.

Docs hurried in, ready to wash up for a continual parade of surgeries. Dorothy stood ready, and during the gloving, focused away from the dark circles under Abner's eyes. Operating under such stress, how could they possibly avoid making errors?

From the wild yells outside, the tramp of army boots, and truck tires winching on the concrete drive, every night looked to be a long one. Cold drafts reached far down the hallway when litter carriers entered, and the nurses kept extra blankets warmed.

Winter had never bothered Dorothy before. But with so many soldiers freezing in foxholes and ever-increasing cases of trench foot, the season lost its enchantment.

As at Anzio, in Sicily, and in North Africa, it seemed this nightmare would never end. Thank goodness for this old building—impossible to calculate what warm air meant to the wounded.

One night toward the end of the month, Millie greeted Dorothy with a mischievous smile when she shuffled into the nurses' quarters. Too weary to ask, she lunged for her bed. Millie could never keep a secret—she'd reveal it soon enough.

"We're having a wedding." Her conspiratorial whisper continued even as Dorothy showed no response. "Wally's—" As she moved closer, her breath testified to a recent smoke.

"Wally said he and Hank wanted to go to a Justice, but found out they have to be married by an American. He's talked to that chaplain who's been recovering from exposure and dysentery."

The one who'd helped Dorothy with the basket case all those months ago—he'd been brought in with the next thing to pneumonia and a doc had put him in bed.

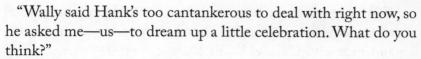

"Wally said Hank's too cantankerous to deal with right now, so he asked me—us—to dream up a little celebration. What do you think?"

"Umm…"

"I take that for a *yes*. So when the paperwork comes through, Wally will let us know. One day when Hank gets off work, he'll be waiting in that empty conference room down from the mess. He'll have the license and a cake, and our job is to get her down there. Shouldn't be too difficult, right?"

Encouraged by Dorothy's grin, Millie went on.

"It will give us something else to think about."

"Mmm. What about her blood test?"

"Oh, that's been taken care of." Millie's snicker surprised Dorothy. "Everybody knows we have accidents with needles all the time. Well, I just happened to have one close to Hank's arm one day."

"You're kidding."

"Nope. Sounds like something you would think of, right? You're rubbing off on me." Millie looked so pleased with herself that Dorothy had to laugh—it was so good to see her finding joy in this little conspiracy.

"Anything for a party. Well, you've got more energy than I do right now. But I'll try to drum some up. What about a gift?"

"We'll think of something. Actually, *you* probably will."

She was right. The idea came to Dorothy the next day between surgeries. They'd need Rig to pull this off, and maybe Jeremy's sergeant. But nothing would make Hank happier.

At long last, the cold eased up and sweaters replaced wool coats. The lines of trucks bearing wounded GIs decreased, along with the tension. When Dorothy asked Lieutenant Eilola for help, she agreed.

"Henrietta's going to hate me for this. Still, this is her *wedding!*"

Hearing Hank gripe was half the fun—*Don't I have enough to do without all these reports to write? What does Eilola do with all her time, anyhow? I oughta be getting extra points.*

Wally went to great lengths to bypass the European theater marriage regulations. One day when he emerged perspiring from an audience with Colonel Ward, Dorothy and Rig were all ears.

"He said every other theater allows marriage, and so does this one, but one of us would normally have to be transferred to another theater or a distant station in Europe. But since we're on the downside of the war, headquarters might make an exception."

Rig nodded. "Bet they will. The Eleventh has never asked for favors."

"Man, if this doesn't work and I get transferred to who-knows-where, Hank's gonna kill me."

Dorothy grinned. "But at least you'd die married."

"Yeah, there's that."

Rig fiddled with his gum wrapper chain—he'd confided in Dorothy that he'd had to split it in two and strung the bulk along his wall. "Well, I think it'll work out. Believe me, soldiers have asked for way more than this and had their wishes granted."

"The Colonel said since I've been making his favorite cookies lately, he'd do his best to put this request through."

When Wally left, Rig turned to Dorothy. "Seems like nothing's ever easy. We'll have to sweat this one out."

In the end, everything worked, and Hank only *looked* like she might kill somebody. The Chaplain, pale but able to get around, performed a short service and added, "The bride and groom have contributed to my ability to stand before you today. Without their ministrations—food and care—I'd still be down in bed."

Colonel Ward said a few words to introduce the new couple and invited everyone to enjoy the cake. Jeremy's sergeant even produced some champagne.

A few minutes into the celebration, Hank approached Dorothy and Millie. "I can tell by your innocent expressions you two had nothing to do with this."

Millie feigned innocence, and Dorothy handed Hank an envelope. "Open it. This is our gift."

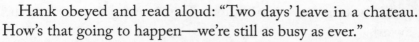

Hank obeyed and read aloud: "Two days' leave in a chateau. How's that going to happen—we're still as busy as ever."

"We're taking your shifts. Lieutenant Eilola helped us figure it out. And by the way, when she gave you all that extra work, she was cooperating with us."

"Oh man, I could just—"

"Thank her? That's the spirit! Anyway, Millie and I think you deserve a little honeymoon, kiddo."

"There's still a war going on, you know. Where would we go, anyway, and how would we get there?"

Wally came up from behind and lifted her off her feet. "We've already got a place, hon, and somebody's driving us there in a few days. Come on—it's time for our wedding dance."

February 27, 1945

"Another briefing—but this time we have no horse flies, mosquitoes, snakes, or braying donkeys to distract us. Oh—and no incoming fire." Chuckles spread through Colonel Ward's audience, and Eric yipped in Hank's arms.

"I've called you together this evening for perhaps the shortest briefing we've experienced. Please welcome the Surgeon, Seventh United States Army for the Commanding General, Seventh US Army."

The surgeon accepted the unit's applause. "Today I present this unit the Meritorious Service Unit Plaque for outstanding devotion to duty in the performance of exceptionally difficult tasks for the period from August 16 1944 November 30, 1944, in France.

"You hard-working men and women deserve accolades for devotion to duty under adverse circumstances. Your service stretches much farther back, as you well know, including Anzio, Sicily and North Africa. You have served above and beyond the call of duty.

"The United States Army may seem slow to honor your work, but believe me, the Seventh Army, on behalf of our greater organization, greatly values your contributions. To this end, I now bestow this award."

He handed the plaque to Colonel Ward, who thanked him and invited everyone to have a look. Even Hank brushed her eyes. But as people swept forward, she held back. "Plaques don't mean a thing, but it's still nice to know somebody noticed."

To resounding cheers, Colonel Ward made another quick announcement. "As our work eases up over the next few weeks, you may want to take leaves—most of you have plenty of days saved up. But I would be remiss not to issue a word of warning. Be careful."

The Rabbi, a bishop from the West Side, and a local priest delivered the sermon at the service for Cecil, Vicar Towsley, and nine other victims of the February attack. Holding Iris in his lap, numbness saw Rupert through, but later, he recalled nothing but Madeleine's hand clenching his.

After the burial, Kathryn and Junior took Iris home with the boys. Junior's supervisor gave him and Anna the morning off, a blessing indeed. Anna, unable to stop weeping, returned home, too. And Gran—she'd never left home this morning. The look on her face allowed no argument.

Madeleine led the way into the church parlors and Rupert followed in a haze not unlike the dust created by the V-2 that wreaked such havoc two days ago. People shook his hand and offered words he barely comprehended.

The church ladies provided hot tea and the closest thing to sweets they could manage—toast dabbled with marmalade. What matter? He could eat nothing anyway. But Madeleine—such a strong woman. She even managed a smile and was the one to thank everyone for their condolences.

As for Rupert, his voice forsook him as the community's tears and murmured sympathies mounted like a flood.

Among the first in line, the Chief Constable's wife asked what they might do, and Madeleine thanked her profusely. During their exchange, the Chief remained quiet. He shook Rupert's hand, holding the grip far longer than normal.

Testimonies proliferated around the table from those who lived or worked near the blast.

"... everything fell silent in a drooping haze, be it cloudy weather or the aftershock..."

"...clay lumps plastered the sides of our house and broke windows, as if someone threw them from a few feet away..."

"...Did you know the rocket was fired from The Hague... travelled faster than the speed of sound..."

"...They say the crater runs nearly 30 feet deep and 70 feet wide..."

"...If only that bugger had gone off a kilometer farther north..."

"...Inside our house, it seemed as though the walls contracted and expanded. Something took my breath away..."

"Elmer had just left for his night shift when our front door blew in all of a sudden..."

"...a huge pall of smoke mushroomed from the top of the crater... seemed to take hours to dissolve..."

"...I lost my hearing during the explosion..."

These recollections made sense, in a distant sort of way—as if the speakers described an event that took place in Ireland or Norway. But when anyone mentioned Cecil's name, his little playmates', or the vicar's, something kept the words separate from Rupert's consciousness.

He held out through the onslaught of kindnesses, and when Madeleine finally grabbed his hand to thank the kitchen ladies, the fog lifted. Still, she did the speaking—he stood inept as a scarecrow.

They started home, but nearly there, Rupert felt he must not proceed. Not yet. Not there, where Cecil's things still sat on his little shelf—his new sweater from the Christmas party, his colored pencils, the maps he had drawn of military positions he heard described on the radio—the conkers he'd labored over so diligently.

He pulled Madeleine back. "I—perhaps—"

"What is it?"

"Perhaps I shall visit the gravesite once more."

"Rupert?" Her eyebrows rose as if he had proposed bringing an elephant into the kitchen.

"Or simply walk a bit more." The sight of their front door down the way unnerved him—the thought of being inside became unbearable. "People will be—"

"Yes, we'll likely have a crowd." Madeleine took a long breath. "You will come home soon?"

"Yes. I need—"

"To be alone for a while?"

That blessed glint of understanding in her eyes created a long pause, and then she smoothed her fingers along his sleeve. When he turned back, she stood watching him with a wan smile.

Then he was off, but proceeded as if in slow time. It seemed his leg muscles had somehow disconnected from the rest of his body.

Back along the pavement the way they had just come, his breath came cleaner. His steps quickened. Minutes passed, and oh, the force that energized him now, directing him on a singular route..

Finagling the church key from his breast pocket with some difficulty, he inserted it into the lock. Because he and Towsley had not met for so long, the churn of iron upon iron sounded odd in his ears.

Silence pervaded the landing, with stairs extending downward to the basement where so recently, women had prepared tea for the mourners. Gratitude for their efforts struck Rupert anew. The warmth and sharpness of that hot drink had renewed him after the burial. The burial of his son and his comrades. The burial of Vicar Towsley.

Once during the short graveside service, Rupert had glanced toward the clergy present, expecting to see Towsley among them.

Burial. Towsley.

That truth reverberated in Rupert's head. Unbelievable. Impossible. For some reason, the memory of the vicar called most strongly at present, and their once-daily discussions crowded Rupert's thoughts.

Past the pulpit, into the nave, with too little sunlight through the windows to cast a shadow. Step-by-step he covered the same length covered by the vicar on his first Sunday after Melvin's attack. Images of his broken visage accompanied Rupert. The wounds had healed to some extent, but had forever altered his countenance.

Yet he bore no ill will. The instant forgiveness he extended toward Melvin Williams swarmed through this holy place. In the narthex, Rupert opened the closet. He did this without thinking, but touching the F L I T container seemed necessary. As he did so, a current traced through his fingers and up his arm.

Chapter Thirty-two

S o many words he and the Vicar had considered. *Behold... hope... glory. Nature... opportunity... pluck. Rest. War.*

When Vicar Towsley initiated this practice, neither of them could have dreamed all they would behold in the ensuing years. This war tore at their *HOPE* and forced them to display *PLUCK* beyond their wildest imaginations.

NATURE? She'd remained faithful through it all, misting and drizzling on them, drenching them, freezing them, and by times, peppering the Green with sunshine. But the nature within—the character people kept quietly obscured lest they draw undue attention. Ah, how the war had drawn out that inner personhood. For better or worse, this inherent nature emerged.

OPPORTUNITY... the Vicar noted this far more often than Rupert, although perhaps he might credit the war for bringing skivs like Avery Ritter into the light and paving the way to their downfall. Because the law had tightened, all might view their woeful fate, should they attempt underhanded dealings.

Of all these words, *GLORY* stood out as he lingered near the cleaning closet.

What, indeed, did this concept mean? Light, for certain. As if to enhance Rupert's musings, the sun burst through the six high windows and spread across his path through the sanctuary.

In this space, the Vicar had pled with his people to reach out to those besought by the war. No one would soon forget Towsley's earnestness that morning.

Slowly, Rupert made his way through the warming rays toward Towsley's study. All the while, he pondered how for decades, people had brought their sorrows to this place, their worries, their despair, their anger. During the Great War, during the Dunkirk debacle, and at so many other precipitous times, men and women gathered here to beseech Heaven for mercy.

MERCY... another shared word. Mercy seemed far off this afternoon, for this world would be far better off had the Vicar remained. No, it was work Rupert sought. Something to do with his hands, some deep well to drown his questions.

With a mix of trepidation and need, he maintained his pursuit, arriving at Towsley's office empty-handed. Nothing could have surprised him more than what he saw... the door wide open and someone in Towsley's chair.

Closer, the figure became clear—'twas Chief Constable Derby. Rupert advanced a few steps, but halted at Towsley's scent emanating from the vestments—ah, his dear friend.

Turning, the Chief rose. "Laudner. I was debating whether I should seek you out."

"Sir?"

"I meant to say this earlier. Do take all the time you need away from work."

"Thank you, but I cannot remain at home."

"I understand, but whatever you need." He leaned his hand against the wall. "You must be wondering why you find me here. It seems that, since the vicar has no close relations in the Green, and with his mother's recent—"

The Chief's sigh touched Rupert. Yes, more than the sight of the vicar's desk, his pencils, his alb and cassock hanging in the open closet.

"The bishop, assailed by so many requests, has asked if we— ahem— That is, whether the police force, might—ah—see to Vicar Towsley's personal effects."

Personal effects. Cecil's sweater swam before Rupert's eyes—his colored pencils, maps, conkers...

The Chief might have struck him in the gut. A full minute passed, with only the sound of a clock ticking, the air heavy with candle wax, linen and wool.

"So I came up here to—" The Chief waved his arm about the study. "To ascertain what sort of endeavor might be required."

Shelves replete with texts and two tall wooden files presumably filled with records surrounded Towsley's worn desk. The walls displayed his ordination certificate and several paintings.

"Such a conglomeration after his long years of service." The Chief grimaced. "And then, we must also attend to his private quarters."

Oh my, the vicarage, too. Quite the undertaking, though Towsley used only three of the rooms, and perhaps the caretaker would manage the kitchen.

For a time, silence united the two men. Some response must be made, but Rupert could think of none.

The Chief evidently endured his own challenges. "We might— What say we— Oh dear." He mopped his head with his kerchief. "What say you and I tackle this together, Laudner? That is—if you've the heart for this work. I might employ some of the younger officers in the vicarage, but here—"

Here, Towsley's scent—his very fingerprints—remained. So recently, he touched the ink well, his writing tools, the handles of the files. Here, he spent hours writing last Sunday's message. Here, he had prepared for that monumental sermon upon his return from the hospital.

Words issued from Rupert's lips with a life of their own. "Yes, of course." And then, something loosened below his breastbone. He breathed even deeper.

"I may begin right now, Sir—this very moment. I came looking for—"

The Chief's eyes declared no need for further explanation.

March 25 Lorquin, France

"Never been so sad to leave a place. Soon we'll be back to camping

318

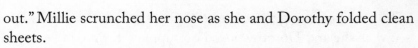

out." Millie scrunched her nose as she and Dorothy folded clean sheets.

"Yeah, but at least it's March 25, and so much warmer. Guess we can't complain. Dorothy wrote something down on a notepad. "That's 300. Now that Jerry's calmed down, we'll never run out again."

"Didn't the Colonel say this'll be our last patient evacuation?"

"Does it make you a little nostalgic? The first truck convoy leaves tomorrow for the bivouac site at Göllheim. Once all the equipment gets shuttled there, they'll be back for us. Wow. How long has it been since we joggled with an IV in a truck box?"

"Can't wait. At least we get one last bath tonight. Then we can kiss them goodbye for a while."

"Hopefully the first echelon can hurry across and we all get there in one piece."

"Well, we've got quite the record—no losses so far. Not from moving, anyway."

"All set up one mile east of Lorsch, Germany, and I won the pot this time!"

Jeremy plopped his tray down next to Dorothy.

"You bet on when we'd get here?"

"Sure did, and I hit it on the nose. March 29, and we've already unpacked."

"And pitched our tents. It's good to breathe good country air again, don't you think?"

But Jeremy gestured to the front of the mess, where the Colonel stood. "All right, ladies and gentlemen. Thus far this month, we have cared for over a thousand patients and evacuated many of them. After unpacking and pitching our tentage, the installation will officially open at 1600 hours.

"We already have patients on the way. Our duty continues."

Before 2400 hours, they'd already admitted 23. The enemy simply had to give up soon.

April, 1945 Schnabringen Bavaria, Germany

In a cool morning breeze from the east, Hank put on her best scowl as she and Dorothy boxed up supplies. Seemed like they'd hardly gotten them out and it was time to move again, to the usual racket of shouts, curses, wheels and brakes grinding.

"Our third set-up in Germany already—rom Lorsch to Lauda to Schnabringen. Isn't this a record number of moves in one month?"

"Probably. But we did our job, and the army's moving on. Better than taking fire on that beach at Anzio—we had so much still ahead of us back then. Hopefully there'll be far fewer casualties at the next place."

"It's all we can do to keep up with the infantry. Guess that's a good sign."

"*Yah vol!*" Rig took a heavy box from Hank. "Wow, you've really developed some arm muscles."

She stuck out her tongue. "Had 'em before I came, buddy."

"Really? I thought maybe some German genes had rubbed off on you."

"Yeah, right."

The docs had operated on such a variety of soldiers in the past weeks—Poles, Frenchmen, Brits, and Germans. They all suffered the same. Agony was agony. But even after all this, that one young man's dying gaze in North Africa still haunted Dorothy—along with the look in Pinky's eyes as they'd said goodbye.

During the past week, she'd come to believe he had lost his life in the final bombing attacks on German cities. If not, with pilots finally having some rest, he would have contacted her. Odd how this reality settled down inside her—a lot like Millie with Del.

And then two days ago, Rig's team delivered the evidence. Pinky must have given his parents her address, or they found it in his effects, because a packet from Scotland arrived as she packed her things.

Thankfully, Millie had left on an errand. At the words "Mail Call," Dorothy peeked out and a private handed her a packet. This delivery, tied in black cord bore the return address of Wigtownshire.

Written in a fine hand, the name froze her in place. She dropped to the tent floor and stared at the return address, written in a fine hand. Pinky's mother? After that, her mind went blank, even as her fingers untied the string.

Prayers came so naturally now as she assisted the docs, who tackled impossible wounds. *Help us…* Now she whispered, *Help me.*

Squeezing the package did little to ward off her worst fears. Soft, pliable, like fabric. Might as well get this over with.

A few seconds later, Pinky's wool tartan flat cap lay on her lap. She'd know it anywhere. He'd used this to introduce her to the Stewart clan design.

Holding the lining to her face, she breathed in. When had he last worn this?

The smooth lining belied its harsh message. When she looked inside the package again, a note drifted out.

"We received news of Pinky's death in an attack on Germany. I know he would have wanted you to have this. He called you his spunky little American girl. The GI's had taught him some of your American terms."

Pinky's full-bodied smile, the touch of his hands, the warmth of his embrace returned as though he stood right here. Then came the tears. Mama's hankie looked the worse for wear when the onslaught subsided.

His mother set aside her own grief to send this—yet another war sacrifice.

A while later, Millie entered. When she saw the cap, her face fell and she held out her hands. Only a week before, Dorothy had done the same for her when final notification of Del's death arrived from Delbert's family. Remnants of his plane had surfaced in the Channel—all seven aboard had died. A fellow pilot had observed Del's plane nose dive and wrote his recollections.

"Oh, Moonbeam—I'm so sorry."

"Pinky's mother sent this. Wasn't that kind of her?"

"Did she say anything about—"

"Just that he crashed somewhere in Germany."

321

"Remember that Hallowe'en party when you two dressed up like—" Millie caught her breath. "You worked so hard getting Pinky's costume ready."

The memory brought a fresh set of sobs. Pinky had been so weary that night, but still full of life. His deep laugh echoed even now, and she could still feel his lips brush hers.

She added his cap to her duffel bag and determined to requisition a trunk somehow. All of the nurses deserved a better place for their treasures.

Writing his mother brought a little comfort. After mailing it she whispered, "May you rest in peace, Houston Pinkstone."

That night, neither of them could sleep, and finally Millie sat up. "I'm going to get my Master's Degree when I get home. I've already sent for information on programs. Want to come along?"

Keep looking ahead. Keep moving and learning. Why not use the GI bill for more education?

"You bet."

Early the next morning in the mess, Rig came looking for Dorothy.

"I meant to deliver that package myself, but the colonel wanted to see me about something. When I didn't find it afterward, I figured—" He threw up his hands.

"It's all right. Millie helped me through."

"Sure wish I could do something to change things."

"Don't we all." Dorothy stirred her scrambled eggs. "But we have to keep on, right?"

"Yeah." He turned quiet, and she noticed the puffiness around his eyes.

"Did you have bad news too?"

"No more than usual, but one of my wife's letters kept me up most of the night. A soldier went missing while under hospital treatment. He was never found, but when his effects arrived at the bureau, she had to decide what to tell his parents."

"That would be tough."

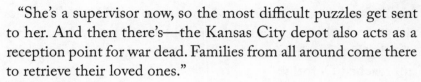

"She's a supervisor now, so the most difficult puzzles get sent to her. And then there's—the Kansas City depot also acts as a reception point for war dead. Families from all around come there to retrieve their loved ones."

"Oh man."

"Yeah. Somebody's got to do this. I just wish it weren't Betty, but she feels— She's met so many grieving families, she says she couldn't stop now—it's too important."

"So she's making a difference."

"Yeah." He got up for some more coffee and sat down again. "Sorry. Didn't mean to depress you."

"No. There's always another side to the war than what I've already considered. The angles never end. Did Betty write about a certain family?"

"A father came for his sons' bodies—three of them. They all died at different times, but somehow the Army managed to return them together. He drove into the city from the northwest with his old farm truck and Betty watched with him while workers loaded up the bodies.

"Now, she can't stop thinking about him driving home to Nebraska all alone. After what happened to the Sullivan brothers, I thought the military wouldn't take that many from one family."

"There's four of us—my three brothers are all in. But we couldn't all be in the same unit. I think losing a sailor at sea would be the worst—no body to claim and no effects. I imagine that's what the Sullivans faced."

Rig shook his head. Not much more to say.

"Hey, Captain." A breathless Jeremy entered the mess and ran over. "Me and Sarge were out gettin' some— saw some deuce-and-a-halfs headed this way loaded down with wounded. Not sure if anybody knows they're comin.' British, I think."

Rig sprang into action. Dorothy raced for the surgery tent.

The next day, the condition of one British soldier in those trucks had deteriorated after abdominal surgery. His paper white skin highlighted eyes as green as Mama's glass salad bowl. The docs debated whether another surgery would do any good. Finally, they decided that might cause even more problems, and one of them approached Dorothy.

"He's too fragile to move, and his blood pressure has dropped a lot. He just drifted off. May not rouse again. Would you stay with him?"

"Sure thing."

An hour into her watch, Millie slipped in and whispered, "Almost 500,000 German troops have surrendered in Italy—thought you'd want to know."

"Oh wow!"

"Our boys have liberated Dachau, partisans have killed Mussolini and his mistress, and word has it that Hitler and Goebbels committed suicide. It's really happening. The war is ending!" As her volume increased, Dorothy's patient stirred.

"Thanks for all the good news."

"Yep." Millie started off but turned back. "Oh, one more thing. The University of Minnesota nursing program has sent us both letters. Bet they've accepted us!"

"You haven't opened yours?"

"Waiting for you. We'll do it all together, start to finish."

"Unnh—" The patient's eyelids trembled, and Dorothy swabbed his face with a warm cloth. When he tried to speak again, she held some water to his lips and helped him drink. As with so many dying men, a story lay in his eyes.

"Where are you from?"

"Beth... East... London."

"I have good news for you. The Germans have surrendered in Italy."

He grabbed her hand, and his burning eyes held her rapt. "My... poc..." He glanced down, so she unbuttoned his breast pocket and waited.

"O... pen..."

She pulled out a woman's hankie. The ghost of a stain outlined its history, yet this soldier clearly had attempted to keep it clean. On the bottom right corner, someone had embroidered M I W.

"Mar...ian." He turned even whiter, if that were possible. His eyes fired so brightly, Dorothy hunkered close.

"Is this your wife's hankie?"

His barely perceptible nod led to more efforts. "T... tube sta... tion. March... forty-three..."

Syllable by labored syllable, his tale unfolded. His last word, "Keep..." demanded a response.

"I will."

"Umm..." His lips upturned slightly before he fell silent. Over the next few minutes, his breathing tapered to nothing.

A doc summoned a corpsman and Dorothy loosened her hold on the patient's hand.

"Thanks for watching him. Sure glad these Brits found us—ship workers recruited to fix machinery at the bulge. We were able to save several."

"This one told such a powerful story, about a tube station accident. His wife and daughter died in a London stairwell. Have you heard about that?"

"Try Rig."

But neither Rig nor Jeremy had heard anything, and Jeremy reminded her, "Don't forget how the war ministry has to control the news. If this story's true, they probably had a good reason to keep it quiet."

Rig agreed. "London's teeming with spies, and Hitler relished every tidbit about the British losing morale."

Dorothy tucked away the hankie with Pinky's cap—you don't lie to a dying soldier. By the time she'd cleaned up, Millie came and produced the letters. The university had accepted both of them.

"It's so good to have something to look forward to, Mil. Don't know how I would've handled saying goodbye to you otherwise."

"Now we know we'll meet again for sure, and it won't be long.

Hey, when are you off duty? Why don't we hitch a ride to Augsburg and find some way to celebrate?"

"All right. For that, I might even wear my new Eisenhower jacket."

"Me too. Nice they finally fitted us for them—we may have to wait forever to get what everybody else in the Army has, but we *do* get it in the end. Wearing that jacket makes me feel so spiffy."

"We could even wash our hair."

"Good idea. Mine's itchy—guess it's been a few days."

Chapter Thirty-three

May 9, 1945

Long tables set end to end in front of St. Peter's School bulged with children. Mums scuttled about, making merry with their offspring. Along with the whole of London and Great Britain at large, Bethnal Green joined in celebrating the German surrender.

Even Junior had taken time from seeking a new job to bring baby Ernest, who wriggled in his arms. Beside them, Kathryn wiped Henry's chin. Not far away, Madeleine and Anna made a determined effort to keep Iris from spoiling her Sunday dress with cream and pound cake. Rupert teared up at Cecil's absence—ah, how he missed that child!

Chief Constable Darby climbed to a short platform for his speech, and Rupert took his post nearby to observe the goings-on. The Chief had aged so much in recent months—fortunately, his son would soon be home to join the force. Then he could retire, leaving the station in good hands.

Such a parade of events—all the changes this war had wrought upon the Green boggled the mind. On the shadowy side, Cecil and Vicar Towsley's absence left an enormous hole today. Oh, how Cecil would have exclaimed when two Spitfires laced the sky in the victory sign!

Little Henry yelled for Rupert to come over, and when he did, Henry promptly spread cream all over his sleeve.

"Oh, my," Kathryn wailed. "Here, let me see to that."

327

But Rupert paid no mind. After all, what were little boys for? Patting Henry's warm head, he allowed the image of Cecil's face to claim him for a moment. As time passed, tenderness and sorrow intermingled when Cecil came to mind.

Such was grief. But a peculiar solace came from knowing that when he introduced Henry to conkers, he would bestow on them Cecil's very own homemade ones. Against that day, Rupert had stored them in the back of the corner cupboard.

When the time came, he would tell his grandsons how their uncle bored the holes himself and baked them with such care. And he would, presumably along with Junior, show them how the game was played.

As for the vicar, he and the Chief had long ago seen to his affairs, and word had it that a new parish vicar might soon be in the offing. One thing for certain, when Madeleine and Iris left for church, Rupert accompanied them. If for nothing else, to keep tabs on that soldier whom he'd befriended.

Of course, he might catch sight of him any day of the week, as the Chief had found work for him in the records department. Oh, the stack of reports the poor fellow faced each day, but seeing his smile return had meant the world.

The plastic surgeon worked a miracle on his nose, certainly not returning him to London scar-free, but serviceable. Of late, a certain young woman had been spied delivering this new worker's lunch. Perhaps soon he would have little boys of his own. When the Chief hired him, Rupert made it clear that the idea had originated with Cecil.

On another front, Sergeant Young had taken it as his personal duty to save the Chief headaches by acting as a hedge between the new man and Sergeant Fletcher. Ah, Young grew wiser by the day.

Anna's eyes brightened at Rupert's approach. When Iris saw him coming, her missing front tooth made her countenance even more winsome.

A lovely family, indeed, and a glorious day here in the Green.

Unforgettable, in fact. No word yet of restrictions lessening, but from now on, no bombs or rockets would fall upon them. That alone required a celebration, as anyone might note from the amount of Union flags decorating the square.

When Rupert squatted down to chat with Iris, she burst forth with all manner of exclamations. "Candy, Papa, and cake. Cream, too—would you like a taste?"

With his mouth agape, he was about to accommodate her when Anna poked him in the ribs. "You're wanted up there with the Chief, Papa."

"Wha—what?"

Someone else pulled at his elbow—Sergeant Young. Rupert rose, and yes, Chief Darby was hailing him forward. Oh my, he'd not paid attention—what had the Chief just said?

Nearly at the podium, Rupert stalled in shock at what he heard.

"Thus it is that Rupert E. Laudner, longtime officer and faithful servant of the people and the Crown, will take on my duties as Chief, commencing on the first of July. His merits, no one doubts. His record, I extol, stemming from his unquestioning loyalty to the Union Jack flying here today, and to the cause of law and order."

Rupert nearly stumbled, but Sergeant Young steadied him. Seconds later, he'd climbed the platform and stood near the Chief.

"And now, Officer Laudner, may we hear from you?"

With the Chief thrusting the megaphone into his hands, Rupert lost Madeleine in the crowd. Then her radiant, dimpled cheeks showed above her clapping hands. The entire crowd applauded with her, and how he wished he could read her eyes. But in spite of the distance, her smile communicated undying love.

The Chief whispered in his ear, "You needn't say much at all." Then he quieted the crowd and waited.

What to say? Breathing alone proved task enough, but Rupert managed to calm himself.

"Why, I—friends and neighbors, and my beloved family. I could not be more surprised. I thought—er—" Staring at the Chief, Rupert's mind went blank.

The Chief whispered, "Go on, then."

"That I should be so honored to serve in this capacity— Thank you, Chief Darby, and anyone else involved. I shall strive to—to act honorably and carry out peace among men here in our community."

More applause, and then the Chief pumped his hand. Other officers gained the platform to thump him on the back.

"Well deserved, sir."

"No one could do a better job."

Even Fletcher came forward. With a nervous nod, he murmured, "These flags since they are not flying from ship's staffs, cannot rightly be called Union Jacks. The Chief ought to have used the correct term, the Union flag."

Some things would never change.

"Wise observation, Fletcher. Jolly good." Rupert made his way from the platform as the program continued. A myriad of friendly shoulder pats landed on his.

Soon the festivities came to a close, and people began to take their children home with full tummies. Walking with Madeleine and all the rest, the scene took on a dreamlike quality. So many alterations during this past year, but this—it would take some time to believe what he had just heard.

Suffering a loss in one's family had come to be expected, and learning that a daughter had gone astray—with all the foreigners about, that, too, had become more commonplace. But this! Never had he felt so completely in the dark.

"We're all so proud of you, dear." Everyone added their comments to Madeleine's, and passersby issued their congratulations. The pressure of her hand on his steadied Rupert as all the talk swarmed his ears in a fog.

Who, after all, was he, to be promoted to this office? When does the son of a barber rise to such prominence? All in all, he'd accomplished nothing outstanding, made no name for himself.

Finally, near home, he voiced his one clear thought. "I should like to know how this decision was reached."

Junior jumped out in front of him. "They took note of the records and you came in far ahead of everyone else, that's how. They asked, 'Whom could we trust to follow in Chief Constable Darby's footsteps?' And then they reasoned, 'Why, Rupert E. Laudner, clearly. Who has more experience? Who does a finer job of it day in and day out?'"

He grabbed Rupert's shoulders. "You are a fine officer, Da! Just this once, leave it to others to analyze the how and why, and accept that you have been chosen." His eyes glinted. "We love you, and everyone else thinks highly of you, too. I daresay you will be working even harder now."

Rupert blinked. With home in sight, everyone—everything—came back into focus. Their street—home and hearth—beckoned on this perfect sunny day.

"Well said, my son."

Mid-June 1945

From their new location near Augsburg, some officers had already left, including Rig and Abner. The rest of the crew claimed stored-up leave time. The nurses took turns manning one recovery tent, so one day, Dorothy and Millie went into the city.

Even with a quarter of the buildings destroyed and destitute citizens everywhere, some noteworthy sites escaped the bombing. At one point, Millie went to find a bathroom, so Dorothy walked along a street as she waited.

"Webbie!"

That voice sent her heart into her throat. She turned to see a tall young man, built like— No, it couldn't be. She stared longer. It was Ewald, in uniform, a medic patch on the shoulder. Its red cross testified to all he must have seen these past months.

He raced forward and grabbed her in a huge hug.

"Hey, little sis. I knew that walk. It had to be you."

Little? But she was—he'd grown several inches since she left home. His face had been so much fuller back then. Now, he'd developed cheekbones.

"You—you made it through!" She dabbed her eyes with Mama's hankie.

"You're still using that hankie?" He choked out the words. "I remember the day Mama gave it to you. Even the pfefferneusse Papa brought home from work couldn't quiet me after you left. I could taste the sadness in our house."

His voice broke, and all she could do was nod.

"Of course, now I know you had to join up. But it wasn't long before Albert left, too. That goodbye was downright awful. Then came my turn, and I thought Mama would never stop crying." He shook his head. "But those days are over now. From here on out, it's going to be *hellos* all over the place!"

He held her at arm's length. "Wow, sis, you've lost weight. Don't the army cooks feed the nurses?"

He looked so much older. No, *old*. Far too old for his age. Finally she could speak. "You're pretty skinny yourself. What have you heard about Vernon and Albert?"

"I got a letter a couple weeks ago. Vernon's in a hospital somewhere—maybe he's made it back to California by now."

"The last I knew, he'd been wounded."

"Yeah. Sounds like he got hit pretty bad—in the head. And as far as I know, Albert's still droppin' bombs on the Japs. Can't you picture him doing that? He always liked playing with airplanes."

"He sure did—do you think he got to meet Eddie Rickenbacker when he toured the South Pacific?"

"Maybe—amazing he survived that plane crash. I'm sure if Albert was anywhere near Argentina or Guadalcanal, he found a way to shake the old man's hand. He was nuts about that British ace James McCudden, too. Remember the way he zoomed through the house with his model, searching for Fokkers and Zeppelins and Albatrosses to shoot down?"

"That was Albert. Do you recall that day we posed in our winter coats on the back steps? The older boys had their ice skates slung over their shoulders, and you and Albert wore matching winter hats. Mama gave me strict orders to make sure you kept them on, but it was a tough job."

"Those chin straps did more harm than good."

"Seems so long ago."

"Yeah. A lifetime. Sure wish I'd had one of those hats last winter."

"It must've been terrible. But you survived the Bulge."

Ewald loosed a shaky breath. "Yeah."

For a minute, silence filled the space. So many things they might say, so much they never would. And then someone approached from behind.

"Moonbeam? I leave you for five minutes, and you—" Millie ran up and halted mid-sentence, her mouth forming an O. "Why, it's Ewald! Oh my goodness."

"Meet my baby brother, Millie—he's been out there sending all those casualties our way." Millie stuck out her hand, but Dorothy pulled them both into a triple hug.

"I can't believe this."

"I know. I was just walking down the street and—"

"We were *supposed* to come today, no doubt about that. So good to meet you, Ewald. Your big sis has told me so much about you, I feel like I know you already."

"We've got another night here. Can you stay long enough for dinner?"

"Sure. Lead the way—I'm starving."

Ewald linked arms with them and they started off. His first question was, "Moonbeam? What's that about?"

Millie gave him all the details, and Dorothy was content to listen. From Gibraltar to Rabat to Sicily, from Naples through Rome, from the Riviera to Lorquin—their long trek sounded unbelievable, like a fairytale. Ewald was full of questions, and Millie supplied plenty of information.

His commander welcomed them, and his buddies joined them

for dinner, happy to share stories of Ewald earning his own nick-name—Trooper. Hearing him laugh and joke reminded Dorothy of days gone by, and as the conversation continued long into the evening, the harsh lines between his eyes eased a little.

When she and Millie had to leave, the entire Woebbeking family might have surrounded them. Ewald insisted on saying, "So long—not goodbye," and hugged her so hard it hurt.

All the way back, Dorothy pinched herself. She could hardly imagine what it would be like to see everyone back home again.

Late July 1945

The Eleventh's latest move to Weinheim stretched a four-hour drive into a full day, with many checkpoint stops along the way and slow passage through Stuttgart. But Dorothy kept thinking, "We'll be this much closer to Bremen."

During off hours these days, Lieutenant Eilola kept the nurses busy with office work while the Eleventh awaited transport to Paris. One day, a colonel was traveling north on an inspection trip, so Dorothy hitched a ride with him.

Getting away from all the paperwork was a treat, but finding this ride seemed miraculous—no one knew how long they would be here, and leaving without seeing Grandma's house would never do. Another officer rode along, leaving Dorothy to view destroyed German countryside from the back seat.

After a day on the road, the officers met several Americans who took her along to dinner with the commanding general and his Bremen staff. By the end of the evening, two officers agreed to help her find Grandma's house.

And the next morning they did, but gray, oppressive skies whispered a warning. Dead calm hung over the streets. Hardly a bird chirped from trees bombed into barrenness. Shattered limbs still peppered the earth, and tree trunks razed of life guarded the area like somber sentries.

Dorothy's memory failed her—the grass had always been green, the yard spotless, the steps swept as clean as the dining room table. Hadn't Grandma believed cleanliness was next to godliness? Like a tune from long ago, her voice came to Dorothy with those very words... *Sauberkeit ist das halbe Leben.*

Now, even the stalwart iron fence bowed in places, as though remaining upright around the property sapped all its energy. Here and there, a weed poked through the iron spikes, once shimmering black, but now marred by flying debris.

Standing near the gate in front of #146 Admiralstrasse, Dorothy's heart broke. Only three walls of the stately old house still stood, but behind them, the interior lay gutted. When her attempts to compose a smile failed, the officer wielding a camera launched her an understanding look.

In the rubble that had once been Bremen, almost every local building had been obliterated—the school, the candy shop, the grocer's where Mama made her daily purchases. Where were the people they had known? Evacuated, she supposed, or buried.

Through the highest windows, blue sky showed through the shattered windows on front wall. Beyond the house a few blocks, the bombing left the *Rathouse* and *Ratskeller* untouched, but the *Dom Kirche*, Grandma's church, lost its roof and many windows. Workers at the site discussed how to erect a roof before bad weather came.

How would these people ever rebuild, if they had survived? She might never know, but Mama would appreciate this photograph. Across the street, one house looked habitable, so Dorothy knocked on the door and a wizened woman greeted her from the shadowy interior.

"I'm Dorothea Webbeking. My family used to live across the street with Tante Lina. Do you remember her?"

The woman shook her head. "They firebombed the house over there. It burned for three days." Her eyes filled. "I thought the flames would never stop."

Dorothy persisted. "Tante Lina was tall and thin. She lived here her whole life."

335

Finally, recognition lighted the woman's face and she nodded. "Yah. I remember her now; I saw her a few years ago."

The officer joined Dorothy and offered, "We can go down to the Provost Marshall's office in the morning and check the records."

Sure enough, the registrant produced a record of Tante Lina's death in February of '42—more to report to Mama. That was the good thing about typing duty—between creating endless reports, she could write letters so much faster.

The other officer remained in Bremen, and the colonel, a surgeon, was much more relaxed than he'd been in surgery, so carrying on a conversation was easy on the return trip. Answering his questions about her family took up the first hour, especially when he realized his son might be in the same unit as Vernon.

Then he asked, "What will you do once you get home?"

"Sleep. Eat Papa's baked goods 'til I'm sick. And then—" She told him about her plans with Millie, and before she knew it, her concern about Paul spilled out.

"His letters keep getting more romantic, and I'm getting to be an old maid. But I could never marry him. I really thought he saw me the way I saw him, as a good friend." She gasped. "Oh, for heaven's sake—I can't believe I told you that. I don't want Hank to know, because she's been predicting this all along."

The colonel burst out laughing. "Hank? You mean Private Pheiffer? No need to worry—I steer clear of walking grenades."

"Well, marriage has calmed her down some."

"I wouldn't know. Like I said, I keep my distance. As for this Paul, I'd say you're one woman who knows how to follow your heart."

What did he mean by that? While she debated asking, he went on.

"Anybody who's survived all you have and still made the best of it—" He drummed his fingers on the steering wheel. "I imagine everyone assumes that in the midst of all the chaos, we doctors took little notice of the rest of you, but some of us did. In fact, Abner told me about your pilot—I'm sorry you lost him."

What was there to say? Dorothy decided to let her silence speak.

At a checkpoint, the doc conversed with a soldier, but resumed right where he left off. "Back in North Africa, I knew the command was all about trapping you into telling them who dropped that note for you, but you withstood their demands. Word got around."

Discomfort wiggled up Dorothy's spine. All this time, doctors had known about Rick's note?

"What I mean is, I respected you for not blabbing the guy's name. He'd probably have lost his post—maybe he should have. Can't imagine what he was thinking when he let that note go for just anybody to find."

More silence.

"Besides, I thought we had far more to worry about than one little incident with a nurse. It was clear to me you meant no harm, and that the guy dropping the note ought to have used his head."

Hmm—wasn't that about the same thing Millie had said?

"Abner may have been the one to tell you that you'd been chosen for surgery—or maybe it was Lieutenant Eilola. But we all had something to say about that, and once we saw how you worked, nobody gave a second thought to that other business."

Yes, it had been the Lieutenant. Remembering her commendation, Dorothy still could think of nothing to say.

"Back to this Paul. I wager he won't be the last fella to fall for you."

"We'll see. He was my professor at Drake University, and we have a lot in common. Maybe I'll give him my medallion from the Pope to ease my refusal."

"There you go. Is he Catholic?"

"Yeah."

"That might work, although if he's set on you, he's in for a rough disappointment. Once we get home and all my photographs are developed, I can send you our picture with the Pope, if you don't have one. You can give that to Paul, too—not everybody gets a private audience."

"Why, thank you."

"As for your future, thousands of men are returning from this mess, ready to settle down. Mark my words—you'll never be an old maid."

Back at camp, Dorothy wrote to Mama about Bremen, and included her latest news—she had the second highest number of work credits among the nurses—108. Would that mean she could leave before the others? Not likely. Everyone who could already had, the latest being Jeremy and his procurement sergeant.

Chances were, Jeremy would never leave North Carolina again. Rig promised to stay in touch. Kansas City wasn't that far away, he said, but once he got home, he'd get so busy, he'd probably never leave, either.

A big shock came when Hank mentioned she might stay in the military. "I'm so tough now, nobody would dare give me any guff."

"You've got a point," Millie said. "And it wouldn't take long for you to rise in the ranks."

Hank pooh-poohed that, but no one liked a challenge better.

As for Millie, she rarely allowed her sorrow to show, and lately she'd declared, "Maybe I'll find exciting work in some unique place after the university. We'll see what happens."

Back on her own cot, Dorothy dreamed of the States. The bakery, the porch steps at 418 Cherry Street, the turn in the stairway, her room in the drafty upstairs. Nothing had changed. A shot of that old photograph flashed before her. They were all adults now, but could still go ice-skating.

Ahh, she could hardly wait.

The next evening in the mess, a visitor stood out. He might have been Rick's twin, but a few years older. When people cleared away, Dorothy approached him.

"Excuse me. You look like somebody I knew once."

His eyes narrowed. "In Cairo?"

"Yes, how did you—"

"I thought you looked familiar. You must be Dorothy. My brother Rick sent me your picture. Never thought about it when I stopped here. Eleventh Evac, yes?" He held out his hand. "I'm Don."

"It's good to meet you. Would you mind waiting here a few minutes? Rick gave me something I've been wanting to return."

A few minutes later, she slipped the family ring Rick had given her into Don's palm. "It wouldn't do to send this through the mail, but I don't feel right about keeping it. I'm sure it'll mean a lot to your family."

"Yes. I think this was my great-grandmother's." He turned the ring over. "A wartime romance, eh? Easy come, easy go?"

"Not exactly."

Before he could go on, she said goodnight, and a puzzle piece slipped into place. Something the colonel had said on their trip from Bremen dovetailed in her consciousness.

I respected you... he'd probably have lost his post. Can't imagine what he was thinking when he dropped that note..."

If he remembered that scenario, the powers-that-be certainly did, too. Maybe that was why she'd had to wait for so long to receive her extra points.

Ah, well. One more goal reached, one more memory sealed in time.

Marseille, France

"Packing is easier this time—I'm finally getting rid of my Great War uniform. You were smart to bury it back in Africa. I'm such a rule-follower, I've lugged it around ever since."

"Yeah, but you can still experience the relief. Want me to help?"

"After dinner?"

"It's a date—find a shovel, ok?"

Millie nodded and continued packing. Scheduled to leave Marseille tomorrow, the nurses tied up odds and ends. Dorothy had finally received her promotion, but so did everyone else—what good had it done to earn all those extra points?

Ah, well. Every experience had expanded her expertise. That was what mattered. She fingered two items at the very bottom of her duffel—a Scottish flat cap and a stained British hankie. A pain still shot through her at the thought of Pinky being shot down.

Easy come, easy go. Breaking up with Rick hadn't been easy, but she knew what she had to do. But losing Pinky—she still had no words.

Across the tent, Millie was humming "We'll meet again some day..." She'd lost her longtime childhood friend, her first and forever boyfriend, her fiancé, and laid to rest her dreams of raising a family with him. Yet she maintained quiet dignity.

"Do we know the name of our ship yet? Remember when we zigzagged across on the *John Erickson*?"

"I haven't heard. And I'll never forget the John E. What a voyage, with 5,000 troops around us in all those ships."

"Yes, and 48 of us debarked at midnight in Casablanca. Who could ever have dreamed what we'd face along the way?"

"March 3, 1943—seems like 20 years ago. If I didn't have pictures from some of these places, they would hardly seem real."

"I wonder how the girls that were sent home are doing."

"Lucy started working at Walter Reed, and I heard Nan joined the Red Cross." Millie shook her head. "Knowing Colonel Scott ended up in the Pentagon recruiting nurses for the rest of his career helps a little."

"Like Wally says, the army moves incompetency up, not out." Hank's snide comment announced her presence. "Well, girls. In the morning, we'll leave our tents behind for the last time."

"In a flash, this whole way of life will vanish." Millie sounded dejected.

"Oh no, we've still got the voyage home." Dorothy added a little levity. "Just think how we can live it up. Meals on time, no duty, no mines to dodge, no German submarines to worry about and peace to look forward to."

"You two are so sentimental. Well, I need to get back to—"

"Wally. We know. You always maintained you'd be an old maid. Well, look at us, old and single, and you happily married."

"For a girl named Hank, I didn't do too bad, did I?" She wandered off and left them to sort and pack.

Dorothy studied the hankie in her hand—what would she ever do with it? Mama would be pleased to see how long hers had lasted, and would probably mention something about its German origins.

But this other one— After hearing the terrible way that British soldier's wife and daughter died, she couldn't throw it away. Of all the dying men's stories she'd heard, this one most piqued her curiosity. And to boot, he wasn't even supposed to be in Germany—the British army had borrowed him from the Navy for his mechanical wizardry, someone said.

What was that unfamiliar part of London he mentioned? *Beth* something. Maybe someday, she'd visit England and see what she could turn up. Maybe she'd go to Scotland, too, and find Wigtownshire.

In the meantime, she only wanted to go home. Placing the initialed cotton square in with Pinky's cap, Dorothy remembered something Mama always said.

A promise is a promise.

Special Thanks

To Camp Algona POW Museum, Algona, Iowa—for providing excellent research resources.

www.pwcamp.algona.org

And to Linda Betsinger McCann, author of
Prisoners of War in Iowa

About the Author

W ords have always been comfort food for **Gail Kittleson**. After instructing expository writing and English as a Second Language, she began writing seriously. Intrigued by the World War II era, Gail creates women's historical fiction from her northern Iowa home and also facilitates writing workshops/retreats.

She and her husband, a retired Army chaplain, enjoy grandchildren and in winter, Arizona's Mogollon Rim Country. You can count on Gail's heroines to ask honest questions, act with integrity, grow in faith, and face hardships with spunk.

Visit Gail online at: GailKittleson.com

Also available from

WordCrafts Press

House of Madness
  by Sara Harris

Angela's Treasures
  by Marian Rizzo

Pipe Dream
  by K.L. Collins

The Mirror Lies
  by Sandy Brownlee

You've Got It, Baby!
  By Mike Carmichael

www.WordCrafts.net

CPSIA information can be obtained
at www.ICGtesting.com
Printed in the USA
BVHW031100230619
551741BV00001B/84/P